LOVE YOU TO DEATH

LOVE YOU ◆ TO DEATH

A NOVEL

——

CHRISTINA DOTSON

BANTAM
NEW YORK

Bantam Books
An imprint of Random House
A division of Penguin Random House LLC
1745 Broadway, New York, NY 10019
randomhousebooks.com
penguinrandomhouse.com

LIBRARY OF CONGRESS CATALOGING-IN-PUBLICATION DATA
Names: Dotson, Christina author
Title: Love you to death : a novel / Christina Dotson.
Description: New York : Bantam, 2025.
Identifiers: LCCN 2025014948 (print) | LCCN 2025014949 (ebook) |
ISBN 9780593874974 hardcover | ISBN 9780593874998 ebook
Subjects: LCGFT: Thrillers (Fiction) | Novels
Classification: LCC PS3604.O869 L68 2025 (print) |
LCC PS3604.O869 (ebook) | DDC 813/.6—dc23/eng/20250407
LC record available at https://lccn.loc.gov/2025014948
LC ebook record available at https://lccn.loc.gov/2025014949

Printed in the United States of America on acid-free paper

1st Printing

First Edition

Book design by Kim Henze Walker

The authorized representative in the EU for product safety
and compliance is Penguin Random House Ireland,
Morrison Chambers, 32 Nassau Street, Dublin D02 YH68, Ireland.
https://eu-contact.penguin.ie

For my parents, Thomas and Olivia.
You always knew.

LOVE YOU TO DEATH

PROLOGUE

———

I shouldn't have come here.

The blood is attracting mosquitoes, and I hate how sticky my skin feels. Before she left, she'd told me, "Sit, stay," as if she were giving a command to a dog, but the bleach was too suffocating. I couldn't stay there. Hell, I couldn't even breathe. It's my own fault—I'd used too much trying to clean up. Years of cleaning up other people's messes, and I almost took myself out inhaling bleach fumes. All that blotting and scrubbing on my hands and knees, making myself dizzy, and for what? The stain is never completely gone. It always leaves behind a mark just beneath the surface, binding itself to whatever it touches. You can scrub or blot or soak until your hands are raw, but it's always there, this tiny imperfection, contaminating everything around it.

I bet she thinks I'm stained. Contaminated. I can tell by the way she looks at me. We were kids the first time I saw that look. And now it's back, or maybe it's always been there, just beneath the surface like a stain. I wrap my arms around myself, not wanting to think about what I've done to her—to both of us.

She'll blame me for this. She's good at that, blaming. I shrink back against the wall, watching her. Does she see me? I want to call out to her, tell her I'm here—but I can't risk it. We're ghosts now, never to be seen or heard from again. I've made sure of it.

A cat scampers out from behind the stairs and makes its way to me. Its fur is dirty and matted on one side, and I wonder if it can smell the blood. There was so much. The cat brushes against my legs and stares up at me like it knows my thoughts. I shoo it away and swat at more mosquitoes. They are relentless. And hungry. One of them lands on my hand where dried blood has collected between my fingers and in the creases of my palm. What I wouldn't give for a long shower. The things we take for granted.

I drop to my knees and rub my stained palms on the grass until they burn. I want to be clean again. But we're never completely clean, are we?

CHAPTER ONE

———

THURSDAY

Housekeeping at the Chamberlain Hotel is a thankless profession. We clean strangers' semen-stained sheets, scrub their pissy toilets, and vacuum their disgusting floors, all for them to fuck up our pristine work as soon as they return to their overpriced rooms with the sad interstate views. I'd quit, but the only job around here willing to pay more per hour than the cost of a value meal at the Tasty Freeze is, well, the Tasty Freeze, and I'd rather wear an apron than a hairnet.

"Room 314 left me twenty dollars, and forty dollars from 322." My best friend, Zorie, waves three crisp twenty-dollar bills at me. "How'd you do?"

"Suite on seven left me a bathtub full of pubes."

We stop at the supply room, and I swipe my ID card across the reader. A green light flashes, followed by a click, and I push open the door. The smell of vinegar is overwhelming. Our hotel manager, Leslie Grace, insists on using vinegar for cleaning, even though guests constantly complain about the smell. I toss two bottles and an armful of toilet paper onto my cart. Zorie swipes two rolls from the shelf and places them inside a laundry bag. She stocks it throughout the day with assorted boxes of cereal from the kitchen, individual soaps, and toilet paper and then empties it into her trunk on her breaks. Good thing we're roommates, or I'd probably starve to death or, worse, never wipe my ass again.

"They're gonna fire you one of these days for stealing," I say.

Zorie winks at me. "They have to catch me first."

Last month, rumors started circulating that Leslie Grace installed cameras inside the housekeeping supply room to catch thieves, but all they caught was the housekeeping manager going down on the sales manager. They were both fired, and Leslie Grace has been on my ass about applying for the housekeeping manager position.

"You know if I become manager, you have to stop stealing from the supply room," I say.

"Does that mean you're applying?"

"Are you gonna stop stealing?"

Zorie lifts her left hand and places her right hand over her heart. "Best friend's honor."

Best friend's honor is our version of swearing, like our own little sworn testimony, minus the Bible. It started in third grade when I accused Zorie of taking my favorite unicorn pen and she declared her innocence by placing her hand over her heart and announcing, "Best friend's honor." Now it's our saying for anything needing more assurance, like Zorie swearing she paid the rent on time or me swearing I didn't use the last tampon.

"I'm serious, Zo. If I do this, no more fucking around."

Zorie looks at me like she's not sure if she should laugh, so she nods instead. "I still don't know why you want that job. More hours and more of Leslie Grace's bullshit. Sounds like hell to me."

"Then it's a good thing you're not applying," I say and poke her in the side with my finger.

"Just the two ladies I wanted to see." Leslie Grace stands in the doorway, her blood-red lips twitching as though she forgot how to smile. The sleeves of her white button-down are rolled up to her elbows, with a visible sweat ring under each arm. Leslie Grace loves to look like she's been hard at work, but the truth is she's just premenopausal. "Would either of you be willing to work second shift tonight?" she asks, fanning herself with her clipboard.

"I can take the shift," Zorie says. Then, to me, she adds, "You have dinner with your folks tonight."

"Right," I say, thinking how I'd much rather spend the evening cleaning extra rooms than enduring another dinner of awkward conversation and insults disguised as encouragement.

"I knew I could count on you two," Leslie Grace says. She shifts her weight from one foot to the other, hugging her clipboard to her chest. "Teamwork and outstanding service are what this company is all about."

I nod and go back to sorting shampoos and lotions on my cart. Nothing gives Leslie Grace a bigger lady boner than reciting the company's mission statement. Her dedication to the Chamberlain Hotel would be impressive if it weren't so pathetic. The woman's entire life's purpose is defined by her ability to fill eight floors of a three-star hotel located in the heart of Redwood Springs, Georgia.

"Kayla is always talking about teamwork," Zorie says.

I drop the shampoo bottle I'm holding, and it rolls across the floor to Leslie Grace's foot. She's wearing open-toed shoes even though her nails are jagged and uneven, with chipped green polish. Leslie Grace picks up the rogue bottle and carefully returns it to my cart.

"Keep up the good work, Kayla," she says. "Teamwork makes the dream work." She turns and takes off toward the door, her sandals slapping hard against her heels in sync with her swinging ponytail.

"What was that?" I say to Zorie.

"You want that manager job, don't you? Think of me as your personal hype woman. I'm just reminding old girl how bomb you are."

I roll my eyes dramatically and smile. "If you expect me to say thank you, I'm not going to."

"Oh, really?" Zorie lifts an eyebrow, and I know what's coming next. She tickles my sides, and I howl with laughter until tears stream from my eyes.

"Okay! Okay! Thank you, Zorie!" I choke out between giggles. I barely have time to catch my breath when I hear footsteps, followed by a loud grunt. Kevin from maintenance is beside me. I know this because I smell him: chewing tobacco, armpits, and beef jerky—his signature scent.

"Morning, friends," he says. "You look awfully pretty today, Kayla."

"She literally looks the same every day. We all do," Zorie says, and gestures to her uniform.

"Can't a man pay a beautiful woman a compliment?" he asks.

"Thanks, Kev," I mumble but keep my eyes on my cart. Maybe if I avoid eye contact, he'll go away. We'd shared a regrettable and drunken mistletoe kiss last year at Leslie Grace's Christmas party, and now he's like my shadow.

"Y'all hear about the lady on seven?" Kevin asks. He leans against Zorie's cart, and she jerks it backward.

"What about her?" Zorie asks. "She die or something?"

Kevin stumbles backward into my cart and laughs. He's close enough for me to see the enormous wad of tobacco stuffed in the middle of his lower lip. "This chick paid for a full week in cash, and I heard she tipped Geraldine a C-note for cleaning off her table at breakfast. That pocketbook must be deep."

"A hundred dollars?" Zorie says, shaking her head. "Damn, how much extra bacon did Geraldine give her? Too bad she's not on my floor."

"She's on mine," I say. I try to keep my expression neutral, but my lips twitch up into a smile. I could really use my own C-note, especially since Freemont Debt Collections keeps garnishing my checks.

"You better get that money, girl!" Zorie high-fives me, and Kevin snorts. A trickle of tobacco juice slides down his chin. God, he's disgusting. He's also nosy as hell, always asking questions and watching us with that goofy grin on his face. Kevin's nosiness has been at an all-time high since he saw me and Zorie going through the lost and found last month in search of outfits to wear to a wedding. Two days later, nosy Kevin spotted us leaving Chapel Ridge Baptist Church in those same floral dresses with an armful of gift bags. He asked me about it in the break room, and I played dumb.

"You must've confused us with some other ladies," I told him.

If Kevin knew I was lying, I couldn't tell. He never asked me about it again, but now he keeps a closer eye on the lost-and-found box, forcing me and Zorie to do our wedding-attire shopping at Goodwill.

Sometimes I wonder if Kevin knows how me and Zorie spend our weekends searching online for weddings we were never invited to, only to show up at their receptions disguised in cheap wigs and stolen dresses. We take what we can from the gift tables and slip out the back during the happy couple's first dance. I should feel guilty, but most weeks, those wedding gifts are the only things keeping the lights on in our apartment.

"I better get back to work. You know how Leslie Grace hates distractions," I say, and back my cart out of the room.

Kevin waves to me and spits out a long, dark string of tobacco juice into a Styrofoam cup.

"Lunch later?" Zorie calls after me.

"Only if you're paying. My funds are kind of low this week."

She smiles and points at me. "I got you, girl."

"You always do. I love you big, Zo."

"I love you bigger," she says, then the door swings shut with a click.

I unhook my clipboard from the cart and scan the page for the remaining rooms in need of cleaning on the seventh floor. Three had DO NOT DISTURB tags on their doors when I checked earlier, and one room requested a late checkout. July is the Chamberlain's busiest month, thanks to all the parents and their bored children who migrate to Redwood Springs every summer to see our one-and-only tourist attraction: the Railroad Museum. Our history class took a field trip to the museum our senior year, and Zorie managed to break away from our group and make out with one of the tour guides. I glance at my Fitbit watch—a gift courtesy of a guest who was dumb enough to leave it unattended on Zorie's floor. Almost checkout time. I push the up button on the elevator, and it opens almost immediately. A middle-aged woman with flaming-red hair, dressed in a green-and-gold blazer and navy pleated pants, is inside. I wait for her to exit, but she doesn't move.

"Going up?" I ask.

"Actually, I'm so glad I ran into you." She holds up a key card. "Doesn't work. Can you let me into my room?"

I jerk my thumb in the direction of the lobby. "The front desk can help you with a new key."

The woman smiles as if my answer was both obvious and dumb. She reaches inside her blazer and holds up a twenty-dollar bill. "Save me a trip, would you, dear?"

I scan the hallway for any sign of Leslie Grace and her swinging ponytail. "Do you have ID? I need to confirm your identity."

"Well, that's a problem, isn't it?" She laughs. "My purse is in my room."

The elevator doors start to close, and the woman stops them with a French-manicured hand.

"Please? You'd be doing me a huge favor, and I'd be sure to tell your manager how helpful you were."

She pushes back the cuff of her blazer and looks at her watch, then back at me, the universal sign of impatience. For every flip-flop-wearing out-of-towner just passing through, there's a guest like this one: entitled and privileged, dangling their threat of complaints in front of you with a smile. They flood the lobby every week, armed with their corporate credit cards, demanding suite upgrades and late checkouts, all while daring the front-desk clerk to deny their requests. The employees know the words awaiting them if they do, the same words always on the tips of the guests' elite tongues: "*I'd like to speak with your manager.*" And if there's one thing Leslie Grace hates more than dust and stains, it's complaints. I can almost hear her voice, proud and stern: "*Teamwork and outstanding service are what this company is all about.*"

"Fine," I say and shove my cart inside the elevator, forcing the woman into the corner. Her citrusy, furniture-polish-smelling perfume invades the tiny space like a smoke bomb, and I hold my breath. "What floor?" I ask in a pinched voice.

"Seven, dear."

I stab the seventh-floor button with my thumb and sink back against the wall. Katy Perry's "Roar" plays on the speakers, and I catch the woman tapping her gold-buckled ballet flats to the beat. I could get fired for letting a guest inside a room without confirming their ID. The woman smiles at me like she knows. The twenty-dollar bill is still in her hand, and I want to ask for it before we leave the elevator, but then the steel doors open and she steps off without a word. She half walks, half runs to the end of the hallway, glancing over her shoulder as if to make sure I'm still there. She stops in front of the Kensington Suite and waits expectantly for me to catch up. I cleaned this suite earlier. I wonder if the bathtub full of pubes belongs to her.

"I really appreciate this, dear," she says.

"And your ID is inside?" I ask. She nods quickly, and I shove my master key into the lock. It lights up green and clicks open. The woman hurries inside and comes back seconds later with a duffel bag.

"Oh, shoot," she groans. "My husband must've taken my bag with my purse."

Of course he did.

She plucks another twenty from the bag and then hands me both bills. "Thank you, dear. The world needs more kind people like you in it."

She shuts the door in my face, and I hear the chain lock slide into place.

═

I use my forty-dollar tip to buy a new maxi dress for tonight's family dinner. Every other Thursday night, like clockwork, I join my dad and his wife, Gloria, at my childhood home and pretend to enjoy their company almost as much as they pretend to enjoy mine. Tonight, however, is a special occasion because my stepsister, Candace, will be making a rare appearance at our dinner table with her fiancé. Last time I saw Candace was on Christmas Eve when she announced her engagement, and we all toasted her with Gloria's disgusting eggnog martinis. And now she's back to remind me of how blissfully happy she is living in Atlanta and that I still live here. Candace wants me to be jealous of her, and maybe I am, but I'd never give her the pleasure of knowing it. She's two years younger than me and three dress sizes smaller, she has a job at an entertainment company working with the who's who of Atlanta R&B, and her fiancé just so happens to be my high school boyfriend, Charles.

I open his Instagram page as I sit in my dad and stepmom's driveway. It's bookmarked on my phone, a fact I'm not proud of. His latest pic is a selfie of him in his white coat. Charles is a medical resident at Emory, another fact Candace never stops reminding me of. It's always *"Charles is so exhausted from doing rounds at the hospital."* Or *"Charles and I will probably move to Buckhead when he finishes his residency."* Zorie and I live in the Riverview District. It's one of those neighborhoods known more for its soaring crime rates than its sweeping landscapes. Not a lot of medical students live in the Riverview District.

I sit with my head against the steering wheel, scrolling through pic after pic of Charles and Candace. They really are a cute couple. She has a pixie cut and cheekbones as sharp as glass. Her teeth are big and sparkling white, like toothpaste-commercial teeth. My own teeth are slightly crooked, but decent. Don't get me wrong, I'm not a dog or anything: five six, brown eyes, thick thighs, and cinnamon-brown hair I've finally managed to grow past my shoulders thanks to Zorie's homemade oils. My face isn't bad: good symmetry, full lips, and nice skin the color of whiskey. If anything, I'm more invisible than ugly.

And then there's Charles with his butterscotch skin and deep dimples. Most of my old classmates have lost what little attractiveness they'd managed to hold on to after graduation. They're balding, fat, and reaping the rewards of leathery skin from years of worshipping the sun. But not Charles. He's still as handsome—if not more—as he was on the day we graduated. He broke up with me the night before he left for college after telling me I wasn't motivated enough. Ten years later, he's in his second year of residency and I'm holding strong as the seventh-floor housekeeper at the Chamberlain Hotel. *"Teamwork and outstanding service are what this company is all about."*

A tap on my window makes me jump, and the phone slips from my hand and onto the floor. Candace stares down at me with one of those pity smiles reserved for funerals and the homeless. Charles is next to her, but he doesn't look at me. I like to think it's harder for him to hide his pity because he used to love me. I sit up straighter, not wanting to look as small as I feel, and flash the biggest smile my lips will allow. For years, Charles avoided coming to any of our family gatherings, sparing me the humiliation of seeing my first love on the arm of my stepsister. Candace would explain away his absence as some hospital-related emergency, and I would quietly sigh with relief. But now they're here, standing in front of me like two shiny objects I can't look away from, and I hate them for it.

"Are you coming in?" Candace asks.

"Be right there," I yell through the window. I pick up my phone from the floor and hold it to my ear. "Just need to finish this call," I say, pointing to my phone.

Candace nods like she doesn't believe me or care, then slips her arm through Charles's. I watch them stride up the walkway in sync, right leg, then left, like little marionette dolls I'd like to run over. Once they're inside, I drop my phone into my purse and smear another coat of lip gloss on my lips. I shouldn't care about these things. Charles is engaged. Taken. Committed. Part of me wonders if they're really happy, but the jealous, petty part of me hopes they aren't.

I push open the car door and stumble out. The espadrilles belong to Zorie, and they're a size too small, but they're the only shoes that go with my yellow maxi dress.

You look like sunshine, Zorie told me when I texted her a pic of me in the dress.

"Sunshine," I mumble. So why do I feel like a thunderstorm?

The screen door is open, and I let myself in. The house reeks of fish grease. I hate fish. Gloria knows this.

"Well, don't you look beautiful," my dad says. He stands from his recliner, his arms outstretched to me.

"Hi, Dad." I kiss his cheek and then wipe away the glossy residue.

"You really look lovely, Kayla. Gloria, doesn't Kayla look lovely?"

From the kitchen island, Gloria cranes her neck to look at me. She's a tall, thin woman with a salt-and-pepper bob and a honey complexion that looks as weathered and cracked as worn leather. Her eyes are too dark for her face, like two flat holes beneath thick, overgrown eyebrows. "New dress?" she asks.

She doesn't answer Dad's question, and he won't ask again.

"I'm gonna wash my hands for dinner," I tell Dad.

He pats my shoulder in a clumsy way that feels like a slap, and I try not to wince from the sting. I used to wonder what he thought of me, especially after Mom died and it was just the two of us. I never wanted him to look at me the way Gloria or Candace did, like I was one humiliation away from slashing my wrists with a razor blade. Thankfully, he never has. Dad might be the only person who looks genuinely proud when he sees me. Mom used to look at me like that. But I guess all mothers do.

I think about the "before" a lot, as in before cancer, when my mom was still the center of my and Dad's lives and we were hers. My happiest memories remain cemented there, in the before, like Mom and Dad slow dancing to Prince in the living room, or Dad bringing me and Mom flowers every week with a little card that read, "To my favorite girls." For our last Halloween together, we'd dressed up as Michael Jackson album covers. I was *Off the Wall* Michael, Mom was *Thriller*, and Dad was *Bad*. Mom made the costumes herself on the sewing machine Dad had gotten for her birthday. She used to tell me Dad spoiled her and then, with a laugh, say, *"Baby girl, I think all this love might keep me around forever."* I miss her laugh. No matter where I was in the house, I could hear it. Dad used to call her laugh sunshine because it made you warm when you heard it. And then the laughter stopped, and my whole world became cold.

Those final days watching her try to hang on in a world that was forcing her out were the worst days of my life. Dad tried to keep things as normal as possible, picking me up from school and making nightly dinners, with the three of us gathered at the table and, later, me pretending not to notice the sound of Mom vomiting in the bathroom after she tucked me in. For a long time, this was our version of normal, always pretending to be happy when all we wanted to do was cry. Mom died a week after my eighth birthday, but the dinners and the pretending kept going, even though we barely touched the food or smiled.

I find the bathroom across the hall from my old bedroom, which Gloria turned into a workout room after I moved out. Candace's bedroom is two doors down and across from the guest bedroom. There's even a full basement, but it's my bedroom she wanted to change. Zorie says I shouldn't be so salty about a bedroom I haven't slept in since I was nineteen years old, but I am. So much of me has been erased from this house.

I wash my hands quickly and return to the dining room, where they're already seated. Gloria and Dad sit on opposite ends of the table, with Candace and Charles occupying one side. I sit on the end closest to my dad, my only ally.

"Let's everyone bow our heads," Dad says, his expression serious. He's ten years younger than Gloria, but you'd never know it looking at him. The lines around his eyes have deepened, and his hair, once as black as oil, is now gray around the temples. It's like their marriage has stolen what remained of his youth and morphed him into this aged man I hardly recognize. Dad sees me watching him, gives me a stern look, and I immediately reach for Gloria's hand and bow my head. Like her personality, Gloria's hand is cold, and I try not to cringe as her long, thin fingers close over mine. "Heavenly Father, we thank you for this delicious meal and for the hands that prepared it. Thank you for the opportunity to gather again as a family."

At this, I look up, since the word *family* in connection with the people at this table is laughable. Candace stares unblinking at me, and I wonder how long she's been watching me.

"In your son, Jesus's name, we pray," Dad continues. "Amen."

I mumble an unenthused amen and wipe my hand on one of Gloria's ugly monogrammed linen napkins.

"I hope everyone enjoys tilapia," Gloria says.

I want to yell, *You know I don't!* but I smile instead.

"So how is work, Kayla? You're still at the hotel downtown?" Candace asks. She knows exactly where I work but pretends like she doesn't every time we see each other. It's like she gets off on having me tell her for the thousandth time that I'm a hotel housekeeper.

"Yep, still at the Chamberlain," I say. I tear off a piece of garlic bread and pop it into my mouth, not because I'm hungry, but because the simple act of chewing distracts me from my thoughts of dumping Gloria's pan of fried tilapia over Candace's head and scalding her perfect bronzed skin.

"My Candace just got a promotion," Gloria says. She loves to differentiate her daughter from my dad's. Everything is *my* Candace and *your* Kayla. I like to refer to Gloria as my dad's bitch.

"Congrats," I say, and pop another piece of bread into my mouth. Carbs do a body good.

"Thanks, but it isn't official yet," Candace says.

"Then why are we talking about it?"

Charles stops chewing, and Gloria drops her fork on her plate. I look at Dad, but he's poking at his fish with intense concentration.

"We're talking about it because it's good news, and in this family, we celebrate good news," Gloria says. Bits of fish collect in the corners of her mouth as she speaks, and she pokes at them with her tongue.

"Then I have good news, too," I say.

At this, Dad looks up, his eyes wide with hope that his only daughter has finally done something better than his stepdaughter.

"I'm applying for housekeeping manager," I continue.

Dad smiles, and pride swells in his eyes. "That's wonderful, sweetheart. My little girl a manager."

And then, for no other reason than I want my dad to keep looking at me like that, I add, "I'm going back to school, too. Thinking about getting a degree in hospitality." It's not a complete lie. I had thought about applying to school back before everything with Zorie happened, but not in the last twenty-four hours or even in the last twenty-four days.

"My goodness, that is quite the news," Candace says. She steeples her fingers under her chin and smiles. "Correct me if I'm wrong, Kayla, but I thought felons couldn't apply for financial aid."

Now it's my turn to drop my fork on my plate. It makes a clattering noise that sounds louder than it should. Gloria muffles a giggle, and Charles clears his throat. I don't look at Dad. I don't have to see his face to know his smile has faded and he's returned to poking his fish.

"Excuse me," I say and shove away from the table so fast my chair falls backward.

I manage to make it to the front door before the first tear falls.

CHAPTER TWO

I'm surprised to see Charles on the front porch instead of Dad when I exhale a plume of cigarette smoke.

"Those are bad for you," he says.

"You would know, wouldn't you?"

"What's that supposed to mean?"

I flick the cigarette onto the driveway and watch the fading ember fight for its life on the asphalt. "Because you're a doctor?"

The tips of his ears turn crimson, and he rubs the back of his neck. "Oh . . . right."

We're both quiet, and I know he's trying to think of something to say. This is the second time we've seen each other since his and Candace's engagement announcement in December and the first time we've been alone with each other since that night he stood on this very porch and told me he wanted to break up. Seven years later, I found out he was dating Candace after they made their relationship Instagram official, posing together with the cheesy caption "Every love story is beautiful, but ours is my favorite."

"Gloria wanted me to tell you dessert is ready," Charles says. His voice sounds shaky, like he's not sure of his own words.

"Yeah well, you can tell Gloria to go fuck herself and her dessert." I reach for my pack of cigarettes on the porch swing and use my teeth to pull one out. My nicotine addiction is getting way out of control. If I could afford insurance, I might see a doctor.

"You look good, Kayla," Charles says, watching me. "Life seems to be treating you well."

I shrug. "You know me, just living the dream."

"I hear that," he says, nodding. Charles is quiet again, thinking, and then manages a weak smile. "I think the last time we were out here together, your dad was congratulating me on getting accepted into Morehouse. Seems like a lifetime ago."

"Dad's always been your biggest fan, whether you're screwing me or his stepdaughter." My words come out bitter. Spiteful, even. But that's how they're intended to sound. I am bitter and spiteful.

"Listen, I don't know what kind of origin story you've dreamed up about my and Candace's relationship, but she and I never planned any of this. We ran into each other at a birthday party in Atlanta, and things just . . . kind of happened."

"Right." I flick open my lighter, light the tip of my cigarette, and inhale deeply. "How exactly did things just kind of happen, Charles?"

He leans against the banister and tugs at his tie. A tie for a fried-fish dinner. Pretentious asshole. "Can we not do this right now, Kayla? You and I were kids when we were together. High school relationships don't last outside of high school."

"Why not?" I ask as smoke billows out of my nostrils. "Why couldn't you and I be together after high school?"

"Jesus, Kayla." Charles rubs his face with his hand and exhales through his fingers. "Do you really want me to say it?"

"I asked, didn't I?"

"You're a housekeeper at a goddamn hotel, okay? You told me once that your dad said you have zero ambition. And he's right, Kayla. You've never wanted to be anything other than . . . what you are."

White-hot anger bubbles inside me, but I refuse to give him the satisfaction of a reaction. He doesn't deserve one. None of them do. It's my own fault for coming here tonight, thinking I could impress them with my forty-dollar Shop 'n' Save dress and my housekeeping promotion. Everyone at the table, besides my dad, thinks I'm a joke. Maybe that's the reason Gloria keeps inviting me to these stupid family dinners, to be her entertainment and make her laugh while she and her bitch of a daughter gnaw on overcooked fish with their shiny veneers.

"The truth is, you changed senior year," Charles says. "And then that thing happened with Zorie after graduation, and you, like, became a different person."

I wince. Almost a decade later, and it still feels like a punch to the gut. Every detail of that day is still burned into my brain, from Gloria's smug expression as the officers escorted me and Zorie into the courtroom to the disappointment etched across every feature of Dad's face. I'd begged Gloria to drop the charges, but she was determined to punish me, and seeing as how her brother was chief of police, she did exactly that. The familiar pang of guilt always manages to needle its way inside my soul whenever I think of that awful year. I've spent every moment since trying to make it up to my best friend for ruining her life.

"You know," Charles says, a little softer this time, "even though things with us didn't work out, I still think about you, Kayla."

My eyes snap back to his face, and I realize he's standing too close. I back up until I'm caught between the wall and the porch swing.

"I've always thought you were the sexiest girl I've ever been with."

He reaches out to touch my face, and I swat his hand away.

"Come on, Kayla. I know you still like me. We could have fun together again. I'm down if you are?"

"Get away from me, Charles," I hiss through clenched teeth.

"Don't be like that, baby." Charles leans in, his breath hot against my cheek, and whispers, "Remember how hard you used to make me?"

He traces the outline of my breast with his finger, and I slap him hard across the face. The impact stings my hand, but I keep it raised in the air in case he needs another.

"What the hell is going on out here?"

We both turn to see Gloria, Candace, and Dad in the doorway, their expressions wavering between anger and confusion.

"Kayla just slapped me for no reason," Charles says. "She's unhinged!"

"You fucking liar!" I shout, and I shove him. Charles stumbles back against the banister, nearly toppling over into Gloria's hydrangeas.

"Don't you touch him!" Candace yells. She sidles between us and shoves me back, but my balance is better than hers. I don't budge. We stand with our faces inches apart and glare at each other.

"Now, girls, that's enough," Dad says. "You two are sisters."

"We aren't sisters," Candace hisses. "We're barely acquaintances."

"You should keep your fiancé on a leash," I say.

Her eyes flash, and for a second, it looks like she might punch me. As luck has it, she spares me her fist and slaps me instead. I stagger back, stunned by her strength, and then lunge for her, but Dad wraps an arm around my waist and holds me against him.

"That's enough!" Gloria shouts. She stands between us with both hands firmly planted on her hips and narrows her black eyes at me. "Kayla, I think it would be best if you leave."

I wriggle free from Dad's hold and wait for him to say something—anything—but he doesn't respond. Or look at me. He stares straight ahead, his brows knitted together.

"Enjoy your dry fish," I say to Gloria as I shove past her. My heart pounds uncomfortably fast inside my chest, but I square my shoulders and walk across the driveway to my car. If Dad is watching me, I'll never know. I don't have the nerve to look back.

———

I don't tell Zorie about the disastrous dinner when I get home. She never asks anyway. She knows I only go to those corny dinners to make Dad happy. In a way, I think it makes him feel closer to Mom, like he's honoring her memory, even though, like me, so much of her has been erased from that house. For months after Mom died, Dad did all the things a widower with a young child is supposed to do— he took a leave of absence from work, cooked every meal, enrolled me in a grief support group for kids at the hospital, and reminded me every day that Mom loved me from here, all the way to heaven, and back again. But it wasn't enough. Eventually, Dad got overwhelmed in his single-father role and started spending less time at home and more time in the bars, guzzling cheap beer and bringing home women whose names he couldn't remember.

When he met Gloria on some dating website four years later, I was more relieved than disappointed. I finally had my dad back, not the hungover version I woke up to every morning, still dressed in last night's clothes and passed out on the living room floor. He cleaned himself up, got sober, started going to church with her on Sundays, and then, on a rainy Tuesday night, introduced twelve-year-old me to Gloria and Candace in a Pizza Hut parking lot across town. I wanted to like them, really I did, but from the very beginning, Gloria was cold and distant. Sure, she was polite, always smiling and asking me about school, but she was never really interested in the things I said. She'd nod while looking past me to admire Candace doing some dance in front of the TV, or tell me that it was time for me to move on when I'd mention missing my mom.

"Life is meant to be enjoyed, Kayla. It's what your mom would have wanted, and you wouldn't want to disappoint your mom, would you?" she'd say with a smile so tight it looked painful.

Candace was no better. She'd make barking noises when I walked past her in the hallway and accuse me of stealing things from her room whenever she and Gloria spent the night. Dad would look at me, more disappointed than angry, and demand that I return Candace's things before the end of the day.

"Fuck Gloria and her stuck-up daughter," Zorie would say. "They give off serious light-skin energy anyway."

"Your mom is light-skinned," I'd tell her, laughing.

"My point exactly."

When I told Dad I didn't like Gloria and her evil spawn, he'd called me selfish for not wanting him to be happy. He even blamed me when they broke up a few years later after Gloria said the stress of a blended family was too much for her. Zorie and I celebrated in her backyard with a bottle of Moscato she'd taken from her mom's bedroom.

For a while, Dad and I were happy again, having conquered the grief of losing Mom together and renewing our bond, but old habits die hard, and Dad found himself frequenting the same bars he'd avoided for so long. Thank God for Zorie during all those nights alone, waiting for Dad to come staggering through the door with his latest skanky bar find. She'd come over with a backpack full of our favorite DVDs, and we'd watch them while she greased my scalp with rosemary oil, like Mom used to do.

"You know you're my ride or die, right?" she'd say.

"Always."

And then, one night, it was Gloria, not some random skank, who came walking through the front door with Dad for a triumphant return.

If I thought Gloria was cold the first time around, she was a block of ice the second. She and Candace moved in right away and immediately took over the house. Photos of Candace and Gloria quickly replaced photos of me and Mom until the only evidence she'd ever existed inside our house was a single framed photo of her by the garage door.

Dad said nothing when Gloria suggested repainting the kitchen an ugly orange color over Mom's favorite pastel blue, or when she moved Mom's furniture to the basement to make room for her gaudy gold couch and love seat. When Gloria suggested I change bedrooms with Candace since mine was bigger and Candace needed more space to practice her cringy dance team routines, Dad agreed. And when Gloria said Zorie was no longer welcome in our home after she called Candace a cross-eyed little bitch for eavesdropping, Dad conceded it was for the best, calling my closest friend a bad influence. I countered that it was Gloria who was the bad influence.

"Why do you let her boss you around like that, Dad? Can't you see she's ruining our lives?" I'd whined.

"I'm not getting any younger, Kayla. I want this to work with Gloria. I know she'll never replace your mother, but she makes me happy," he'd told me, his eyes brimming with tears. "It's time for all of us to move on and start the next chapter of our lives."

I consider my own next chapter as I kick off the too-tight espadrilles and collapse on top of my bed. I open my laptop, type in the Chamberlain Hotel website address, and click on Employment Opportunities. There are only three openings: one for housekeeping, one for the front desk, and one for housekeeping manager. I click that box.

In the morning, I wake to loud voices coming from the kitchen and the smell of burning bacon. Zorie never cooks, mostly because she's terrible at it, but also because she hates washing dishes. Something about dishwashing detergent being murder on her cuticles. Weirdly, rubber gloves are the one item she never steals from the supply closet. I shuffle down the hall in my floppy slippers and find her at the stove, humming and scraping a scalded skillet with a spatula. Her braids are piled high on top of her head in a bun, and she's wearing her favorite green pajamas that complement her mahogany skin. When she turns to smile at me, I am once again reminded of how beautiful my best friend is. Her features are sharp and defined, like they were drawn on her face with a fine-point pen, from her jawline and straight nose to her big, round eyes that disappear into half-moons when she laughs, like she's doing now.

"Hey, girl, hey!" she says, waving the spatula at me.

"What are you so cheery about this morning?" I ask and plop down at the table.

Seconds later, I have my answer in the form of a big, beefy man with a bald head and biceps the size of watermelons. He pulls out a chair and sits down across from me as if he's done it a thousand times before.

"Morning," he grunts.

I nod my response.

He smells like my strawberry bodywash, which means he took a shower here. Which also means he spent the night. I shoot Zorie a murderous glare, and she mouths, *Sorry.* Our landlord has a strict no-overnight-guests policy because of all the complaints about un-authorized occupants, and if you're caught, it's an automatic evic-tion. We've been late with our rent two months in a row and can't risk giving our landlord another reason to kick us out. Lord knows Gloria would not be very psyched to have me living under her roof again.

"How many pancakes do you want, sweetie?" Zorie asks him.

Sweetie?

"I'm low-carbing it this week, babe."

Babe?

"Shit. I forgot," she says with a wink.

I wait for her to introduce me to the strange man who smells like Bath & Body Works sitting at our kitchen table, but she doesn't. She goes right on humming and scrambling eggs at the stove while I try to avoid eye contact with her new "sweetie."

"You must be Kayla," he says after a while.

I nod again.

"I'm Isaiah, Zorie's man." He offers his hand across the table, and I reluctantly shake it. It's the size of my face.

"I wasn't aware Zorie had a man," I say and twist in my seat to look at her.

"I told you about him . . . the guy from The Spot?" Zorie says and smiles over her shoulder at Isaiah. "We met on trivia night. He's been my baby ever since."

I try to remember the last time Zorie and I were at The Spot together since bars aren't really my thing. Zorie calls them her hunting grounds, and The Spot is pretty much the only bar in Redwood Springs with a decent mix of semiattractive men. I met my last boyfriend there a year ago on one of the rare nights I joined Zorie for two-for-one margaritas. His name was Trevor, a fast-talking truck driver from Baltimore looking to settle down and start a family. Three months into our relationship, he did just that, but with his exgirlfriend. He'd called me "emotionally immature," and I'd called him an asshole with a four-inch dick.

"Isaiah has his own business," Zorie says, interrupting my thoughts. "He's a designer."

This is the part where I'm supposed to look impressed. Isaiah stares at me, tilting his head as I take in his pockmarked skin and wide-set eyes and the chunky cubic zirconia studs in his ears.

"This here is one of my bestsellers," he says and points to his black T-shirt with the words *All My Bitches Love Me*.

I study the T-shirt's slanted text, thinking I'd seen the same shirt on Zorie three nights ago, wrinkled and stained, like she'd pulled it out of a hamper.

"My baby made this," she'd said, grinning proudly and reeking of tequila. I didn't ask for details as I helped her to her room since, in Zorie language, "my baby" can mean anyone from the barista who gives her free lattes to the bartender at The Spot who gives extragenerous pours.

"I take special orders, too," Isaiah says, as if he'd answered a question I never asked.

"Is that right?" I trace a scratch on the table with my finger, feeling like I've been dropped into the middle of an infomercial.

"Isn't my baby talented?" Zorie says, pride swelling in her voice. She dumps a skillet full of scrambled eggs onto his plate and slides the pan of extra-crispy bacon in front of him. "Isaiah could probably make you one for free, since we're best friends."

"I'll think about it."

Zorie kisses him, and I ignore the tiny pang of jealousy twisting around my insides. I miss dating and all the feels that come with meeting someone new. After Trevor, dating felt more like a chore, swiping right on apps and meeting for dinners with men whose pics never quite matched the live versions. We'd talk about our mundane lives over meals as bland as their personalities and then, after an awkward side hug in the parking lot, politely agree to do it again soon—which, of course, never happens. And then there were the occasional one-night stands with bored guests passing through the Chamberlain Hotel on business. I'd pretend not to notice their wedding rings, and they'd pretend not to know me when I showed up to strip their beds the next morning. As much as I wanted a real relationship, finding someone in Redwood Springs was a lost cause.

"I need to get ready for work," I say and push back my chair.

"You're on your own today, girl," Zorie says. "Leslie Grace gave me the day off since I took second shift yesterday. All this teamwork energy I'm giving, Leslie Grace might give *me* that management job."

"Oh sure, right, like that would ever happen." I laugh and start past her, but she catches my arm.

"What's that supposed to mean?"

I blink at her and wait for the smile that doesn't come. Her face is serious. Hurt, even.

"What? You don't think I'm management material?"

"Of course I do. You know I think you'd be great at anything," I say earnestly. "I'm your biggest fan."

Zorie's face softens, and a new smile appears on her lips. "Wouldn't it be funny if we were both promoted?"

"We'd be the best damn management team the Chamberlain has ever seen," I say and kiss her cheek. "We'll talk later, okay?"

I go back to my room to change and see a missed call from the Chamberlain Hotel and a text from Leslie Grace: *Come see me as soon as you get here.* It's really happening. Finally. I smile my first real smile in the past twenty-four hours.

CHAPTER THREE

———

FRIDAY

The Chamberlain Hotel parking lot is a flurry of guests zigzagging through rows of cars with their rolling suitcases. I envy them for leaving this town that I now feel like a permanent fixture of. Once inside, I wave to Geraldine setting up the breakfast bar and to Serena checking out guests with the kind of all-teeth smile Leslie Grace encourages.

Mornings behind the front desk are always hectic: copy machines humming, phones ringing, keyboards tapping, and the aroma of coffee and hard-boiled eggs permeating the air from the dining room. I enter my code to open the door that leads to the back offices and make my way down the short hallway, past the conference room, to Leslie Grace's office. She sits at her desk, squinting at her computer screen and mumbling to herself. A knife and an apple sliced in half with peanut butter smeared on its insides are on a saucer next to her keyboard. I knock on the door, and she waves me in without looking up.

"Take a seat, Kayla."

I pull out the lint-covered chair across from her and sit, wincing as the seat creaks under my weight.

"Almost done," she says.

I glance around her office, thinking of the last time I sat across from her in this very chair and asked—no, begged—for a raise. Most of her framed photos are of her dog: an ugly white furball with bulging eyes and a flat nose. What's his name? Biscuit? Cupcake? Something yeasty, I'm sure of it. From what I've learned about Leslie Grace over the years, she's a loner, a recluse. She doesn't have friends. No husband. No ex-husband. No boyfriend. No ex-boyfriend. Her entire existence is dedicated to this hotel. Looking at her now, I feel sorry for her.

"Cute dog," I say.

At this, Leslie Grace finally looks up and smiles. Her eyes are bloodshot and ringed with dark circles like she hasn't slept in years, let alone days. "Donut is such a good boy."

Donut! I knew it was something yeasty!

"I won't keep you in suspense any longer, Kayla." She takes a bite of the apple and sucks the peanut butter off her thumb. "I called this meeting because there's some important business I'd like to discuss with you."

I shift in the chair, and it lets out another painful groan. "Is this about my application?"

She steeples her fingers under her chin and leans forward. "What application?"

"My application for housekeeping manager."

"You applied?" Leslie Grace swivels in her chair and leans in close to her computer screen. "So you did. If I'm being honest, I was hoping you'd apply, Kayla. I think you'd make a brilliant leader." She swivels back to face me, and I brace myself for the job offer coming next. "Which is why I was so incredibly disappointed when it was brought to my attention what you did yesterday."

"Wait, what? I don't understand."

"The guest on the seventh floor—Mrs. Sherman? Did you or did you not allow Mrs. Sherman to enter the Kensington Suite without first confirming her ID?"

I blink slowly, waiting for my brain to catch up to my other senses. Fuck my life. I knew those forty bucks weren't worth it. "I was just trying to be a team player," I say. My voice comes out in a tremble, and I swallow hard. "It won't happen again."

"Kayla, I shouldn't have to remind you how dangerous it is to let guests into rooms without confirming their ID. Do you remember last year when someone stole five hundred dollars from one of the suites?"

I nod. I do remember. Because it was Zorie.

"Unfortunately for you, it was Mrs. Sherman's husband who was registered to the Kensington Suite, not Mrs. Sherman, and thanks to your careless actions, she was able to gain access to his belongings as well as his, um, companion's."

Every muscle in my body tightens, and the chair feels less sturdy beneath me. I'd let a scorned woman enter the room of her husband and his side chick. How dumb could I be?

"As you can imagine, Mr. Sherman was very upset. He wanted to have you arrested for trespassing or unlawful entry. Now, I don't know how the laws work regarding this type of thing, but given your history with the legal system, I managed to talk him out of it." She pauses and waits for me to thank her, but all I can offer is a nod. If I open my mouth to say anything, I might burst into tears. "Are you aware that the Chamberlain was one of the first fully integrated hotels in Georgia in the 1960s?"

She pauses again, but I don't nod this time or care about this impromptu black-history lesson.

"The owners of the Chamberlain, Mr. and Mrs. Bennett, are very compassionate people. They were willing to let you and Zorie work here despite your special circumstances, but your actions have put all our jobs at risk. Can you imagine the damage it would do to the Chamberlain's reputation if the media found out our housekeepers were allowing strangers to enter guests' rooms?" Leslie Grace places her hand on her chest and exhales. "Thankfully, the Bennetts have graciously agreed not to pursue legal action against you and instead will take the seven hundred dollars for damages to the room and Mr. Sherman's belongings out of your paycheck."

Her words suck the oxygen from the room. I grip the sides of the chair and inhale deeply as my brain does the math. "That's almost my entire check. How am I supposed to survive on a hundred bucks? Can't they use insurance or something to pay for the damages?"

"I'm sorry, Kayla, but these are the consequences of your actions." Leslie Grace gives a noncommittal shrug, and I officially hate her now. "You'll receive your final check at the end of the month."

"You're really doing this? After seven years here?" My voice cracks, and I feel the tears behind my eyes. "Please don't do this, Leslie Grace. It will never happen again, I swear."

Leslie Grace leans forward on her elbows, and I steel myself for what I know is coming. My next chapter has ended before it began.

"As much as it breaks my heart to lose such a valuable employee, I have no choice," she says. "Kayla, you're fired."

The reality of what took place inside Leslie Grace's office doesn't hit me until I'm in the Tasty Freeze's drive-thru and ordering a spicy chicken biscuit and a side of hash browns. I devour them before I leave the parking lot. The chicken is tough, like chewing a leather shoe, and the biscuits are tasteless and dry, but I eat every last bite, even lick the greasy wrapper, which is a new low for me.

Fired.

I've never been fired from anything, unless you count that summer at the Rib Shack when the manager told me not to come back if I wasn't ready to work hard. So I didn't.

But that was high school, and I've been at the Chamberlain for almost seven years. I'm supposed to be a responsible adult. A reliable one. And now I'm the fired one.

"I'll just find another job," I say, feeling the wheels of my brain start to move again. And then the wheels screech to a halt as I remember this is the only job I've had since my felony charge and that the Chamberlain Hotel took some convincing to hire not only me but also my best friend. Fucking Gloria and her bullshit about consequences for bad behavior. If it weren't for her, Zorie and I might not have wasted an entire year of our lives in the Sumner State Prison for burglary.

And now I am jobless. My and Zorie's combined salaries were barely enough to live on, which is why Zorie suggested stealing the gift box from the first wedding we ever crashed two summers ago, right there in the Chamberlain Hotel's grand ballroom. We scored eleven hundred dollars that night. It was enough for Zorie to convince me to do it again. And again. And again. Until it became our part-time job and Zorie's addiction. Thirteen weddings later, we've furnished our entire apartment with our hauls, not to mention the cash we've collected across the great state of Georgia. Last month's wedding brought our grand total to $5,385. We'd counted it twice, stretched out on Zorie's bed, marveling at how we'd never seen this much cash in our lives. She'd wanted to take a trip, somewhere tropical, but I'd insisted that we save enough for emergencies and getting our raggedy cars fixed. To think, only a month ago, our biggest problem was deciding between the Caribbean and new tires, and now I'm one paycheck away from qualifying for food stamps.

Thank God for our emergency stash. I drive home quickly, thinking my panic was premature. Zorie isn't in the apartment when I get there. Probably somewhere making T-shirts with her new baby. I make a beeline to our kitchen and to the cabinet with the Folgers coffee jug. I twist open the top and dig through the coffee grounds for the Ziploc bag full of cash, but it's gone. I dump the contents of the jug into the sink and watch as coffee grounds slide down the drain.

"We were robbed!" I shout.

"No, we weren't." I jump at the sound of Zorie's voice. She leans against the refrigerator, watching me. "I was going to tell you, Kayla. I swear."

Dread quickens my pulse. "Tell me what?"

"Don't be mad, okay?" Her voice sounds small, like it doesn't belong to her. "Promise me you won't be mad."

I speak slowly, as if to a child. "Zorie, what did you do with our money?"

She paces in front of me, chewing her thumbnail. "You promised you wouldn't get mad."

"I didn't promise shit. Where's our money, Zorie?"

"Think of it as an investment—an opportunity to support a black-owned business."

"Oh my God." I groan. I sink to my knees with my face in my hands. "You gave all of our savings to Isaiah for his dumbass bootleg T-shirt business, didn't you? How long have you even known this guy?"

"Three weeks."

"Oh my God." I groan again.

"Isaiah says he can double our money, maybe even triple it." Zorie stares at me with big, pleading eyes. "I did this for us, Kayla. You're always so worried about money, so I figured if we had more of it, you wouldn't be so stressed all the time and we could finally live."

"We had a plan for what we were going to do with that money, Zorie. We were going to get our cars fixed and save the rest for emergencies. That was the plan."

"No, that was *your* plan. *I* wanted to go on a vacation, and now we can go wherever we want because we'll have plenty of money."

"Because Isaiah's raggedy T-shirts are gonna make us millionaires?" I say and roll my eyes. "The man scammed you, and now we're broke."

Zorie frowns at me. "Why are you so pressed right now? It's just one little investment. God, it's not like it was our rent money. That's what our jobs are for, remember?"

"Except I don't have a job!" I snap. "I got fired today. Someone narced on me about a guest. I don't want to talk about it."

I've never seen someone turn gray before, especially another black person, but that's exactly what happens to Zorie's face. "Fired? Damn, girl. What happened?"

"Didn't I just say I don't want to talk about it?"

She shifts her weight from one foot to the other. "Guess I didn't think Leslie Grace would ever fire you. I'm so sorry, Kayla."

I narrow my eyes at her. "Are you, though?"

Zorie looks confused for a moment, then nods. "Of course I am. I'm your best friend." She takes a step forward and holds out her phone. "It's okay, we can fix this. There's a wedding we can go to in Jasper Falls tomorrow. It's small, but we can probably get enough to cover our rent for a month or two until—"

"Until what?" I yell. "Until I get the big executive job? Oh wait, that's right—they're saving that job for the girl without the felony." I tilt my head back and exhale to the ceiling. "When we crashed that wedding last month in Shepherdsville, the flower girl saw us take the gift box. She cried, Zorie, and we just left like two heartless thieves. Aren't you tired of being a criminal? Crashing weddings . . . stealing from the bride and groom . . . doesn't it ever get old? Don't you want something better for yourself?"

Zorie's mouth presses into a thin line, and she lowers her phone to her side. "That's why I invested in Isaiah's company—so we can both have a better life."

"Don't be an idiot, Zorie! I'm talking about something *real*—an actual career—one that comes with respect *and* money. I'm tired of living like this." I take out a cigarette and place it between my lips. I don't have the energy to feel sorry for Zorie. Not this time. "You know what your problem is?" I pluck the cigarette from my lips and point it at her. "You lack ambition."

"You sound like your dad right now," she says, rolling her eyes.

"Yeah? Well, maybe he's right. Look at us! We never change. Our lives are just as shitty now as they were ten years ago. Shittier, even!"

Zorie stares at me, her expression a combination of shock and frustration. "And whose fault is that?" she yells. This is met with loud knocks from the apartment below. Miss Eugena. Zorie moves closer, her chest rising and falling beneath her thin T-shirt. "I had dreams, too, and I threw them away because of you and your petty bullshit. You were the one who broke in and trashed that place the night before your dad's wedding. And when everyone blamed me for your little tantrum, I took the hit, because that's what best friends do—they protect each other." She holds up her wrist with our tattooed initials: KD+ZA. They're the same letters tattooed on the inside of my own wrist. "You know what this means." She stabs at her wrist with her thumb. "It means ride or die. You know I don't have anyone else." Tears pour down her cheeks, and she doesn't bother wiping them away. "You're it for me, Kayla. You're my family."

She'd said the same words to me the night she showed up at my front door, soaked to the bone from running in the rain to my house, nearly three miles. She'd looked so small standing there, her tiny ten-year-old body shivering against the biting October wind. I made her hot chocolate in the microwave while she changed into a pair of my pajamas, and then, through her tears, she told me Miss Patrice hit her after an argument about Zorie's grandmother. Something to do with a fire and her grandmother being badly burned.

"She told me it was my fault for not watching the stove, and then she hit me. I didn't know where to go, so I came here," Zorie said, sobbing against my shoulder. "I don't have anyone else, Kayla. You're my family."

"You're safe now. I won't let anything happen to you, Zo. I'll always keep you safe. I promise," I said.

Zorie nodded, and then, smoothing back her hair, she showed me the deep-purple bruise under her left eye. I immediately called Dad, and he rushed home, half-drunk and, ironically, ranting about what an unfit mother Miss Patrice was.

"God is my witness, you're never going back to that woman again," he said.

And she didn't—at least, not right away. Zorie spent the next seven months with us, until the court decided Miss Patrice was a suitable mother again. I used to ask Zorie why she didn't live with her father if Miss Patrice was so cruel, and she'd tell me the only thing she shared with Omar Andrews was a last name. He and Miss Patrice had met at a party, and after a night of drunken sex, she found out she was pregnant. For his part, Omar did his best to do right by Miss Patrice, sending her money every month for Zorie's care, but he had zero interest in being a part of her life or her mother's. When he died in a car accident our junior year, he designated twenty thousand dollars of his life insurance policy to Zorie, which Miss Patrice promptly deposited into an account she claimed Zorie could access when she turned eighteen. By the time we were released from prison, the account had been completely depleted. She'd told Zorie the money went toward her legal fees, even though we both had public defenders. Zorie never spoke to Miss Patrice again after that, except to offer a sarcastic "Hello, Mother" in passing if they happened to run into each other. Miss Patrice would pretend not to hear her, and Zorie would laugh, even though her expression looked hurt.

"Kayla? Did you hear what I said?" Zorie asks, snapping her fingers at me.

"I heard you." I stare down at my own wrist and trace the initials with my finger. Ride or die.

"I'll fix this." Zorie swings her purse over her shoulder and digs out her car keys. "I promise."

She leaves me on the kitchen floor, still clutching the empty Folgers jug.

CHAPTER FOUR

———

One hour later, I peel myself off the linoleum, determined not to feel sorry for myself. The Chamberlain Hotel isn't the only hotel in Redwood Springs. I open the job-seeker app on my phone, and a new email notification pops up from Bank of Redwood. My account is overdrawn. Again. Clearly breakfast at the Tasty Freeze was a mistake.

I take a deep breath and will myself not to panic. Rent is due in three days, but I still have a paycheck coming from the Chamberlain, minus seven hundred bucks. I'll ask our landlord, Garrett, for an extension. He's in his late thirties and flirts with me when I drop off our rent at the office. Maybe all my extra giggling at his corny jokes will finally pay off. I smile, feeling hopeful again. We'll be fine. Of course, in the meantime, we'll be forced to live off our stolen supply of Lucky Charms and Cinnamon Toast Crunch since we won't be able to afford groceries. But who cares about a balanced diet at this point? And once our water is shut off, Zorie can use her key to let me into the hotel for showers after hours. Oh, and we'll use candlelight once the electric company disconnects our power. Easy.

I take out my phone and find Garrett's number. My thumbs move quickly over the keypad, alternating between happy-face emojis and sad-face emojis and then a heart. The ellipsis moves on the screen, and I hold my breath, waiting. Garrett's reply to my request for an extension is short and sweet: *NO*, followed by, *wyd*?

"Asshole!" I yell at the screen. Miss Eugena immediately responds with three annoyed knocks. I shove back from the table and go to the fridge to take inventory of our sad food supply: three Chobani yogurts, a wilted bag of salad, a half-eaten Hot Pocket, and an empty jug of milk. Zorie burned what was left of our bacon and scrambled an entire carton of eggs for her shady boyfriend. I slam the refrigerator door.

"Don't panic. Do not panic."

I unlock my phone again and scroll through my list of contacts. Asking Dad and Gloria for money is obviously out of the question. I'd rather starve to death than hear one of her self-righteous "Told you so" lectures. My finger stops on the Chamberlain Hotel's preferred guest and owner of the biggest penis I've ever seen: Rodney, full-time Cherry Crisp Soda rep and part-time adulterer. I press his name with the eggplant emoji next to it and wait. He answers on the first ring.

"This is Rodney," he says in a voice I don't recognize. Very corporate and very fake.

"Rodney? It's Kayla?" I say, as if I'm unsure of my own name.

"Who?"

He sounds annoyed, and I'm tempted to hang up, but then I remember his last words to me as I slipped out of room 622 three Sundays ago with my panties tucked inside my purse: *"Call me if you ever need anything, beautiful."*

I clear my throat and start again. "This is Kayla . . . from the Chamberlain Hotel." I pause and wait for some sign of recognition, but there isn't one. Someone in the background yells something about a meeting, and then everything sounds muffled, like he's covering the phone.

"If this is about a bill, you'll need to call Cherry Crisp's corporate office," he says.

"This isn't about a bill, Rodney. I'm Kayla . . . the housekeeper," I repeat, louder.

"Kayla the housekeeper . . . from the Chamberlain Hotel," Rodney says, letting my name roll around on his tongue. For a second, I picture his face as the memory forms in his brain of us in the shower that last night together. "Kayla the housekeeper," he says again. "How'd you get this number?"

"You gave it to me. You said to call if I ever needed anything, and I need something."

"Is that right?" His voice is softer now. It's the same one he uses when we're alone. "And what do you need from your boy?"

"Money," I blurt out.

He doesn't say anything. I can't blame him. I know how ridiculous I sound. Even worse, I know how ridiculous he thinks I sound. We've hooked up three, maybe four times at the Chamberlain. I don't even know his last name and only found out where he worked because I wore his Cherry Crisp T-shirt home one night. And here I am asking Rodney Eggplant Emoji for money.

"Are you stupid, Kayla?" he asks. "My God, you cannot be this stupid. We hook up a few times, and you thought, what? You could just call me up and ask for money like you're my woman? Do me a favor, Kayla from the Chamberlain Hotel, and don't call this number again."

He hangs up.

And just like that, there went one of our best corporate accounts.

I close my eyes, taking in long, deep breaths. Clearly if I'm going to find money, I'm on my own. No one-night stands. No parents. No emergency stash. I press my fingers to my temples to slow down my mind. Think, Kayla. Think. I need quick cash. And where do you go for quick cash?

The pawn shop.

I open the cabinets below the sink and grab two Keurigs, an Instant Pot, a sous vide kit, and a Vitamix blender and carefully stack each on the kitchen table. There's at least six hundred dollars' worth of appliances here. It would've been more if Zorie hadn't pawned a food processor and an espresso machine last month to get her hair done and if I hadn't pawned a mixer and a cheese board for gas and groceries. I take out my phone to text Zorie my plan and then decide against it. She didn't text me when she decided to give Isaiah our entire emergency stash. I tuck my phone back inside my pocket and grab my keys.

====

Quik Dollaz Pawn Shop is surprisingly busy when I arrive with my trash bags of appliances. It's one of the few local pawn shops we've visited to avoid drawing suspicion. I wait in line behind a woman holding a trumpet case. She shifts her weight from one foot to the other, and I wonder if the case is too heavy for her. When it's her turn, she sets the case on the counter and opens it slowly, carefully, wiping away smudges with the hem of her shirt. The man behind the counter lifts the trumpet from the case, his thick fingers leaving ugly black smears up and down its golden frame. The woman looks as if she's on the verge of tears watching him, and she goes back to shifting her weight from foot to foot. Finally, the man squints at her and barks, "Two hundred."

The woman looks almost horrified. "It's worth a thousand!"

"It's worth two hundred here." He takes a toothpick from his shirt pocket and chews the end of it. "Take it or leave it."

She turns to look at me as if she wants my approval, but I look away and pretend to be interested in the display of power drills.

"I'll take it," she says, her voice barely a whisper.

He checks her ID, and then she signs a form and hurries out the door with two hundred-dollar bills in her hand. I watch her as she stands on the sidewalk, looking mournfully through the window. I've never been attached to the things I pawned. How could I? They don't belong to me. The woman wipes away a tear, and I look away. What must her life be like to have to give up something she clearly loves?

"Can I help you?" the man asks me.

I make my way to the counter and unpack my bag of goods.

"This stuff belong to you?" he asks, opening the boxes.

"Of course it does."

I can't tell if he believes me.

"You guys still hiring?" I ask, pointing at the handwritten HELP WANTED sign by the register.

"Third shift only," he says. "You can apply online if you're interested." He goes back to examining the appliances and simultaneously typing on his computer. I watch his hands as they move from one appliance to the next. Every nail is bitten down to the quick, and every knuckle is tattooed with an X.

"Two hundred," he says without looking up.

"What?"

He removes the toothpick as if this made his words difficult to understand. "Two hundred," he repeats.

"There's six hundred dollars' worth of shit here," I say.

"Stolen shit."

Sweat beads on my forehead. He's clearly better at this game than me. A career of lies and manipulation has given him an advantage. I shift my gaze to see who's watching, then lower my voice. "I told you—this stuff is mine."

The man smiles like he knows my words are bullshit. "Two hundred, and I won't call the police."

"Fine. Whatever. Just give me the money." My throat tightens, and I hate the way it sounds like I'm about to cry as I hand over my ID.

"Oh, and don't bother applying for the job, Miss Davenport. We don't hire thieves. You have yourself a good day now." He smiles, looking pleased with himself.

I turn and catch sight of my reflection in the glass door. But it isn't my reflection. It's the woman who just pawned her trumpet. We are the same.

———

LOVE YOU TO DEATH

I decide to use ten dollars of my two hundred and treat myself to a second meal with no nutritional value and hit up the drive-thru at the Tasty Freeze again. Old habits die hard. The car in front of me takes forever to order, and I'm about to honk my horn when I see the driver's eyes watching me in their rearview mirror. I give them the finger, and the driver twists around in the front seat to look at me, her lips curled up in an ugly smile. I'd recognize that Botox smile anywhere. Candace.

"Shit." I shift gears into reverse, but a pickup truck is practically touching my bumper.

Candace opens her car door, and I watch in what feels like slow motion as she climbs out and walks toward me.

Shit. Shit. Shit.

The driver of the pickup gives an impatient honk, and Candace flashes her oversize veneers. She taps my window, and I stare straight ahead, feeling like a trapped rat. Her tapping is relentless, and so is the honking behind me. I finally give in.

"Shouldn't you be on your broom back to Atlanta?" I ask.

"There's that charming Kayla sense of humor we all adore. You really did miss your comedic calling," she says through my cracked window. "And if you must know, Charles's parents are throwing us an engagement party this weekend, so we've extended our stay. I would've invited you, but—"

"What do you want, Candace?" I snap, my eyes still fixed on her 2BLESSD license plate.

"Can't I say good morning to my big sister?"

I grit my teeth. "Like I said, what do you want?"

She leans a hip against the door, drumming her nails on the Starbucks cup in her hand. "Mrs. Charles Phillips" is written above the cup sleeve because of course it is. "Charles told me how you came on to him last night. Honestly, Kayla, it's so sad how obsessed you are with him. Trust me, I get it. Charles is perfect. But he's mine. I'm sorry it's so hard for you to find a man who wants a maid and a felon for a girlfriend."

And then I feel it—coffee—warm and wet on my skin. My eyes snap back to Candace's smiling face, and she lifts the Starbucks cup at me in a mock salute.

"Have a nice day, sis, and stay away from Charles," she says before giving me the finger and tossing the empty cup on my hood.

I will myself to stay calm as my hands grip the steering wheel so tightly my knuckles turn white. Candace's car moves forward, and so do I. Right into her bumper. The impact pushes her car past the drive-thru window and into the path of an SUV whose driver manages to slam on their brakes before colliding with Candace's BMW. Tasty Freeze employees and customers spill out of the restaurant and into the parking lot, their concerned eyes darting from Candace's car to my 1997 Nissan Sentra.

"Call the police!" someone shouts.

"Ma'am? Are you okay?" a man in a Tasty Freeze uniform asks through my cracked window. The name tag on his shirt says "Jimmy" and, beneath it, "Manager." It was a last resort to work here, but now my chances of getting hired are gone just like the funds in my bank account.

"Ma'am? Should I call someone?" he asks, his voice more urgent than before.

I shake my head but don't look at him. Candace is still inside her car. Probably calling Gloria as we speak. I have no insurance. I have no job. I have two hundred dollars to my name.

I take out my phone and shoot a text to Zorie. *One last time.* It's only three words, but she'll know what it means.

CHAPTER FIVE

Leaving the scene of an accident is a crime. Everyone knows this. I know this. But it doesn't stop me from leaving the Tasty Freeze's parking lot and driving across town to the Chamberlain, where Zorie is waiting. She climbs inside my car and immediately hugs me.

"You okay, girl? You sounded so freaked out when you called." Zorie pulls away to look me up and down, and hugs me again. I don't realize I'm crying until I see the dark, wet spot on the shoulder of her gray housekeeping uniform. "You better not get snot on me," she says with a grin.

"Too late," I say and wipe my nose with the back of my hand. "Why are you working today, anyway? Thought you had the day off."

"Picked up an extra shift seeing as how we need the money now that you're . . . unemployed." She sighs and wipes the tears from my cheeks with her thumbs. "You want to tell me why you were so freaked out on the phone?"

I lean forward and fold my arms on the steering wheel. "This is so bad, Zo. Gloria is going to send me back to prison."

"You're always so dramatic. Whatever it is, it can't be that bad."

"It is. Very." I go over the whole awful story with Zorie: how Candace poured coffee inside my car and, after temporarily losing my mind, how I rammed my car into hers.

"Wow," she says when I finish. I wait for her to say something else, something comforting, maybe, but she laughs instead. "If I was with you, we would've really fucked some shit up."

She laughs harder. Louder. It's contagious. I hunch forward and laugh with her until my sides ache and tears stream down my cheeks. A woman wearing a sweater-vest in the middle of summer watches us carefully as she passes my car, and I do my best to regain my composure. The last thing I need is for her to complain to the manager about the two loud black women loitering in the parking lot and for Leslie Grace to ban me from the Chamberlain Hotel forever.

"I bet the thought of sending you back to prison has your step-mommy's panties wet right now," Zorie says, wiping her eyes with the back of her hand.

This only makes me laugh harder. Then, as if summoned by the devil himself, my phone buzzes, and Gloria's number flashes on the screen. I hit decline. Seconds later, it buzzes again. This time it's Dad's number. I consider letting it go to voicemail, but I know he'll only call again. Anything Gloria-related is always an emergency with him. She could be calling to ask if I swiped one of her linen napkins from last night's dinner, and Dad would blow up my phone until I told him I haven't seen it. I take a deep breath, clear my throat, and stab the screen with my thumb.

"Hi, Dad."

"You answered," he says. I can tell by his voice he's smiling. Hopeful, even.

"It's not a good time. Can I call you later?"

"You won't." The smile in his voice fades, and a new tone replaces it. Disappointment? Sadness? "Listen, Kayla, I'm not mad. I just want to talk."

I don't say anything. I wait.

"Kayla? Are you there, sweetheart?"

I heave a long sigh. It's time to rip off the Band-Aid. I look at Zorie and mouth, *So annoying.*

"What did she tell you, Dad?"

"That the two of you exchanged words."

"Exchanged words?" I laugh. "Did she also tell you that she poured coffee inside my car?"

"I know the two of you have never been close, but all this animosity between you and Candace has to stop. If this is about . . . him—"

"It's not about Charles!" I snap.

We've been here before, Dad and I, tiptoeing around any mention of Charles, as if saying his name might send me into some kind of emotional spiral. Weirdly, it was Dad who looked as though he might burst into tears that night at dinner three years ago when he told me Candace and Charles were dating. He'd hugged me so tight I thought my bones might crack. I'd told him I was fine, not wanting to give Gloria the pleasure of seeing me looking hurt.

"I don't want Charles, okay, Dad?" I say into the phone. "He and Candace can ride off into the sunset for all I care." Or over a goddamn cliff. "I just want you to see that it's not me doing the fighting, it's her. Candace and Gloria have made my life a living hell since the day they moved in, and you always pretend not to see it."

"That isn't true, sweetheart," Dad says, and I picture him shaking his graying head at my words. "The only thing I've ever wanted is for all of us to try to be a family. When your mom died, I felt like you were robbed of the chance to grow up with a mother. I wanted you to have that experience, Kayla. Gloria isn't perfect, but she means well, and I know she cares about you very much."

I bite my tongue until I taste blood. Gloria cares about me. The words are so ridiculous they're not even worth a laugh. Yes, Gloria *cares about me* so much that when I was sixteen, she donated all my summer clothes to the Goodwill and replaced them with smaller sizes to motivate me to lose weight. Zorie and I searched the donation bins until we'd collected every single piece of my wardrobe and then dumped a garbage bag full of Gloria's shoes into the same bins.

"She only wants the best for you," Dad is saying. "We both do."

I shake my head, thinking how much Gloria *only wants the best for me* that she "forgot" to invite me to Dad's retirement party from the warehouse last fall. The photo from that night of Gloria and Candace beaming proudly with my only living parent is still prominently displayed on the living room wall.

"Why do you always choose them?" I blurt out.

Zorie stops scrolling on her phone and blinks at me with her huge black eyes.

Within seconds, all the anger, hurt, and disappointment of the last few years spills out of me like vomit right there on the fuzzy pink steering-wheel cover. "Since you and Gloria met, it's always been about her and Candace—whatever they want, whatever they need," I say, my voice rising. The couple loading their luggage into the car next to us stare, but I don't care. "You let her erase me from our family, Dad. Just like you erased Mom."

My mind flashes back to that first month after my release from prison and the way Gloria monitored my every move inside the house, like I was a virus threatening to contaminate her perfect world. She and Candace locked their bedroom doors at night, making sure I heard the lock click when I walked past their rooms. By the end of the month, Gloria had convinced Dad that my presence in the house made her and Candace uncomfortable, and he asked me to leave. Zorie picked me up in her boyfriend's Mustang, and I sprinted across the lawn without looking back. I spent almost a year on Zorie's boyfriend's couch before we landed jobs at the Chamberlain and saved enough money for our own place.

"You made me feel like I didn't belong anywhere, Dad," I say. "You made me feel alone."

Now it's Dad's turn to be quiet. He clears his throat, and I imagine his brain working overtime to come up with an excuse for being a shitty father.

"I never meant to hurt you, sweetheart," he says finally. "I love you more than anything in this world. That's why I told Candace not to press charges on the condition that you pay for the damages. She told the police it was a family disagreement."

"But it wasn't a family disagreement. She started it. *She* poured her drink inside *my* car." I hate how whiny my voice sounds, but I can't help it. Talking to Dad about anything involving Gloria or Candace always makes me feel like I'm twelve years old again.

"How long are you going to keep doing this, Kayla? You're almost thirty years old. Don't you think it's time for you to start accepting responsibility for your own actions, or will it always be someone else's fault?"

"Daddy, I'm telling the truth. Candace started it!"

He lets out a long sigh, and I picture him sinking back into the worn cushions of his recliner. "Candace is being very gracious here by not pressing charges."

He pauses, like he's waiting for me to say something, maybe for me to thank him for keeping me out of jail this time. But I can't bring myself to say the words.

"I'm tired, Kayla. I really am," Dad says after a beat. "I'm tired of apologizing to Gloria and Candace for the things you do over and over again."

"Then stop!" I yell and hang up.

"You okay?" Zorie asks, watching me.

"I just wish he'd take my side for once, you know? He acts like he's doing me a favor by convincing Princess Candace not to press charges if I pay the damages."

A flash of uncertainty crosses her face. "I mean, isn't that a good thing?"

"It's just one more thing for them to hang over my head. No matter what I do, she will always be the better daughter—the one he's the proudest of." I take a deep breath and swallow the growing lump in my throat. "The one he wishes was his."

"Hey, fuck your dad," Zorie says. "If he can't see the perfect human he created for what you are, then fuck him. His loss."

This is what I love about Zorie, how she can instantly turn into my very own hype woman just when I need it. "I know Candace is waiting for me to screw up again so she can have me arrested. Bet she has her chief-of-police uncle on speed dial."

Zorie nudges me with her elbow. "Don't worry. We'll get the money. We always make ends meet somehow, don't we?"

I press my forehead against the steering wheel as if trying to push out a new plan. "Do you ever feel guilty after?" I ask.

Zorie is quiet for a moment, watching me. "Do you?"

I shrug but don't answer. Truth is, I'd never felt guilty until the last wedding, when the flower girl burst into tears watching our theft in action. Until that moment, I'd always felt like some kind of sociopath for never caring that I was stealing a piece of two strangers' happiness.

"Doesn't matter anyway," Zorie says, still watching me. "This is the last time, right?"

"It has to be."

She holds up her phone and points at the screen. A man and woman wearing matching cowboy hats hold hands in the middle of a cotton field. "Meet the future Mr. and Mrs. Brett Fletcher. Their reception is at some little community center in Jasper Falls. We can go tomorrow."

"Jasper Falls, huh? Isn't that, like, two hours away? We've never been to that part of Georgia before."

By "that part of Georgia," I mean the redneck side. Hillbilly, USA, to be exact. It's a risk. A real gamble. Two black women in the middle of backwoods Georgia, where Confederate flags hang from almost every porch and people still use words like *colored* to describe our skin.

"You sure it's a good idea?" I ask. "We might . . . stick out."

"The couple posted the band they hired on their Instagram. Solar Sonics. The lead singer and drummer are black, so maybe to be on the safe side, we can blend in as part of the entertainment."

"Because we're black? That feels low-key racist, Zo," I say, laughing.

"I'm just keeping it real. Maybe they don't have black friends, and in a town like that, you *know* how many black friends you have. The band is our in." She leans closer and swipes at the phone screen with her pinky. "Look," she says, pointing. "They all wear the same T-shirts. I was thinking Isaiah could make us a couple."

I consider Isaiah's inventory of tacky tees. "You think he's up for it?"

"He is if we are."

I sink back into the seat and fold my arms. "Okay. But this is definitely the last time. I'm not doing this again, Zorie. I mean it."

She clenches her jaw and drums her cotton-candy-pink nails on her phone screen. I know what she's thinking—that I don't mean it. Maybe I don't. I say the same thing after every wedding.

"You're right," Zorie says after a while. "It's getting too risky anyway."

"Then you agree? We're done?" I try to keep my voice even. I need Zorie to think this is her decision, not mine. She's weird like that. When she wanted to get matching butterfly tattoos on our ankles, I told her how much I loved the way our names sounded together— like we were part of some badass nineties R&B group. Kayla and Zorie. K and Z. A few days later, Zorie decided we should get our initials tattooed on the insides of our wrists.

"After this, we're done," Zorie says. She lifts her left hand and places her right hand over her heart. "Best friend's honor."

I nod and do the same.

"Best friend's honor."

CHAPTER SIX

SATURDAY

What little confidence I have fades the closer we get to the Jasper Falls Community Center parking lot. We're surrounded by cars and trucks with MAKE AMERICA GREAT AGAIN bumper stickers.

"This is a bad idea. We should go," I tell Zorie. Between the bumper stickers and the community center looking more like an abandoned warehouse, everything about this wedding reception is starting to feel like the beginning of a bad horror movie. On top of that, turns out Isaiah isn't as talented as he pretends to be. Shocker. The Solar Sonics logo is crooked on our T-shirts. Even worse, *solar* is spelled *soler*.

"I can't believe this is what you used our emergency stash on," I say.

"You worry too much, Kayla. It doesn't look that bad. The guests won't know the difference anyway. We'll be in and out faster than they can do the boot scootin' boogie."

I frown. "The what?"

She waves a dismissive hand. "Never mind. Just act like you're supposed to be here." Zorie pats my arm as if she's trying to comfort a child. "If anything happens, I got you."

I stare down at her hand on top of mine, our contrasting skin tones, the matching tattoos painted on the insides of our wrists with our initials.

"Do you trust me?" Zorie asks.

I nod. I do trust her. I've trusted Zorie every day since we met on the playground in first grade, when she told me I had dandruff the size of cornflakes and then punched a sixth grader in the nose for saying the same thing. We became instant best friends and, from that day forward, a fierce team.

But being Zorie's best friend also came with its challenges, especially when she'd lose control, like sophomore year when two cheerleaders made the mistake of calling us ghetto bitches in the bathroom, unaware that Zorie and I were in the last two stalls. Seconds later, we shot out in perfect synchronization just in time to see one of them make a beeline for the door while the other, now cornered, considered her options. Unfortunately for her, she'd run out of time. From the corner of my eye, I saw Zorie reach out and grab her ponytail, then swing her around the room before shoving her so hard she fell backward into a stall and banged her head on the toilet.

I'd never seen so much blood, like paint sliding down the porcelain. Zorie reached out and unhooked the heart pendant necklace from around the girl's neck, then smiled at me as she placed it in my hand.

"A gift for my bestie," she whispered.

I never told Zorie how a million goosebumps broke out over my skin at that moment, or that the image of the girl's blood-soaked cheerleader uniform is seared into my brain. By some miracle, it was only a flesh wound, and her parents eventually transferred her to another school out of the district, but not before she named Zorie and me as the violent duo who assaulted her. Of course we denied it. Even when Principal Medina interviewed us separately, I stuck to our story that we'd found the girl like that, bleeding and confused on the bathroom floor.

Zorie always had my back, and I always had hers.

"I trust you," I say.

She slides her fingers into the spaces between mine and squeezes. "One last time."

====

Twelve minutes.

That's how long I give us to finish. Last month, it was eighteen, but there were more people then. More distractions. This time, it's us inside a banquet hall of around fifty white folks with their eyes on us. They know we're not supposed to be here. Two black women at an antebellum-themed wedding reception? Zorie was right. These folks would *know* if the newlyweds had any black friends.

A backdrop of a plantation house hangs on one wall, where two women pose with lace parasols and their gaudy ruffled pastel dresses. A photographer who looks uncomfortable, either from the heat or from this racist-themed reception, instructs them to smile in an exaggerated Southern accent.

"Well now, don't y'all look as pretty as a Georgia peach," he coos as the women giggle, and I gag.

To the right of us, a red banner is draped across the buffet table with the words THE SOUTH SHALL RISE AGAIN in huge block letters. I roll my eyes. It's all so ridiculous, from the Confederate flag tablecloths with the magnolia centerpieces to the rows of white wisteria hanging from the ceiling and making me sneeze.

"What the hell, Zo?" I whisper.

"I swear their wedding website didn't say anything about them cosplaying the 1800s. Except there was that one photo of the groom dressed up as a Confederate soldier."

"Zorie!"

"We're going to need more time."

"No way. Not here," I say. "Twelve minutes tops and we're out."

The black bartender across from us is dressed like Colonel Sanders, that is, if Colonel Sanders was the color of coffee and had an Afro. He looks up and lifts a champagne flute in a mock salute. I nod, feeling almost sorry for him. Did he know he'd be serving cocktails while dressed like the fried-chicken mogul at a wedding reception celebrating the Old South? He's cute, though, even in his cringy costume. I'm tempted to go over there, but I can't afford to be distracted. If I don't get the money to pay the damages for Candace's car, I'm headed back behind bars for God knows how long with a hit-and-run charge.

"So what's the plan?" Zorie asks.

With a jolt, my brain snaps back into focus. The stage is across the room, centered between two emergency-exit doors. To the left is the kitchen, and to the right, the gift table with a bedazzled box labeled GIFTS AND CARDS.

"It's too close to the stage. It won't work. Too many people will see." I glance around the room at the service staff organizing dishes on the tables. "Unless we move it," I say.

"There's a table close to the doors near the picture display," Zorie says. "Ugly-ass couple." She bristles and I laugh. We wait until a woman dressed in a peach petticoat gown finishes arranging magnolias in a mason jar and then disappears into the kitchen before we make our move. Carefully, Zorie lifts the gift box and carries it to the table closest to the entrance doors. I follow with one of the flower arrangements from the table, but trip over my own feet and fall into a man wearing a black suit without a tie.

"Careful there," he says, steadying me. He smiles, flashing two identical dimples in each cheek. "You have to use both feet when you walk."

I resist the urge to crack a smile. Corny, but cute. "Thanks." I start past him, and Mr. Corny blocks my path.

"My friends call me Dez." He extends his hand to me, and I reluctantly shake it. "And you are?"

"Busy."

He squints at my T-shirt. "Solar Sonics, huh?"

"That's what it says on my shirt." I start past him again, and he slides into my path with his square-toed shoes.

"Did you know *solar* is misspelled?"

I look down at my T-shirt and feign surprise. "Oh wow—you're right! I can't believe I didn't catch that."

He stares at me, looking unconvinced. "Wait . . . did Frankie hire you? Is he changing the logo again?"

Behind him, Zorie has arranged the gift-card box in the middle of the photo display. If we play this right, we can grab the box during the bride and groom's first dance.

"Dang it, Frankie's always doing this—hiring new background singers without clearing it first. He did the same thing last month in Macon," Mr. Corny says.

"Who are you?" I ask, narrowing my eyes at him.

"I'm Dez, and you're . . . busy, right?"

I sigh and shift the flower arrangement to my opposite hip. "Listen, if this is your attempt at flirting, you should know I have a boyfriend."

"Well, that's too bad, isn't it?" He runs his fingers through his dark curls and cocks his head. "I was giving you some of my best material."

I stare at him for a long moment, wondering if he knows I'm an impostor, but something about the way he looks at me, with his eyes slightly narrowed and lips pursed, changes my mind. It's almost like he's memorizing my face.

"I really have to go." I fluff my hair so that it falls over my eyes, and move past him, my shoulder colliding with his biceps.

"Can I at least get your name?" he calls after me.

I keep walking and join Zorie at the doors.

"What was that all about?" she asks.

"I'm not sure. He was either flirting with me or trying to figure out if I'm lying about being a member of Solar Sonics."

"Do you think we should leave?"

I glance over my shoulder at Mr. Corny. He's still watching.

I have two options, really: Option A—hightail it out of the 1800s and risk adding another offense to my growing criminal record, courtesy of my wicked stepsister, or Option B—go through with the plan and pay off Candace.

And then, as if God himself chose my answer, the doors open and the room is flooded with guests, the women decked out in hoop skirts embellished with ribbons and bows.

They pause briefly at the gift-card box and deposit envelope after envelope inside. I imagine the money-stuffed envelopes, thick with hundred-dollar bills tucked in cards with clichéd phrases like "two hearts, one soul." Zorie and I pretend to busy ourselves with arranging a tray of champagne flutes left unoccupied.

"I'll have one of those," a voice says behind me.

I turn, and it's Mr. Corny. Again. What is with this guy?

"Funny thing, I texted Frankie, and he has no idea who you are," he says.

"Seriously, what is your obsession with the band? You a fan or something?"

He smiles. "Something like that."

I roll my eyes. "Fine. If you must know, I was hired by the drummer to be part of the band's hype crew."

He gives me a long look. "Hype crew?"

"I mingle with the guests and get them on the dance floor." The lie slips easily from my mouth. I'm better at this than I thought I'd be.

"Interesting." Mr. Corny nods slowly and strokes his chin. "Didn't know that was a thing."

"And now you do," I say with an impatient sigh. "Anyway, don't you have something better to do than stalk me?"

He lifts an eyebrow. "Stalk you? That's a pretty strong word, don't you think? Maybe I'm just thirsty."

I hand him a flute. "Clearly."

It's then that I notice the microphone now occupying his left hand.

He downs the champagne in one gulp, hands the flute back to me, and lifts the microphone to his mouth.

"I want to thank everyone here this evening for coming out to celebrate the happy couple, Julianna and Brett Fletcher, as they make their debut into this thing called marriage," he shouts into the microphone. "My name is Dez of Solar Sonics, and I'll be serenading you with my band tonight."

Oh shit.

I lift a hand to cover my gaping mouth, and he winks at me. I'd studied every band member's photo on their Instagram page, and this guy looks nothing like Dez. I try to recall the profile picture of the band posing against a sunset background and the lead singer holding a microphone with one hand and flashing a peace sign with the other. He was at least a hundred pounds heavier in the photo, but it was definitely Dez. No wonder I didn't recognize him.

"Now what?" Zorie hisses next to me.

I open my mouth to answer her as Dez slips an arm around my shoulders and pulls me against him.

"I'd like to introduce y'all to a very special new member of Solar Sonics and part of our hype crew, Miss—" He shoves the microphone at me, and I flash a nervous smile. "Come on, now. Don't be shy. Tell the good folks your name."

My fake name is on the tip of my tongue. It's at the forefront of my brain. Jane. Just say Jane.

"Kayla," I blurt out.

"Give it up for my bandmate Miss Kayla, y'all!"

The room erupts with applause, and I stand there like an idiot, wishing the hardwood floor would open up and swallow me whole. I can't even look at Zorie. I've ruined everything. They know my name.

"Save a dance for me, Miss Kayla," Dez whispers. He saunters off through the crowd, breaking into song as he climbs the stage. "Uptown Funk."

"We need to go," I tell Zorie. But she's not listening. Her eyes are fixed on the gift-card box and the endless line of guests dropping their envelopes inside. "Did you hear me? We need to go." I tug at her arm, and she jerks away from me.

"There's probably hundreds inside that box, Kayla, and there's still more coming in. Never underestimate these country folks. They have deep pockets and keep it hidden. I mean, look at that line. Bet it will be enough to pay off Candace and our rent. Isn't that what you wanted?"

"It is . . . I mean, it was. But our cover's blown now. I said my name—my *real* name. We have to get out of here."

Zorie smiles, but only halfway. "*Your* cover's blown. Not mine. Sorry, girl, but I'm not leaving here without that box."

She says something else, but I can't hear her. The band has started playing, and Dez's voice booms over the speakers. "I'd like to dedicate this next song to a very special lady who caught my eye this evening," he says, then sings the first verse of "Can't Take My Eyes Off You." He smiles at me from the stage, and heat rises into my cheeks. I have to bite my lip to keep from grinning like an idiot.

"I'll wait for you in the car," I say to Zorie. I start past her, and she grabs my arm.

"Don't go. Give me ten minutes. I can do this. Please?"

My phone vibrates, and I open a text from Dad. The damage on Candace's BMW totals five thousand dollars. Fuck my life.

"Ten minutes and then we're out of here," I say, then turn and push my way through the crowd. Dez is still singing his dedicated song, but I refuse to look at him. I need him to sing a fast song. One that will get the crowd hyped and on the floor—far away from Zorie.

I stop at the buffet table and take my time plucking little smokies from a Crock-Pot. The BBQ sauce soaks through the thin plate immediately, and I hold the sagging bottom with my hand to avoid the sausages landing at my feet like severed fingers.

"Careful with those," says a voice next to me. "Wouldn't want you to ruin your nice shirt."

Nice? He must be drunk.

"You sure are a pretty little thing."

The stink of sour beer floats out from the man's mouth and up my nostrils, but I don't look up. It's important to make as little eye contact as possible to avoid being recognized later. The music stops, and Dez calls for everyone to join the bride and groom on the dance floor. He sings a song I don't recognize, but apparently the entire room does, because they bolt to the dance floor.

"How 'bout a dance with an old man?" my buffet stalker asks. Before I can object, he jerks me forward, and I stumble behind him to the center of the floor. The women stop dancing to watch me as I attempt to stay on beat. I'm not a good dancer, but they all seem impressed with my two-step. White folks are always impressed by black folks' dancing. To them, we're all Beyoncé or the King of Pop himself. I run my hands down the front of my body as Dez sings something about country girls. I do a quick spin and see Zorie still lingering at the gift table. She holds up five fingers.

Five minutes.

This is my cue to go harder. I need more eyes on me and fewer eyes on Zorie, so I crouch down low and bounce my ass in the most obscene and mesmerizing twerk my knees can handle.

It works.

A crowd forms around me, cheering and clapping. And then I feel someone grab my arm. Panic seizes my body. We've been caught. The police are probably minutes—no, seconds—away from turning me and Zorie into a Black Lives Matter poster.

"Very impressive." It's the same voice from the buffet table, and this time I look up at his face. He smiles and then moves his hips with mine, and suddenly we're dancing. Sort of. "I'm Billy," he says, still smiling. "You from around here, beautiful?"

I turn my back to him and push out my ass so that it's nestled snugly in his crotch. Billy's breath hitches, and I know he won't be asking any more questions for the rest of the song. He places both hands on my hips and moves with me, or at least he tries to move with me. Bless his heart. Poor Billy can't keep up. Dez is in his final chorus of whatever this song is, and I give my audience one last dip before excusing myself to the ladies' room. By now, everyone is hyped, and Dez sings a Bruno Mars song from his very basic playlist.

"Thanks for the dance," I say and squeeze through the crowd of gyrating, sweaty bodies.

"You're not running from me, now, are you?"

I smell Billy behind me, thick and pungent. The room suddenly feels tight and claustrophobic, like I'm one breath away from full-on suffocation. Billy's hand reaches for mine just as I disappear inside the bathroom and close the door. But I'm not alone. A woman with wide-set eyes and a wig almost as terrible as mine shrinks back against the stall door.

"Sorry, ma'am. Didn't know this bathroom was occupied," I say in the most sugary sweet voice I can muster.

The woman nods but doesn't move. Her shaking hands tighten around her purse strap, and I know she'll remember this moment if she hears about me and Zorie on the news. Fucking Zorie. She just had to pick Jasper Falls.

I briefly consider going back to the dance floor, maybe even joining Dez onstage. I can twerk on him while Zorie takes the box. It will be vulgar enough that the audience can't look away.

"I'll let you get back to your business," I tell the frightened woman and yank open the door. Billy is waiting with his thumbs hooked around the belt loops of his jeans. He has a Confederate flag bow tie and white suspenders. The secondhand embarrassment I have for this man is on another level.

"That didn't take long, now, did it?" He flashes a smile that reveals too much of his gums. "How 'bout another dance?"

I fluff the curls on my wig and return what I hope is a convincing smile. "Sorry, hon, but my friend is waiting outside."

"You leaving?" His smile fades. "They haven't even cut the cake yet."

"I'm diabetic," I say quickly, and squeeze past him. His fingers brush against my hand, but I swat them away. The stretch of hallway between me and the back door feels miles long, and I'm tempted to break into a run. I quicken my pace and hear Billy's boots close the space between us.

"You sure are a fast little thing," he says almost gleefully.

I extend both hands out in front of me, prepared to shove open the back door and make my getaway when I hear someone yell, "Stop!"

The blood drains from my face, and I'm suddenly dizzy. Shit. I was too sloppy with my distraction. Should've known we'd never pull off crashing a wedding where the tablecloths were Confederate flags. I turn slowly, imagining the local news headlines with photos of me and Zorie in our lopsided wigs posted side by side.

"I can explain," I say to the confused woman in the lemon-colored apron a few feet away.

The line between her brows deepens, and she waves the wooden spoon she's holding out in front of her. "That door is the emergency exit. You'll set off the alarm."

I glance behind me at the door with EMERGENCY EXIT clearly marked in bold red letters. It's so in-your-face obvious I almost laugh. "My bad."

She ignores me and fixes her disapproving stare on Billy. "Make sure this one uses the front door."

I let the "this one" comment roll off my shoulders. No time to be offended. I need to find Zorie.

"After you, sweetheart," Billy says, and bows as though he were ushering royalty. If I were drunk enough and he were thirty years younger, I might find this charming.

I hurry past him and the apron lady but stop dead in my tracks when I spot Zorie chatting it up with the bride. Fucking Zorie. It's one thing to twerk on a drunk guest, but any direct contact with the wedding party is completely off-limits. Too risky. Zorie knows this. It's her own rule. Then, as if reading my thoughts, the bride's heavily outlined eyes find mine, and her surprised expression changes into a snarl. She lifts a finger to point at me and yells something, but it doesn't register until I feel Zorie's hand on my elbow and she's yanking me forward. The word *thieves* bounces off the bride's lips and above Dez's voice telling the crowd to "get jiggy with it." We shove through the crowd of confused faces and paper plates of wet potato salad. One of the bridesmaids spits on me, and I resist the urge to grab her braided ponytail and drag her across the floor in her ruffled lilac dress.

Hands grab at us. They want to keep us here. They want to punish us for what we've done. Zorie elbows the apron lady in the face, and she falls back against Billy with her hands covering her nose. I use my free hand to scoop a handful of potato salad from the buffet table and toss it behind me like confetti. A woman screams, and from the corner of my eye, I see the bride swipe her face. Bull's-eye.

We reach the front doors, shove them open, and race down the steps to Zorie's car. For the first time since she'd bought the 1975 Cadillac Eldorado at an auction, I'm thankful it's a convertible. We hop in without bothering to use the doors, a move right out of a *Mission: Impossible* movie. Two men chugging beers next to a pickup stop to watch us as if deciding whether we're worth chasing. Turns out, we are. Zorie cranks the engine, and it rumbles to life just as the men close in on us. She takes off, the tires squealing on the asphalt. Terror or adrenaline or, hell, both pulse through my veins, and I sit on my hands to stop them from shaking.

"What the hell were you thinking talking to the bride?" I yell.

"She was asking me about you and why you were grinding on her dad. I was trying to stop her from kicking your ass!" Zorie shouts.

The women from the reception spot us and race across the parking lot in our direction in a flurry of cheap, synthetic fabrics. One of them hurls a sequined stiletto at Zorie's head, but she ducks, and it lands in my lap with its daggerlike heel stabbing my thigh. I pluck it by the strap and chuck it at the parking lot, but it misses the asphalt, because of course it does, and lands squarely between the eyes of an old man wearing an embarrassing ruffled ascot and a top hat. He staggers backward, then forward into the path of the Eldorado. Zorie swerves and nearly sideswipes the bride, ripping away her veil beneath the tires, just as a flash of chiffon and tulle darts in front of the car. There's a sickening bump as a woman's body bounces, then rolls across the hood of the car.

Zorie slams on the brakes, and I look behind me at the growing crowd. They've stopped chasing us and are huddled around the woman awkwardly splayed on the asphalt. I twist back around in my seat and stare straight ahead as a disturbing realization washes over me.

"What did you do, Zorie?" My voice is barely a whisper, and I doubt she hears me above the screams. Hers. Mine. Theirs. I can't tell. She wraps her fingers around the steering wheel and presses down hard on the gas. The car lurches forward, and we take off in a cloud of dust as the screams disappear behind us.

CHAPTER SEVEN

We take the back roads and veer off the long stretch of highway onto a secondary road, whipping in and out of hollers. It's gravel and hell on the Eldorado's cheap tires, but it's the fastest route back to Redwood Springs, according to my phone.

"Maybe I should drive," I say.

"I'm fine."

We're halfway through the first holler when two deer dart in front of us. Zorie slams on the brakes, and the Eldorado skids to a stop. She sinks back in the seat, inhales deeply, and closes her eyes. I do the same and wait for my heartbeat to slow down. The last thing we need is to wreck her car on some backwoods gravel road. Cell phones barely work out here as it is, and we'd be forced to walk to one of the sketchy trailers lining the road.

"You okay?" I ask.

Zorie opens one eye and squints at me. "I said I'm fine. You don't have to keep asking."

I take a deep breath and stare straight ahead, trying my best to concentrate on breathing normally. The sound of the woman's body hitting the hood of the car reverberates inside my ears. I shove open the door and vomit into the mossy grass.

"I'm scared," Zorie says, her voice cracking. "I think I killed her."

I wipe my mouth with the back of my hand and twist in my seat to face her. "You don't know that."

"She hit the car pretty hard, Kayla. She's dead." Zorie is in full-fledged crying mode now. An ugly cry at that—the kind where her tears mix with snot and her eyes squeeze shut like tiny slits on her face. "I'm a fucking murderer!"

I want to grab her by the shoulders and tell her to calm the hell down, but my hands are shaking too badly to hold on to anything. "Listen to me. We have to stay calm. It was clearly an accident. We'll go to the police and—"

"The police?" she snaps. "Are you kidding me right now? No way I'm going to the police. Ever."

"We kind of don't have a choice at this point. Everyone saw us. I told them my real name. Who knows if the photographer took one of our photos. They will find us, Zo, and it will be worse when they do. Our best chance is to turn ourselves in. Explain what happened."

Zorie stares at me like she wants to laugh. "You want us to explain that we stole the bride and groom's wedding gifts and then hit a woman in the parking lot? What exactly do you think they'll say, Kayla? No problem? Don't worry about it?" She yanks off her wig and tosses it into the field. "I can't go back to prison. I won't. Not even for you." She shifts gears, and the Eldorado jerks forward, spraying gravel into the air.

"Wait, where are you going?"

"To Isaiah's. We can park the car in his garage until we figure out what to do."

"What's to figure out? We're going to the police." I swipe at my phone screen. "There's a station twenty-two miles from here."

"No!" Zorie bangs the dashboard with her fist, and the windows shake. "Don't you get it, Kayla? I'm the one who took the gift box, and I'm the one who hit that woman with my car." She yanks the gift box from under her shirt and sets it on the seat between us. It's slick with Zorie's sweat, and one side is dented. "I'm fucked," she says, and bursts into tears. I reach for her, but she shoves me away. It's just like that night ten years ago—me in the passenger seat of Zorie's mom's Honda Civic outside of Rudolph's Tea Room with Gloria's ripped wedding dress draped across my lap and the empty spray-paint cans at my feet. I'd told the police Zorie had nothing to do with it, that it was my idea, but they'd ignored me and handcuffed us both. Maybe I could've fought harder for her freedom, but part of me wanted her with me. I needed her with me. My ride or die.

Officer Perry had been relentless with his questions that night inside the interrogation room of the north precinct, asking me again whose idea the break-in was and if I'd been armed. At times, his voice sounded muffled, like he was speaking underwater, and no matter which way I tilted my head, nothing made sense, until the word *burglary*.

"I'll be honest with you, Kayla. You're looking at a burglary charge, which is a felony in Georgia and punishable by a prison sentence of up to twenty years," Officer Perry said.

"Prison? Wait, no . . . I can't go to prison. I'm barely out of high school!" I searched his face for some indication he was just being an asshole, giving me a hard time, or maybe teaching me a lesson through some twisted scare tactic. But Officer Perry's cold eyes remained unblinking, his expression hard.

"At least you'll have your friend to keep you company," he said with a smirk.

Right then was my opportunity to tell him I'd done this solo, that Zorie was innocent, but the words seemed jammed inside my throat, and no matter how I formed my lips, they remained there. The truth was, if prison was my future, it was a less scary fate with Zorie by my side. We were each other's shields. Protectors. I pictured Zorie sitting inside the interrogation room down the hall, poised and confident, like always. Knowing Zorie, she probably had the arresting officer hanging on her every word. What had she told them? Some exaggerated form of the truth? Had she sacrificed her freedom for mine?

I considered all the times I'd let her fight my battles, at school, with Gloria—Dad, even. If I was hurt, Zorie was devastated. If I was heartbroken, she was vengeful. In return, I gave her my unconditional love and loyalty. I was completely devoted to her. Zorie didn't deserve my betrayal, and yet, staring down at my handcuffed wrists, I knew I wouldn't survive a prison sentence without her. Guilt settled in the pit of my stomach and remained there, tucked away next to regret from that moment on, gnawing away at my insides. That night, I committed the ultimate best-friend betrayal: treason.

"I'll tell them the truth. I won't let you go down for this," I say to Zorie.

"Oh, like how you let me go down for burglary, trespassing, and vandalism?" she snaps. The Eldorado swerves slightly, and her hands tense on the steering wheel.

"I told you the cops twisted my words," I say, surprised how easily the lie slips out of my mouth.

"When I told you to do something big that night, I had no idea you'd do something like that." Zorie's chin quivers, and she swipes at her tear-soaked cheeks. "I spent an entire year of my life locked up because of you, and here we are again, headed back to prison if that woman dies because you threw a tantrum and rear-ended your stepsister's car."

"So now you're blaming me for the fact that you made roadkill out of a wedding guest?"

"Why would I blame you, Kayla? According to you, you never do anything wrong. Nothing's ever your fault, right?" Zorie makes a sharp left, and my shoulder knocks painfully against the door. I lean out the window and wait for the wave of nausea to pass. "Trust and believe, I'm not going down for this alone. This was your idea. 'One last time,'" she mimics in a voice that sounds nothing like me. "You have just as much blood on your hands as I do!"

My chest tightens as a sickening feeling grows in my gut. Zorie is right. I may not have hit that woman, but I was there to initiate the chaos with my twerking and flirting. They will remember me, and we're never supposed to be remembered.

We drive the next hour in total silence until Zorie's loud sobs force me to turn on the radio. I don't want to think about what we've done, or the consequences. I lean against the door and breathe in hot and humid air while Mariah Carey distracts me from my thoughts. When we finally reach Redwood and Isaiah's neighborhood an hour later, I almost cry with relief. No cops. No arrests. No interrogations. We're safe. Zorie pulls into the oil-stained driveway of a house with dingy siding and crooked shutters. She honks twice, and Isaiah appears in the doorway, yawning and scratching his belly.

"Open your garage door!" Zorie shouts.

He nods and disappears back inside the house. Seconds later, the garage door lifts, and Zorie pulls forward.

"Look, I'm sorry for what I said. I'm just really scared, okay? If that woman dies, I'll turn myself in. I promise." Zorie doesn't look at me as she says this, and I'm not sure I want her to.

"I'll turn myself in, too," I say, and will myself not to cry.

She kills the engine and reaches for my hand. "Really? You'd do that for me?"

"If one goes down, we both go down," I tell her, then, forcing a small smile, say, "Best friend's honor."

The overhead light turns on, and Isaiah stands in the doorway, his thumbs hooked in the front pockets of his jeans. "Y'all coming in or what?" he asks.

"We're coming, just finishing up business talk," Zorie says. She blows him a kiss, but he's not paying attention. His eyes are on the hood of her car. Isaiah squints and then runs his hand along the front.

"You hit something, baby?"

I look at Zorie, and she lifts a finger to her lips and shakes her head.

"Damn, baby. You must've hit something big. Hood's all dented, and something else." He pauses to tug at the "something else" with a loud grunt and holds up a piece of ripped tulle. "You run over a princess or something?" he says with a laugh.

I shove open the door, lean forward with hands on my knees, and vomit until my body aches from dry heaves.

"I hope you're cleaning that up," Isaiah says.

===

The news coverage of the wedding is immediate. As I feared, the woman in the bathroom remembered me and gives a very embellished interview to Channel 5 news reporter Cassidy Sullivan.

"She came into the bathroom, cornered me like a dog, and tried to take my purse. But I fought back. I had my Lord and Savior, Jesus Christ, on my side," the woman says to the camera.

Awesome. Not only am I a thief, but apparently I attack little old ladies in bathrooms. That'll go over really well at my trial. I turn off my phone and try to focus on the sound of Isaiah's cat purring next to me on the couch. It's surprisingly soothing, and I give in to the stress of today's events, dozing off, but I'm immediately jolted awake by the sound of hysterical crying. My eyes dart around the room before they settle on Zorie curled into a ball on the floor.

"She's been like this for the past hour," Isaiah says from the doorway, making me jump. "What the hell happened today?"

I don't answer him. The fewer details Isaiah knows about Jasper Falls, the better for all of us. Can't have the T-shirt king being a witness for the prosecution. I slide onto the floor next to Zorie, aligning my body with hers, and slip a hand over her waist.

"The news says she's still alive, Zo," I whisper against her shoulder.

Zorie sniffles, and I feel snot or tears on my forearm. "Channel 5 says she's in critical condition."

"That's still alive, right?"

At this, she jerks away from me and sits up, pulling her knees to her chest. "She's alive for now, but who knows for how long."

I glance behind me to see if Isaiah is still watching us. He's not, but his shadow is. I scoot closer to Zorie on the floor so that our shoulders touch, and lower my voice.

"What happened to that woman today wasn't your fault, Zorie. It was an accident. She came out of nowhere."

"She didn't come out of nowhere. Be real. She was chasing us because I stole the goddamn gift box." Zorie's voice is rising, and the shadow on the wall is still there, growing against the floral wallpaper. We shouldn't have come here, to his place, but Zorie was so desperate to hide the car. It was either here or abandon it at the park downtown and pray it was stolen by a pack of crackheads. "It's all my fault," she says. "If I'd left when you wanted to go, none of this would've happened."

I rest my head on her shoulder, and she rests hers on mine. "Hey, we've had a pretty good success rate until now," I say. "All good things must come to an end, right?"

I feel her nod and then the vibration of sobbing as she bursts into tears all over again.

"I'm so sorry, Kayla. I messed everything up, didn't I?"

"We both messed up." I reach for Zorie's hand and hold it between us, thinking how so much of our lives have been defined by devastating moments—the death of my mom, Zorie's toxic relationship with her own mother, prison. Dad used to say chaos always found Zorie, but maybe it found me, too, like a ruthless hunter sniffing out my desperation. Tears brim my eyes, and I rub them with my knuckle.

"I'm sorry, too," I say, my voice wavering. "For everything."

Zorie sniffles and swipes at her cheeks. "I need a cigarette."

"You don't smoke."

She cuts her eyes at me. "Today I smoke."

"I'm all out, but I'll see if I can bum one off Isaiah," I say, standing. She curls into a ball again on the floor and wipes her runny nose with one of Isaiah's T-shirts. At least they're useful for something.

I make my way to the back of the house, past Isaiah's cheesy collection of framed gangster-movie posters. It must be some kind of rite of passage to hang Tony Montana on your wall, like it somehow gives off big-dick energy. I find Isaiah sitting on the back steps with a Corona in one hand and a cigarette in the other. He looks surprised when he sees me, even though I watched him sprint out the back door seconds ago.

"Mind if I bum a couple of those for me and Zorie?" I ask.

"Zorie doesn't smoke," he says.

"Today she does."

He nods like he understands and tosses his pack to me. I pull out two, slide one into my back pocket, and wait for him to light the one I'm holding.

"Sit. You're making me nervous," Isaiah says, and pats the space next to him.

I take a long drag of the cigarette, and it's so good I could cry. "Really just came out here for a cigarette, not a conversation." It comes out harsher than I mean it to, but I don't apologize. I owe him nothing.

"I get that." Isaiah nods and blows out a white plume of smoke through his nose. "I know we just met and all, but real talk, I feel like me and you have a lot in common. You're a hustler like me. So from one hustler to another, it sounds like you and my girl in there are in some deep shit."

I want to tell him we're drowning in it. But I don't. I take another long drag and shift my weight uncomfortably from one foot to the other.

"Ain't too many folks around here drive a yellow Eldorado," he says.

"Is there something you want to ask me, Isaiah?"

He shrugs and flicks at his cigarette with the tip of his thumb. "You look like you need a friend is all."

"I have a friend." I walk to the opposite side of the deck and stare off into the darkness. "Zorie's the only friend I need."

"I feel that." He stands, and the deck bounces under his weight. "You know, I envy you and Zorie. You two really hold each other down. I respect that." Isaiah holds out his fist for me to dap. I don't. "Listen, from one hustler to another, I hope y'all know what you're doing."

"We'll be fine," I say, turning my back to him.

"An arrogant hustler is a caught hustler," he says.

"For your information—" I spin around to face him, but he's gone. The red ember of his cigarette disappears inside the Corona bottle as the back door closes.

CHAPTER EIGHT

———

SUNDAY

Isaiah's cigarette doesn't relax Zorie like I'd hoped, but another part of him does. After hours of me hearing the kinds of sounds one should only hear from two people who are mortally wounded, they both finally call it a night, leaving me alone with my thoughts—my dark, disturbed thoughts that involve replaying a woman being tossed onto the hood of the Eldorado and discarded onto the pavement, broken. I force myself to push them as far from my mind as my brain will allow, but they always return like some unstoppable, morbid loop.

Clogging my thoughts even more is Dad and his relentless calls and texts. No doubt he and Gloria saw the news coverage of the wedding crashers, the very unoriginal and generic name we've been dubbed by the local media. It's another proud father-daughter moment for Dad to add to his sparse collection, along with my discharge from the Sumner State Prison as a shiny new felon on probation. And yet now I've somehow managed to outdo even that by riding shotgun through a parking lot and colliding with a woman dressed like a ruffled idiot.

I take out my phone and go to Channel 5's website, surprised to see that ours is no longer the top trending story. We've been replaced by a story about a woman suing an all-you-can-eat buffet for promoting obesity. It's the kind of ridiculous story Zorie and I would laugh about for hours, but I couldn't laugh right now even if I wanted to. I scroll down the page to the wedding-crasher story and click on a new interview posted with the bride and groom, still decked out in their antebellum gear and looking very out of place among the black doctors and nurses who side-eye them in the background.

"Anything you'd like to say to your wedding crashers, Julianna?" the reporter asks, and thrusts a microphone in the bride's face.

The camera zooms in, and Julianna smiles in an odd way that makes her look like a sock puppet, with her bottom lip tucked under her top one. Flecks of dried potato salad are still visible in her hair and along the side of her overly bronzed face. "We're all just so blessed to be alive. And prayers for my best friend, Amber. She's fighting for her life right now," she says before her new husband yanks the microphone from the reporter and points a finger at the camera.

"You two bitches better get ready because when me and my family find you—"

A hairy-knuckled hand grabs the microphone, and the camera quickly shifts back to the reporter, who looks both confused and frightened. "Back to you in the studio, Jim," she says with a forced, wooden smile.

Lovely. Not only are the police looking for us, but now so is the Confederate general himself. I turn off my phone and stare up at the water-stained ceiling. From this angle, the brown marks kind of resemble angel wings, which is strangely comforting. If Amber pulls through, I swear I'll never steal another thing. I'll even return the collection of *People* magazines I swiped from the Chamberlain lobby. Swear. But since I'm a holiday Christian, my prayers are probably pretty low on God's playlist.

"Please let Amber live," I whisper to the angel wings before I close my eyes and wait for sleep.

═══

The house is quiet when I open my eyes. There's a half-eaten Pop-Tart on the table next to a note from Zorie.

At work. Call you later.
Z

"Work?"

I read the note again and wait for the context of her words to register in my brain.

"No, no, no, no, no!" I jump off the couch and sprint down the hallway to the garage, feeling panic creep up my chest and into my throat. It stays there, clutching my esophagus and holding my breath hostage while I fumble with the dead bolt.

Work?

The panic squeezes until I'm panting, choking, and forced to my knees. I stay there, staring out into the empty garage, where all that remains of the Eldorado is a black oil stain on the concrete floor.

"Zorie!" I shout into the empty space.

It's over. We're done. Finished. Every cop in town from here to Atlanta and every county in between is looking for that car, and Zorie's dumb ass drove it to work. Probably even parked it on full display right in front of the Chamberlain's dining room, like always. Little kids got a kick out of seeing the long yellow car, and their grandparents loved reminiscing with Zorie about the things they used to do in the back seat.

"Fucking Zorie."

I take out my phone and do something I'm not proud of.

I call Kevin.

He answers on the first ring.

"I need a ride," I say quickly.

"Well, good morning to you, too." He laughs, but I can tell it's not a real one. His voice is different, strained. "You, uh, okay?"

"Can you pick me up in front of the Shop 'n' Save?"

"Sure, but—"

"I'll meet you there in fifteen minutes," I say and hang up.

━━

It takes me ten minutes to walk the six blocks to the Shop 'n' Save. I park myself on a bench in front of the store and wait to hear the rattling engine of Kevin's minivan. Such an odd thing for a thirtysomething single man with no kids to own a minivan. It's a bold choice, maybe even a weird one, but today I'm grateful for the ride. The van sputters to a stop in front of me and backfires. Guess that's my cue to get in.

"Got you a coffee from that new place on Third," Kevin says when I climb in. He's wearing jean shorts that expose too much of his thighs and a tank top that exposes too much of everything else.

"I really appreciate this, Kevin," I say.

He grins and blots the sweat from his face with his tank top. "It's no trouble. And hey, maybe we can go sometime. My treat."

It takes me a second to realize he's talking about the coffee, not the ride. I give a noncommittal shrug. "Maybe."

"Great, you and me," Kevin says, clearly ignoring my lack of enthusiasm. He reaches for another cup in the holder, pops off the lid with his thumb, and spits out a long string of tobacco. Coffee sloshes over the sides and onto those thick, pale thighs, and he jumps behind the wheel.

"Ah, shitfire! Don't drink that, Kayla. I gave you my goddamn spit cup!"

I toss the cup at him as if it's on fire, and he manages to catch it before his personal collection of phlegm coats him and the inside of the van.

"I appreciate the gesture, Kevin, really I do, but can you please just drive me to the hotel? It's kind of an emergency."

"Picking up an extra shift today?"

I reach for the handle to roll the window down more, but it's stuck. "Zorie took something important when she left for work this morning, and I need to get it back. God, Kev, will you circulate some air in here? It's suffocating."

"Your wish is my command," he snorts, and shifts gears. The van rumbles and jerks forward, releasing another round of embarrassing backfire into the parking lot. An elderly couple crossing in front of us takes cover behind a lamppost, and I shout my apologies at them for Kevin's piece-of-shit vehicle.

We take off across the parking lot to the main highway, with the wind whipping the fast-food wrappers covering the floor into a frenzy. I try to stop them from escaping with my feet, but it's too late. Three Whopper wrappers are sucked out in a matter of seconds.

"So what'd you and Zorie get into yesterday?" Kevin asks, watching me.

I expected this question, just thought he'd at least wait until we reached the first intersection before he asked it. "Watched some Netflix. You?"

Kevin purses and chews his lips like he's trying to stop the words from coming out, but they slip out anyway, and in one long breath, he says, "The car that hit that lady in Jasper Falls looked an awful lot like Zorie's."

I will myself to stay calm. Everything is perfectly fine. I rehearsed my response on the walk to the Shop 'n' Save. I've got this.

"I heard about that on the news. Crazy how much it looks like Zorie's car," I say, shaking my head. "And that poor woman. So sad. I hope she'll be okay."

"Okay? She's dead," he blurts out.

His words suck the air out of the car, and I find myself leaning farther out the window. Panic pulses through me. I clearly heard him wrong. It's my paranoia messing with me, that's all. "What did you say?" I manage to choke out between gasps.

"I said that woman from the wedding hit-and-run is dead. Saw it on the news while I was buying these coffees. Something about her going into cardiac arrest." Kevin doesn't say anything for what feels like a full minute, and then, weirdly, he laughs. "Guess it's a good thing it wasn't you and Zorie driving, 'cause y'all sure would be in a shitload of trouble!"

I taste vomit. I feel it. Right there in the back of my throat, inching its way to the front of my mouth and pressing itself against my teeth. Dead. Not just dead, *murdered*. And we did it.

If one goes down, we both go down.

"You okay, Kayla?" Kevin asks, watching me.

I fan myself with both hands, thinking of our promise. We have to turn ourselves in. "A promise is a promise," Leslie Grace would always say if we agreed to clean a guest's room at a specific time. "Our word is our value."

"Pull over!" I shout.

"What's that now?"

"Pull! Over!"

Kevin jerks onto the shoulder of the road, and I shove open the door and inhale deeply.

"You ain't sick, are you? 'Cause I got to work this weekend," Kevin says.

I lean against the seat and wipe the sweat from my brow with the back of my hand. "Just get me to the Chamberlain, okay, Kev?"

"Whatever you say. Your good friend Kev will have you at the front entrance in two shakes of a lamb's tail."

"I hope that means fast," I mumble.

Kevin presses the gas as if to demonstrate his commitment, and the van explodes with another round of backfire. I keep my face pressed against the window, sucking in humid air to suffocate the nausea. It works, until we reach the Chamberlain parking lot and I

don't see the Eldorado parked in its usual space. In its place is a police cruiser and an officer with a thick black beard leaning against its
hood and talking to Leslie Grace. Damn. I'm too late.

"Wonder what that's about," Kevin says.

I press my fingers to my temples as if it will help slow down my
brain. It doesn't. "Do you have your keys on you?" I ask.

"Always do. Why?"

I twist in my seat to look at him but move too fast and am suddenly
dizzy and struck by another wave of nausea. "I need to borrow them
to go through the back."

Kevin frowns. "What's wrong with the front?"

"For fuck's sake, Kevin. I was fired the other day, and I'm sure Leslie Grace doesn't want me on the premises."

"You were fired?" He feigns shock, and I roll my eyes.

"Like you didn't know. Can I borrow your keys or not?"

Kevin digs in his jean shorts pocket and fishes out a key ring with
a million keys and a plastic key card. "I could get in trouble for this,"
he says.

"I won't let that happen." I reach for the keys, but he yanks them
back against his shoulder. "Don't worry. You can trust me. I promise."

"I need my job, Kayla. They're raising my rent, and like my mama
always says, you can't squeeze blood from a turnip." Kevin does that
lip-pursing thing again and spits into his cup. "The family of that
dead woman are offering a twenty-five-thousand-dollar reward for
the drivers of that car. That's a lot of money, ain't it?" He places his
hand on mine, and I try not to flinch. "Course I'd be just as happy
with a beautiful lady by my side instead. Hell, what's the use of having money if you ain't got no one to spend it on?" Kevin grins at me,
and I know what he's telling me without saying the words.

"You know what, Kev? Forget the keys. Thanks for the ride." I yank
my hand away and fish out a crumpled twenty-dollar bill from my
pocket, courtesy of Julianna and Brett's gift box. "For your trouble.

Thanks for being a good friend," I say, with a heavy emphasis on *friend,* and press it into his calloused palm. It's not twenty-five thousand dollars, but maybe it's enough to shut him up for a little while.

I slide out of the minivan and half walk, half run past Leslie Grace and the officer and through the sliding glass doors of the lobby. Geraldine calls out to me from the dining room, but I pretend not to hear her. I didn't get a good look inside the police cruiser, so if Zorie is still here—and free—I have to warn her. Halfway through my sprint to the elevators, I'm stopped by Serena from the front desk, who grabs me by the arm and yanks me behind one of the fake ficus trees.

"Is this Zorie's car?" she whispers, holding up her phone. The video of the Eldorado has made its way to TikTok. I squint at the screen, tilting my head from side to side as if examining each pixel.

"Wow. That's so weird. It totally looks like it," I say.

"I know, right?" Serena leans in close, and I get a whiff of hard-boiled egg on her breath. "Everyone here is talking about it, and they swear it's her car. But I keep telling them there's no way it's hers, because, like, why would she be in Jasper Falls? They don't even have a Walmart."

I nod. "Exactly."

Serena opens her mouth to say something else, but I can't stomach any more of her questions, or her breath.

"Gotta run. Text me more of those videos! So wild!" I say. My phone pings with four texts from Serena before I make it to the elevator. She gives me a little wave as the doors close. I steady myself against the back wall, panic mounting in my chest. Not only do I have to worry about Kevin turning us in, but now I have to worry about the Chamberlain Hotel employees vying for a chance at the twenty-five-thousand-dollar reward.

I take the elevator to the third floor, Zorie's floor, and almost burst into hysterical giggles when I step off and see her standing there with her cart.

"Kayla?"

I throw my arms around her neck, relieved to see my best friend still a free woman. "I saw the police outside and freaked out," I say.

"Girl, I know. I was about to text you," she says before pulling away from me. "Rumor is, Leslie Grace has a new man . . . Officer Joe or something. He does security downtown at Club Neuvo. Kayla, if that woman can get a man, there's hope for you!" Zorie laughs, but stops when I don't join her. "Wait, why are you here? Did Leslie Grace give you back your job?"

"Why are *you* here? We're supposed to be keeping a low profile."

"What do you think I'm doing? If we act like something's wrong, everyone will know something's wrong. The second I don't show up for work, people around here will start running their mouths even more than they already do, especially now with my car all over the news. You know how they are, Kayla."

I scan the hallway to make sure no one's listening, and whisper, "Where's the Eldorado?"

Zorie whispers back, "In Isaiah's garage."

I stare at her, confused. "Are you messing with me?"

"Why would I be messing with you? Miss Geraldine picked me up. I told her I had a flat." Worry settles on her face. "Kayla, what's going on?"

I open my mouth to explain, but close it when a woman in a sports bra, leggings, and a full face of makeup strolls past us. Zorie blurts out a cheery Chamberlain good morning, flashing all her teeth, which the woman ignores.

"Bitch," Zorie mumbles, which the woman also ignores.

"The Eldorado wasn't in the garage this morning, and I thought—"

"That I was stupid enough to drive it to work?" Zorie cuts in. "Wow, Kayla."

"I'm sorry, okay? Everything is so messed up right now." I lean against the wall and squeeze my eyes shut, feeling the painful prick of tears behind the lids. "She's dead, Zo," I say in a pinched voice. "It happened this morning. Cardiac arrest or something."

Zorie's knees buckle, and she steadies herself against her cart just as the elevator doors open. A woman balancing a child on her hip steps out in her bare feet, looks at me and then at Zorie, and asks, "What time does the pool open?"

"Ten," I answer, but she ignores me, her eyes still fixed on Zorie. Without my housekeeping uniform, I'm invisible.

"Ten," Zorie repeats.

"Thanks so much," the woman says, and disappears back inside the elevator.

"When I left Isaiah's this morning, my car was still in his garage and that woman was still alive," Zorie says as soon as the doors close. She paces in front of me, chewing her thumbnail. "None of this makes sense."

"Isaiah must've taken it. Kevin says the woman's family is offering a reward for any information about the drivers."

Zorie stops pacing and glares at me, her eyes narrowed. "You told Kevin about this?"

"Of course not," I say a little too loudly. A door down the hall opens, and a man peers out.

"Good Chamberlain morning to you, sir!" Zorie shouts, but this time, no smile accompanies her greeting. The man frowns and quickly shuts the door.

"I would never tell Kevin, or anyone, what we did, but he's not an idiot, Zo. I mean, he is, but he's convinced the car on the news is yours." I take a deep breath, prepared to deliver the next news that will change both our lives forever. "I think he's going to turn us in for the reward money, and if he doesn't, there's a growing line of folks in this hotel who will."

The elevator doors open as if they've been queued up for this interruption, and the same woman with the child appears in the hallway again. "Did you say the pool opens at ten or eleven?" she asks Zorie. I'm still invisible.

"Did it ever occur to you to say 'Excuse me' when you see two people talking?" Zorie hisses through clenched teeth. "Or are you used to just inserting yourself into other people's conversations?"

The woman blinks in surprise while simultaneously turning three shades of red. She moves her kid to her other hip and staggers back inside the elevator. The doors take their time closing, despite her multiple stabs at the buttons, and I watch the numbers climb to the eighth floor. When I turn to face Zorie again, she's crying and shaking her head.

"No, it's not true," she says. "I checked the news an hour ago, and that woman was still alive. How can she be dead?"

I reach for her hand, but she jerks away from me. "Zorie, we have to go to the police now and tell them what happened, before Kevin or Isaiah does it for us."

She's quiet for a moment, pacing and sobbing, then stops to look at me. "What if we don't?" she says, her eyes wide and unfocused. "What if we left right now and . . . like . . . disappeared. Not forever, but just until things calm down? We can stay with my great-aunt Ruby in New Orleans."

I tilt my head, confused. "That's not what we promised each other. We said we'd turn ourselves in if that lady died, because it's the right thing to do."

Zorie folds her arms across her chest and lifts her chin, defiant. "Maybe I changed my mind."

"This isn't like changing your mind on an order at the Tasty Freeze. A woman is dead." I move closer and lower my voice. "And we killed her."

More tears fall from her eyes, but she doesn't wipe them. I hold out my hand to her, wait for her to give in.

"It's the right thing to do," I say, and press the down button on the elevator.

"I can't," she says, shaking her head. "Please don't make me do this, Kayla. I won't survive going to prison again."

"Don't worry. This time it wasn't your fault."

"It wasn't my fault last time, either," she snaps, then claps a hand over her mouth. "I'm sorry. That came out wrong. I just meant, maybe you could do this one thing for me because I did that one thing for you."

A sharp stab of guilt pierces my insides. *That one thing for you.* As if that one thing was something as simple as picking up takeout from the Dragon Express and not sacrificing a year of her life to spend in prison.

"Kayla, *please.*"

I don't look at her. If I do, even for a second, I'll give in. Zorie knows this and reaches out to lift my chin with her hand.

"Do this one thing for me," she says, her black eyes boring into mine. "You know how this town is. They'll crucify us even though it was an accident. I need us to be on the same team with this."

Uncertainty twists in my gut. I try to imagine a life on the run with Zorie and the life left behind here, without Dad. "What about my dad and your job?"

"You think I care about this job?" Zorie laughs and yanks off her name tag. "I care about you and me, not the Chamberlain Hotel," she says, and tosses the name tag and her apron into the trash bin on her cart. "And as for your dad, Kayla, that man has his family. Me and you—we're family." I try to look away, but Zorie keeps her hand on my chin. "Ride or die, remember?"

My head moves, but I'm unsure of which direction. Is it a nod or a shake? Do I agree or disagree? Zorie grins slowly, and I have my answer.

"Yes, girl! We're really doing this!" Zorie squeals, and rushes at me with outstretched arms.

"The police will be looking for both of our cars, so we'll need a new one," I say. "We can go to one of those buy-here, pay-here lots. Do you think there's enough in that gift box?"

"At least eight thousand, last I checked." Zorie releases me and takes a step back, the enthusiasm in her expression suddenly fading. "Is that enough?"

"Maybe." Numbers slide and crash into each other inside my brain as I add and subtract what's left of our livelihood. "New Orleans is, what? Eight hours from here? We can buy a cheap car and keep enough for gas and food."

"Don't worry about food. I got you," Zorie says and dangles her housekeeping key card in front of me. "And you already know Miss Geraldine will hook us up with whatever we need. She loves me, says I remind her of her grandbaby."

She tucks the key card back inside her front pocket and stabs the elevator button. We both watch in silence as the numbers descend from the eighth floor to the third.

"You really think we can start over after all this?" Zorie asks when the doors open.

I think of my mom's words and the sincerity in her eyes as she'd say them to me, then focus my own eyes on Zorie. "Listen to me—there's nothing in this world God won't forgive you for as long as you ask for it with a clean heart."

"Yeah, well, me and God aren't exactly besties these days," Zorie says.

"You're in luck, then, because my mom and God are like this." I hold up my crossed fingers. "She'll put in a good word for us because Lord knows my heart doesn't feel too clean at the moment." I reach for Zorie's hand and give it a small squeeze. "Do you trust me, Zorie?"

She flashes a smile that doesn't quite reach her eyes. "Always."

CHAPTER NINE

———

The Eldorado and Isaiah are still MIA when Geraldine drops us off. It took forever slipping out of the Chamberlain to avoid Serena and the rest of the hotel staff shoving more videos of the Eldorado in our faces. Zorie does a sweep of the home, looking for what I assume is evidence of cheating. She emerges looking more panicked than when we'd left the hotel.

"What's the matter? Found some size-two thongs in your man's closet?" I ask as I stuff what's left of our belongings inside a garbage bag. The past hour feels like a dream that doesn't belong to me. I'd watched Zorie and Geraldine clear out an entire shelf of assorted cereal boxes and dump them inside a laundry bag as if they moved in slow motion. And when Zorie emptied the contents of the lost-and-found box into a garbage bag and handed it to me, I'd stared at it like an idiot until Zorie shook me awake again.

"Don't be mad, okay?" Zorie says, pacing in the doorway.

"Why would I be mad?"

I try to speak in a calm voice, but I'm sure my words come out annoyed and agitated. If they do, Zorie doesn't seem to care. She stops pacing and stares at me, her big black eyes wide and unblinking.

"The money in the gift box is . . . gone." Zorie sighs and sinks down next to me on the pullout. "I fucked up again."

I lunge at her, and she slips off the bed and lands awkwardly on top of a Gino's Pizza box.

"I'm sorry!" she shouts. "I thought I could trust him!"

"You thought you could trust the man you've only known for three weeks?" This is the annoying version of Zorie that works my nerves: the man-obsessed, dick-crazed woman who can't see straight after she starts sleeping with a man. Her last attempt at a relationship began on Tinder and ended with her maxing out her credit card to fund her boyfriend's three-day Airbnb with his fiancée. She cried herself to sleep that night while I contacted the bank to report the card as stolen. Six months later, when my own attempt at a relationship with Trevor came to a screeching halt, Zorie surprised me with our own mini-vacay using her new credit card to book a suite at a five-star hotel in Atlanta. We spent the weekend dining on porterhouse steaks and lobster tails and drinking champagne by the pool.

I'm tempted to kick her as she curls into a ball at my feet. Instead, I reach for the empty Pepsi bottle on the coffee table and hurl it at Zorie's head. She jerks to the right, and it bounces against the wall and rolls under the recliner. "How much cash do you have on you right now?"

Zorie lowers her hands in front of her face and stares up at me with wet eyes. "Maybe thirty bucks?"

"I have two hundred. That might be enough for two tickets."

"Tickets for what?"

"The bus. We have to get out of here, don't we?"

Zorie sits up on her elbows and squints at me like I'm suddenly out of focus. "Hold up . . . you're still coming with me?"

"The way I see it, I'm in this mess as deep as you are, and in case you forgot, Georgia has the death penalty. So unless you want to die young, we need to get out of this state ASAP." I grab Zorie's backpack off the recliner and stuff my ripped leggings and Soler Sonics T-shirt inside. Before he robbed us blind, Isaiah had been more than generous last night with letting us borrow some shirts from his product inventory. Zorie picked a bubblegum-pink T-shirt with the words MY BODY IS YOUR BLESSING stamped across the front in glittery red letters. I opted for a less ridiculous plain black tank top and a pair of shorts that were two sizes too big but held up nicely with the help of one of Zorie's hair ties.

"What will we do for money?" Zorie asks, watching me.

"Isaiah's a hustler, right? I'm sure he has some valuable junk in here somewhere," I say, waving my arms out in front of me. "We'll take an inventory of anything of value and then pawn it when we get to New Orleans."

A quick sweep of Isaiah's house produces an iPhone with a cracked screen, two pairs of Jordans, and forty bucks. The T-shirt mogul really lives a frugal life.

"How much do you think we can get for the sneakers?" I ask Zorie.

She shrugs and stuffs the Jordans inside a pillowcase. "Three hundred if we're lucky. I can call Kevin. He sells a lot of junk on eBay."

She takes out her phone, and I yank it from her hands. "Kevin wants to turn us in for reward money, remember?" I power off the phone and tuck it safely inside my back pocket. "Probably best if we keep our phones off from now on, you know, in case Kev actually told the police about us and they're tracking us. We can buy new ones when we get to New Orleans."

"Damn, you're bossy when you're scared," Zorie says. "I'll allow it. For now." She winks at me and slings the pillowcase over her shoulder. "I'll meet you in the garage."

"Why the garage?"

Zorie doesn't answer me. I join her at the garage-door steps and stare out at the empty space that previously housed her Eldorado.

"What's going on, Zo?"

She smiles, stomps down the steps, and takes one of the spray-paint cans from the shelf next to Isaiah's makeshift work area.

"I want to leave a goodbye note for my baby," she says, shaking one of the cans.

I open my mouth to object, but it's too late. The word *bitch* is already being inscribed onto the concrete wall in huge, sweeping black letters. She writes "Asshole" on the opposite wall before dropping to her knees on the concrete floor. "Ain't this some shit?" she says before bursting into tears and hysterical sobs.

For a second, I'm not entirely sure if she's crying about her stolen car, her broken relationship, or the fact that we are most definitely going to prison. Maybe all three.

"I really thought we could do this, Kayla. Just disappear and start over with what, two hundred seventy dollars? God, you must think I'm an idiot."

I do, but I'd never say it out loud. "I think you're scared, like me."

She sniffles and nods. "I just wish we could catch a fucking break for once in our lives, you know? Like, why is everything always so damn hard for us?"

I stagger to my feet, feeling my own eyes brim with tears, and start down the steps toward her, but I stop when the garage door opens. Zorie shoots me a panicked look, and I gesture for her to come to me, but she doesn't move. Her gaze has shifted to the black hatchback slowly entering the garage and to the driver who looks painfully stuck inside.

"You stupid motherfucker!" Zorie shouts. She jumps to her feet and pounds the hood of the car before it comes to a complete stop in front of her.

Isaiah unfolds himself from inside and takes in Zorie's new artwork on his garage walls. "What the hell did you two bitches do to my house?"

"Where's my car?" Zorie shouts. Her hood pounding has now moved to Isaiah's chest, and he grabs her wrists. I charge at him, and it's clear he's overpowered. He raises his hands in surrender, and we back off. "If the two of you would please calm the hell down, I'll explain everything."

Zorie and I exchange looks, and I wait for her cue to back off or scratch out his eyes. She nods, and I join her against the wall closest to the door.

"Didn't you get my text saying I was on my way home?" he asks Zorie.

She doesn't say anything.

"I know you two ladies are pissed, and trust me, you have every right to be. I mean, I did kind of take your money."

We both charge at him, and he grabs a fire extinguisher from the shelf and aims it at us. "Calm down!"

I lock arms with Zorie, and we stand there like a human barricade. Isaiah drops the fire extinguisher and holds both hands out in front of him, palms forward, like he's trying to calm wild animals. We are feral.

"Now, listen, I only took the money because I wanted to help."

"How does stealing eight thousand dollars help us?" Zorie asks.

Isaiah holds up a key. "I used the money to buy you a new ride. You two want to get out of here without the police on your ass, don't you?"

I wait for another biting comment from Zorie, but there isn't one. She yanks the key from him and jumps into his arms, wrapping her long legs around his hips.

"I love you so much, baby!" she says, kissing every inch of his face.

I watch them, feeling dizzy with whiplash. What just happened? Zorie might trust him, but I sure as hell don't. He looks at me from behind Zorie's braided bun, and I know he knows it, too.

"What makes you think the police are on our ass?" I ask him.

"I've got eyes, don't I? All that crying and whispering y'all been doing . . . the shit on the news . . . I knew something was going down, so I hooked y'all up." He flashes a smile, and I wait for my bullshit detector to activate, but I get nothing.

"This entire car cost eight thousand dollars?" I ask, taking in the compact sedan with the chipped paint, cracked windshield, and rusty doors.

"I mean, it's no Maserati, but it'll get you ladies out of here," Isaiah says.

Zorie slides off him and nods. "He's right, Kayla. No one will be looking for us in this car."

"But they'll still be looking for the Eldorado," I say. Then, narrowing my eyes at Isaiah, I ask, "What did you do with it?"

He shrugs. "Left it with a buddy of mine. He's cool people. He'll keep it safe."

"If the police find that car, your friend could be in some serious shit, Isaiah," Zorie says. She reaches up and holds his face in her hands. "You could be, too."

"Don't worry about me, baby. Your man's got this," he says with a wink. Zorie leans in to kiss him, but he steps back, his expression suddenly serious. "The two of you better hit the road. The police started putting up roadblocks at all the interstate ramps."

I grab the pillowcases filled with Isaiah's shoes and, for a brief moment, consider leaving them, but there's no time. All our money is wrapped up in this car. We'll need his Jordans money later.

"Thanks for doing this, Isaiah. I mean it," I say, and I do mean it. Hustler to hustler.

He leans on the hood of the car and smiles at me in a way that suddenly makes me sad.

"I got into some trouble when I was a kid," Isaiah says. "Almost spent my entire childhood in juvie, but this retired cop from my neighborhood stuck his neck out to save my ass. He died a few years ago, and I always said if I ever saw someone backed into a corner like I was, I'd pay it forward." He nods at Zorie, then at me. "You two take care of each other."

"We always do." I force a small smile and take the key from Zorie. "I'm driving this time."

CHAPTER TEN

———

Apparently in Redwood Springs, Georgia, eight thousand dollars will buy you a car with not only a dashboard full of dead flies but also an interior that smells like rancid Taco Bell.

"Does your window roll down any more than that?" I yell at Zorie over the loud engine.

"I'm trying," she says, pushing down hard on the handle. The window lowers another half inch and then stops. At this rate, with only a sliver of air circulating throughout this steel coffin of a car, and no air-conditioning, we'll both die of suffocation before we reach the state line.

"It's just a few more hours until dark, and then it'll be cooler," Zorie adds.

"A few hours? Try six," I say.

"Then in *six* hours, it will be dark and cooler," she says.

This might be true in most states, but not in Georgia, where the temperature goes from hotter than hell to just plain hell once the sun goes down.

"We'll stop at the next gas station and get some ice," I say.

From the corner of my eye, I see Zorie pull out a small bag. "I hope that ice is free because between our money, Isaiah's, and the change I found in the trunk, we only have $283.19 to get us to New Orleans."

"That's more than enough. The trip is ten hours taking the back roads, and this car gets good gas mileage, so we'll probably only need to fill up a few times."

She lets out a long, exasperated sigh. "What about food? We're really eating dry cereal and bananas the entire trip?"

"We don't have a choice, Zo. We have to save money. And hey, worst-case scenario, we still have Isaiah's Jordans. You said yourself they're worth at least three hundred bucks."

"Maybe," she mumbles.

"God, would you stop being so negative? Damn." I can't help feeling a jolt of annoyance at my travel companion. Between her constant need to state the obvious ("It's raining! Turn on the wipers!") and her nonstop complaining for the past two hours, I'm tempted to pull over and take my chances hitchhiking. "At least I'm trying to think of ideas for money. The only thing I've seen you do since we started this trip is complain!"

"Let's not forget that it was *my* boyfriend who found this car for us. If it wasn't for him, we'd still be looking for a way out of Redwood Springs."

"Oh, Zorie, I could never forget your boyfriend's generosity. I mean, if it weren't for you giving him our entire emergency stash and him stealing our money—because clearly once wasn't enough—and then buying us this disgusting piece of shit, we'd still be riding around in your car with a dead woman's DNA across the hood!"

As soon as the words come out, I want to swallow them back down and hide them deep inside my bowels. Zorie sinks into her seat and presses her lips together.

"I'm sorry," I say quickly, even though I know it's too late.

"No, you're not." She twists away from me and stares out the window. "I know you, Kayla, and I know you've wanted to say that since yesterday. Surprised it took you this long."

Two headlights appear in the distance, and I check the speedometer to make sure I'm not speeding. The SUV passes quickly, and I steady my shaking hands on the steering wheel.

"Look, I don't want to fight," I say. My voice is controlled and calm, like I'm speaking to a child. I don't need a Zorie tantrum while we're fugitives on a backwoods highway. "We're over an hour away from the Alabama state line," I say, and hold up the map I swiped at the last gas station. My late-night thou-shalt-not-steal deal with God is officially off the table. "We'll stop for food then and cool off."

I reach for the knob to turn on the radio, and Zorie swats my hand.

"I don't want to listen to music," she says.

"Fine. We'll just ride in silence."

"I don't want to do that, either."

A sharp pain stabs me between my eyes, and I pinch the bridge of my nose. Fucking Zorie. "You don't want the music on, and you don't want quiet, so what do you want, Zorie?"

She folds her arms across her chest. "I want to stop at the next gas station."

"It's better if we wait until we get to the next state."

Zorie twists in her seat to look at me, and her face contorts into an ugly snarl. "I said I want to stop at the next gas station."

"The police are all over this state looking for two black women, and if Kevin actually turned us in, then they're looking for *us*. We have to be smart about this. We're fugitives now." I bristle at the word. Saying it out loud makes it real. *Fugitives.*

To my surprise, Zorie laughs. "You really can't help it, can you? You always have to be the smartest one. Well, you know what? I'm smart, too."

"Never said you weren't," I scoff.

"Sometimes I think you forget. Whose idea was it to start this wedding-crashing thing? Mine. We'd still be struggling to pay our bills if it wasn't for me. But I fixed it, didn't I? I always fix it, and I'll fix this, too."

We're both quiet, the uncomfortable kind when you want to say something to break the tension but have no clue what to say or how to say it. My mind wanders to the first wedding we ever crashed on that balmy summer night in June two years ago. The air conditioner had stopped working at the Chamberlain, and Leslie Grace called for all hands on deck to set up portable fans to cover every inch of the ballroom. Zorie and I loomed in the doorway and watched the new bride and groom take the floor for their first dance to Ella Fitzgerald's "At Last." No one seemed to care that the cake's frosting was melting or that the ice sculpture of the couple's new last name had long since melted into a puddle near the party favors and now spelled out *Gross* instead of *Grossman*.

I'd been too mesmerized by the romance of it all, or maybe I was so delirious from heat exhaustion, that I hadn't noticed Zorie by the gift table.

"Kayla!" she'd shouted at me before tugging me away from my post by the life-size cardboard cutout of the couple, Tammy and Levi Grossman.

"Put the gift-card box under your shirt," she'd whispered.

I'd stared blankly at her, thinking I'd misunderstood, until she shoved me forward.

"Take it," she'd insisted.

I shook my head defiantly as the music crescendoed behind us. Levi had dipped Tammy and kissed her inside the warm glow of the spotlight. Guests applauded and whistled, and for one brief moment, they no longer cared about the overcooked roast beef being placed in front of them or the cheap, flat champagne being poured to the rim of their glasses. And they no longer cared about the two housekeepers lingering much too long at the gift table.

"Take it. Now," Zorie urged. And then the box was in her hands, and then mine, as we half walked, half ran out of the ballroom and into the lobby of sweltering guests too hot to give a second glance in our direction.

It wasn't until we were in the hotel parking lot that the gravity of what we'd done finally sank in.

"Are you insane?" I yelled.

Zorie laughed and collapsed on the hood of her car in a fit of hysterical giggles. "You should see your face right now!"

"What if someone saw us, Zo? We could've been fired or, hell, arrested."

"But they didn't see us," she said between giggles. She yanked the box from my shaking hands and opened it. "Oh my God." She reached inside the small opening and pulled out handfuls of ten-, twenty-, and hundred-dollar bills. "Are you seeing this right now? Can you imagine if we did this all the time?"

I didn't have to imagine. We did it again the following weekend. And then again and again—each time scoring more money and in less time.

Looking back, I should have stopped it. It had gone on longer than either of us planned, but Zorie was so convincing with all her talk about the two of us deserving a better life and how crashing weddings was our head start. Only now, our greed and carelessness have made an even bigger mess of our lives.

Dad used to warn me that being friends with Zorie would guarantee a life of messes. He even called our friendship toxic because of her influence over me. I always thought his so-called concern came from Gloria until he said Zorie would be my downfall because I don't know how to walk away from her. He'd said the same thing when we were thirteen and he caught Zorie taking one of his beers from our refrigerator. Zorie was convincingly apologetic, telling him she'd confused it with soda. Dad believed her, until he found us both giggling in my bedroom with the stink of Coors Light on our breath.

And then, when we were fifteen, Zorie and I thought it would be fun to drive Miss Patrice's car to the mall, only we T-boned a minivan along the way. Zorie sprained her neck, and I broke my arm, but we still managed to laugh about our injuries in the ambulance on the way to the hospital. Dad blamed Zorie for the crash, even though I was the one who'd insisted on driving that night. He'd never looked more disappointed than he had at the hospital when he and Gloria arrived to take me home.

"One day, that girl is gonna lead you somewhere you can't get out of," he'd told me. "I know you care about Zorie, but maybe it's time to walk away from her and make some new friends."

But I didn't need new friends. I had Zorie. New friends only got in the way.

That's the thing about being best friends with Zorie. There wasn't room for anyone else. KD+ZA. Even if someone tried to turn our duo into a trio, they never stuck around. Maybe I liked it that way. Maybe subconsciously it was me who didn't want to share Zorie. She made me feel special and seen, like I existed inside a life that made me feel invisible. But with Zorie, her light always shined on me, bold and bright, and mine on her. The truth is, we don't know how to walk away from each other, and even if we did, I'm not sure I ever could.

"Take this exit," Zorie says, jolting me from my thoughts.

"I think we should keep driving."

"And I need to pee, so take the exit."

I roll my eyes and switch lanes onto the exit ramp. Doing anything other than pulling over will only piss her off more. As much as I hate to admit it, I'd rather make this journey with Zorie than alone, even if our final destination is still unknown.

"Make it quick," I say and pull in next to a pump. "Might as well get gas while we're here and save us some time. Twenty on pump four."

"Whatever you say, boss."

Zorie pulls Isaiah's Atlanta Braves hat down over her forehead and heads inside with her mile-long braids bouncing against her bare shoulders. I yell for her to get ice, but the door closes behind her before I finish. A red Ford pickup pulls up to the pump next to mine, and a man in a cowboy hat with a deep-purple birthmark covering half his face steps out. I turn my back to him, thinking I should've worn a hat, too, and pray the sunglasses are enough to make my face forgettable. Just in case.

"Hot enough for you?" the man asks.

"Yes, sir. I think it is," I say.

He chuckles, even though nothing's funny, and I adjust my tank top so it covers more of my boobs.

"Sho'nuff a hot one," the man says again. Then in a low growl, he says, "Now don't you go meltin' on me, darlin'."

I return the nozzle to its place on the pump and decide to join Zorie inside, where it's air-conditioned and far away from my new cowboy suitor. I jog across the asphalt and am almost to the door when I see Zorie inside aiming a gun at the cashier's face.

"Oh shit!" I shout, and break into a run back to the car. The cowboy, still chuckling to himself about God knows what, barely notices the commotion until Zorie zips past him with her gun in the air.

"Start the car!" she yells. It's a stupid command, given the fact that I've already started the car and shifted gears.

Zorie jumps inside, and I press the accelerator before she can close the door completely. The bag with Isaiah's shoes and our phones falls out, but there's no time to go back for them, especially with the shotgun-toting cashier now circling the pump.

"What the hell just happened?" I ask as I take a sharp right turn into a holler. I veer down a narrow gravel road before gunning it across a field to an abandoned barn.

"We needed cash, didn't we?"

I slam the brakes before we hit the back wall and carefully tuck the car inside. "I can't believe you did that."

"What are you doing? We should keep driving," she says.

I shake my head. Bombs of pain explode in my skull. There isn't enough Tylenol in the world to make this migraine disappear. "It's too risky to keep driving now, seeing as how you just robbed a gas station. Safer to sit still."

She fans my face with the wad of cash. "At least I got us an extra three hundred dollars."

I smack her hands away, and the bills go flying. If the windows actually rolled down, they might have floated away on the hot breeze.

"You could be a little more grateful," she says, collecting the bills from the dashboard. "We needed this, Kayla. You really think we'd make it to New Orleans with that little bit of change we managed to scrounge together?"

"Yes, actually, I do, and now, thanks to you, we're completely fucked." I sink back into the worn leather upholstery and try to catch my breath. "Where did you even get a gun?"

"Isaiah gave it to me before we left." Zorie says this like it's the most normal thing in the world. "He wanted us to be safe."

"You definitely made sure of that, didn't you?" I scoff. "Do you have any idea what you've done?"

"Yeah, I got us three hundred extra bucks."

"No, idiot, you've added another charge and guaranteed a longer prison sentence for us if we're caught. We might as well turn ourselves in now and ask the judge for leniency." I rub my eyes with the heels of my hands as if to push the tears back inside, but they come anyway. Zorie rubs my back, but I shove away from her. "You want to be the smarter one so bad, then how are we supposed to get to New Orleans now with the police looking for a rusty black sedan that, only a few minutes earlier, was practically invisible?"

"You worry too much," Zorie says. She takes out a bag of Doritos, opens it, and pops a chip into her mouth. Somehow, during her armed robbery at the Citgo, she managed to grab snacks. "We'll be halfway to New Orleans by tonight and stuffing our faces with beignets by morning." She pushes back the seat and props her dirty feet on the dashboard, licking cheese dust from her fingers.

I stare at Zorie, and then at the gun in her lap. I know I shouldn't be scared. Every part of me knows this. It's irrational to be scared of a woman I've known my entire life and who, up until this point, I knew better than she knew herself. But looking at Zorie now with that cheese-dust smirk and her wild eyes, I'm scared pieces of Zorie may be slipping away. I felt that the first time I saw her after we were both released from prison. We'd met for lunch to celebrate our new freedom, but Zorie seemed distant and distracted, like she'd forgotten how to live outside of the prison's concrete walls. She barely spoke as she poked at her lo mein and gave only a half-hearted smile when I joked about the two of us surviving on baloney sandwiches for almost a year. Over the next few months, I'd see flashes of my best friend that reminded me she was still there, but different in a way I never could describe, almost like she was fighting to keep the new version tucked away. Gone was the fearless and confident Zorie I'd known since we were kids. This new Zorie was anxious and paranoid and flinched sometimes when I touched her.

It was my fault for believing we could protect each other. In reality, we were separated almost as soon as we entered the prison doors. I'd see her at meals and in the yard, but even then, she seemed distant, like she'd folded up into herself. A few weeks later, I was told by another inmate that Zorie was sent to the SHU, or solitary confinement, as I later learned, for fighting one of the guards. Zorie once said being alone with only your thoughts for an entire month was a thousand times worse than any prison sentence she could ever imagine. She never said much else on the subject, and I didn't ask. The shadow of prison can be very dark and cold.

"I have a good feeling about this, Kayla," she says, watching me.

My eyes move to the gun again. "If you expect me to concentrate on driving, you need to put that thing away."

Zorie rolls her eyes and slips the gun inside the glove compartment. "Happy?"

"Elated." I lift the key to the ignition, but stop when I hear sirens. My body tenses, and I'm not sure if it's vomit or fear I taste in the back of my throat. I swallow them both down and will myself to stop shaking.

"Relax. We're safe." Zorie pats my arm. "They're headed for the interstate. Guarantee it."

"You're right," I say, and exhale. "They'd be stupid not to take the most obvious route out of this town." But as soon as the words come out, we hear the sirens louder. Closer.

"Shit. We can't just sit here and wait for them to find us. We need to move, Kayla. Now." Zorie's nails dig into my skin, and I bite the inside of my cheek to stop myself from screaming. "Drive."

I take a deep breath and start the engine.

CHAPTER ELEVEN

—

Zorie's quiet for the next hour. I want to ask her what she's thinking, but I'm also scared she'll tell me, so I keep my focus on the road, cutting through neighborhoods and trailer parks. Every few miles, I catch Zorie staring at me, only to quickly look away and turn toward the window. We've never fought like this. Ever. Even after what went down with my dad and Gloria's wedding, my friendship with Zorie was stronger than ever. Losing an entire year of our lives made us very aware of everything we'd taken for granted, including each other. What little reputations we had in Redwood Springs were tarnished. We'd shamed our families and been stamped with a permanent criminal label by the judicial system. And still, through it all, the one constant in our lives was each other. But this? Now I'm not sure how we'll ever come back from this.

We pass a sign that reads, MAMAW'S STATELINE RESTAURANT, 86 MILES. The road ahead has never felt longer. The last and only road trip I'd ever taken with Zorie had been eight hours, but it didn't involve vehicular homicide or robbery. We'd driven to Daytona Beach with Miss Patrice and her boyfriend Jeremiah. The trip was meant to celebrate their one-year anniversary, but since she couldn't leave Zorie home alone and she'd been banned from my house, Miss Patrice had taken us both, promising my dad we'd be under the strictest supervision. Two hours after checking into our suite, Miss Patrice and Jeremiah left us to board a five-day cruise ship in Port Canaveral. Zorie and I spent the week taking shots of Fireball on the beach with the college crowd and hosting parties in our suite, catered by room service. The bill for a week's worth of burgers, pizza, chocolate cake, chicken tenders, and steak was well over a thousand dollars, including charges for movie rentals and damages to the room.

"You're always showing your ass!" Miss Patrice had told Zorie. "Why can't you be more like Kayla?"

"Why can't you be more like a mom?" Zorie snapped.

The drive home that Saturday had felt twice as long with Zorie and Miss Patrice arguing nonstop. At one point, Zorie threatened to tell my dad about Miss Patrice and Jeremiah leaving two minors alone in a hotel room for an entire week, and Jeremiah reached over the front seat to grab her. I'd used my iPad to deliver three swift blows to his bald head before he relented and sulked back down in his seat. By the time we reached the next exit, Miss Patrice and Jeremiah had broken up.

"I'm not a bad person, Kayla," Zorie says. She shoots me a sidelong glance and shoves her giant leopard-print sunglasses onto her face. Another free gift from the Citgo. "We're even now. You did that stuff with your dad's wedding, and I did this."

I don't say anything. I stare straight ahead and squeeze the steering wheel tighter and tighter until my fingers ache.

"Really? This is how it's gonna be? You're not talking to me anymore? Gonna be a pretty boring friendship if we never talk again." Zorie laughs and fans herself with an old McDonald's bag she found in the back seat. "I know what we need." She opens the glove compartment and pulls out a folded Ziploc bag. "Isaiah gave it to me. He thought it might come in handy to help us relax. One hit of this, and we'll both be good as new." She holds up a joint and dangles it in front of my face.

"Awesome. We now have an unregistered gun and drugs in the car while we're on the run from the police for robbing a gas station and killing a woman," I sneer, and push her hand away. "Did that boyfriend of yours happen to give you anything legal when we left, or are you planning to pull out a bag of heroin next?"

"I'm just trying to be a good best friend and take your mind off things." She lights the joint with the car lighter and takes a long drag, then holds it inches from my face, making my eyes water. "I guarantee it will make all your Gloria problems disappear."

"What about my Zorie problems?" I shout. "We're not in high school anymore. This isn't one of our after-school smoke sessions. This is real life! We're in a lot of fucking trouble, and you need to start acting like it!" I shove her hand away again, and the joint falls from her fingers and onto the seat between my legs.

"Shit!" Zorie looks down to retrieve the smoldering joint just as I slam on the brakes and nearly collide with the van in front of us.

"What the hell, Kayla?" she shouts, and punches my shoulder.

"That van slammed on its brakes. What was I supposed to do?"

Zorie opens her door and cranes her neck outside. "Fuck. Looks like a police roadblock."

The blood drains from my face. Guess we're adding drug possession to our growing list of felonies.

"Do you realize what will happen to us if the police stop us and smell inside this car?" I ask.

"Girl, relax. We'll handle it."

But I can't relax—mainly because I'm not high. My pulse races so fast I'm dizzy. I'm on the brink of a total breakdown. Then, as if things can't get any worse, I have to pee.

It takes thirty minutes to move one mile before we're stopped by a short, tattooed officer directing traffic around three police cruisers and an ambulance parked haphazardly in the middle of the highway.

"Afternoon, Officer," Zorie says, leaning over the console. Her voice is the same one she uses when she calls the electric company to ask for an extension on our bill. "Sure is hot out today." She squeezes her boobs together with her arms so that her cleavage spills out of her T-shirt. "I'm so hot I can barely keep my clothes on."

The officer ignores her and keeps his steely gaze locked on me.

"Is everything okay, Officer?" I ask, trying to keep the tremble out of my voice.

"Driver hit a pedestrian about a mile up. Y'all need to turn around and take the detour to Gravel Hill Road. Just take a left at the intersection by the highway, and you'll run right into it," the officer shouts.

I nod but don't move. I stare straight ahead with my hands still gripping the steering wheel. I could put the car in park, get out, and run to the officer with my hands in the air. I could surrender. End it all. Take the L for both of us. I glance at Zorie, and she mouths, *Be cool.*

"Ma'am? Did you hear what I said?" the officer shouts through the window.

I blink, as if waking from a dream, and squint up at him. He stares at each of us, his face looking more annoyed than before.

"Move along," he says.

Judging by his sharp tone, he has no intention of repeating himself. I nod and shift gears into reverse.

"Damn, that was close," Zorie says and exhales a long breath.

I swing the car around and watch the officer in the rearview mirror until I can't see him anymore.

═══

The sun is still a blazing ball of fire by the time we cross the state line into Alabama. I almost cry with relief when I finally empty my bladder for the second time on the side of the road. Somehow, we've managed to make it to another state without being pulled over. Zorie seems less enthused and more interested in finding a Taco Bell on the map. She settles for a Dairy Queen that I nearly crash into when she takes the steering wheel.

"Are you trying to get us killed?" I yell at her.

"I'm trying to get us fed!"

I leave Zorie in the car this time and order us cheeseburgers and onion rings that I know I won't finish. She looks disappointed when I hand her the bag.

"No milkshake?" she asks.

"Milkshakes were five apiece. Even the small ones. We have to save money." I hand her a water. "Take it. It's good for you."

She rolls her eyes and stretches back on the hood of the car. It still feels suffocatingly hot, but I'm grateful for the fresh air and the shaded parking spot. I climb on top of the hood next to her and bite into an onion ring. Hot grease coats my tongue, and I force myself to swallow.

"We should probably check the news at some point and see if Kevin turned us in," I say.

"How? On our imaginary phones?"

"I'm sure there's a library around here that will let us use the internet."

Zorie watches me over her cheeseburger, a slight smirk on her face. "You really are enjoying this, aren't you?"

"Enjoying what?"

"Being in charge. It's turned you into a different person, all bossy and shit."

I tear open a ketchup packet with my teeth and smear its contents on my burger wrapper. "Someone has to be the responsible one."

"So you nominated yourself." Zorie snorts. "Got it."

I try to drown my annoyance with a gulp of water, but it doesn't work. My patience jumped out of the car miles ago. For all I know, it hitchhiked back to Redwood Springs on the back of a pickup en route to my old life that no longer feels ordinary and boring. My job—or former job—at the Chamberlain Hotel is a dream compared to being homeless and on the run from the police with an overgrown toddler.

"I never wanted any of this," I say. "I wanted to get enough money to pay off Candace and then start over. Go to college, maybe. Do something with my life."

Zorie finishes off the last of her burger and tosses the wrapper at the trash bin a few feet away. It misses and lands on the ground. She doesn't pick it up.

"I was going to be a business major. Thought I'd be pretty good at that," I say. "But then you wanted me to take a year off with you so we could travel. Do you remember that?"

"Oh, I definitely remember that," Zorie says. She stares off, as if suddenly lost in a memory. "I had it all planned out. First, New York, then Chicago, Vegas, and we'd end in California. Best trip of our lives. And do you remember where we ended up spending that year?" she asks, a new edge in her voice.

I pick at my chipping nail polish, unable to look at her or force down another grease-soaked onion ring. She doesn't want me to answer her question. She wants me to feel it, and I do.

"It wasn't traveling with my best friend across the country, unless you count that one month when we were transferred to the Harlin County Jail because of overcrowding. That was an adventure, wasn't it?"

"All right, stop!" I shout. A few drivers in the drive-thru lane crane their necks to look at us, and I shift my body away from them. "I've apologized a million times for what happened that year. If I could take it back, I would. But I can't. When you picked me up from Dad's that night after he kicked me out, you told me you forgave me. And here you are again throwing it back in my face. Zorie, you have got to stop punishing me for this. I'm begging you."

Zorie twists her braids into a bun on top of her head and slides on her sunglasses. In this light, she looks as if she's glowing from the inside out. I don't think Zorie will ever know how beautiful she truly is.

"My mom used to tell me all the time how much she wished I was more like you," Zorie says. "It was always 'Kayla is so pretty' and 'Kayla is so polite.'" She lowers her sunglasses to look at me. "'Kayla can do no wrong.'"

"We should go if we're going to make it to New Orleans before midnight," I say. Not in the mood for this trip down dysfunctional lane, I start to slide off the hood, but she grabs my arm. She's determined to keep me here inside this memory with her.

"When that shit went down with Gloria and your dad, my mom was the first one to come to your defense. She blamed me. My own mother. Said I was a bad influence on you." Zorie laughs and shakes her head. "She never was much of a mother anyway. If she had to choose between me and some man, she'd choose the man every time."

Growing up, I used to think Zorie was being overdramatic about her mom in the way most kids are about their parents, but that week in Daytona was more enlightening than anything Zorie had ever told me when it came to Miss Patrice. Theirs was a relationship doomed from the very beginning. Miss Patrice had Zorie at sixteen and was always resentful of the pregnancy. For most of Zorie's childhood, she treated Zorie more like an annoying little sister than a daughter. I was always jealous of all the freedom Zorie had back then: no curfew, sleepovers with boys, easy access to Miss Patrice's weed stash. But Zorie's rule-free life wasn't because she had some crunchy granola mom who believed in her child's self-expression. No, Zorie's life had no rules because her mom didn't care. Period.

"I think Mama would've preferred you as her daughter instead of me," Zorie says. "I was her bad seed."

"Am I supposed to apologize for that, too?" I ask, my voice rising. "Fine. I'm sorry."

"Do you realize you say you're sorry more than you say you love me?" The hurt behind her voice stings, and I can't look at her.

"All I've ever wanted was for us to have a good life like everyone else—like Candace and Charles," I say. "Why do horrible people like them get to live like that while we're out here barely surviving? It's not fair, Zorie."

"That's your problem, right there. You're too focused on what everyone else has instead of appreciating your own shit. Girl, if people don't believe in you, then fuck them. I've always believed in you, Kayla. I just wish you believed in me, too."

My mouth is fixed to say I'm sorry again, but it feels meaningless now. Generic, even. That night at the Tea Room, I'd only wanted to rip off a sleeve of Gloria's wedding dress. One tiny imperfection to make Gloria lose her mind. But Zorie said I was thinking too small.

"If you're gonna do something, do it big," she said and handed me the spray-paint cans. She'd swiped them from the Shop 'n' Save earlier that day to "decorate" a cheating boyfriend's car.

I didn't want to do it. As much as I hated Gloria, I loved my dad and would never want to intentionally hurt him. But there we were, tipsy in the parking lot of a building that in less than twenty-four hours would officially make Gloria and Candace my family.

"It'll be hilarious," Zorie urged, slipping the cans into my hands. "I'll be your lookout."

Half an hour later, I'd spray-painted every version of "homewrecking whore" on every wall in the building and drawn a supersized penis on Candace's maid-of-honor dress. I topped off my clever artwork by smearing the contents of the Tea Room's refrigerator all over every countertop and plucking the heads off every flower I found. For my grand finale, I sliced Gloria's dress to ribbons and stuffed all her jewelry into a garment bag before walking outside to Zorie's mom's car. We'd sat in the parking lot, laughing at the looks on their faces in the morning when they showed up to find my handiwork. And then, as we were illuminated by flashing red-and-blue lights, our laughter stopped, and we were dragged out of the car, handcuffed, and forced into the back seat of a police cruiser.

"I think about that night at the Tea Room a lot, Zo," I say. "Everything felt so out of control with my dad, you know? He's the only parent I have left, and I felt like I was losing him, too." Tears brim my eyes, and I blink them back. "Never in a million years did I think we'd be arrested and sent to prison over something so stupid. I hate that I fucked up our futures like this."

Zorie smiles at me. "Hey, your future is my future. Remember that."

I swipe at my tears and smile back. "And for the record, I've always believed in you, too."

"You better, bitch," she says with a wink.

"Look at us being all emo," I say, laughing. "We should go. We're losing time." I open the car door to climb back inside, and I hear Britney Spears's "I'm a Slave 4 U" on full blast from a car in the drive-thru. Zorie and I studied the entire routine in high school and did the dance in matching pink bodysuits for a very shocked and surprisingly horned-up audience at the senior talent show. That performance earned us a front-page write-up in the student newspaper with the headline: "Senior Stars Slay Competition with Iconic Dance." I glance at Zorie, and she's already sliding off the hood in time for the chorus. Without missing a beat, I join her in front of the car, and suddenly, we're KD+ZA again, our rhythm restored. We're so deep into our routine that we don't notice the growing crowd with their phones aimed at us. I stop mid-twirl and instinctively cover my face.

"Please don't film us," I say.

"You guys are so good! Yes, queens!" a girl with neon-pink braids says, and snaps her fingers approvingly. The crowd agrees with her and begs us to go on, but I'm already opening the door.

Zorie is trying to do the same when the girl with the braids grabs her arm. She immediately whips around and smacks the girl hard with an open hand. The girl falls back into an older lady who'd been tentatively watching from a distance but is now eagerly filming the entire scene.

"I'm sorry," Zorie stammers, but it's too late. The crowd has turned on her—on us. Milkshakes fly at my window as Zorie struggles to open the passenger door. Someone strikes her on the shoulder, and she yelps as she falls forward against the car.

"Get away from her!" I shout and jump out, fists raised. I shove through the crowd until I'm swinging at random Dairy Queen patrons.

"Are you okay?" I ask Zorie, and place a protective arm around her shoulders.

She nods and yanks open the car door. I give my new audience the finger before climbing back inside and taking off.

"Thanks for having my back," Zorie says, fastening her seatbelt.

"I can't believe we made it out of there without someone dumping ice cream on us," I say.

"I wouldn't mind, seeing as how we're too poor to buy any ourselves," Zorie says.

It's not funny, but we both laugh like maniacs, tears brimming our eyes, and don't stop until a loud thumping sound forces us off the road and into a gas station parking lot.

"Why are we stopping?" Zorie asks, peering out the window.

"Something's wrong." I park next to pump five, get out, and circle the car slowly, expecting to see the smashed remains of some unfortunate animal embedded in the tread of the tires. But what I find instead is so much worse. "Are you fucking kidding me?" I shout.

Zorie is next to me immediately and staring with the same horrified expression at the back tire, now completely shredded. She looks at me, and I feel her panic. Taste it, even. It rises in my throat, and I swallow it back down.

"This is so bad, Kayla," Zorie says in a voice much smaller than I expect.

I lean forward on the hood of the car and close my eyes. God clearly hates me. Hell, he clearly hates both of us. Why else would he keep punishing us like this?

"We're not good at this," I groan. Then, turning to look Zorie straight in the eyes, I shout, "We have to turn ourselves in!"

Zorie sinks back against the gas pump and blinks at me as if to see me better, then frowns. "Come again?"

"God is clearly pissed at us. This is a sign that it's time to do the right thing. We barely have enough money to survive, we have no phone, and now our tire is fucked. Look at us, we're in the middle of nowhere," I say, and wave my hands out in front of me. "We might as well take the L and go to the police. At least we'd get an air-conditioned cell, a shower, and a free meal."

Zorie is quiet for a moment, and then smiles. "You forgot one little thing," she says, and reaches inside the car's glove compartment for the gun. "We have this. Give me three minutes, and I'll get us a new ride and enough cash to make it out of this town." She starts to close the door, and I grab her by the shirt and yank her back.

"No! We're not robbing another gas station!"

She jerks away from me, but the gun slips from her hand and bounces on the seat. We both stare at it, but neither of us makes a move to take it.

"You realize if we do this, I'm a dead woman walking," Zorie says after a while.

"We'll find a good lawyer."

She laughs. "With what money?"

Tears sting my eyes, and the air suddenly feels suffocating, like I can't get enough oxygen into my lungs fast enough. I reach for Zorie, wrapping my arms around her shoulders, and she collapses against me.

"We're going to be okay, Zo. Best friend's honor," I whisper against her shoulder. Her body vibrates against mine, and I hold her tighter, knowing with more certainty than I've felt in a long time that we will never be okay again.

CHAPTER TWELVE

———

Two things go through my mind as we approach the doors of the Juniper Circle Minit Mart: One, I may never see Zorie again after this, and two, I may never see Dad again, either. The weird thing is, never seeing Zorie again hurts more.

"You sure you want to do this?" I ask her again for the fifth time since making the thirty-second walk to the double doors.

"No, but you're right—we can't go on like this. We're not made for this kind of life," she says. "Not like this is a Liam Neeson movie or something where the good guys win."

"Are we the good guys?"

Zorie smiles and shrugs. "I hope so."

I reach for her and hug her to me in a tight hold. She squeezes back and kisses my cheek. "I'm sorry I got you into this."

"I'm a grown-ass woman. I agreed to do this, and I'll tell anyone who asks." I release her from my hold and swipe at my eyes. "I love you big."

"I love you bigger."

We pull open the door together, her hand over mine, and walk in like two badass boss bitches and are met with a bored gaze from the woman behind the counter.

"We need to use your phone," I tell her. "There's been an accident."

The woman cranes her neck to look out the door behind me. "What kind of accident?"

"A bad one," Zorie answers. "Can we use your phone or not?"

The woman clenches her jaw and drags her fingers through the ends of her tangled bob. Her nails are dirty, like she rakes mud with her fingers for a living. Finally, after thirty agonizing seconds, she shoves the phone at me.

"No collect calls," she says.

I nod my thanks and lift the receiver to dial 911 with shaking hands.

"911. What is your emergency?" the operator's robotic voice asks over the speakerphone.

"I-I need to report an accident," I say, then, to the woman, "What's the address here?"

"7856 Drakes Creek Road," she says.

"I need to report an accident at 7856 Drakes Creek Road," I tell the operator.

"I'm sorry, hon, can you repeat that? The connection is bad, I can barely hear you."

"7856 Drakes Creek Road," I repeat through clenched teeth.

"Hon? Can you hear me?" The phone crackles and pops before becoming a busy signal.

"What happened?" Zorie asks. She shakes so hard her braids bounce against her shoulders. This is the most terrified I've ever seen her.

"The phone disconnected or something." I lower the phone, but I'm not sure if it makes it back to the receiver. I reach for Zorie again and hold her against me.

The woman watches us carefully from behind the counter and reaches for her cell phone next to the register. I think she's going to hand it to me, but she texts something instead. She looks up, sees me watching her, and lowers the phone to her side.

"This was a bad idea. We should go," I say to Zorie.

"You sure? I may not have the guts to do this again if we leave."

"I won't ask you to do it again. Promise." I grab her hand and pull her behind me toward the doors, when a police cruiser pulls up and catches us both inside its high beams.

"I guess all good things come to an end," Zorie says, her eyes fixed on the officer approaching the doors.

I have an immediate urge to run. But where? We can't exactly hide behind the display of Cheez-Its. The gas station is the size of a shoebox.

"Be cool," I whisper to Zorie.

"What else would I be?" she whispers back.

We step away from the door slowly and busy ourselves sifting through magazines and crossword puzzles at the display by the slushie machine. The door chimes, and I hear the officer's heavy boots on the floor and the static of his radio. His presence envelops the tiny convenience store, and even though our backs are to him, I feel his eyes burning holes into us.

"Dispatch traced a call from this location about an accident," he says in a deep, authoritative voice.

Zorie reaches for my hand and locks her pinky with mine.

"These girls were in a *bad* accident," the woman behind the counter says.

I don't like the mocking way she says *bad*. When I glance at her, she smiles and takes a long swig of Mountain Dew.

"An accident, huh?" The officer's boots move closer until I can feel him inches away from us. He smells sour, like when wet clothes are forgotten and left in the washing machine overnight. "You ladies hurt?" he asks. His voice is impatient, and I know he won't be happy if he has to ask the same question twice.

I suck in my breath and turn, prepared to meet whatever fate God has in store for us, but before I can lift my arms and surrender, a man in a black baseball cap with neon lettering walks in. I squint at the familiar words sewn into his cap: *Solar Sonics*. He meets my stare and stops dead in his tracks.

"Evening, ladies," he says.

I open my mouth to speak but realize my vocal cords are frozen and so is my stare. Dez stands in front of me, grinning like he had onstage before the wedding took a tragic turn. My hands instinctively go to my face, but there's nothing to hide under—no hat, no wig, no sunglasses. It's my full face. On full display.

"Does anyone own that Ford Focus at pump five? The back tire is totally shredded," he says and jerks a thumb behind him.

Zorie and I exchange looks.

"We do," I say quickly. Then to the officer, I add, "That was the accident we reported. A shredded tire."

The officer's hands move to his holster, and I try to ignore the fact that they're now in close proximity to his gun. Uncertainty etches itself across every feature on his face. "Shredded tire, huh?"

I nod and wonder if I can be arrested for calling in a nonemergency emergency. "We were scared," I tell him. "It's going to get dark, and we don't know the area."

He cocks his head to the side and drums his holster with his fingers. "Next time you ladies have a flat, call AAA. Not the police," he says and turns to leave.

"Night, Bobby Ray! See you at church Sunday!" the woman behind the counter calls after him, and he waves without turning around.

"So about that tire—I can change it for you if you have a spare so you ladies can get back on the road?" Dez offers.

I stand there for a second. For some reason, this strikes me as hilarious. Back on the road. As if this were some fun, adventurous road trip and not us running for our lives all the way to the land of beignets and gumbo. I throw my head back and laugh at the ceiling until my sides ache.

"You okay, girl?" Zorie asks, watching me. Her voice is low and gentle, like she's comforting a small child, which makes me laugh harder. I take a deep breath and hold my sides, trying to contain my laughter, but every time I look at Zorie's confused face, it starts again. I've clearly gone insane. The stress of the past twenty-four hours combined with possible heatstroke has made me lose my mind. I hunch forward and laugh until no sounds come out.

"Y'all gonna buy something or not?" the woman behind the counter asks, and points to the NO LOITERING sign by the doors.

"Or not," Zorie snaps, which sends me into more giggles.

"Is everything okay?" Dez asks, looking more and more uncomfortable by the second and probably regretting his offer to change our tire.

"She's not usually like this," Zorie says. "We're kind of having a bad day. Lost our phones and now the tire."

"Here," Dez says, handing us his phone with its metallic Solar Sonics emblem on the case. This guy is a walking promotion for his cheesy band. He swipes across the screen, frowns, and lifts the phone above his head. "Shoot. This dang phone. Gets terrible reception."

"Don't worry about it," I say, and wipe my eyes with the heel of my hand. "Maybe you could still help us with the tire?"

He smiles and flashes those adorable dimples I remember. "Okey dokey."

Still corny, but still very cute. I start past him and trip over my laces and into a sunglasses rack.

"Careful there," he says, steadying me.

I wait for him to make a joke about using my feet to walk, but he doesn't. He stands awkwardly behind me and rubs the back of his neck before extending a hand to me.

"I'm Dez, by the way."

I stare at his hand as if the concept of handshaking is new to me.

"And you are?" he asks, watching me.

Oh my God. He has no fucking clue who I am. Of course he doesn't! Poor guy only saw half my face thanks to the wig's awful bangs.

"Do you have a name, or should I just call you Giggles?" Dez asks.

I laugh, mostly from relief, and look up at him through my lashes. "Right. Sorry. I'm Michelle, and that's—"

"Star," Zorie says with a little pinky wave.

I roll my eyes. Of course she picked the stripper name.

"After you, Michelle." Dez lifts his lips in a half smile and holds the door open. "Um . . . and Star."

Going from air-conditioning to the swampy outside is like someone throwing a wet blanket over my head. I swipe at the fresh beads of sweat on my forehead and try to walk like a normal human next to Dez.

"You two headed back to New York?" he asks.

"Why would we go to New York?"

Dez points at our car. "Saw the New York license plate and figured you were out-of-towners."

I stop walking, and Zorie slams into me. How had we missed the very obvious New York license plate? Zorie shoots me a panicked look, and I shrug, unsure of how to answer his question.

"It's a rental," Zorie says quickly.

"Hey, it's cool." Dez laughs. "I promise I'm not interrogating you ladies. When I saw your plates, I figured we came from the same direction and thought I'd ask if you heard about those two women who killed that woman in Georgia yesterday."

I don't look at Zorie, even though I can feel her eyes burning a fiery hole into the back of my head. "We don't really keep up with the news. Too depressing," I tell him.

"You should google it later. Wild story. I was actually at the wedding and—I kid you not—the killers were dressed up like members of the band!" He points to the white van with the words LET SOLAR SONICS SERENADE YOUR NEXT EVENT stenciled on the side in big neon block letters. Three heads look out the window at us and wave. "We were the band! How's that for wild?"

I imagine saying back to him, *And we're the killers! How's that for wild?* But I say, "That's crazy," instead, then do my best to look both shocked and horrified, even throw in a few *bless your hearts* before popping the trunk. The inside of the trunk smells worse than the car, and I'm convinced it carried a dead body at some point. What it doesn't hold is a spare tire.

"Seriously?" I groan.

Zorie peers over my shoulder and into the trunk as if I somehow overlooked a whole tire.

"No luck?" Dez asks.

I shake my head and close the trunk. A trickle of sweat drips into my eyes, and I rub them hard until I realize I'm crying. Zorie slides an arm around my shoulders, but I push her away. It's too damn hot for comforting. I settle for an empathetic pat on my back instead.

"Maybe we can call your rental company and they can send someone to pick up the car?" Dez offers.

We all look back at the gas station, and the woman has placed a CLOSED sign in the window and turned out the lights.

"Fucking Karen," Zorie mumbles.

"You know what, it's fine. We'll figure it out," I say, and swipe the snot from my nose with the back of my hand.

Dez shifts his weight from one foot to the other. He clearly wants to leave, but his gentleman manners tether him here with us.

"We'll be fine. We'll get a friend to pick us up. You can go," I say.

Zorie frowns at me. "He can?"

"Star's right. I can't go," Dez says, and shoves his hands into the front pockets of his jeans. "Listen, I know we just met and all, but my grandmother would roll over in her grave if she knew I left two young ladies stranded and all alone in the middle of nowhere. The guys and I are on our way to our next gig. We can drop you off in town, somewhere less deserted, and you can wait for your ride there."

Right. We'll wait for our phantom ride that will never come.

"We're not dangerous," he says, and places a hand over his heart. "I promise."

Poor, sweet, innocent Dez. He has no idea who the real dangerous ones are.

"Michelle?" He stares at me with big, concerned eyes. I've been quiet too long.

"We can't ask you to do that, Dez," I say.

"You didn't. I volunteered."

I look at Zorie, and her expression is so hopeful that I'd hate to disappoint her.

"If it's not too much trouble," I say.

Dez smiles, flashing those adorable damn dimples. "It would be my pleasure."

"I bet," Zorie says under her breath, and I nudge her in the ribs. Hope I leave a bruise.

CHAPTER THIRTEEN

The other members of Solar Sonics aren't as welcoming as their hospitable lead singer. They eye us suspiciously as we squeeze past them to the back of the van with our pillowcases full of clothes. We force ourselves onto the sliver of seat remaining between the tower of suitcases, a keyboard, and two guitars.

"Fellas, I'd like you to meet Michelle and Star—two new friends in need of a little help," Dez says. Even without an audience of wedding guests, he still sounds like a wedding singer announcing his next performance. "And this motley crew is Frankie, Gunther, and Ryan."

"Star, huh?" says the guy riding shotgun with the platinum-blond mohawk. I recognize him immediately as the keyboard player, Frankie, or the cringeworthy name he uses on Instagram: Magic Fingers. "Must be an old family name."

Zorie opens her mouth to respond, and I squeeze her knee. We need to make it at least to town before they throw us out of their van because of Zorie's mouth.

"So where are we taking you?" asks the lead guitarist, Gunther, who looks a lot different in person than in his photos. From what I remember, his skin was crystal clear and almost translucent in the photos, but inside the van, it's covered in cystic acne, and his hair is thinning at the crown.

"We're taking them to the next gas station so they can arrange for a tow truck to pick up their car," Dez answers. He sits in the driver's seat, diagonal from the drummer, Ryan, who has yet to acknowledge us or look up from the sheet music in his hands.

"That might be a problem, Dez," Frankie says. "The next gas station isn't until exit 281, which is forty-seven miles away."

Dez twists in his seat to look at us and flashes his dimples. "What do you ladies think? You okay driving with a bunch of dorks?"

"If it's not too much trouble," I answer. Frankie mumbles something under his breath, which makes Gunther laugh, and I suddenly feel like a trespasser. An intruder. We're clearly not wanted inside this van, but we're not wanted at the Juniper Circle Minit Mart, either. Dez and Gunther were thoughtful enough to push our car to the side of the road and off the gas station's property, but that doesn't mean some meth head won't steal our tires in the middle of the night. What's left of them anyway.

"Don't mind them," Dez says, watching me. "It's been a long twenty-four hours, and Frankie's worried about the bad publicity for our band after that woman was killed."

Zorie stiffens next to me, and I shift in my seat. "We'll get out of your hair as soon as we get to the gas station," I say.

Dez opens his mouth like he wants to say something else, then closes it and twists back around in his seat. I stare at the back of his head and try to imagine what he must be thinking. Does he regret offering us a ride? What if he recognized us and this is a setup to drive us to the police station and collect the reward money? He seems a little too eager to help two complete strangers. This is beginning to feel like a mistake.

"Hungry?" Zorie whispers. She hands me a bag of Cheez-Its courtesy of her five-finger discount. It's frightening how skilled she is at taking things that don't belong to her.

"Thanks," I say and take the bag. God only knows when and where our next real meal will be. I lean against the guitar case and pop a

Cheez-It into my mouth. "We need a new plan," I whisper. "Kind of hard to make it to New Orleans without a vehicle."

Zorie shrugs. "We'll take this one."

"I'm serious."

"So am I." She laughs a little too loudly and a little too long. Frankie and Gunther twist in their seats to look at her, and I nudge her with my knee.

"I still think we should do the Skynyrd," Ryan says suddenly. His voice surprises me. It's high-pitched and feminine, a direct contrast to his broad, muscular frame.

"I told you, this is an older couple—an older, sophisticated crowd. They'll want the classics—the Temptations, Etta James, Neil Diamond," Dez says.

Ryan shakes his head. "I think we're making a mistake. People want something they can really move to."

"You just want to play your little drum solo," Frankie says with a laugh.

"Maybe I'm tired of playing the same boring songs at every wedding," Ryan scoffs.

I glance at Zorie, and she smiles. She loves watching a good fight. That's why she's obsessed with every *Real Housewives of Wherever*. Me, not so much.

"Why don't we let the ladies decide," Dez says.

I shake my head defiantly. The less we piss off this group, the better our chances of maintaining our anonymity. "Thanks, but we'll sit this one out," I say.

"I think it should be Skynyrd," Zorie chimes.

The van swerves onto the shoulder and then back onto the road as Dez glances in the rearview mirror at Zorie.

"I mean, who doesn't like Skynyrd? They're rock royalty," she continues, and leans over the seat so that her face is parallel to Ryan's. Her hands are purposely tucked under her boobs to push them up and out, and I hide my grin as I watch Gunther and Ryan try their best not to notice. "I bet your drum solo is fire," she says to Ryan. A blush crawls up his neck and across his cheeks. Zorie looks at me and smiles. This is what she does, makes men feel like they're the most desired person in the room. It's in the way she tilts her head to make it look as if she's riveted by their words, and how she lightly sucks her bottom lip and touches her collarbone to look just the tiniest bit turned on. Before they know it, they've revealed parts of themselves they never intended to share, and Zorie hangs on their every word, filing away information. "Guys, we're in Alabama. And what's the most famous Alabama song ever?" Zorie asks.

"She's right," Gunther says, nodding. "Once they hear that guitar chord, the crowd is gonna go bananas."

Ryan grins, looking pleased with himself. "Skynyrd it is."

And just like that, Zorie—aka Star—has won them all over. She sinks back into the seat with her arms folded behind her head, and we ride.

———

By the time we make it to the next city, Zorie has performed six Lynyrd Skynyrd songs for her captivated audience and even twerked on the back of Ryan's head. I wonder, if things had gone differently yesterday and we hadn't gone through with stealing the gift box, what might've become of our connection with Solar Sonics. Would Dez and I have eventually reconnected, and would that connection have led to him and Zorie becoming the front man and woman of the band?

I'm still considering Zorie's life as an international pop star when the van rattles to a stop in front of a gas station.

"Guess this is your stop," Dez says. He gets out and slides open the van door, and I peer out at our new destination. It's crawling with sketchy characters, including one woman who lost her pants and is now bare-assed in front of us. "On second thought, maybe we'll try the next station."

"I have a better idea," chimes Ryan, who has become a lot more talkative since the life-changing twerk Zorie did on his head. "Why don't we head on to Montgomery? We can grab dinner at the hotel. It's comped anyway, and room service is 24/7." His gaze shifts to Zorie, and he smiles. "We can get to know each other better."

Yep. Life-changing twerk.

Zorie gives a coy smile to match her half shrug. It's enough of a commitment to satisfy Ryan, and he yells for Dez to drive to the Blythewood Hotel.

"Do you guys always get free dinner at the Blythewood?" I ask. Leslie Grace considers the Blythewood our biggest competition in the three-star-hotel market. What the Chamberlain lacked in aesthetics, we made up for in outstanding customer service. Except for those times when we didn't.

"Our gig tomorrow is in the Blythewood's ballroom, so the bride and groom comp our rooms and meals as part of our contract," Dez says.

"A Monday wedding? Seriously?" I ask.

"We've played at a few weekday weddings. Mostly backyard gigs. Glad it's at the Blythewood this time. Food's awesome, especially the taco bar, and the front desk lets us use the pool after hours. One of the perks of being in a band."

My stomach growls at the mention of tacos, and I cover it with my hands. Dez laughs, and Zorie hands me another bag of Cheez-Its. The bag feels warm, and I wonder where on her body she'd hidden it since leaving the Juniper Circle Minit Mart.

"How did you guys end up stranded anyway? I mean, doesn't everyone have a phone these days?" Frankie asks.

I think of our phones somewhere on Highway 109 with Isaiah's Jordans. RIP.

"Actually, we lost our phones," Zorie says.

I nod quickly, thinking how grateful I am for her quick response since all I can think about now are tacos.

"That's why we stopped at the gas station in the first place—to use their phone because of our flat tire," I add.

"Oh." A small frown creases his forehead. I know what he's thinking: how ridiculous our story sounds with our raggedy "rental" that's one oil leak away from death, our missing phones, and our overstuffed pillowcases. Even I wouldn't believe me.

"We were robbed!" Zorie blurts out. "They took everything and left us with that awful car! Our luggage, our phones, our money—gone! They said they'd kill us if we called the police." She leans forward and sobs into her hands. I cry, too, and I know we're both crying about the same thing, and it has zero to do with our phones.

"Dude, do something," says Gunther.

I'm not sure which "dude" he's talking to, but Ryan responds first. "They always comp us an extra room, you know, for our equipment. You girls are more than welcome to it."

"Hey!" Frankie yells. "We can't go giving up our rooms just because you think you're getting a piece of ass tonight."

"Dude! Not cool!" Gunther snaps.

"It's fine," Zorie says, wiping her eyes on her sleeve. "It's just that, I was thinking what a great story this would make for the news when we tell them how your band came to our rescue."

Frankie's quiet for a moment, and I watch his eyes dart between us. I know what his next words will be before he says them.

"Okay, fine. But make sure you mention *all* of our names."

Zorie smiles triumphantly, and for the millionth time in the past hour, I'm grateful she's with me. I mouth *Thank you*, and she mouths back, *I got you.*

━━

The lobby of the Blythewood Hotel is at least three times the size of the Chamberlain's and ten times as stunning. If I had my phone, weren't on the run from the police, and were still employed, I'd snap a pic and text it to Leslie Grace.

"You ladies wait here, and I'll grab our room keys," Dez says.

There was something about the way he said "our room" that made it sound as though this was always the plan. An impromptu vacay with our Solar Sonic friends at the Blythewood Hotel in Montgomery, Alabama. He takes off across the checkered marble floor, leaving Zorie and me alone by the elevators with an unaccompanied luggage cart. One of the suitcases is metallic pink with a sticker of the Eiffel Tower on its side beneath another sticker with the words *Future Mrs.*

"Is that what I think it is?" Zorie asks, following my gaze.

"A new wardrobe?" She stands in front of me, in case we're being filmed, and I carefully remove the suitcase from its corner of the cart before ducking inside the bathroom a few feet away. Zorie doesn't follow me. She knows it's better to separate and distract when we're . . . working.

I find an empty stall at the end of the row and lift the suitcase on top of the toilet. It's unlocked but still takes some work to pry open. The back wheel slips off the seat into the toilet and splashes my face with whatever hepatitis-infused water lives inside these porcelain bowls.

"Fuck this." I push open the stall door, but freeze when I hear a voice. I duck back inside the stall, climb on top of the toilet seat, and crouch down with the hundred-pound suitcase hugged to my chest.

The woman's shoes click hard against the tile floor as she paces in front of the sinks. "Mom, I'm freaking out," she whines. "Don't tell me to calm down! All my bridesmaids' gifts are in there!" She gives an impatient grunt. "It was on the luggage cart. On the luggage cart, Mom! I think that ghetto black girl by the elevators stole it."

My body tenses as I contemplate bashing her head into the mirror.

And in what feels like slow motion, the damn suitcase slips from between my legs and onto the floor.

"Mom, I'll call you back," the woman says, then louder, "I said I'll call you back!"

I suck in my breath. Really not in the mood to fight a bitch. I reach down and lift the suitcase between my legs again and squeeze.

"Hello?" the woman calls. She paces up and down the aisle before coming to a stop in front of my stall. I look down and see a pair of yellow strappy sandals under the door. "I'm sorry to disturb you, but I'm hoping you can help me."

"This is really not a good time," I say. Through the crack in the door, I see a flash of blond hair as she turns to walk away. I wait to hear the door open and close, but it doesn't. She's still here. With me. More punishments from God.

"I'm sorry again, ma'am, but there was a lady by the elevators— a black one—and I think she may have taken my suitcase."

I roll my eyes and will myself to stay calm. I am a fugitive on the run with my best friend and am currently holding this future bride's suitcase. One cry of mistreatment from this lady and the police will be here with handcuffs.

"Actually, I did see someone by the luggage cart," I say. "A white guy with a blond mohawk."

"A white guy? You're sure?" She asks this as if a white thief were inconceivable.

"Very suspicious looking," I say. "Now, if you don't mind, I really need to get back to my business. I ate at the taco bar earlier."

The woman doesn't say anything else, and I hear the door swing closed. I hop off the seat and work quickly to pry open the suitcase with what little fingernails I have. Finally, it creaks open, and I snatch a maxi dress, a pair of shorts, and a halter top from inside.

"Girl, what is taking so long?" Zorie's voice echoes inside the small space, making me jump.

"Put these in your pillowcase," I say, and toss her the stolen clothes.

"This is cute. Expensive, too," Zorie says, taking in the green-and-gold maxi dress.

"Zorie!"

She nods and jams the clothes inside the pillowcase with our T-shirts. I stuff the suitcase into one of the trash cans and cover it with paper towels. The lid barely fits, but there's no time to care. Dez is waiting by the elevators when we emerge and holds up two chocolate chip cookies.

"The Blythewood is known for their homemade cookies at check-in," he says proudly, like he gets a commission each time he says it.

I take one of the cookies and am tempted to stuff the entire thing into my mouth, but I don't. "Thank you again, Dez. For everything."

He smiles and ushers us both inside the elevator. As the doors close, I see a tall, thin blonde with yellow strappy sandals yelling at a very confused Frankie in the middle of the lobby.

CHAPTER FOURTEEN

———

"Sorry, they're adjoining rooms," Dez says. He holds open the door to room 416, and we pass under his arm. The room is smaller than I expect, given the spacious lobby, and one of the double beds is covered in the band's equipment.

"I can move that stuff if you want," Dez offers.

"It's fine. We'll take care of it." I wave a dismissive hand and sink down into the rolling chair by the desk. Zorie sits on the bed opposite me and stares at the floor. Since the elevator ride, she's barely spoken except to mumble a half-hearted thanks to Dez when he handed her a room key.

"Guess I'll let you two do your thing. I'll be over there if you need me," Dez says, and motions to the door connecting his room to ours.

I wait until the door clicks shut before I open the menu on the desk. "I'm thinking we skip the taco bar and order room service. I mean, how many more chances will we have to eat free steak?"

"Sure. Sounds good," Zorie says, but doesn't look up. Her expression is somber, and her chin quivers as if she's on the verge of tears.

"Hey, you know what we need right now? Ice cream. I'll order us a couple of sundaes with extra nuts." I twist in my chair to dial room service and watch Zorie in the mirror while I wait for someone to pick up. "Yes, I'd like to order two chocolate sundaes with extra nuts for room 416 and two steaks, medium, with loaded baked potatoes. Oh, and a couple of Sprites," I say to the bored voice on the other end. When I hang up, Zorie is curled on top of the bed with her back to me.

"Zo? You okay?" She doesn't answer me, and I join her on the bed and gently rub her back. When we were kids, she'd beg me to do the "Crisscross Applesauce" song with my fingers on her back. It's basically me drawing lines up and down her back with my fingers, but she loved it. I start to do it now, but she scoots away from me.

"Zorie, talk to me," I say, but she only curls tighter into a ball. She's always been the taller one of our duo. Looking at her now, with her knees pulled into her chest and her arms folded under her cheek, she looks almost childlike. I cover her with a blanket from the closet and tell her I'm going to shower before the food gets here. Zorie doesn't move or respond.

I take a long shower with the hotel-provided toiletries and slip on the stolen halter top. The shorts are too small, but wearable if I leave the top button undone. I brush my hair into a tight bun and step back to marvel at my reflection. All in all, not bad for someone on the run. Could use a toothbrush and maybe a little deodorant, but I look surprisingly decent.

"*You really look lovely, Kayla.*" Dad's voice needles its way inside my brain. Instinctively, I reach into my back pocket for my phone to call him, and remember my phone is gone and these aren't my shorts. How humiliated he must be, his only daughter accused of running over a bridesmaid at a wedding she was stealing from. Bet when the truth comes out, Gloria will force him to sit down for a TV interview so they can tell the world what a terrible person I am.

And they'll be right.

When I open the bathroom door, Zorie is sitting cross-legged in the middle of the bed with our steaks and two of the biggest chocolate sundaes I've ever seen. She looks up when she notices me and smiles.

"You look pretty," she says.

"I bet that maxi dress you liked will look really good on you. It's in the bathroom, if you want it."

Zorie shrugs. "Maybe."

I sit across from her and pop open the can of Sprite with my middle finger. "Food looks good." It really does. The steaks are cooked perfectly, and the baked potato is dripping with butter and sour cream. I could eat everything on the plate with just my hands, starting with the chocolate sundae. I reach for it, but Zorie grabs my wrist.

"Both of these aren't for you," I say and shove her hand away.

"I need to talk to you about something before your sugar high hits."

I don't like her tone. It's melancholy. Sad. If we were dating, this is the moment she'd tell me we should see other people.

"Let's talk after we eat," I say, and reach for my spoon, but she places her hand over mine.

"You should go home," she says flatly.

"Right. I'm sure Dad and Gloria are waiting to throw me a huge welcome-home party." I laugh and wait for her to join me, but she doesn't. Her eyes remain locked on mine, her face expressionless.

"I called my aunt in New Orleans on Ryan's phone when you were in the bathroom with that chick's luggage. She doesn't want us there." Zorie pauses. Takes a deep breath. "She knows what we did. It's all over the news, and she doesn't want to get involved."

Now it's my turn to take a deep breath. "What do you mean it's all over the news?"

"Kevin turned us in, the pussy. A detective called Aunt Ruby, asking questions about me. She told them she hasn't spoken to me in years."

"That's it, then," I say hoarsely. "It's over."

"It doesn't have to be. I talked to Ryan, and he's thinking about going solo and moving to Texas."

A sick feeling swells in the pit of my stomach. I know what's coming next, what Zorie's already decided. I don't look at her, but it doesn't stop her.

"This could work for me," she says. "I can live in Texas, and Ryan will take care of me."

The ice cream is starting to melt. It drips down the sides of the silver bowls and onto the comforter, forming a milk-chocolate river along the side of Zorie's bare foot.

"What about Isaiah?" I ask. Like it matters. Zorie and Isaiah's short-lived romance ended the second we backed out of his driveway. I look at her, but her outline is blurred by fresh tears. "What about . . . me?"

"You come from a good family, Kayla. This was never supposed to be your life. Working at the hotel, going to prison . . . being on the run with me. None of it." She pokes at the cherry on top of her sundae, and it disappears inside its whipped-cream grave. "Let's be real, this would've eventually been my life no matter what. I'm destined for it. You're not."

I shake my head. "That's not true, and you know it."

"Oh, I know it." Zorie laughs. "Look at us—how different we are. We were never meant to be friends."

"You're right." I hold up my right arm and point to its tattooed wrist. "We weren't meant to be friends. We were meant to be *best* friends, and I'm not leaving you."

Zorie closes her eyes and rubs them with the backs of her hands. "You don't get it. There's nothing for me back home. You have a family to go home to. They'll help you make things right again. They always do. Tell them it was all my fault—that I forced you to go on the run with me. They'll believe you."

"This is all wrong," I groan. "What do you even know about this Ryan guy?"

She shrugs. "I know he likes me. That's enough."

There's a knock at the adjoining door, and we both jump. Zorie starts to stand, but I reach for her. "Don't. We're not finished."

She smiles and smooths back my hair with both her hands. "Yes, we are."

I reach for her again, but she's already on her feet and headed for the door. Dez is on the other side when she opens it, dressed in a neon-yellow Solar Sonics T-shirt, black skinny jeans, and Chuck Taylors.

"Everything okay in your room?" he asks.

"Great. Perfect," Zorie says, her voice dripping with sarcasm.

Dez looks to me as if for reassurance, and I force a small smile. "Everything's fine," I say, trying my best to sound upbeat.

He looks relieved and takes a tentative step inside, eyeing our steak dinners on the bed. Technically he never gave us a budget, but the steaks were definitely the most expensive items on the menu.

"That's some spread," he says. Dez is quiet for a moment, his eyes fixed on the bed, with his lower lip caught between his teeth.

"Do you want a bite or something?" Zorie asks.

The tips of his ears turn crimson. "Sorry, I wanted to ask Michelle something, and I was trying to think of a way to do it without being weird."

"Too late." Zorie trudges back to the bed, leaving Dez to stand awkwardly in the doorway with his hands shoved inside his front pockets.

"Uh, well, I was thinking, if you're not too tired . . . and if I'm not interrupting your dinner—"

"You are," Zorie chimes in with a smile.

I shoot her an annoyed look, and she shrugs. "You're not," I say. "What's up?"

"I, uh, thought you might want to check out the rooftop garden. They remodeled it since the last time I was here. Really cool space. But only if you want to."

I start to shake my head. Leaving Zorie alone with this unfinished conversation hanging thick in the air is not an option. But she interjects before I can decline Dez's invitation.

"Go. Have fun," she says. "We'll talk when you get back."

I want to protest, but she's already turned her back to me. There will be no further negotiations tonight.

"I guess I'm all yours," I say to Dez.

"Shall we?" He offers me his arm, and I reluctantly link mine with his.

"Don't do anything I wouldn't do!" Zorie calls after us.

Dez laughs, but I want to burst into tears.

═══

Acting like a normal person is incredibly hard when you don't feel normal at all. Normal people don't steal strangers' clothes or strangers' names. I'd chosen the name Michelle thinking it was ordinary enough to be forgettable. People don't remember Michelles unless you're Michelle Obama. But now, walking arm in arm with Dez, I realize my chosen moniker is one he can't stop saying: "Tell me about yourself, Michelle. What brings you to Alabama, Michelle? How is a woman like you not in a relationship, Michelle?" I try to pivot his questions back to him, like asking about the band and his favorite songs, thinking these are safe topics. They're not. Seconds into his answer about his favorite song, he tells me about yesterday's wedding and the chaos that ensued in the middle of his rendition of "Stand by Me." I'm trying so hard to look shocked by his words and not guilty that I don't notice we've stopped walking.

"We're here," Dez says. He opens the door to a staircase that smells faintly of weed, and I follow him inside. The staircase is misleading since it's three flights instead of one. By the time we reach the doors leading to the rooftop, I'm sweaty and hyperventilating.

"Beautiful, huh?" he says, waving his arms out in front of him.

It's dark, except for the sad string of lights pinned to a table, and I can barely make out if what I'm standing on is fake grass or a wet, spongy rug.

"Beautiful," I repeat.

Dez takes my hand and guides me to the table, and I take a seat on one of the mismatched vinyl chairs. He's clearly planned this little impromptu adventure, right down to the two glasses of wine and the platter of tacos and guacamole.

"You don't have to eat them if you don't want to," Dez says.

"Are you kidding me? I'm starving, and these look delicious." I grab one of the tacos that isn't swarming with flies and take a small bite. It's soggy, and the meat is weirdly crunchy. "Delicious."

I pick at the wilted lettuce and stare down at the city below, thinking how far away Redwood Springs seems now. I picture Dad alone in his bedroom, head bowed, praying for the salvation I no longer deserve. Zorie's wrong about me having a family to go home to. My family stopped existing the moment the cancer stole my mother's final breath. Even in those last moments with Dad and the hospice nurse, Mom reminded me to be brave. "Be fearless, Kayla," she'd whispered. "You're a part of me, and that means you're strong." I'd held on to her with all my strength, like she might float away if I let go. But no matter how much I clung to her, I couldn't keep her there with me. I swallow the lump that forms in my throat at the memory.

"Were you able to report those people who robbed you?" Dez asks, jolting me from my thoughts.

"In the morning. Star and I are too exhausted to be interrogated by the police tonight," I say. He nods at me, and I'm convinced he sees the guilt and lies ooze through my rayon-blend shirt like a flashing neon sign pointed at my head: Liar. Liar. Liar. "Thank you so much for your help, Dez. Star and I really appreciate it."

He laughs. "You don't have to keep thanking me. I was happy to help. Not every day I run into a beautiful woman in the middle of nowhere."

Heat rises into my cheeks, and I self-consciously run a hand over my hair. The humidity has made it unmanageable at this point, but I do my best to smooth the sides.

"Can I ask you something, Michelle?"

It takes me a minute to realize he's talking to me. "Sure."

"You seem like a woman who has her stuff together. Probably smarter than half the women me and the guys meet on the road."

"That's not a question."

Dez leans forward on his elbows. "I guess I don't get why you hang out with a girl like Star."

I frown. "What's that supposed to mean?"

I know exactly what he means. We don't match. We never have. Zorie was always the outspoken one of our duo, the uninhibited, fearless one. In high school, I played the role of the dutiful sidekick who watched shit go down and kept my mouth shut. If Zorie wanted to throw ham at the fat kid in the cafeteria, I told her it was hilarious. If she wanted to tape condoms to the pregnant freshman's locker, I helped. But somewhere between senior year and the awful year that followed, our dynamic shifted, and I became the outspoken one, reining in my best friend and her wild antics. While Zorie made her rounds at the local bars, I was home tracking her location on my phone and ready to save her from herself. If someone tested Zorie's temper, I stepped in to defuse it. Our lives together became safer, more controlled, and part of me thinks Zorie resents me for it.

"Star's my best friend," I say to Dez.

"I'm sorry. That came out wrong." Dez shakes his head and shoves a hand through his hair. "It's just, earlier, I caught her going through Ryan's bag by the elevator. I didn't tell Ryan, but it's kind of messed up that she'd steal from him when it was his idea to bring you both here in the first place. Just seems like she's more of a liability than a friend."

My frown deepens. "And you've decided all of this after knowing us for, what? Four hours? How do you know I'm not the liability?"

"You're right. I'm an idiot. I shouldn't have said anything."

Dez twists away from me and stares up at the sky. I want to tell him that my entire outfit came from someone else's luggage and that forty-eight hours ago, I'd sold six hundred dollars' worth of stolen shit to a shady pawn shop owner. Zorie sifting through Ryan's bag of undies and T-shirts that were probably stained under the arms and crotch is the least of his worries.

"It's late. We should probably go." I start to stand, but Dez doesn't move. He stares straight ahead, unblinking. "Dez?"

"I hate my band," he says flatly. "Frankie, Gunther, Ryan—I hate them all."

I slide back in my seat, unsure of what to do or say next. "Oh."

"They don't respect me. I'm the lead singer, you know. I deserve respect." He leans forward and cracks his knuckles, shaking his head. "We're scheduled to play at the country club across town in a few days for a couple in their early twenties. Do you think they want to hear Barry Manilow or Paul Anka ballads?"

I take a sip of warm wine and wince as it slides down my throat, thick and tart. This rooftop tour is feeling more and more like a huge mistake. Zorie is probably in Ryan's room, twerking him into submission.

"I should get back to my room," I say. Then, for extra emphasis, I feign a long, dramatic yawn.

"Right." Hurt registers on his face. He can't think this date—or whatever this is—is going well. Can he?

"Listen, if it's any consolation, I think you're an amazing singer." I place my hand on his, grazing my thumb across his knuckles. "They're lucky to have you."

Dez stares at me with his brows furrowed, and I immediately know I've messed up. Kayla has heard Dez sing, but Michelle has not.

Dez opens his mouth to ask me the perfectly logical question that has no doubt formed in his mind. "How do you—"

Before he can finish, I lean in, grab his face with both hands, and kiss him hard on the mouth. He kisses me back. Harder. My hands slip into his hair, tugging and pulling, and I kiss him until I forget about the past twenty-four hours and my last conversation with Zorie.

"You taste amazing," I say, surprised by how turned on I am. My last hookup was over a month ago, and I could really use a stress reliever right about now.

"You taste amazing, too," Dez whispers against my lips. He stands and lifts me onto the table. "Is this okay, Michelle?"

Really wish he'd stop calling me that.

"Yes," I say in a deep, throaty voice I don't recognize. I move his hands down the front of my body to my shorts and wait for him to take them off, but he doesn't move. He stares down at me as if unsure what to do next. This has definitely never happened before. "What's wrong?" I ask.

"Nothing. You're great. Perfect, actually. It's just that . . . I don't usually do things like this."

"Things like what? Sex?" I prop myself up on my elbows and cock my head to the side. "Dez, are you a virgin?"

My question surprises him, and he gives a loud, strangled laugh. "No, of course not."

"Then take off my shorts." This time, he doesn't hesitate. He slides my shorts down over my flip-flops, and I pull him to me, wrapping my legs around his waist.

"You're beautiful, Michelle." He grazes the curve of my hip with his fingertips, sending shivers over my body. "So beautiful."

Dez lifts my legs onto his shoulders, and I give in to him. Completely.

CHAPTER FIFTEEN

I'm a terrible person.

I've called myself that in the past. Even in the last few hours. But now I mean it. I really, genuinely mean it because I'm standing in the lobby of the Blythewood Hotel with the smell of sex on my skin.

"Want to grab a drink? There's a bar across the street," Dez says. He takes my hand and slides his fingers between mine. I stare at our reflections in the mirrored wall and wonder what other people must think of us. Can they tell we just boned on the rooftop? My eyes shift to Dez's flushed face. His hair sticks to his forehead, and the collar of his T-shirt is damp with sweat. He looks feverish, like he's one breath away from passing out. He smiles at me inside the mirror like he knows my thoughts, and I look away, embarrassed.

"I'm going to run to the bathroom," I say.

"Should I wait for you?"

"I'll meet you there."

He smiles again and lifts my hand to his lips. "Whiskey and Rye."

"What?"

"The bar across the street—the name of it is Whiskey and Rye."

Dez leans in to kiss me, but I turn too quickly, and he kisses my hair instead. Poor Dez. He's fallen in love with a wanted criminal. A murderer. I watch him walk out the sliding glass doors, glancing over his shoulder every few steps to wave at me. Bless his heart.

I turn on my heel in the direction of the bathroom but stop when I spot a shirtless man in Hawaiian swim trunks and bare feet seated in front of a computer inside the business center. I duck inside and slide into the chair farthest away from him.

"Internet here is a piece of shit!" the man slurs. From where I sit, I can make out a Google image of a scantily clad Kim Kardashian on his screen.

"Perv," I mumble, and tap the keyboard to wake up my own computer. My hands shake as I type "Julianna Fletcher wedding" and "Jasper Falls, Georgia," into the search box. Photos and articles with headlines like "Red Wedding" and "Forever Hold Your Peace" immediately fill the screen. I click through the photos of Julianna and Brett's love story and Amber Childress, the bride's best friend, as the growing knot in my stomach tightens.

"Goddamn firewall!" the shirtless man shouts.

I ignore him and focus on Amber, with her bright-blue eyes. She smiles at me from inside the computer as she points to Julianna's engagement ring. The caption reads, "Amber and Julianna in happier times." Each mouse click reveals a new fact about the woman described as "magical" by her friends. Amber volunteered at the humane society. Amber was a hospice nurse. Amber adopted a dog missing one leg. Tears sting my eyes, but I force myself to keep clicking. I deserve every ounce of guilt and shame that pulsates through my body.

The last few articles are filled with photos from the wedding. Amber and another bridesmaid playfully pose for the cameras as they make their way down the aisle after the happy couple. Her lipstick is smeared, and there's a smudge of mascara on her cheek, but she looks too happy to care. Zorie and I were probably moving centerpieces at this exact moment to make it easier for us to take a piece of the bride and groom's joy. According to Channel 5 news, no arrests have been made, but apparently the press has renamed Zorie and me the Wedding Crasher Killers and described us as "armed and danger-ous." Video from that day shows us walking across the parking lot in our Soler Sonics T-shirts and entering the building before racing out of it half an hour later. I click on a video embedded in the article of Frankie giving an interview with the rest of the band.

"This has been a messed-up day, and our thoughts and prayers go out to the family of this beautiful woman," he says into the micro-phone with the huge Channel 5 logo attached. Then, shifting his stare from reporter Courtney Cunningham, Frankie looks directly into the camera and says, "Our band is not affiliated with those thieves. They stole our identities, but we are innocent and avail-able for bookings through the fall." I shake my head, thinking Dez is right to hate Frankie.

So far, there have been no Zorie-and-Kayla sightings. But thanks to Kevin's interview, the police are close.

"If I could speak directly to my friends, I'd tell them to stop and come back home," he says to the camera. "Don't throw your life away like this." As the camera pans away, Kevin asks, "When do I get the money?"

I roll my eyes and scroll farther down on the page, stopping when I see the headline of the next article: "Man Arrested in Connection with the Wedding Crasher Killers." Panic seizes me, and I squeeze the mouse so tight I think it might break. A photo of a white guy follows the article, with a caption identifying him as the driver of the Eldo-rado. Shit. I think back to Isaiah standing in his garage with the key to our new ride, saying, *Left it with a buddy of mine. He's cool people. He'll keep it safe.* If this buddy of his hasn't narced on him yet, it's definitely coming.

I clear my internet search history and push back from the desk and into Frankie. He stands behind me, wet from the pool and smelling of chlorine, a towel draped around his neck.

"Just the Michelle I wanted to see," he says.

"I was just on my way back," I say, but he doesn't move. Frankie stands as still as a statue, watching me with bloodshot eyes.

"You see, I have a problem, Michelle, and I could really use your help to figure it out." His lips curl up into a grin, and he moves closer, the heat of his body invading my space. "Can you help me, Michelle?"

I back up until I'm caught between the desk and a wall. "I really need to get to my room."

"Your room," he says, biting back a smirk. "Don't you mean the free room you and your friend managed to hustle from us?" Frankie laughs, and the drunk pervert in the next row glances over his shoulder at us. My eyes plead with him to help, but he turns back to his monitor. Back to Kim.

"The thing is," Frankie continues, "I've been trying to figure out where I know you and your friend from, and I think I finally figured it out."

"Good. Then you don't need my help."

I try to squeeze past him, but he blocks me.

"Yesterday was a really messed-up day for the Solar Sonics. The news was calling our band some kind of criminal ring that uses gigs to rob our audiences. Do you know what that kind of press does to a band's reputation?"

"I thought all press was good press."

"Not quite." He cocks his head to one side, making his features look weirdly distorted beneath this incredibly unflattering light. "That band is our livelihood. Our purpose. And yesterday, two grifting murderers threatened to take that from us."

Panic replaces the guilt and shame pulsating through my body, and I glance at the drunk dude again. He's found a Corona from somewhere and chugs half the bottle before belching loudly.

"Is there something you want to ask me, Frankie?"

His grin widens. "Is there something you want to tell me, Michelle?"

Frankie's close enough for me to smell the whiskey on his breath. His eyes are glassy like they don't belong to him. Drunk asshole. He smiles, as if reading my thoughts, and I get an even closer view of his huge yellow teeth, which may as well be fangs at this point. I suck in my breath and wait for his next move. Neither of us speaks. We stand there, staring, daring each other to look away.

"So I was thinking about the little proposition your friend made in the van about Solar Sonics rescuing two stranded ladies," Frankie says. "I think the better story would be Solar Sonics capturing the Wedding Crasher Killers. What do you think?"

At this point, I have two choices: scream and draw more attention to myself and possibly the police or run like hell and pray he's too drunk to keep up.

I opt for the second choice and break into a run, but drunk Frankie's reflexes are surprisingly quick. He slides two thick arms around my waist and yanks me backward against him.

"Let go of me," I say through clenched teeth.

Frankie rests his chin on my shoulder with his lips parallel to my ear. "We'll be on every news program across the country for this. People will be lining up to see the band who captured the Wedding Crasher Killers."

I elbow him hard in the ribs and instantly regret it. He puts me in a choke hold and I scratch at his arms to free myself, but he only squeezes harder until I'm gasping for breath and seconds from passing out. Pieces of the business center begin to fade, like it's being ripped apart, corner by corner, before my eyes. A dark figure emerges from somewhere in the room, and I feel myself start to fall.

"I've got you."

I gaze up through half-open eyes at Hawaiian-Swim-Trunks Guy and realize I've fallen into his arms. He helps me to my feet as I try to catch my breath and regain some semblance of consciousness.

"I think you broke my nose, you fat bastard!" a muffled voice groans behind me.

I turn to see Frankie curled into a ball on the floor, with his hands pressed to his face and blood pouring through his fingers.

"Maybe now you'll learn not to put your hands on women," Hawaiian Trunks says. Then to me, he asks, "You okay?"

I nod and mumble a quick thank-you before taking off toward the staircase. If Frankie was pissed before, he's enraged now. And probably sober thanks to Hawaiian-Trunks Dude's massive fist.

I climb the stairs quickly, taking two at a time. The recent choke hold and my cigarette addiction don't help with my athleticism, but I manage to make it to the fourth-floor door. Loud voices float down the corridor from the direction of our room. I move closer and stop at our cracked door. Zorie's and Dez's voices crash into each other, belligerent and angry.

"What's going on in here?" I ask, shoving open the door.

"Why don't you ask your friend?" Dez shouts. His eyes bulge, and his face is the deepest shade of purple, like he's one shout away from choking on anger. He turns and disappears back inside his room. Part of me wants to go after him, but I can't sacrifice the time, not when Frankie is probably calling the police as we speak.

"We need to go," I say to Zorie.

"Not until that asshole gives me my bags," she says, half shouting. Her eyes bulge like Dez's, and every vein in her neck is on full display.

"You mean your luggage?" Dez peers around the corner from his room and dangles two pillowcases in front of him.

I look at Zorie for an explanation, but she only shrugs. Whatever happened in this room before I got here had gone horribly wrong.

"Listen to me," I say slowly. Calmly. I place my hands on Zorie's forearms and feel myself vibrate with her. "They know our names. The police found your car back in Redwood and took the driver for questioning. If he hasn't already told them about Isaiah, he will, and then Isaiah will tell them about us. Everything about us. We need to go. Now."

"The police? I should've known the two of you were up to no good," Dez says. "I came back here to look for you when you didn't show up at the bar, and then I find your partner here going through my stuff."

He looks genuinely hurt. The hate I feel for myself in this moment can't be measured. Fucking Zorie. Maybe she was right about being destined for this life, or maybe the thrill of theft has evolved into some kind of compulsion.

"It wasn't like that, Dez. I wish I could tell you the truth, but I can't."

As if in response to my pathetic excuse, Dez dumps the contents of each pillowcase onto the floor. I watch in horror as Dez's shoes and wallet fall out on top of the pile of T-shirts.

"Guess this was your plan all along, right? Seduce me while your partner robs me? Is Michelle even your real name?" He shakes his head and bends down to pluck his wallet and shoes from the pile, but stops when he sees one of Isaiah's T-shirt creations. "Even my clothes?" he says. Dez leans in and squints at one of the shirts. He looks at Zorie, then me, as realization washes over his face. "You're them, aren't you?"

I look at Zorie, unsure of what to say. It's pointless to deny. The evidence is all right there at his feet. If I can convince him it was all a misunderstanding, then maybe he'll convince Frankie.

"Listen to me, Dez," I begin, but his eyes don't meet mine. They're focused on something else. *Someone* else, actually.

"Get in the bathroom! Now!" Zorie yells. She holds out Isaiah's gun in front of her and aims it at Dez.

I freeze, trying to control my breathing, trying to think. "What the hell are you doing?" I shout.

"He's obviously going to call the police, so I'm buying us some time."

"By pointing a gun at him? Are you insane?"

"Insane? Me?" Zorie grins in a way I don't recognize, with her lips pulled back and her full teeth exposed. "Actually, I've never felt more clearheaded in my life."

"I'm sorry. You ladies are obviously under a lot of pressure, and I'm only adding to that," Dez says. He lifts his hands in the air and focuses his terrified stare on me. "I won't call the police. I swear. I was just a little upset, but it's all good, okay?"

"Take his phone," Zorie orders.

I don't want to, but I've seen what a desperate Zorie is capable of. I go to him, digging inside each of his pants pockets, then finding his iPhone in the front pocket of his shirt.

"You don't have to do this, Michelle," he says.

It's too much. Everything is too much. I feel sick. No, worse than sick. Infuriated. Salty tears dampen my lips. "Yes, I do," I say. "I'm sorry." Then, for good measure, I yank the hotel's phone cord from the wall and stuff it inside the pillowcase.

"Good. That's real good. Smart," Zorie says. "Now grab his wallet and his keys."

I do as I'm instructed. My movements are no longer my own, and I work robotically according to Zorie's commands. He hates me. I disgust him, but I can't worry about that now. My only goal in this moment is to keep Dez alive and Zorie from doing something she might regret.

"Take off his clothes," Zorie says.

I stop and stare quizzically at her, unable to compute her latest order. "Why would I do that?"

"To make sure he doesn't leave this room," she answers, as if it's the most logical explanation. Then, taking a step forward, she adds, "If you don't, I will."

"Just do it," Dez says. I look at him, and he squeezes his eyes shut.

"Any time, Michelle," Zorie says.

Her gun mocks me inside the mirror, and I once again do what I'm told. I undress Dez until he's naked in the middle of the room and then take his bags. He holds his junk with both hands as tears stream down his face.

"I'm so sorry," I whisper, but I doubt he hears me over his sobs. I lift the pregnant bag over my shoulder and will myself not to cry. Crying is for the weak. "Let's go. The police are probably already on their way."

"He needs to get in the bathroom first," Zorie says.

"That's enough, Zorie!" I hiss. "The man is butt-ass naked, and we have his clothes. Do you really think he's leaving this room?"

"Actually, yes, I do." Zorie's expression contorts into an ugly scowl, and for a moment, she no longer looks human. She cocks the gun, and I have an irrational thought that she might shoot me.

"Fine, whatever. But I hate the way you're acting right now." I lift my hands in a nonthreatening manner and duck out of her way.

In the mirror, I watch as Dez walks to the bathroom on shaking legs. Zorie follows and closes the door before sliding a chair beneath the knob. She's ruined everything for us. Whether I stay or go, I'm connected to this moment now. I am an accomplice to armed robbery and false imprisonment. We are ruined.

"Now we can go," she says, and tucks the gun into the waistband of her leggings. She saunters past me as if we've just completed a shopping spree at Lenox Square in Atlanta. As she grabs the handle of Dez's rolling suitcase, I realize I don't know this woman anymore, and after what just went down inside this room, I'm not sure if she knows herself.

I follow Zorie into the hallway, and she slides a DO NOT DISTURB sign onto the door handle—first to our room, then to Dez's.

"You said my name in there. Was that on purpose?" she asks as we half walk, half run to the stairwell.

"I'm sorry, it's kind of hard to keep my cool when you have a gun pointed at me."

"Stop being so dramatic. It wasn't pointed at you, it was pointed at him."

"Who was standing directly behind me!"

She stops walking, and I slam into her. I step back, putting some distance between us, and try to slow my racing heart.

"I told you to go home, didn't I? But you were determined to stay, even after I told you this was never supposed to be your life. So I'm sorry, Kayla, but this is how we survive now. If you have a problem with it, you can walk away right now. I won't stop you."

Zorie yanks open the door to the stairwell, and it slams closed behind her. I look back at the corridor, which suddenly feels darker and miles long. My entire body shakes as a million emotions swirl inside me. What happens if I go back to that room? Back to Dez? Would he even trust me at this point or believe that I genuinely want to help him? And what happens if I get into that van with this new version of Zorie? The desperate one who has nothing left to lose? I shake my head free of those thoughts. She's my best friend. We've come this far together. I don't owe Dez anything. Not my friendship or my loyalty. But Zorie? I owe her everything.

I yank open the door just as the elevator opens and Ryan appears in the hallway carrying a bouquet of red roses. He turns in the direction of our room and doesn't look back.

Neither do I.

CHAPTER SIXTEEN

MONDAY

"Aunt Ruby used to say New Orleans was the perfect place to disappear. It's surrounded by swamps and alcoholics. If anyone recognized you, they'd forget you the next day. Isn't that funny?" Zorie laughs and adjusts the rearview mirror. "Want to hear something else funny? I think I might keep the name Star. It's really growing on me. What do you think?"

I bite my lip to keep from saying something that might piss off my gun-toting, trigger-happy travel companion and pretend to be interested in the flat, gray countryside that makes up Chickasaw, Alabama. We'd driven through three towns in the Solar Sonics van since making our grand exit out of the Blythewood parking lot. Zorie managed to tediously peel off most of the cheesy Solar Sonics decal from the side of the van using the steak knife she'd swiped from our room. It now reads, YOUR NEXT EVENT, which is ironic given we literally have no idea what our next "event" will be. Or even if we'll survive it. With the growing miles between the van and the Blythewood, we've yet to see another vehicle on the road. If anyone is chasing us, they're taking their sweet time.

"Are you really not gonna talk to me?" Zorie asks. "Don't tell me you're still mad. It's been two hours."

I close my eyes, resisting the urge to look at her. Somewhere along the route from Georgia to Alabama, my best friend was abducted and replaced by this darker, crueler version who thinks nothing of pulling a gun on strangers in the name of survival.

"Come on, don't be mad, Kayla."

She pokes at my side, tickling me, but I don't laugh. I couldn't laugh even if I wanted to.

"Is no one off-limits for you?" I snap. "Dez wanted to help us!"

"Right, the wedding singer with the heart of gold wanted to save us from a life on the streets and expected absolutely nothing in return. God, you can be so naïve sometimes." Zorie lets out a long, exasperated sigh. "Dez was weak, and he was making you weak and distracted. If we're gonna pull this thing off, we have to be focused and resourceful. I saw an opportunity, and I took it. The guy had five hundred dollars in his wallet, which means we now have a little over a thousand dollars. Trust me, I did you a favor. You should be thanking me right now instead of acting like a salty bitch." She switches on the radio, and I quickly switch it off.

"Did it ever occur to you that I had the Dez situation handled?"

"By fucking him on the rooftop?" She smiles so wide I think the corners of her mouth might split in two. "Did you really think you two were alone up there? That's what I mean about being naïve, Kayla. But I gotta say, I was pretty impressed. Guess I'm finally rubbing off on you."

I roll my eyes. "You say that like it's a compliment."

"Because it is." She turns to me, her expression cold and flat. "The way I see it, I've given you every chance to walk away and go back to being the good girl you want everyone to believe you are. But here you sit, riding shotgun inside your lover's stolen van. Face it, Kayla, you're exactly where you want to be. You love the chaos as much as I do. Always have."

"Where I wanted to be was on my way to New Orleans with my best friend, not with some crazy person who's become a little too comfortable holding a gun."

"It's called adapting to your environment," Zorie hisses, spit flying from her lips. "Animals do it all the time for survival, and that's what we're doing. Surviving."

She'd used that word the morning of our arraignment: *adapt.* "We have to adapt to our new lives. No tears." I'd swiped the last of my tears on my sleeve and squared my shoulders like Zorie, my head held high while the judge read our charges to the courtroom. *Adapt.* I used to think Zorie was stronger than me, but the truth is, she's just better at pretending.

We pass a new sign: WELCOME TO MOBILE COUNTY. Every passing mile peels off another layer of our old lives, exposing a new, ugly, raw wound. Maybe I do want to be on this morbid road trip with Zorie. Maybe on some subconscious level, I enjoy the lies. Thrive on them. Get off on them. And yet the guilt of what we've done in the past forty-eight hours gnaws at my insides, infecting the wound. Rotting the flesh.

"Amber Childress was a good person," I say, more to myself than Zorie. "This never should have happened."

To my surprise and absolute horror, Zorie laughs—and not just any laugh, but a deep and robust laugh that makes her eyes disappear and her shoulders shake.

" 'This never should have happened,' " she mimics in a whiny, high-pitched voice. "Girl, you made all of this happen the second you had your little temper tantrum and hit your stepsister's car. It's time you start taking responsibility for your actions."

The van swerves, and my hands instinctively wrap around my seatbelt. Zorie never drives well at night. Or in the daytime. Or ever.

"It's just like with your job," she says. "Think about it, Kayla—when you were fired, you didn't take ownership for what you did. You blamed someone else for narcing on you about not checking a guest's ID."

I blink, thinking I heard her wrong. My whole body stiffens. "What did you say?"

Zorie doesn't respond. Or look at me. She stares straight ahead, her microbladed brows knitted together.

"I never told you it was about an ID," I say.

She shrugs and runs a hand over her braids. "Then I heard it from someone at the hotel. Kevin, probably. You know he loves telling everyone's business."

"Oh my God," I say slowly. "It was you, wasn't it? You're the narc who got me fired."

She bites her lip, still focused on the road, and I know I'm right. I suddenly feel breathless, like I've been kicked in the gut multiple times.

"Oh please. You hated that job. Did you honestly think becoming manager would change that?" she asks, disgust in her voice. "I admit I never thought Leslie Grace would fire you, but honestly, it was the best thing that could've happened. You would've never left that place voluntarily." Zorie sighs and shakes her head. "I thought I was help- ing you, Kayla. I thought maybe with our investment in Isaiah's busi- ness, we could do our own thing for a while and finally live, do some traveling, see the world. I mean, did you really want to end up like Leslie Grace, stuck at a hotel in Redwood Springs for the rest of your life? I did you a favor by setting you free."

I laugh. "Set me free? That's your explanation? Look at us, Zorie. Am I free constantly looking over my shoulder for the police? Or how about right now inside a stolen van in the middle of God knows where? Does that look like freedom to you?" I close my eyes for a min- ute as all the hurt and confusion do laps around my brain. I don't say anything for a long time. When I do, the first words that bubble to the surface are "You're supposed to be my friend."

Zorie twists in her seat to look at me, her eyebrows pinched in a deep frown. "I *am* your friend. I'm your goddamn *best* friend."

I stare at her, thinking how good she is at pretending. When we were kids, Zorie pretended she was my sister, convincing even our teachers of our biological connection that didn't exist. In high school, she pretended to have a terminal illness when the principal threatened to expel her for photoshopping the head of our math teacher onto a porn star's body. She even created a doctor's note confirming her tragic diagnosis. Soon after, Principal Medina dropped the expulsion threat, deciding that the stress of being kicked out of school would be detrimental to Zorie's health. And now, Zorie is pretending again. Only this time, she's pretending to be a supportive friend. Hell, at this point, pretending to be human would be a stretch for my soulless companion.

"You were jealous," I hiss.

"Of you?" Zorie flicks her hand at me. "Girl, bye."

A surge of anger races through my veins, and I'm tempted to yank every braid from her scalp, one by one. "You were always jealous," I say. "You knew Leslie Grace wanted me to have that job, but you knew if I got it, you'd have to stop stealing from the rooms."

Zorie snorts. "Okay, Scooby-Doo. You caught me. I totally narced on you because I desperately wanted to keep stealing toilet paper." She rolls her eyes. "Seriously, get over yourself, Kayla."

"And you were jealous that I'd be moving up without you." I nod, assured of my conclusion. "That's it, isn't it? You thought I'd become successful and leave you behind. We can't have separate things and separate lives, can we? It's always K and Z."

"God, you are so conceited, you know that? You really think I can't live my life without you? If you walked away right now, I'd be just fine. Trust and believe."

I take a deep breath, trying to hold in the rage, but it pulses through me like acid, and suddenly I'm reaching for the steering wheel. "Then let me out. Stop the van," I say sharply.

"Are you trying to get us killed?" Zorie shouts.

But I can't hear her over the roar of blood in my ears. I lunge for the wheel again, but this time, Zorie backhands me hard across the face. My own hand flies to my cheek, and I blink back fresh tears. I think I taste blood. Zorie stares at me, a look of shock and sadness etched across her features. It's the first time she's ever hit me. The impact stings, but the overwhelming feeling of betrayal hurts more.

"I-I'm sorry. It was an accident," Zorie says. The van swerves, and I yell for Zorie to watch the road just as a deer darts out into our path. She slams on the brakes, and the van fishtails and we slam hard into the guardrail. The engine sputters as if it can't catch its breath, then stops on the shoulder.

"You okay?" Zorie asks.

I push open the door and stumble out onto the grass. The smell of burnt rubber swells in my nostrils.

"Great! The van won't start!" Zorie groans. She gets out of the car and comes to stand over me, watching me with anxious eyes. "What the hell are we supposed to do now?"

I roll onto my side and press my throbbing cheek into the dewy, cool grass. "You can do whatever you want because this road trip ends here."

Zorie laughs. "You're not serious. What are you gonna do? Hitch-hike in the middle of Trump country?"

I clamber to my feet and stagger forward, away from her. "You told me to walk away. This is me walking away."

As if in response to my dramatic exit, a flash of lightning divides the sky, followed by a low rumble of thunder. Perfect timing, God. The way my day is going, I'm most definitely getting struck by light-ning. Probably twice.

"Will you please stop being a brat?" Zorie calls after me. "It isn't safe out here."

"It isn't safe with you, either."

I climb over the guardrail so that I'm off the highway and pray there are no snakes hiding in the thick brush. Zorie follows, and I walk faster, then faster, until I'm running. The sky explodes, and the rain feels like tiny pellets on my skin. Running in the rain is harder than I expect, and I immediately trip and roll down the muddy embankment into a ditch of soggy cigarette butts. Seconds later, Zorie rolls down the hill like a human bowling ball and slides face-first into a mound of mud.

"See what you made me do?" she shouts.

"What happened to taking accountability for your own choices?" I shout back, spitting water droplets with each word.

Zorie staggers to her knees and squints at me through the rain. Her braids cling to her face, and she shoves them back, mud and all. "I'm sorry I hit you, okay? It was a reflex or something. Now can we please go back to the van and out of this rain?"

"You don't get it, Zorie. I can't keep doing this with you. You're a liability." I run a hand over my face and heave a sigh. "Being friends with you isn't worth the risk. Not anymore."

Her face darkens, and she clambers to her feet. "This is just like you! Always so goddamn selfish! All I've ever done is try to be a good friend—a best friend—and this is what you think of me? That I'm a liability?"

"It's not all I think of you," I say. "I think you're sad, and desperate. You're a grown woman who can barely take care of herself, or function without a man, and gets off on stealing from newlyweds instead of, I don't know, trying to better yourself. It's honestly pathetic. I feel sorry for you."

As soon as the words come out, I want to suck them back in. But it's too late. Years of resentment have bled out of me and landed between us on the muddy embankment.

"You feel sorry for me?" Zorie repeats. A slow smile creeps across her face. "Oh, that's hilarious. Truly. This from the girl who can't even get her own life together. All you ever do is complain about being mistreated, but you don't do anything to fix it. Just admit it, Kayla. You love being the victim. Your dad was right about you. Zero ambition." She makes a circle with her thumb and forefinger. "Zero."

"And what about you, huh? What are you even doing with your life? Robbing weddings? Giving our money away to randoms? Have a nice life, Zorie, or Star, or whatever bullshit you want to call yourself from this point on. How's that for ambition?" I turn to start the climb back up the hill to the highway and feel her hand on my elbow. She jerks me around to face her, and for the first time in our decades-long friendship, I'm actually afraid of her.

"You can go if you want to, but you won't survive out here without me. You're weak. Always have been," she says and shoves my elbow back.

I take a step forward, suddenly feeling bold. I've spent most of my life justifying my friendship with Zorie and ignoring all the times she made our friendship feel transactional. Every moment—every secret—had a cost, and she never stopped reminding me of it. When I'd hooked up with the guidance counselor from our old high school, and his wife showed up at the Chamberlain demanding to see me, Zorie pretended to be me and managed to scare the woman off, saving me from an ass kicking. When it was my turn to return the favor, I did, handing over Gloria's church-treasurer keys to Zorie so she could sneak in and steal the petty cash box from her office. *Do this one thing for me because I did that one thing for you.* Sometimes I wondered if I was Zorie's friend because I was indebted to our friendship, not because I wanted it.

"We're done!" I shout over the rain.

Zorie makes a fist, then drops her hand to her side.

"You're going to hit me now? Why not shoot me in the face with Isaiah's gun?" I laugh. "But don't forget to cut off my tattoo so my family can never identify the body."

She shakes her head and laughs. "You're not even worth it. It would be like punching a puppy. I hope some disgusting, deranged hitchhiker finds you and skins you alive."

I frown. "Wow. That was weirdly specific."

We both turn and walk in opposite directions. I have no idea where

I am, what time it is, or even what I'll do once the Alabama sun comes back out to bake me. How did everything get so messed up? Kayla and Zorie. KD+ZA. Our friendship feels like tiny snapshots of time over the years, intertwined with life-changing moments, like Mom's death and Zorie's grandmother's house burning down. We'd leaned on each other so much after that, until Zorie turned thirteen and Miss Patrice decided she needed more structure. Two weeks after school let out, Zorie was sent to New Orleans to spend the summer with her aunt Ruby.

"Gregory, the child makes up more lies than I can keep up with," she'd told my dad when she picked up Zorie the night before the trip. She sat across from him at our dining room table, leaned forward on her elbows with her head in her hands, her blond hair and black roots bouncing as she sobbed. "I used to think Zorie lied to piss me off, but now I think she does it because she likes it, like she enjoys hurting people. I don't know what to do with her anymore."

I'd listened from the hallway as she described a version of Zorie I didn't know—a devious, manipulative version who lied and schemed to get what she wanted. None of it made sense. It was Miss Patrice who was the liar, not Zorie. I remember turning to walk away and seeing Zorie watching me from my bedroom door, smiling.

Goosebumps break out over my skin as I recall the memory, and I rub my arms.

"Okay, fine!" Zorie shouts behind me. "I'm scared! But so are you, and since we're out here in the middle of nowhere, I think our chances for survival are better together than apart."

I stop walking but don't turn around. "That's the difference between you and me, Zorie. I'm okay on my own."

A clap of thunder booms above us, and I will myself to stay calm. If Zorie wants to act like a little bitch, she can do it alone.

"Whatever, Kayla. I'm not begging you to go with me. I'm okay being alone, too. I've been alone most of my life."

"Only because no one can stand to be around you!"

This was probably the wrong thing to say. Something warm and wet smacks hard against the back of my head. Mud.

"You bitch!" I shriek.

Zorie hurls another hunk of mud at me. This one smacks against my forehead and drips into my eyes. Not one to be outdone, I scoop up the biggest, most disgusting pile of worm-infested mud I can find and hurl it at her, but she ducks, and the mud pie lands with a splat behind her.

"Gotta be quicker than that, babe," Zorie says. She launches another mud attack and strikes me in the shoulder. "Why can't you see that everything I do—everything I've ever done—is for the both of us?"

She doesn't wait for me to answer since we're both suddenly caught inside the path of a bright light.

"Shit! Run!" Zorie shouts.

We take off down the hill with a car's horn blaring in our ears. If I thought running in the rain is hard, running down a muddy, wet hill is even harder. Seconds into my sprint, I slip on a patch of mud and fall on my ass.

"Hurry! Get up!" Zorie yells.

"I'm trying!"

She grabs my wrists and hauls me to my feet. I take a clumsy step forward, but slip again. Zorie is immediately at my side, yanking my arms until I clamber awkwardly to my feet. We duck behind a tree, which every weatherman on the planet says is the absolute worst thing you could do in a thunderstorm. And yet, here we are, clinging to its scratchy bark and peering around its thick sides.

A dark figure emerges from the car and stands next to the guardrail, holding a black umbrella. They crane their neck in our direction, watching.

"You think it's the police?" Zorie asks.

"Maybe." I squint in the darkness. "Probably."

The figure gives the brush one final sweep with their flashlight before climbing back inside the car and driving away.

I should feel relieved, but don't. Whoever was in that car saw the abandoned Solar Sonics van—the *stolen* Solar Sonics van.

"We should keep running," I say.

"Together?"

"For now." My tone is sharp, biting, but Zorie nods anyway.

Lightning streaks across the sky as something howls in the distance, and we take off up the hill. Together.

CHAPTER SEVENTEEN

———

We tear through the maze of trees, with me punching branches and Zorie holding the hem of my shirt. Seeing in the dark is not a skill either of us possesses, but apparently my eyes are better than hers. Thank God for moonlight.

"Do you think they're chasing us?" Zorie asks in a breathless whisper.

"Do you want to stop and find out?"

This is the only answer Zorie needs to hear to pick up the pace. She steps on my heels, sending us both torpedoing down another hill and into a creek.

"Looks like we're going to have to swim across," I say, carefully wading into the water.

Zorie takes a tentative step forward, then back again. "I'm not crossing that."

"It's the only way to the other side."

She's quiet for a second before letting out a long, exasperated sigh. "I can't swim."

I can't tell if she's joking, and I squint at her silhouette in the darkness in search of a smile. "Why are you being so extra right now? You literally go with me to the water park every summer."

"To look cute in a two-piece," she says. "Have you ever actually seen me get in the water, Kayla? For real?"

"Two summers ago, you told me you went snorkeling with some guy at a resort in Cancún. Now all of a sudden you can't swim?"

"I might've lied."

"Shocker."

"I was embarrassed, okay? He played me."

"They always play you, Zorie, and you never learn." I roll my eyes and turn my back to her. "I guess this is where I leave you, then."

"You can't leave me in the woods alone like this. What if an animal attacks me or something?"

"You're resourceful. You'll figure it out."

I wade deeper into the creek. Truth be told, my parents were amazing swimmers. Like, Olympic amazing. Growing up, they taught some of the older kids at our church how to swim. I'm amazing, too. Mom took me to my first swim lessons when I was two years old. Even then, she said I was the best little swimmer in the class. If I wasn't worried about the damage to my hair from chlorine, I might have trained for the Junior Olympics, like Mom did when she was a teen. Maybe then I wouldn't have been so distracted by Dad's relationship with Gloria and Candace.

"Kayla, please don't leave me! I need you!" Zorie calls out.

I tilt my head back and stare up at the moon. If God is watching us, I hope this is his version of a truce and all is forgiven. "Stop whining. You know I'd never leave you." I heave a deep sigh and turn around. "Here, get on my back," I say and squat in front of Zorie.

"You're joking, right? I'll weigh you down," she says. "We'll both drown."

"Someone didn't pay attention in Mr. Harvey's science class. Don't you realize we're weightless in water? Shut up and get on my back, Zorie. Now!"

She slips her arms around my neck and leans forward, resting her chin on my shoulder. Water rushes at us full force, and I point out that she's choking me.

"Oh, sorry." Zorie loosens her grip and buries her face in the back of my hair. The water is lukewarm and sloshes over our shoulders and into our faces. Each step takes us deeper into darkness until I take off, arms stretched out in front of me, with a 135-pound woman on my back. I move effortlessly in the water, even with Zorie holding on to me for dear life.

Every muscle in my body aches by the time we reach the shore, and I wonder how long we were in the water. Zorie helps me up the steep incline before collapsing next to me. I peel off my halter top and wring out the water over a pile of rocks before slipping it back on.

"I could really use some deodorant right about now," Zorie says.

"We should try to find a gas station and find out how far we are from the next town." I stare out at the moonlit creek and wonder if the figure at the guardrail followed us and is watching us right now. "We can't stay out here exposed like this. It isn't safe. If that person with the flashlight doesn't get us, some wild animal will."

"Shit!" Zorie stands and pats her front pockets and lets out a low, frustrated groan. "I lost the gun. And the money. I had them both before I got in that stupid creek."

"I guess that was my fault, right?"

"You were the one who wanted to go all Michael Phelps across the creek, and now we probably have a bunch of flesh-eating parasites inside our ears."

A light flickers on in the distance, and a man's voice calls out for Old Millie to come back inside.

"Did you hear that?" I ask. "I think there's a house on the other side of that hill. Maybe they'll give us a ride to the next town." What we'd do in that next town is still up for debate, but the less time we spend here, the better.

"You really think whoever that voice belongs to is gonna open the door this early in the morning and invite two random black women inside?" Zorie smirks. "This ain't Redwood Springs, Kayla. We're in the Deep South, babe. The only things folks this far in the country say yes to are guns and Mountain Dew."

I glance at the creek again with the strange feeling we're being watched. "We have to at least try."

Zorie gives a reluctant nod, and we stagger forward like two broken soldiers marching to our executions.

By the time we reach the other side of the hill, we're barely walking. We shuffle up the long gravel driveway to the farmhouse, where we're greeted by a small brown dog that growls and barks at us before scurrying away underneath the porch. Good thing. I'm so hungry I might eat it.

"Who's out there?" A man who looks to be at least in his late seventies comes to the screen door before we reach the porch and squints at us over the rim of his bifocal glasses. When we don't immediately answer, he lifts a long-barrel rifle and points it at the door. "I said who's out there?"

"We are, sir," I say quickly.

The man opens the door slowly and steps out onto the porch, his rifle at his side. Zorie and I hide behind a Buick with a JESUS IS MY BOSS bumper sticker parked in the driveway just in case Gramps gets a little trigger happy.

"What the hell you think you're doing out here on my property at this hour?"

I peer out around the Buick's bumper, and the old man makes a face, like he's surprised and disgusted at the same time. We must look like a duo of hot messes—muddy, wet, and covered in scratches from the branches.

"Y'all come from around that car and show your faces," he says.

I take a tentative step to the side but keep a safe distance from the porch. Not that bullets discriminate when it comes to distance. Zorie does the same thing beside me.

"If the two of you are thinking of robbing me, ain't no money here. So you better get 'fore I shoot you dead on my porch," the man says.

"No problem, thanks," Zorie says, and turns to leave, but I grab her arm and pull her back.

"What are you doing?" I whisper.

"Trying to stay alive. I'm a black woman standing in a white man's driveway in the middle of nowhere before the sun is even up. I'm seconds away from my name being a hashtag."

I roll my eyes. Clearly convincing this man and his gun to trust us enough to give us a ride to town is all up to me. I sigh and turn slowly to face him, palms forward, and paste on the biggest fake smile I can muster. "We're so sorry to have disturbed you, sir. It's just that, we were in an accident on the other side of the creek and could really use your help."

"Is that right?" He scratches at his long white beard like something's crawling through it. The man lowers his gun, his expression suddenly serious. "You two cross that creek?"

We both nod. Our sullen expressions seem to be enough to convince him we're not dangerous.

"Wouldn't be very Christian of me not to at least offer you ladies shelter from the storm," he says. "Tornado watches are all over this county. Come on in and wait it out."

"Thank you, sir," I say and hurry up the porch steps behind him. Zorie is less enthused but follows anyway.

The inside of the farmhouse is cluttered with stacks of books and magazines that, judging from the thick layer of dust, haven't been touched in years. Something that also looks like it hasn't been touched in years is our host, whose overalls are a dingy brown in the seat area. Worse still, the air inside the house smells sour, spoiled, like rotten meat. We follow the man through the kitchen, where the smell is the strongest. The sink overflows with dirty dishes, and roaches crawl in and out of open cans of dog food.

"The name's Paul," the man says over his shoulder.

"I'm Kay—Michelle, and this is Star," I say.

Paul gives a quick nod of acknowledgment and tucks the rifle inside the pantry, next to a bag of chicken feed. "Excuse the mess, ladies. My maid has the week off."

I give a polite laugh. "We know the feeling."

Zorie frowns at me, and I shrug.

"You sure are up awfully early, Mr. Paul," I say.

"The Bible says all hard work brings a profit, and there are chores to be done." Paul nods at the mud-caked boots by the door. "Got some chickens and a few pigs out yonder." He ushers us into a room with a couch, a recliner, and two TVs, one turned on to an old Western and the other to the local news. A half-eaten jelly donut is on a TV tray next to the recliner, and Paul tears off a piece and pops it into his mouth.

"You ladies hungry?" he asks, licking his fingers.

I am. Starving, actually. But all hunger disappears at the sight of two roaches crawling over the donut.

"No, thank you," we say in unison.

Paul eases into the recliner and lifts a burning cigar from the ashtray on the coffee table. Zorie and I cram together on the couch, shoulder to shoulder, and watch him like we have no idea what to do next. My eyes shift to the TV displaying a man wearing an Atlanta Braves T-shirt with a huge pink #JUSTICE4AMBER button. He stands across from a reporter in a parking lot full of people holding candles and singing "This Little Light of Mine" in the background. I recognize him immediately. Brett Fletcher. The other half of the newlywed couple Julianna and Brett. I clap a hand over my mouth and swallow hard as the taste of bile rises in the back of my throat. I look over at Zorie, who has her hands clenched so tightly the knuckles are white.

"Tell me about your friend," the reporter says. She's an overly tan, middle-aged woman with wide, cartoonish eyebrows that move when she talks.

"She was magic," Brett says. "She had the most amazing laugh, and her smile . . . man, that smile . . ." He tugs at his hair and stares down at the framed picture of Amber in his hands. He looks thoughtful for a moment before bursting into tears. The camera pans out, and I spot Julianna a few feet behind him, holding a neon-pink JUSTICE FOR AMBER poster.

The reporter gives a weird, constipated smile at the camera. "This is Kelly Rivers reporting at the site of last night's emotional candlelight vigil honoring the late Amber Childress, the woman who was tragically run over at her best friend's wedding. Back to you in the studio."

"Shame what happened to that poor woman," a small voice says behind us.

We both turn to see a petite woman in a wheelchair roll into the room, cradling a cordless phone in her lap.

"This is my wife, Ruthann," Paul says. "This here is Michelle and Star. They were in an accident on the other side of the creek. I told them they could wait out the storm here."

"Well, good morning, and my goodness, you ladies are soaked to the bone. I should get you some fresh towels," Ruthann says. She's a thin woman with sunken eyes and hollowed cheekbones. Her skin is the color of oatmeal, and her hair hangs in long gray waves over her shoulders. Even with her gaunt features, I can tell she's pretty or, at least, she used to be.

"Paul and I have been following that horrible case since last night," she says, collecting two towels from a basket on the floor. I wonder if the towels smell like the house. She wheels over to us and hands us each a stiff, discolored towel with the overwhelming scent of bleach. Zorie and I voice our appreciation and dab at our skin with the scratchy material.

"This country went to hell in a handbasket when they took prayer out of schools," Paul says, his eyes locked on the TV. "No God-fearing person would do such a thing."

Zorie and I share a look, and I stare down at my hands. My entire body vibrates on the couch, and I wonder if Ruthann and Paul notice.

"Well, the good Lord saw to it to bring her home," Ruthann says. "She's in a better place now."

"Amen," Paul says, nodding.

We're all quiet for a moment, listening to the news drone on about the weather, when Zorie blurts out, "Why do people always say that?"

Paul and Ruthann stare blankly at her, confused. I stare, too, because what the hell?

"Say what?" Paul asks.

Zorie shrugs and leans back on the cracked leather couch. "Why do people always say someone's in a better place when they die? Like, how do they know?"

I hear myself gasp, then cough. Fucking Zorie. Too far. Even for her.

"I think I would like something to eat after all," I say, thinking this is a safe transition. "Got any more of those donuts?" I nod at the bug-infested pastry on the TV tray.

"Certainly, dear," Ruthann says. She smiles at me, but I can tell it's only a polite one, not a real one. She's uncomfortable. Zorie and her cringy comment have made Ruthann second-guess her hospitality. She rolls her wheelchair in the direction of the kitchen, and I'm tempted to follow, but I don't trust Zorie and her big mouth alone with Paul. We need to stay here long enough to figure out a new plan, and in order to do that and avoid being kicked out in the middle of a tornado, I need Zorie to shut the hell up.

"You make a good point," Paul says. He removes his glasses, wipes them on his shirt, and replaces them as if he can see Zorie's insanity clearer now. "I suppose we never can understand God's plans for our lives."

"No, we can't," Zorie says. She cuts her eyes at me, and my entire body goes numb. Something about the way her eyes flash chills my insides. "We never know what's in store, do we?"

CHAPTER EIGHTEEN

—

Midway through our third episode of *Bonanza* and my fifth jelly donut, the tornado warning sirens force us into the basement for safety. Thick sheets of rain pound the roof and rattle the windows, with every wind gust making me more doubtful of the stability of the old farmhouse.

"Don't you girls worry. This house may be seventy years old, but it has good bones. It's been through worse," Paul says, watching me. He carefully lifts Ruthann from her wheelchair and over his shoulder as if he's done it a hundred times before. I wonder what it must feel like to trust someone so completely with your life.

"Not too fast down the stairs, Paulie," Ruthann warns. She grabs hold of his belt loops with each hand, and I think how tiny she suddenly looks in his arms.

"I've got you, darlin'," Paul says.

We follow them down a rotted wooden staircase that creaks and groans under our weight. I balance the tray of baloney sandwiches and Mountain Dew that Ruthann prepared in case of a power outage, and Zorie carries the cordless phone and a weather radio. Ruthann didn't say much when she handed us the supplies, but I noticed the way her hands trembled. I'm not used to people being afraid of me. Not sure how I feel about it.

"Here we are," Paul says. He flips on a light switch at the bottom of the stairs, and I brace myself for the scattering of oversize rats and roaches, but the space is surprisingly clean. The smell, however, is worse than upstairs, and I try my best to breathe through my mouth without looking too obvious.

"Y'all make yourselves comfortable. We may be here for a while," Paul says. He places Ruthann on a futon near the water heater, and I join Zorie on the beanbag across from them. I tear off a piece of a sandwich's crust and pop it into my mouth. It's hard and stale, but I manage to swallow it.

"You girls from around here?" Ruthann asks. I know she's making small talk, but there's something in her tone that makes me wonder if she's collecting information to piece together later. Zorie's outburst upstairs didn't help Ruthann and Paul's growing suspicion of us. Neither did her comment about the couple's antique hutch being worth a lot of money.

"We're just passing through," I say, hoping this is a satisfying enough answer.

Ruthann nods, and her strange, wooden smile widens. "On your way back home?"

This time it's Zorie who answers. "We're on our way to our destination," she says flatly.

"I see." Ruthann's smile fades, and she stares down at her apron. A red Bible with a cracked, worn cover peeks out from inside one of the pockets, and she rests both hands on top of it. My mom had the same red Bible, equally worn, with her name engraved in gold letters on the bottom-right corner. I'd find her reading it alone at the kitchen table, her brow furrowed in deep concentration as her yellow highlighter moved across the page. She'd look up, see me watching, and open her arms for me to climb into her lap. "This book is our homework from God, Kayla," she'd say. "He's like our teacher, and he wants us to learn from it. If you ever need help figuring out a problem, it's all in here." I'd nod, and Mom would hold me close while she read God's lessons. Sitting here now, I can't remember a single one.

"Well then, we certainly hope the two of you won't run into any more awful weather on your journey," Ruthann says, her eyes still on her Bible.

Zorie smiles. "I'm sure we won't."

I try to think of something upbeat or interesting to say to break the weird tension filling the basement and suffocating us along with what is most definitely mold.

"When I was a kid, my mom would tell me to be quiet when it storms. She said it's how God communicates with us," I say.

At this, Ruthann looks up, and her smile returns. A real one this time. "Your mother is a very wise woman. It absolutely is how the good Lord communicates with us."

"It's right there in the Bible," Paul says. " 'Be still, and know that I am God.' "

"Does it work?" Zorie asks. She takes a long swig of Mountain Dew and belches loudly. I glare at her, but she ignores me. Her gaze is focused on Ruthann.

"It most certainly works," Ruthann insists. "In the quiet is when God is the loudest. Close your eyes and wait for the Lord to give you instructions."

"Let's try it, then," Zorie says. "We'll close our eyes and listen. All of us."

When I look at Ruthann and Paul again, their eyes are already closed. I do the same and listen as rain strikes the house and thunder rattles the windows. But if there is some hidden Godly message waiting to be discovered in this quiet, I can't hear it. What I do hear are footsteps on the staircase, and when I open my eyes, I see Zorie slip out the basement door. Where's she going? I glance at Ruthann and Paul. Their heads are bowed, eyes squeezed shut. They must've received God's incoming call.

I bow my own head and wait once more for God's message. It

comes to me in the form of more snapshots of my dad, like blurry Polaroids flashing across my mind. In one image, he sits cross-legged on the floor with me and Zorie while we braid the synthetic strands of my dolls' hair. Then in another shot, Zorie is helping me apply eyelashes in her bedroom for prom. The last snapshot is darker, with distorted shapes and colors, but I can make out my mother's casket and my dad on one side of me and Zorie on the other. Every meaningful moment of my life—every snapshot—has Zorie's imprint. Is this God's message to me? That we should remain together? I rub my eyes and realize I'm crying, but I'm not sure what I'm crying for—my own betrayal or Zorie's.

A loud beeping sound interrupts my thoughts. I open my eyes and see Ruthann and Paul staring at me with matching curious expressions. Zorie is still gone, and I'm anxious for her to come back. The beeping sound is courtesy of the weather radio, and Paul reaches for it on the floor between us. A robotic voice comes on, and we lean in to listen for new updates about the tornado. I wonder if the Solar Sonics' van has been sucked up and spit out in another city miles from here.

"The Mobile Police Department is investigating reports of two armed-and-dangerous females in the area thought to be in their late twenties and African American. Members of the general public should shelter in place, lock all doors and windows, and notify the police of any suspicious persons matching this description."

The voice repeats the message a second and a third time.

A knot of fear tightens in my stomach with each word.

Holy fucking shit. We are so screwed.

I don't look up, even though I know they're looking at me. I will myself to stay calm and poke at the sandwich with my finger. The middle is soggy, and the ketchup soaks through the bread like a bloodstain.

"Where's your friend?" Paul asks. His voice is different now, sharp and annoyed. He won't be quoting any more Bible verses.

"Bathroom," I say quickly, even as a new, terrifying thought enters my mind. What if Zorie is gone, like, really gone? What if during our moment of silence, she found Paul's car keys and took off without me?

"This was never supposed to be your life."

"I think we better find her, and then the two of y'all best be on your way," Paul says. He's on his feet and headed to the staircase before I can object. I don't know where we'll go or what we'll do for money. At this point, I don't even know if we'll survive. I look up at Ruthann, thinking maybe I can plead with her to stay until after the storm. It's the Christian thing to do. But when our eyes meet, her face is as hard and stale as the crust of my sandwich.

"You two best be on your way now," she repeats.

I place the tray on the floor and climb to my feet. The mud stains have dried on my clothes, making the material feel stiff against my skin. I want to ask Ruthann if I can borrow some clean clothes, but asking for anything at this point will probably result in Paul aiming his rifle at my head.

"Thank you for your hospitality," I say.

Ruthann lifts the Bible from her apron and holds it out in front of her like a shield. "My grandmother used to say certain people are born with the devil in them. No matter what they do, that kind of evil sticks to them like a stink they can't wash clean. And that friend of yours has the stink of the devil all over her."

As if to emphasize her observation, gunshots ring out above us, followed by a loud crash and heavy footsteps. He shot her. Paul shot Zorie! I don't know if I say the words out loud or in my head, but Ruthann doesn't move. Her terrified gaze is on the basement door. I want to run, but I doubt I'm fast enough to outrun a gun. I feel my body go limp like a wet washcloth, and I lift my hands above my head in silent surrender. But when the basement door opens, it's not Paul's silhouette that stands in the dimly lit hallway. It's Zorie's.

She bounds down the stairs with Paul's rifle in tow and stops at the foot of the futon. Streaks of red cover her clothes in a gruesome pattern that makes my stomach lurch.

"You okay? You're bleeding," I say, and point at her shirt.

"It's not my blood," she says flatly.

At this, Ruthann lets out a bloodcurdling scream, filling the basement with her hysteria. She pushes herself off the bed, crawling across the floor with surprising speed to the bottom of the stairs.

"Paulie!" she shouts through her tears. "Sweetheart, answer me!"

"He can't," Zorie says. She sinks down on the futon and leans forward on her elbows. "I didn't want to hurt him. I swear. But he was trying to kill me. I had no choice."

"Is he—" The word sticks in my throat. I stumble back against the wall and rub my face. "You . . . killed him?"

"It was self-defense!" Zorie shouts. "I had no choice! He was trying to kill *me*!"

This only makes Ruthann scream louder. Her nails scratch at the stairs as she tries to pull herself up, but she's too weak. She slides back down onto the floor and sobs into the concrete.

"Oh my God! I can't think with all this screaming!" Zorie says, jumping to her feet. She paces in front of the futon with the gun like she's guarding the space. Her eyes are wild, and I'm not sure I recognize her anymore. She stops pacing and fixes her frenzied gaze on me. "You believe me, don't you? That it was self-defense?"

Nausea rolls in waves deep inside my gut. Did I believe Zorie? She'd robbed a gas station at gunpoint and threatened to shoot Dez in his hotel room, but she never actually fired the gun. If she was a cold-blooded killer, wouldn't she have killed them when she had the chance? Hell, wouldn't she have killed me? No, Zorie wasn't a murderer. She'd simply adapted. Survived.

"Devils! Both of you!" Ruthann screams.

My heart thumps in my ears so loudly I can barely think. I need to do something—say something—to calm Zorie down. I know better than anyone that this newest version of Zorie can be a very unpredictable thing, especially while holding a gun.

"The police know we're in the area. They sent out an alert on the radio," I say. "We have to go."

"And leave this one here to tell the police about us? She'll turn us in the second we walk out that door. We can't let that happen."

Her words hang in the air between us, and I find myself shaking my head so violently I'm dizzy. She wouldn't. She can't. "Zorie, hold on. Let's talk about this."

"Talk about it?" She looks at me, surprised, and narrows her eyes. "You don't believe me, do you? You think I'm lying that it was self-defense."

"Of course I believe you." I should be hysterical. Everything about this situation calls for extreme hysteria. But I'm weirdly calm. *Adapting.* I don't scream or move. I just stand there staring at the woman who's supposed to be my best friend and the one person outside my family who knows me better than anyone. I'm supposed to know her better than anyone, too. But I don't know this Zorie Andrews in front of me at all. Not anymore.

"Look at her," I say. "She's old, frail. Poor woman can't even walk. She's not a threat." I kneel beside Ruthann, thinking how the last person I watched die was my mom. I won't let it happen again. "By the time someone shows up to check on her, we'll be long gone and starting our new lives. We don't need more blood on our hands."

Zorie watches me, as if absorbing my words. Her eyes widen, shiny and wet. "More blood on our hands? Wait, do you think I'm going to shoot her?"

Yes.

"Are you kidding me? That's insane." I force a small laugh and hope it's convincing. "Come on, let's get some fresh clothes and get out of here."

"It *is* insane, isn't it?" Zorie gives a weak smile in return and helps me to my feet. I wait for her to start upstairs and then grab the phone from the beanbag.

"What are you doing?" she asks.

I freeze, my fingers tightening around the phone. Tremors of fear run through my body. Is this the moment when my best friend shoots me in the back? I swallow hard and turn to face her. "We don't want her calling the police as soon as we leave, do we?"

She sucks her teeth. "Right."

"We should probably leave her some food, too. In case she's down here for a while." I slide the tray of Mountain Dew and sandwiches across the floor to Ruthann, who hasn't stopped crying since her last failed attempt to climb the stairs. She jumps as the tray crashes into her side and one of the cans rolls under the stairs.

"That's enough, Michelle. She's fine," Zorie says. Aggravation coats every word, and I know I'm trying my luck by delaying the inevitable. I have to leave with Zorie. She's too far gone now, lost in her own delusions, and if I don't go with her, she could hurt more people in the name of survival. I step over Ruthann and drop her Bible next to her.

"I'm sorry about this," I whisper and pray my best friend doesn't hear me.

CHAPTER NINETEEN

—

Paul's lifeless body is on full display when I enter his bedroom. He's face down on the blood-soaked carpet with a bullet hole in the back of his head. The gory scene stuns me as much as it frightens me, like walking into a horror movie midway through. I've never seen a dead body like this before, except on TV, especially not one with part of the brain exposed. The room suddenly feels tight and stuffy, and I drop to my knees and dry heave next to the bed. How had this morning turned into such a nightmare? We were only supposed to stay until the storm cleared. That was the plan. And now Paul is dead with his blood and possibly brain matter drying on my best friend's clothes.

I retch again.

"Here," Zorie says, and tosses me a sheet from the bed. "Let's cover him up so you'll stop gagging."

I wipe the string of saliva from my lips with the sheet and sink back against the wall. I have so many questions, like why was Zorie in Paul and Ruthann's bedroom? And if it was self-defense, why is there a hole in the *back* of Paul's head? Was he running from Zorie? Did she sneak up on him?

"I found a thousand dollars in a shoebox and some old watches that might be worth something," Zorie says, peeking out from the closet. "You should check his pockets for any cash and throw some of these trash bags over him while you're at it. They're scented. He may be here awhile."

I don't want to think about Paul's decomposing body or the smell of death that will inevitably invade every inch of the old farmhouse. I cover him with the sheet and trash bags and force myself to stand on legs that don't feel like they belong to me. "The police will be here soon, Zo. They know we're in the area. We need to get out of here."

"Guess they found the van, huh?" she says and continues her task of yanking clothes off their hangers.

I watch her, feeling hot and feverish, as she stuffs the clothes into a duffel bag on the floor. "We only need a few things, not the poor woman's entire wardrobe. Ruthann's still alive down there, you know."

Zorie stares at me like I'm an idiot. "The lady was wearing an apron as an outfit. She probably never even goes inside her closet. I think we're good." She peels off her shirt, rolls it into a ball, and stuffs it inside the trash can by the bed. Then, yanking a fresh T-shirt over her head with the words WORLD'S BEST GRANDMA on it, she tosses me a pink one with the same words. "We match."

I feel powerless and, more than anything, guilty. It gnaws at my insides and turns to bile in my throat. I want to vomit it all out. Retch and heave until I ache. All these years, have I missed the signs? Has my best friend—my only friend, really—been a certifiable psychopath this entire time, and I've been too stupid to notice? I hear Zorie's words to me in the van: "*God, you can be so naïve sometimes.*" Maybe she's right.

"What happened in here, Zorie?"

She shrugs. "I told you."

"No, you told me it was self-defense, and now I want details."

"Jesus, Kayla. You want details? Fine." She stops mid-yank, but doesn't look at me. "I was looking for the bathroom and got lost. Next thing I know, Paul and his gun are staring me in the face. He said if we didn't leave his house, he'd bury us in it. Some Christians, right?" she says with a little laugh. "I told him I was going to get you and we'd get out of his hair, but he wouldn't let me back into the basement." At this, she turns around, her eyes boring into mine. "I couldn't leave you here with these . . . these people. So I tried to move past him to the basement door, and he jabbed me in the stomach with the gun. I grabbed the closest thing I could find"—she nods at the blood-splattered lamp on the floor with the lopsided shade—"and I hit him as hard as I could. He dropped the gun, and we both grabbed it. Next thing I know, the gun went off, and Paul was dead." Zorie kneels next to me and smiles tenderly. Flecks of dried blood cover her cheeks. "Don't you see? I was protecting you, Kayla. You're the most important person in the world to me. Swear to God, I'll never let anything happen to you. Ever."

I glance at Paul's lifeless body and at the growing crimson circle where part of his skull used to be.

"You believe me, don't you?" Zorie cups my face, forces me to look at her. I have two choices: believe my best friend killed Paul to protect us or believe Zorie killed Paul because she wanted to. I shake my head, as if to release the morbid thought from its hold inside my subconscious.

"You were protecting us," I say slowly.

"That's right. I was protecting us. And you know what? Because of me, we're going to be okay."

I nod, or maybe Zorie moves my head. I'm not sure I'm in control of my own movements anymore. She stands, her eyes still on me, and holds out her hand.

"Let's go."

═══

Paul and Ruthann are the proud owners of a Buick, a minivan, and a Toyota Camry, whose keys we find on a hook inside the garage. There's a framed drawing of a sunflower with the name Avery written beneath it in red crayon. She must've given Ruthann the world's-best-grandma title. I trace the sunflower with my finger and wonder for the hundredth time if Ruthann is okay.

"Come on. We'll take the Camry," Zorie says. She's already tossing the bags into the back seat but keeps the gun with her. We just have to make it to New Orleans, and then I can cut ties with Zorie for good. Freedom is only a few hours away.

I climb in next to Zorie and wait for her to start the car, but she doesn't. She stares out into the garage and chews her bottom lip.

"You know I'd never hurt you, right?" she says.

"I know that." Then, for extra reassurance, I place my hand over hers. "We'll get to New Orleans and put all of this behind us. We can be free again."

"What if we don't make it to New Orleans?"

"Well, we won't get anywhere unless we hit the road," I say and give a weird, high-pitched laugh I don't recognize.

Zorie twists in her seat to look at me, and my body tenses. God, what I wouldn't do for a cigarette right now. "I'm serious, Kayla. I've killed two people. If the police find us, I'm dead."

"First of all, Amber was an accident, and Paul was self-defense."

"Right." She nods, but her expression is hard and flat. "But what if they don't believe me?"

"Then you'll fight it in court." I try to look convincing, but my face refuses to cooperate. Fear will not leave my face, and Zorie's expression mirrors mine.

"I can't spend the rest of my life in prison, Kayla, and I don't want to die." Her eyes widen, glassy with tears. "You have to promise me that if we reach the point of no return, we end this. Together."

My gaze shifts to the gun propped against the dashboard and then back to her. Goosebumps break out over my skin, and I rub my arms. I know what she's asking me, what she's saying without providing the words. A final sacrifice in the name of friendship. Love. We end this. Together. *"You know I'd never hurt you, right?"*

"Kayla, do you promise?"

Thunder rattles the garage doors, and I jump, prompting a burst of laughter from Zorie. She hunches forward in her seat and grips her sides as tears stream down her face.

"Oh my God! You should see your face right now!" She snorts. "A murder-suicide pact? I really had you going, didn't I?" She punches my shoulder, and I wince from the sting. "Girl, you watch too many movies."

I let out a shaky breath and wait for my heartbeat to slow down. I want to scream or cry or both. My head throbs, a combination of fear and aggravation.

"Can we please just go before the police show up? Or would you prefer to try your stand-up routine on them?" I ask.

"Are you mad at me? Please don't be mad, Kayla. I don't like it when you're mad at me." She sticks out her bottom lip and pretends to pout. I hate when she does that. Makes her look like an overgrown toddler, which, at this point, she basically is. "Look. I got you a surprise." She lifts her shirt and points to a half-empty bottle of bourbon stuffed inside the waistband of her leggings. "Found it in the closet. Who knows how long this shit's been in there. Bet it's ripe as hell."

She unscrews the top, takes a long swig, and passes it to me, but I shove her hand away. "Not in the mood."

Zorie shrugs. "More for me, then." Another blast of thunder flickers the garage lights, and Zorie starts the car. "If you'll please do the honors," she says and hands me the garage-door opener. I click it, and we twist in our seats to watch as it rumbles to life. The door lifts slowly, like it's unsure if it should keep us inside or let us go. I'm unsure, too. When it finally lifts completely, headlights greet us, and a man in a yellow rain hat leaning out of an SUV. I open my mouth to scream, and Zorie slaps her hand over it.

"Doesn't look like a police cruiser," she says. "We'll get rid of him."

I don't like the way she says "get rid of him" or that her hand smells like the lemon-scented trash bags we used to cover Paul's body.

"Be cool." She drops her hand, but I still feel the warmth of her palm on my lips.

The man opens his door and steps out onto the gravel driveway in a yellow poncho. He looks our age, maybe a few years older, and stands in front of his SUV, squinting at the Camry.

"I should run his ass over," Zorie says.

"No!" I blurt out.

She stares at me, looking me over as if she's trying to figure out what to make of me. "Seriously, what's your problem? Why are you acting like I'm a monster?"

Before I can answer her, the man taps on the window with his umbrella handle, making us both jump.

"Morning, ladies," he shouts through the glass, then motions for Zorie to roll down the window. She doesn't. "My name's Brian. I'm Paul and Ruthann's neighbor."

Zorie shrugs, and I nudge her with my elbow. She cuts her eyes at me, annoyed, and I nod at Paul's gun against the dashboard.

"Shit." She slips it beside her seat and clenches the steering wheel. I think she's about to reverse but remembers this Brian guy's SUV is parked behind us.

"Maybe if you just listen to what he has to say, he'll go away," I say.

Zorie rolls her eyes and cracks the window. "Can we help you with something?" she shouts.

"I don't mean to disturb you—"

"You are," Zorie snaps.

Brian flashes a smile that reveals too many teeth. "I knocked on the front door, but no one answered. I was just about to leave and saw the garage door open." He wrings the umbrella in his hands, twisting it so hard his knuckles are white. I can see his brain working overtime to decide if he should ask who we are or go back to his SUV. I want to help him out, yell at him to go home and pretend he never saw us, but I can tell by his stance next to the Camry—arms folded, head cocked to one side—that he is not one to walk away without answers.

"Are you two friends of Paul and Ruthann?" he asks.

Goddamn it, Brian.

Zorie's hand reaches for the gun. Her fingers clench on the barrel. He won't survive this interrogation much longer. I lean across the console, surprising Zorie, and shout through the cracked window, "We're hospice nurses!"

Zorie looks both relieved and confused, but nods in agreement. "Taking care of business!" she says.

"Wow, you people really are dedicated," Brian says. "Even in a tornado, you're taking care of the sick and needy." His expression changes then to a forlorn one. "I had no idea Paul and Ruthann were sick."

"We can't say anything more about their conditions," I shout through the window. "HIPAA and all."

"Understood. Say no more." Brian makes a zipper motion across his lips.

"Well, have a good rest of your day." I wave at him. He waves back but doesn't move. My annoyance with our new friend has reached its boiling point.

"You should go now, Brian. Paul and Ruthann need their rest. We'll tell them you stopped by," I say.

He takes a step backward, then forward again. Oh, Brian. Bless your little idiot heart.

"It's just that, I saw Paul and Ruthann two nights ago at church, and they looked fine," Brian says. "If they're sick, they shouldn't be alone in this storm and with those two armed and dangerous . . ." His voice trails off, and his eyes widen with a new realization I hate to see. "I'll leave you two to your business, then." He turns to walk away but slips in his own rain puddle. Zorie is out of the car immediately, gun drawn and pointed at Brian's dumb rain hat.

"I don't want any trouble," he says, his voice cracking.

"Neither do we," Zorie says.

She doesn't flinch when the gun cocks, but I do. My eyes dart around the garage as if the solution to Zorie's sudden bloodthirst lies somewhere wedged between the Weed eater and the bag of mulch in the corner.

"Wait! Don't hurt him!" I shout and stumble out of the car.

"I wasn't," Zorie growls.

I race around to them, but Zorie blocks my path. She won't allow me to throw myself in front of her gun again after what happened with Dez. "We can tie him up and put him in the basement with Ruthann," I say quickly.

Zorie's right eye twitches, and for a second I honestly think she's gone insane. "Get up," she yells at Brian. He clumsily climbs to his feet and stands in front of us, hands raised to the ceiling.

"I won't say anything," he says, chin quivering. "I'll go home and never talk about today with anyone."

Zorie laughs. "Best friend's honor?"

It's at that moment I realize I can't stand her. I hate my best friend. Despise her. I grab an extension cord from the wall, and she jerks her head at me like she knows what I'm thinking, what I want to do. I picture her face as I do it, her eyes rolling back inside her head, her hands scratching at her neck as the cord slowly tightens around her throat.

"Girl!" Zorie snaps. "What are you waiting for? Tie him up!"

I take a tentative step toward him. He flinches but doesn't run. I tell Brian to give me his hands, and he does. The extension cord is thick, and it pinches his skin as it wraps around his wrists. I don't look at Brian as I work. I can't. His eyes will haunt me for the rest of my life.

I take the last extension cord and wrap it around his legs so that he has to jump to move. He does this all the way to the basement door, with the rifle pressed into his back.

"I'll help him down the stairs," I say and sidle between Brian and the gun's barrel. Zorie doesn't object, but when I unlock the basement door, Brian falls inside. He rolls and bounces down the stairs and lands next to Ruthann, who barely moves. Blood sputters from his mouth, and I think I see a tooth pop out. I slam the door and whirl around to face her, this stranger in front of me.

"What the fuck is wrong with you?" I shout, spraying her face with spittle. "Are you cosplaying some deranged serial killer now?"

"He isn't dead!" she shouts back and reaches past me to open the door. "Look! He's still moving!"

"Then what are you waiting for? Don't you want to finish him off?" I shove her away and stomp down the hallway. I'm almost to the kitchen when I realize I'm running.

"I didn't touch him, Kayla! He must've tripped!" Zorie screams after me, but I ignore her.

Brian's SUV is still running in the driveway, and I get in, lock the doors, and start to reverse, when gunfire and glass stop my efforts. A sound escapes me, guttural and animalistic, and I duck down in the seat with my hands covering my head. Am I shot? Bleeding? I search my body for bullet holes but find none.

"Kayla! Oh my God! Are you okay?" I hear Zorie shout over the rain.

I lift my head and peer over the dashboard. The front windshield is shattered, and the bullet formed a clean path through the passenger headrest. Zorie stands in front of the SUV, still clutching Paul's gun and craning her neck to see beyond the shattered windshield.

"Kayla? Please say something!"

I open the door and step out into the rain on shaky legs. My pants feel wet, and I'm pretty sure I pissed myself. Zorie rushes at me, arms outstretched, and hugs me so tightly I whimper.

"Kayla! Thank God you're okay!"

"Okay? You fucking shot at me!" I scream at her, my entire body trembling. "You could've killed me!"

Tears fill her eyes, and she shakes her head. "I'm so sorry. The gun must've misfired or something." Zorie swipes at her tears, but more fall. "Oh God, I don't know what I'd do if anything ever happened to you."

She kisses me lightly on the cheek. I try not to shudder.

CHAPTER TWENTY

——

The Cardinal Inn's NO VACANCY sign mocks us from the road, but Zorie stops anyway, desperate for sleep and convinced she can negotiate a room for us. I'd rather sleep in a field on the side of the highway than share a room with a woman I'm pretty sure is a sociopath who might smother me in my sleep, but I'm too exhausted from the events of the past forty-eight hours to protest. Every mile since leaving the farmhouse felt like driving into another dimension, separating us even further from our former lives and selves. We'd come under siege by heavy hail and torrential rain as we crossed into Mississippi, both threatening to swallow us whole and forcing us to wait out their wrath beneath an overpass.

"Peace offering," Zorie says, and hands me a crumpled pack of Marlboro Lights. Flecks of blood dot the cellophane wrapping, and I shove her hand away, feeling my guts churn. "God, for the last time, Kayla, the gun misfired. I'm sorry."

"Why?"

"Why what?"

My face feels hot and sweaty, and I swipe at it with the back of my hand. "Why are you sorry?"

"Because you're my entire world. You can't seriously believe I'd try to kill you."

"I don't know what I believe anymore."

"Well, that's too bad, isn't it?"

Zorie doesn't say anything else, and I'm grateful for the silence. I'm also terrified of it. Quiet gives my thoughts time to roam around, grow, and then claw their way out of my brain. I don't trust my thoughts anymore. I fear them.

"Only one of us should go in," Zorie says after a while. "They're looking for two black females, not one."

I peer out the window at the hotel entrance and the bald man watching our car from beneath the awning. He lifts a cigarette to his lips, inhales deeply, and flicks it onto the sidewalk. "I don't want to go in," I say.

"Then wait in the car."

"No." I risk a glance at my best friend. "I don't want to go in, because I don't want to spend another second with you."

Zorie's expression shifts from confusion to hurt. "You don't mean that."

I unfasten my seatbelt and twist in my seat to face her. I need her to look at me so there's no mistaking my words. "I do mean it. I don't want to do this with you anymore, Zorie. I'm tired of running, and I'm tired of this cruel, heartless person you're turning into." I pause, take a deep breath, and try to breathe normally before I pass out. "I'm going home."

Zorie laughs like I've just said something hilarious. "Home? What does that even mean? It doesn't mean your *family*, you know why? Because *I'm* your family. And it doesn't mean love, because *I'm* the only one who really loves you." Her face darkens, and her lips pull back from her teeth. "It's time you start recognizing it."

She glares at me with cold black eyes, and I glare back. Fury flashes through me. This self-righteous bitch is telling me about love after getting me fired from my job and going on this bootleg Thelma and Louise road trip?

"This is what you call love and family?" I shout. I don't know where I find the strength or the courage, but within seconds, I'm on top of her, grabbing her neck and shoving her head against the window.

"I hate you!" I yell.

Zorie shakes her head at me, and even though I have her by the neck, she laughs like a maniac. "You never were a good liar, Kayla."

I squeeze tighter, watching with sick amusement as her eyes bulge and new veins crawl up the sides of her face. My hands ache from gripping so tightly, but I don't care. And I don't stop.

"Okay, okay. Message received. You can stop choking me now," Zorie says in a pinched voice.

She scratches at my face and arms, but I keep right on squeezing. Even when I hear the car door open and a man's voice shout for me to stop, I squeeze tighter and tighter until my fingers are numb.

"Stop it or I'll call the cops!" the voice says. Thick, pale fingers grab mine and pry them from Zorie's bruised neck. She hunches forward, coughing and gasping for breath.

"Everything's fine," Zorie manages to cough out. "We were just having a conversation, weren't we, Michelle?"

All the blood rushes out of my head. I'm dizzy. I look up and see the bald man from under the awning who was watching us moments earlier. The name tag pinned to his yellow polo shirt says DUSTIN and, beneath that, MANAGER.

"It was a conversation, Dustin. That's all," I mumble, and climb off Zorie.

Dustin stares at me for a long time. He picks at the skin around his nails, and I notice his hands are shaking. I know he's waiting for me to say something else, like a more believable explanation for almost killing Zorie. I don't have one.

"We need a room," I tell him. I lean against the side of the car. I'm tired, traumatized, and too damn hungry to fight anymore. "How much?"

He shifts his weight from one Crocs-adorned foot to the other, his eyes darting between the two black women in front of him. "Three hundred a night."

"For this roach motel?" Zorie scoffs. "You have got to be kidding me." She climbs out of the car and stands next to me. One of her braids has fallen out, and her hair sticks out in a long, crimped line. "What's your problem"—she leans in and squints at his name tag—"Dustin? You don't want two black women staying at your motel?"

Dustin steps backward, putting some distance between the three of us. "Price just went up to six," he says, and folds his arms with a smirk.

Oh God. I watch the veins in Zorie's neck appear as she grits her teeth, then glance at the rifle through the windshield. She wouldn't use it. Not here in the Cardinal Inn's parking lot with occupied guest rooms only a few feet away. I move in front of the driver's door, surprising Zorie.

"We'll take the room," I say quickly.

"The hell we will!" Zorie protests.

Dustin stands awkwardly in his too-tight polo shirt and khaki pants that don't quite reach his ankles. Zorie wants control. But I want it, too, and there's only one way to make us equal players in whatever twisted game this is. I'd have to be the better manipulator.

"We'll take the room, and we'll pay in cash," I say.

Zorie's eyes snap back to look at me. "What are you doing?"

"Surviving."

"If you ladies will follow me, I'll get you checked in," Dustin says, gesturing for us to come with him.

I wait for Zorie to start walking, but she doesn't move. She remains cemented in front of me on the oil-slicked asphalt.

"Wow, that was really dumb. I thought you were supposed to be the smart one," she says. Then, leaning in close to my face, she whispers, "See you inside, friend." The corners of her mouth turn up into a smile, and I know I've made a mistake.

A big one.

══

Our six-hundred-dollar room turns out to be a tiny, windowless box with one bed and a stained red comforter. The air is stale, and there's a rancid smell coming from the bathroom. If I didn't know any better, I'd say there was a dead body decomposing in the tub.

"Enjoy, ladies," Dustin says, but it sounds mocking, like a warning. He closes the door, and I sit on the corner of the comforter with the fewest stains.

"You're not gonna follow him?" Zorie asks, watching me. "I thought you were *so* ready to get away from me."

I kick off my shoes and curl into a ball on the bed. The rancid smell swells in my nostrils, but I'm too tired to care.

"What's the matter? Don't feel like talking now? You were real chatty in the parking lot with your boy Dustin when you offered up half our money." Zorie kicks the bed, but I don't move. Starvation has made me too weak to do anything beyond gaze up at her while she paces in front of me. "How the hell are we supposed to get by on four hundred dollars?" She stops pacing and squats in front of me so we're eye to eye. Her breath stinks of whiskey. "Guess this means I'm gonna have to be a lot more creative getting more."

"Do whatever you want. It's blood money anyway." I roll over onto my side and close my eyes defiantly. "I don't care anymore," I say through a yawn.

"Okay, fine. I'll let you be in your feelings right now because you're tired. You'll feel better once you get some sleep." She places a scratchy, foul-smelling blanket over me, and I kick it off.

"You're not listening," I snap, jerking upright. "I don't like who I am with you, Zorie. And after today, I don't want to know you anymore."

"Like I said, you're tired," Zorie says, her voice cracking on the last syllable. She sweeps her braids to one side and then turns toward the door. "I'm going to the vending machine. When I get back, I hope you check that stank attitude."

She reaches for the door handle, and I call her name. She stops but doesn't turn around. Doesn't matter. I don't need to see her face for what I say next.

"I meant what I said, Zo. After today, we're done."

Zorie yanks open the door and slams it behind her. A clap of thunder rattles the windows.

I close my eyes.

CHAPTER TWENTY-ONE

———

Sleep comes immediately, but a restless one. I toss and turn between my sweat-soaked sheets while images of a very alive Paul and smiling Ruthann and Brian haunt my dreams. Together they eat baloney sandwiches and watch the news inside the dilapidated farmhouse. I watch them from a distance and even call their names, but they don't hear me, or maybe they don't want to. From somewhere in the house, a dark figure emerges carrying a rifle. I shout their names again, but they keep right on eating sandwiches and watching TV, and then it's too late. The figure shoots all three of them, one by one, until each of them jerk and writhe on the floor in a pool of their own blood. The figure shoots them again and again until every feature of their faces is erased. And then the figure turns and looks right at me.

Zorie.

Her lips don't move, but somehow I hear her voice repeating the same words she'd spoken only a few hours earlier. "I'd never hurt you!"

I jerk upright, untangle myself from the stinky sheets, and sit on the edge of the bed. My pulse races so fast the room spins around me.

"It was just a dream, stupid." And then, like an afterthought, I remember Zorie is in the room with me. I look at the clock, 8:32 P.M., and turn on the lamp, illuminating the space in a creepy glow. The bed is empty, and her side is still carefully made up, with the pillow on top.

She left me. She actually abandoned me in Hick Town, USA, with not a single dollar to my name. Not that I blame her. My last words to her were "We're done." But Zorie and I are never done. There's always something holding us together, binding us, like an invisible chain.

"Zorie?"

I hear a low moan and realize it's coming from the bathroom. I pad across the room in my bare feet to the closed bathroom door.

"Zorie? You in there?" I ask and twist the knob. It's locked, and I immediately fear the worst. "Zorie, open the door." When her last boyfriend dumped her to go back to his wife, Zorie threatened to kill herself by taking a bottle of Tylenol. He left a Walgreens bag with two bottles on our doorstep with a note that said "Sweet dreams, bitch." She only managed to swallow six pills, but it was enough to convince me never to call her bluff.

The lock clicks, and I hold my breath, half expecting to see a semi-conscious Zorie splayed on the bathroom floor and surrounded by pills, but she's all smiles when the door swings open. And nearly bald.

"You like?" She does an odd little twirl and strikes a pose against the doorframe with a hand on her hip. Behind her, I see the evidence of her creation, with her former braids and chunks of hair pushed together into a pile by the toilet.

"Your turn," she says, and holds up a pair of scissors. Crimson streaks stretch across the inside of her tattooed wrist, dividing our initials, and drip down her forearm. She follows my eyes to the wound and smiles. "Just a scratch."

"Zorie, what did you do?"

She steps toward me with the scissors, still grinning like a maniac. "You said you don't want to know Zorie anymore, so I got rid of her. This is the new me."

I take a deep, ragged breath, my eyes still fixed on the dark streaks trailing down the inside of her arm. "We need to get you to a doctor, Zo. I think you need help."

"I don't need help, silly," she says, laughing. "I gave you what you wanted—a new and improved ride or die. I just had to get rid of all evidence of the old one." She nods at her wrist. "And now we can start over. You and me. Forever. Give me your wrist." Zorie holds out her hand expectantly, and I back away.

"I'm going to call for help."

"Why are you acting like you're afraid of me?" Her eyebrows knit together in a deep frown. "Are you afraid of me, Kayla?"

I swallow hard and press my trembling hands together. "Please. You're like the least scary person I know." My heart pounds uncomfortably fast inside my chest, and I steady myself against the wall. "I like your hair. It suits you. The *new* you."

At this, Zorie hunches over in a fit of laughter and drops the scissors, which I promptly kick away from her. "Oh my God. I tried to hold it together for as long as I could, but your face! You're such a bad liar, Kayla." She pushes past me and collapses on top of the bed, wiping her wrist on the comforter.

"You shouldn't do that. Could get infected," I warn.

"Guess I shouldn't do this either, then." She lifts her wrist to her mouth and licks hungrily at it until no evidence of blood remains. "Tomato juice," she says, holding out her puncture-free wrist. "Gotcha."

I want to pounce on her and claw off every piece of skin on her face. "You think that's funny? You're sick!" I shout to a symphony of banging on the wall.

"Relax, it was funny. You're so uptight. I wanted to make you laugh." She stretches out her long body, folding her arms behind her head. "You know what I have a craving for? Chinese. We should definitely order Chinese for dinner."

"Fuck this." My annoyance with Zorie has reached its boiling point. I snatch my shoes by the desk and stuff a pillowcase with the few pieces of Ruthann's wardrobe I manage to grab from the duffel bag on the floor.

"What are you doing?" Zorie asks.

"What's it look like I'm doing?" I heave the pillowcase over my shoulder like a ghetto Santa. "I'm done. I'll hitchhike my way back home if I have to—anything to get away from you. You're a fucking psycho, and I'm done pretending you're not."

"Oh, so now I'm a psycho? Because of a dumb prank? Where's your sense of humor, Kayla? You used to crack up at shit like this."

"Maybe because back then, I didn't realize how fucked up you are!" I cock my head to the side and narrow my eyes. "Did your mom even hit you when we were kids, or was that a dumb prank, too?"

Zorie's expression changes to a scowl. "Why would you even ask me that? You saw the bruise on my face."

"Right, I saw a bruise," I say with a smirk. "And just a few minutes ago, I saw what looked like blood on your wrist. How could I have been so stupid? I can't believe I missed the signs that you're insane."

Zorie laughs. "If I'm insane, then what does that make you? Oh wait, I know, you're the normal one, right? Because *normal* people vandalize the place their dad is getting married in the night before his wedding. And *normal* people drive their car into their stepsister's car. And something else . . ." She taps her chin and pretends to think. "Oh, got it!" she says, snapping her fingers. "*Normal* people crash weddings and steal the bride and groom's gifts."

"Is there a point to this?" I ask.

"The point, bestie, is that you and I are just alike. So if I'm insane, so are you. Or do you still think you're so much better than me?"

"Yes! I do!" I shout. There's a loud bang on the opposite wall, followed by a muffled voice telling me to shut the fuck up.

Zorie pushes herself off the bed and aligns her body with mine. She moves in closer, and I feel the heat of her body and her breath hot against my cheek. "You walk out that door, and I swear to God I'll do it for real." She somehow manages to grab the pair of scissors before I do and holds the blade against her wrist.

"You're not serious," I say, calling her bluff, something I vowed to never do.

"You really want to find out how serious I am? If I die, it'll be your fault," she whispers. "Do you really want my blood on your hands?"

"Give me the scissors, Zorie." I reach for them, but she snatches them back toward her shoulder.

"I'll take that as a no." She lifts her lips in a half smile and sinks back down onto the bed. "I know you think I'm this cold, heartless monster or whatever, but I really am looking out for you—for both of us. It's not safe out there, Kayla. The police are sniffing around everywhere. Dustin was watching the news in the office when I went to the vending machine. They found Paul, Ruthann, and Brian. I guess Brian's girlfriend got worried and went looking for him."

She grabs the remote from the nightstand and aims it at the TV. Brian's bruised and swollen face immediately fills the screen. He looks directly at the camera and says through his newly missing front teeth, "They twied thew thill me." Seconds later, a video of me and Zorie dancing in the Dairy Queen parking lot appears onscreen, followed by one of Zorie hitting the girl with the neon-pink braids and me flipping off the crowd. The final video is in slow motion and shows Zorie pulling a gun on the gas station cashier and the two of us running across the parking lot to our getaway car. It's clear to anyone who knows us that we are the two women in the videos.

My heart sinks to my feet. I'm not mentally prepared to see my face in all its high-definition glory with the word *murderer* plastered across CNN and the new reward for our capture totaling seventy-five thousand dollars.

"You should've let me kill that girl at Dairy Queen when we had the chance," Zorie says. Then, with a smile I'm not sure is sincere, she adds, "I'm kidding."

My throat tightens, then my chest. I think of Dad and Gloria watching this on their obnoxiously large eighty-five-inch TV. "Turn it off," I mumble.

"It's gonna be okay, Kayla. I promise. You know why?" Zorie doesn't wait for me to answer. "Because we're better together than apart."

The invisible chain tightens around me.

I can't breathe.

———

Zorie's hand holds on to mine so tightly my fingers throb. She's been like this for hours, her legs wrapped around mine and her head pressed between my shoulder blades. I try to wriggle free from her hold, but it's pointless. She won't let go.

I tuck my free hand under my cheek and watch the headlights from the highway grow and shrink against the wall. Sleep won't come for me. Not tonight. The nights are always the hardest. My first night in prison, I'd spent hours wondering how I'd ever fall asleep in a place that felt so confined and claustrophobic. And then the shadow would come, moving and growing, and I'd make myself small on top of my bed. It was enough to keep me awake every night for the next three months until I finally gave in to my exhaustion, only to wake up hours later with my cellmate watching me. I always thought nothing would ever be as frightening as that moment.

Until tonight.

Now it's Zorie's shadow that grows and moves against the wall, suffocating me inside this confined space. It is Zorie who watches me in the dark and who makes me feel so small. I roll onto my back, thinking survival will not allow me the luxury of sleep. Zorie sighs contently and rests her head on my shoulder. Her hand still grips mine. She'll never let go.

———

In the morning, Zorie manages to slip in and out of the drugstore unnoticed wearing a JESUS IS MY BOSS baseball cap she swiped from Paul and Ruthann's closet and a pair of oversize sunglasses she'd taken from God knows where. She returns to our car, grinning from ear to ear, having successfully stolen two boxes of hair dye and a bag of Twizzlers.

"Blond for me and red for you," she says, handing me the box.

"Wild cherry? Really?" I say, reading the box. The words EMBRACE YOUR INNER WILD SIDE are stamped beneath a photo of a white woman with flaming-red hair.

"We have to change our looks, don't we?" Zorie says.

Back at the hotel, Zorie is first with our homemade makeover, and then me. Neither color looks good with our complexions, but at least we no longer match the photos of Alabama's most wanted murderous duo. I sit on the bed, forcing down my third bag of Funyuns and watch Zorie cross off back roads along I-10 to New Orleans. She's convinced we can still make a life for ourselves without her aunt's help.

I remember Zorie had said, *"Aunt Ruby used to say New Orleans was the perfect place to disappear. It's surrounded by swamps and alcoholics. If anyone recognized you, they'd forget you the next day."*

For our sake, I hope she's right.

I spend most of the morning watching news coverage of our murderous spree across the great state of Alabama, with random people calling in to give updates on our whereabouts. One woman said she spotted us at the Piggly Wiggly in Goodwater, Alabama. Another said we were in Miami. But maybe the most telling interview of them all was with Desmond Reynolds, aka Dez, who sat down with a CNN news anchor to tell the world how I seduced and then robbed him.

"Truth is, I've never been intimate with anyone . . . until her," Dez says. He sits in a chair that makes him look much smaller than I remember, with his Solar Sonics hat pulled down low on his forehead.

"Do you mean to tell me the alleged killer was your first lover?" the anchor asks, biting back a smile.

Dez nods. "That's right."

The anchor leans in, his brows furrowed behind his tortoiseshell frames. "Not only did this woman steal your belongings, but she also stole your virginity . . . and perhaps even your heart?"

"Told you he was weak," Zorie says before turning it off.

"He was a good guy," I say, sinking back into the pillows. Shame and guilt form a knot deep inside my stomach. I'd taken something from Dez he can never get back, something more valuable than his iPhone or Chuck Taylors. "And I ruined him. I'm a horrible person."

"Why? Because some dude chose to pop his cherry with some random woman he picked up at a gas station? Girl, that's his fault. He clearly wanted it to happen the way it did, or he would've stopped it. You have nothing to feel guilty about."

I nod, even though I still feel guilty. Very. Nothing I can do about it now but hope that our brief encounter on a table of soggy tacos doesn't scar him for life.

"We should probably leave and think about getting another car now that we've made the national news," I say as Zorie draws another *X* on her map. "And we'll need jobs when we get there."

"Look at you thinking ahead," she says and nods her approval.

I am thinking ahead. The only thing tying me to Zorie right now is money. The sooner I get my hands on more of it, the sooner I can break that tie for good. She's made sure going home is no longer an option for me, thanks to our little home invasion and Paul's murder— sorry, self-defense killing. I'm connected to Zorie's crimes now as much as she's connected to mine, and maybe that's exactly the way she wanted it. Me, forever tied to her, indebted to her. If I go down, you go down. Until a few days ago, I'd never questioned our friendship or my loyalty to a woman I can barely stomach to be around now. I had no reason to. Then again, maybe there was always a reason bubbling just beneath the surface but I was too dumb to notice. *"You're naïve, Kayla."* Dad always said Zorie would be my downfall. And here we are, sharing a disgusting hotel room in this country-ass town, with the police hot on our asses. Zorie isn't just my downfall. She's my demise.

"We need to change our names again," I say.

Zorie frowns. "What's wrong with Star and Michelle?"

"Um, everything. Star and Michelle are wanted by the police. Their victims are giving interviews to the media. Star and Michelle can't exist anymore."

She purses her lips, thinking. "I'll be Wilhelmina. I saw it on a business card in the office last night. What do you think?"

"We're trying to blend in, not stand out." I reach for the archaic phone book on the nightstand and flip it open. "What about Diane?"

"Do I look like a Diane to you?"

"You're right. Too elegant," I say and flip to the back of the book. "Rhonda?"

Zorie scrunches her eyebrows together, thinking. "I can get behind Rhonda, I guess."

I flip the book back to the front and scroll down the page. "I'll be . . . Hope."

"I can see you as a Hope." She grins up at me, and I manage to give her a less enthusiastic one back.

I hate her for enjoying this; for turning this horrific road trip to hell into some kind of girls' trip, where we explore our newfound identities.

"I was thinking," I say through my forced grin. "If we're going to do this—I mean *really* do this—we need to establish some rules."

"What kind of rules?"

I want to grab her by the shoulders, shake her, and scream, *The kind that stops you from committing crimes!* But I don't. Something has changed in Zorie. Snapped. When she looks at me, her eyes are wild and unfocused. It's this strange version of my old friend, my sister, that frightens me in a way I've never felt before.

"Rules so we don't get caught," I say, my voice calm and controlled. "Like . . . no more guns."

Zorie waves a dismissive hand. "Don't be stupid, Kayla. We have to protect ourselves."

"I'm serious." I look her straight in the eye so there's no mistaking my words. "No guns."

We stare at each other, her jaw clenched and my eyes unblinking. I scoot to the edge of the bed closest to the door in case I need to run.

"Fine," she says with a long, relenting sigh. "No guns. But I'm keeping the knife." She lifts her shirt and points to the hunting knife tucked into the waistband of her leggings. I don't bother asking where or when she took the knife, and she doesn't volunteer it.

"Also . . . I need to call my dad," I say.

At this, she looks up, her face contorted in confusion, or anger. I can't tell anymore. "Wait, weren't you the one who said no phone calls home because the police will track us?"

"If I'm never going to see him again, I need to at least say goodbye. He's the only family I've got." Her eyes flash, and I quickly add, "Besides you."

Zorie blows out another sigh. "Fine. But only on our way out. And keep it short. We don't need police on our ass again."

I don't mention that I'm not planning to talk when I call Dad. I only want to hear his voice, see if I can detect worry in his words.

"Since we're making rules, you think I can make one, too?" Zorie asks.

My body tenses, but I nod anyway.

"My rule is . . . when we get to New Orleans, we start over. Clean slate."

"Wasn't that always the plan?"

"It was—I mean, it is." She drops her pen on the bed and scoots closer to me, and I catch another glimpse of the hunting knife inside her waistband. "I see the way you look at me now, and I don't like it," Zorie says. "It's like you hate me or something."

"I don't—"

Zorie holds up a hand to shut me up. I do.

"What I'm saying is, I want you to be proud to be my best friend." She reaches for my hand, and I notice how dirty her fingernails are. Zorie has always prided herself on her nail game. The Kardashians don't have shit on Zorie Andrews's nails. But that was the old Zorie. This Zorie has used those hands to tie up innocent people, to rob them at gunpoint, and to shoot them dead inside their own home. These are the hands of a stranger.

"When we cross that state line, it'll be like going into the future. The past won't matter anymore." She squeezes my hand, her jagged, dirty nails digging into my palm. "I hate what's happening with us. Can we start over, Kayla? For real?"

I nod without hesitation. "Of course we can. I want that, too." My throat feels tight, and I'm not even sure if I say actual words. Zorie seems satisfied with my answer and pulls me into her. The hunting knife presses against my stomach, but it doesn't hurt.

I'm numb now.

There's no sign of Dustin in the office, only a petite blond woman with black roots and hoop earrings big enough to stick my arm through. I slide my room key across the desk and tell her I'm checking out, but she ignores me. It's only when I help myself to the bowl of peppermints in front of her that she lifts her heavily outlined eyes to look at me.

"Can I help you?" she asks in her slow Southern drawl.

"Checking out. Room 118," I say and nod at the room key between us.

"We do express checkout here. Your bill is delivered under the door." She licks chocolate from her thumb courtesy of the half-eaten donut next to her keyboard.

"Actually, I was wondering if I could use your phone?"

She lifts a pencil-thin eyebrow. "One in your room not working?"

I shake my head. "Lost my cell phone, too."

She drums her turquoise talon nails on the desk. One of them is broken, and dried blood is gathered at the cuticle. Finally, after the longest staring contest ever, she shoves the phone at me.

"If it's long-distance, I'll need to charge it to your room," she says.

"Of course. Thanks so much." I lift the receiver. Red lipstick covers the mouthpiece, and I wipe it on my shirt before dialing Dad's cell. He answers on the first ring.

"Hello?"

I have to bite the inside of my cheek to stop myself from answering.

"Hello?" he says again, louder. Frantic.

I hold my breath.

I wait.

And then I hear it. A whisper so soft and low I almost mistake it for a sigh. But there's no mistaking the syllables that form my name.

"Kayla? That you?" Dad whispers.

I close my eyes to stop the tears pressing against my lids. What will his life be like now without me? Will he miss me? Will he be relieved that I'm gone? His last words to me were how tired he was of apologizing to Gloria and Candace for the things I've done. Maybe now the three of them can become the family they've always wanted to be, and I will become a face inside a frame by the garage door, like my mom.

"If it is you, please come home. I'm worried about you, sweetheart." His voice cracks, and he sounds on the verge of tears. "You're my little girl. Let me help you."

The urge to give in, to say yes, forces me to bite down so hard on my lip I taste blood. I want to tell him I'm tired of running and that I'm ready to be rescued, not from Zorie, but from myself. My mouth opens, and I feel the words forming on my tongue: *Please help me,*

Daddy. But any thoughts of a family reunion quickly disappear when I hear Gloria's voice.

"Kayla, it's Gloria," she says, as if I don't recognize the nasal, high-pitched sound piercing my ears. "Listen, I talked to an attorney, and she feels strongly that if we can get you into a psychiatric treatment facility, you can avoid jail time. I explained to her how you snapped on Charles and my Candace last week and that your jealousy may have caused this psychotic break. Anyway, your father and I agree it's for the best."

My fingers tighten around the phone as her words reverberate inside my head. *"Your father and I agree it's for the best."* Even now, in my darkest moment, Dad has once again sided with Gloria, deciding that his daughter is not only a homicidal maniac, but also a jealous, vengeful, mentally ill woman driven to her breaking point because of a broken heart. I want to laugh or scream at the ridiculousness of it all, but I don't do either. I hang up and back away from the phone as if it's on fire. I'd rather take my chances at freedom than be locked inside a padded room where my sanity is questioned.

"Fuck you both," I say under my breath.

The woman eyes me curiously from behind the desk. Her features twist into a concerned frown as she watches me swipe the snot from my nose with my shirt collar.

"You okay, hon?" she asks.

I force a small smile. "I'm great," I choke out.

The woman looks unconvinced but nods anyway. Damn. I fucked up. Why didn't I hang up sooner? I look at the clock behind her. Bet the police are camped out in every corner of the house with Dad and Gloria, waiting for me to screw up, like now. I wonder if that was enough time for them to trace the call. What if officers are en route right now to the Cardinal Inn? I look at the clock again. Zorie and I have minutes, maybe even seconds, to get the hell out of here.

"You have a nice day now," the woman says, and gives a little wave with two chocolate-covered fingers. I start to wave back, when the phone rings, making me jump. It's my dad calling back. He'll ask what the person who called looks like, and she'll tell him I have big brown eyes, toffee skin, and freckles across my nose and cheeks. He'll know those features belong to me because I belong to him.

"Cardinal Inn?" the woman says, and takes a bite of her donut. Her eyes linger briefly on me and then move back to the computer screen. "I'm sorry, I can't understand you . . . Who are you looking for?"

I swipe my hand under my nose again as her confused eyes return to my face. Her mouth opens, revealing bits of chewed donut on her tongue.

Run, Kayla! Run!

My subconscious screams at me—demands I move, but I can't. My legs refuse to cooperate with my brain. Dad is looking for me. I want her to tell him I'm here, that I'm okay and not insane.

"I don't understand . . . Can you repeat that, hon?" she says, cradling the phone against her shoulder. She reaches for a notepad, her gaze still fixed on me. "Spell that for me, hon?"

I feel myself lean in, as if I can somehow hear the person's voice on the other end. She frowns at me and turns her back just as a shirtless man carrying a small child on his hip walks into the office. The front of the child's shirt is covered in slobber, which he—or she, I can't tell—happily wipes on the man's hair-covered belly.

"Toilet in room 311 is clogged again," he shouts.

The woman holds up a finger, telling him to wait, but he ignores her.

"What y'all need to do is update the plumbing in this place." The child giggles and dangles a set of keys over the man's shoulder. They fall to the floor behind him, but he doesn't turn to pick them up. He leans across the desk, his large belly pressing into the ledge like Silly Putty. "This is the second time it's clogged in two days," he says. "I want the room comped."

The woman covers the phone receiver with one hand and, through a braces-covered smile, says, "Sir, maybe you should take smaller shits."

This is my cue to leave, but I can't. Not yet. I glance down at the keys with the Florida State University keychain, then at the child watching me with curious eyes.

"Mine!" the kid says and holds out a grimy palm as a string of drool slides down their chin. The man switches the child to his other hip and continues his rant about the size of the toilet seats. The woman behind the desk looks less than amused.

Screw this hillbilly showdown. I grab the keys from the floor and take off through the double doors to Zorie and the Camry parked underneath the awning.

"Oh God. What did Mr. Davenport say? Or was it his bitch wife?" Zorie asks as I climb inside next to her.

"He didn't answer," I say.

"I'm sorry, girl." Zorie reaches for my hand and looks deep into my eyes. "You need to let him go now, Kayla. If we're gonna start a new life, you need to let go of everything in our past. And that includes your dad."

The keys cut into my palm. I don't want to think about Dad. Not now. I swallow hard and stare out into the parking lot. A gray Buick LeSabre is parked a few feet away, with its trunk open like an invitation.

"Park next to the Buick," I say, pointing.

Zorie frowns. "Why?"

I trace the Buick emblem on the key in my hand. "Because I think it belongs to this key, and to our new ride."

"You didn't . . ." she says slowly. Then, squealing, she pulls me to her in a tight embrace. "See? I told you we'd be okay. Just think, in a few hours, we'll be in New Orleans, living our best lives. KD and ZA forever!"

I hug her back, even though it hurts.

CHAPTER TWENTY-TWO

—

TUESDAY

Jazz vibrates the Buick.

The windows are down, and a sweet and earthy smell wafts inside. I lift my head to peer out at the trumpet and saxophone players on the sidewalk. Two women with flashing light-up novelty cups dance in front of the musicians, arms raised and the cups' pink contents sloshing over the rims and down their forearms.

"Welcome to our new life," Zorie says, watching me. Dark circles have made a home under her eyes. She looks as though she's aged ten years in only a few days.

"We're really here? In New Orleans?"

She nods and waves her hands out in front of her. "Home sweet home."

I lean out the window and inhale deeply. After years of binge-watching a TV show about sexy Louisiana vampires, of fangirling over the state's queen herself, Miss Britney Spears, I'm finally in the land of beignets and gumbo. Home sweet home.

"No reports of a stolen Buick or the Camry still," Zorie says.

I glance behind me at the two license plates tucked inside the car seat. We'd switched out the Camry's license plate for a Georgia one we'd found in the parking lot and exchanged the Buick's Florida plate for a Michigan one. We were as invisible as two black women with cartoonish red and blond hair can be.

"We need to find a cheap place to stay for a few days, until we can find jobs," I tell Zorie.

"Already on top of it."

I duck back inside the car and stare up at the giant flashing marquee with the words QUEEN'S INN.

"Fit for two queens," Zorie says.

"Two exiled queens," I mumble, taking in the dingy, cracked siding and the overgrown shrubs crawling over nearly every window on the first floor.

"Sign says rates are thirty-nine dollars a night. It's the best we can afford since we gave Dustin over half our money for the other piece-of-shit room."

I sink back into the seat and close my eyes. New beginnings. A clean slate. "It's fine," I say with a sigh. "We'll make it work."

"We always do."

Zorie backs into a parking space near the office, and I start to get out, but she stops me. "The police are looking for two black females, remember? Only one of us should go in."

"Fine. Go." I look away and focus on a couple making their way across the parking lot. The woman, dressed in a crop top and shorts that might as well be denim panties, slips her arm through the man's, and he shoves her away. He walks faster, almost running, as she struggles to catch up in her sky-high platform heels.

"Don't worry. It's only temporary," Zorie says.

She gets out, and I lock the doors. The couple are arguing now. The man lifts a fist as if to hit her, and the woman shrinks away.

"What a classy establishment," I mumble.

As if he heard me, the man's eyes briefly meet mine. I duck down in my seat and wait a beat before peering over the dashboard. He's gone. I let out a long sigh of relief, but it's short-lived. When I pull myself upright again, the man is standing next to my window. He smiles down at me like he can read my thoughts or, worse, smell my fear. I go to roll up the window, and he places his hand on it, shoving it back down with impressive strength.

"We know each other?" he asks.

I shake my head quickly and lean as far back as I can against the console. His smile widens, and he runs his tongue over chipped, rotten teeth.

"Figured we must know each other the way you were staring." The man rests his forearms on my window and peers in. A sharp, pungent odor immediately fills the small space, and I choke back a gag. "Would you like to get to know each other?"

"Please get away from my car." My voice comes out low and shaky and does little to move him from his stance at my window.

The man reaches inside his jacket pocket and pulls out two twenty-dollar bills that he shakes at me. "I've got money," he says. "How much?"

It strikes me then that this heavily intoxicated, disgusting man thinks I'm a prostitute. I don't know whether to be offended or terrified.

"How much?" he asks again, louder. This time, he doesn't wait for me to answer. His arm shoots out and grabs mine, yanking me forward against the door. The tiny black hairs on his upper lip move as he exhales rancid breath against my cheek. "How much?"

I'm too stunned to scream or call for help. I reach behind me on the seat and grab the first thing my fingers touch. Zorie's bourbon. My fingers wrap around the bottle's neck, and I slice it through the air and against the side of the man's face. He staggers back with both hands pressed against the bleeding gash that divides his cheek.

"You stupid motherfucker!" I shout.

He drops to his knees and moans at the asphalt. I shove open the door and stand over him, my fingers still gripping the bottle's neck, now slick with blood.

"Keep your hands off me next time!" For emphasis, I kick him hard in the stomach and watch as he curls into a ball at my feet. I stay like that, poised over him with the bottle, until the sound of someone clapping breaks my concentration. I spin around, expecting to see Zorie, but it's a woman with ebony skin and cotton-candy-pink hair, watching me from the sidewalk.

"Bravo!" she says, grinning wildly. "I was wondering when someone would finally knock out his old pervert ass!"

I drop the bottle, and it shatters at my feet, sending shards of glass sliding across the parking lot.

"Don't worry. I'll clean that up," the woman says.

"You don't have to do that."

"Actually, I do. Part of the job," she says, and nods at the housekeeping cart parked in front of one of the rooms. "I've told Uncle Delphin over and over again that if he keeps propositioning the guests, he'll get what he deserves. Looks like my premonition finally came true."

"Oh God. He's your uncle? I'm so sorry."

"Don't worry about it. Uncle Delphin had this coming for a while now, haven't you, Unc?" She nudges his leg with her sneaker, and he gives an angry grunt. "I don't know why my parents still keep him around. Guess they feel sorry for him. My folks own the hotel and let him stay here for free."

"Oh." I bite my lip and stare down at her uncle. He swipes absently at his face, smearing blood into his thick black hair. "He's bleeding pretty bad. Maybe we should call for help?"

She waves a dismissive hand. "Please. He's had a lot worse done to his face. Trust me. Mama will put some Neosporin on it, and he'll be good as new. I'm Olympia, by the way." She holds out her hand to me, revealing a huge red-and-yellow dragon tattoo on her inner forearm. Olympia follows my gaze and laughs. "It was a dare. One too many Jell-O shots at a high school party."

"I like it," I lie. It's hideous. The dragon looks like a toddler drew it and some of the color bled outside the lines.

"I think you might be the only one who does. You got a name?"

I shake her hand and say, "Hope."

"Funny. You don't look like a Hope to me." She crouches in front of me and begins collecting shards of glass from the ground.

"Let me help you," I say.

"My grandmother would kill me if she saw a guest cleaning at her hotel. Good old family business. Shitty work and shittier benefits." She laughs and plucks a shard of glass from Delphin's pants. He watches her movements carefully, then fixes his eyes, or at least what I can see of his eyes, on me. Half his face is covered in blood. "You checking in, Hope?" Olympia asks.

"My friend is." My friend who's taking her sweet-ass time and who's been gone long enough for me to slice a man's face in half.

"Well, I hope you and your friend will check out our pool while you're here," Olympia says. Then, lowering her voice, she adds, "The health department finally cleared us for reopening." She's quiet for a moment, watching me, then lets out a round of high-pitched giggles. "Girl, I'm just messing with you!"

I laugh, too, but nervously. I glance at the office with its bright-orange double doors. What is taking Zorie so long?

"Ow! Damn it!" Olympia groans.

My gaze shifts back to her, and she's sucking her finger.

"Cut myself," she says.

"You should use bread. Easier to pick up broken glass," I say.

Olympia lifts a pierced eyebrow. "Bread? Really?"

"Kind of works like a sponge. An old trick I used to use in house-keeping."

"You're a housekeeper?" She says it like she's impressed, not disgusted, which is the reaction I usually get.

"I was," I tell her. "Back home."

Olympia stands and cradles her handful of broken glass. Her palm is bleeding, but I don't tell her. "And where's back home?"

I know what she's asking: *Where are you running from?* A black girl named Hope must be running from something. I look her straight in the eye and say, "Far away."

She gives a knowing smile. "It's none of my business. I shouldn't have asked. Mama is always telling me how nosy I am." She looks down at her hand, notices the blood, and winces. "Bet this wouldn't have happened if I'd used bread. Damn. We could use someone like you with cleaning tips around the hotel. Too bad you don't live here."

My chest tightens, and I almost shout, *Yes! We do live here!* but I give a shrug instead. She'll sense my desperation, smell it coming through my pores, and then the questions will come fast and furious, because desperate people have secrets.

"You don't live here, do you?" Olympia asks.

The sun is hot on my face, and sweat stings my eyes. I don't want to be here anymore, in this interrogation. She's baiting me. I press my lips into a thin line to keep the truth from coming out.

"Listen, I don't want to get in your business, but if you and your friend are trying to keep a low profile, you've come to the right place." She leans in conspiratorially. "The Queen's Inn prides itself on discretion."

"Oh, we're not—"

Olympia lifts a hand to shut me up. "My family has a saying, '*Bondye fe san di.*' It's Haitian for 'God acts and doesn't talk.' I think me and you meeting like this is God acting." She smiles, and I notice for the first time she's missing one of her front teeth. "If you're interested in a job, meet me in the office tomorrow morning at nine sharp. If not, no worries. Just trying to help out a new friend."

"Are we friends?"

"*Bondye fe san di,*" she says with a wink.

I repeat the melodic phrase in my head as hope bubbles up inside me. If God did create this moment, then he must have new plans for me and Zorie. An actual chance to start over. I begin to cross the parking lot toward the office, feeling hopeful about our futures, when Delphin's hand grabs my ankle. I kick the side of his face, staining the tip of my shoe with his blood, but he doesn't relent.

"Let her go, Uncle D!" Olympia shouts, and pulls me away from him.

"We have another saying," he says, squinting up at me. " *'Bat Chen an, tann mèt li.'* "

I look back at Olympia to translate.

" 'Beat the dog, wait for its master,' " she says. "It means if you hurt someone, you'll get what's coming to you."

Delphin grins at me with his bloodstained teeth.

I shiver.

CHAPTER TWENTY-THREE

I find Zorie leaning across the front desk with her arms pressed against the sides of her boobs to emphasize her cleavage. It's what she does when she's flirting, and judging by the way the dreadlocked guy on the other side of the desk stares hungrily at her chest, it's working.

"Glad to see you're still alive. I thought something might've happened to you since you've been in here forever," I say from the doorway.

Zorie turns to look at me, surprised, as if she just realized I was outside waiting. "Girl, me and Lamont got to talking about food, and you know how I am when it comes to food," she says. "Guess I lost track of time."

Her eyes drift back to Mr. Dreadlocks, and the hope I felt seconds ago disappears. It's starting again. Zorie has found a new distraction. I wonder how long it will take her to give him all our money and tell him everything about the last few days, right down to the seventy-five-thousand-dollar reward for turning us in.

"So . . . are we staying here or not?" I ask, not bothering to hide my impatience. Or annoyance.

"Damn, Hope. Will you relax? Lamont totally hooked us up."

Mr. Dreadlocks—or, I guess, Lamont—smiles at me. Every tooth is covered in gold. Gross.

"Room 106 is the best room we got," Lamont says proudly. "Even got a jacuzzi in there."

Again. Gross.

"Well, aren't you gonna say thank you to Lamont for hooking us up?" Zorie asks, frowning.

"I'm a grown-ass woman, Rhonda. I don't need you telling me when to say thank you." I look at Lamont and force a smile. "Thanks."

Zorie gives a satisfied nod, and Lamont slides a room key across the desk.

"Y'all need anything, you come see me," he says, but more to Zorie than to me.

"Oh, I'm definitely coming to see you," she says.

I want to roll my eyes, but I'm too exhausted to move any muscle on my face. Zorie tucks the key inside her tank top, a move I'm sure she thinks is sexy but looks awkward since the key's outline is visible beneath the thin material. She does her best walk toward me, swaying her hips from side to side, with Lamont's hungry eyes following every step. When she finally reaches me, I grab her arm and yank her outside behind me.

"What the hell, Kayla," she yells, and jerks away from me.

I scan the parking lot for any sign of Delphin and Olympia, but they're gone. So is her housekeeping cart.

"Is it too much to ask for you to keep your panties on when you meet a man?" I hiss.

"Says the girl who hooks up with randoms at the hotel after hours." Her lips curl into a smile. "If I were you, I wouldn't be so quick to judge. Remember, you and me? We're the same."

Zorie saunters past me in that same hip-swinging way. She stops in front of the same door Olympia's housekeeping cart had been parked at earlier. "You coming?" she calls.

I swipe the sweat from my hairline and move forward. It's all I can do. Move forward.

———

I wait until after we've both showered and changed to tell Zorie about Olympia's job offer. By her reaction, you'd think Olympia offered to have us join her on the pole at some seedy strip club. Zorie paces in front of me, waving her arms and grunting at the ceiling like a maniac.

"We're supposed to be starting new lives, Kayla—not going back to the same old shit we did in Redwood Springs. Hotel housekeeping again? How stupid can you be?"

"We need jobs, don't we? Or were you planning to shack up with Mr. Dreadlocks?"

She frowns at me. "Who?"

"Lamont!" I shout. "You always do this! You meet someone, and then everything turns to shit. This is our one chance to right all the wrongs we've done in the past few days—to be better people."

Zorie watches me from the cracked mirror on the wall. A slow smile spreads across her lips. "You think taking a housekeeping job at some shitty hotel is gonna cleanse you of your sins? Is that what this new-found love of scrubbing toilets is all about?"

I pull my knees to my chest on top of the bed. The emerald comforter smells like Febreze, and I wonder how long it's been since it was actually washed. "God acts and doesn't talk," I say.

Zorie turns away from the mirror to look at me. She's put some of the complimentary lotion in her hair, making it look plastered to her head. "Is that what your daddy tells you?"

"It's what I know!" I snap. "Us coming here was God intervening. He wants to help put us on the right path."

"Oh, does he, now?" She folds her arms and cocks her head. "The path to righteousness. Zorie and Kayla. Reborn under his will. Is that what you mean?"

"Go ahead and make fun, but I'm taking the job." I lean back against the pillows and close my eyes, no longer caring that Zorie is here. Sleep comes immediately, and I welcome it. In my dreams, I see Dad and Mom holding hands and waving at me. I run toward them, arms outstretched, but the closer I get, the farther away they appear until I can't see their faces anymore. They transform into abstract shadows before my eyes, and I drop to my knees, screaming their names.

===

"Kayla! Wake up, girl!"

My eyes flutter open, and Zorie is standing over me, wearing a white belly-baring halter top and black skinny jeans. Somehow, during my nap, she managed to find makeup and fake eyelashes so long they curl and almost touch her eyebrows.

"Why are you dressed like Kylie Jenner?" I ask, rubbing my eyes.

"I went shopping. We're going out."

"I don't want to go out. I want to sleep."

Zorie points at the window. "It's already dark out. You've been asleep since we got here and screaming for your parents. You were so loud the room next door called the office to complain."

"I was dreaming about my parents," I say through a long yawn. "I miss them."

"Remember what we talked about? Letting go of our past?" Zorie sits down next to me and reaches for my hand. Acrylic nails with pointy tips have transformed her fingers into talons.

"You got your nails done? We're supposed to be saving money," I say.

"Don't worry. With our new jobs, we'll be set."

I frown at her. "What new jobs?"

"Duh." Zorie rolls her eyes. "Our housekeeping jobs. I've decided I'm in." She pauses as if to wait for applause. Maybe a standing ovation. I roll over onto my side instead. "Did you hear what I said? I'm going to work with you here."

"Congratulations," I mumble.

Zorie lets out a loud groan and hits me with a pillow. It hurts more than it's probably supposed to, but I remain perfectly still.

"I'm trying here, Kayla. Isn't that what you wanted?"

"What I want is for you to have some goddamn remorse instead of acting like this is some kind of vacation." I roll onto my back again and stare up at her, holding eye contact even though she can't bring herself to look at me. "I know we can't change the past, but we should at least *want* to."

Zorie chews her bottom lip and traces the floral pattern on the comforter with one of her talon nails. I wait for her to say something, an acknowledgment that she understands. But she doesn't say anything. She stands, checks her makeup in the mirror, and heads to the door.

And then she's gone.

CHAPTER TWENTY-FOUR

———

Starvation forces me to rifle through Zorie's bag in search of cash for the vending machine. She's been gone for over an hour now, and part of me thinks she won't be back this time. The other part of me is even a little hopeful she won't be back. I find the receipt for her new outfit on the bathroom counter: fifty-seven dollars. So much for saving money. We'll be broke before our first paychecks—that is, if we're hired at all. We have no IDs, and forget about using our Social Security numbers. There's no Rhonda or Hope attached to those numbers. Only Kayla and Zorie: two of America's most wanted.

I find six dollars and a crumpled piece of paper with the words *Aunt Ruby* and a telephone number with a 504 area code. Zorie's words echo in my ears: *"She knows what we did . . . She doesn't want to get involved."* I drum my nails against the counter. Growing up, Zorie always talked about her aunt Ruby like she was the only adult she ever trusted. I sit on the bed and smooth the paper against my knee. No way Zorie's beloved aunt would turn her back on her favorite niece now when she needs her the most. I lift the phone's receiver, dial 9 for an outside line, and then the number.

"Yes?" a voice answers on the second ring and sounds much too young to belong to a woman in her mid-seventies.

"Yes . . . um . . . hi . . . is this Miss Ruby?" I ask.

The other end of the phone goes silent, and then a new voice comes on, annoyed. "Hello? Ruby's been gone seven years. Who is this?"

I hang up and stare at the paper in my lap with a dead woman's name and phone number. Aunt Ruby died seven years ago? Wouldn't Zorie know this? Why had she suggested a dead woman as our New Orleans connection? I stand and start across the room to return the paper to Zorie's bag but stop when I hear a light knock on the door. I duck behind a wall and hold my breath. It can't be Zorie. She has a key. And she would announce herself. The knocking continues until, at last, I hear Olympia say my name, or at least the name I gave her.

I inch slowly to the door, still uncertain if I should open it. What if Olympia discovered who we are, and this is some kind of trap? Worse, what if she's being escorted by the Louisiana State Police?

"I brought food," she says. I can tell by the muffled sound of her voice that her lips are pressed against the door. "If you're in there, would you mind opening the door? This Crock-Pot is kind of heavy."

I unlock the dead bolt, unchain the lock, and open the door. Olympia stands in the doorway with a white Crock-Pot filled to its rim with thick red sauce.

"Gumbo," she says, following my stare. "Saw your light on and thought you and your friend might want some real New Orleans cooking."

My stomach rumbles.

"Unless you're busy?" Olympia says.

I consider sending her on her way, but then wonder if that might look suspicious. She already thinks I'm hiding something. Closing the door in her face with her oversize Crock-Pot of gumbo will only make me look guilty.

"I'm not busy at all. Please, come in." I move to the side, and she squeezes past me through the doorway.

"Hope you don't mind. I got your room number from the registry. You and your friend are the only new arrivals today, so I figured this was you." She sets the Crock-Pot on the desk next to the TV and looks around. "Where's your friend?"

I have no idea.

"Out," I say.

"She'll have plenty to dig into when she gets back. I hope the two of you aren't the kind of ladies who don't eat, because one thing my family's gonna do is feed you. You'll never go hungry around here." She removes the backpack she's carrying, takes out a baguette, and points it at me. "You know what? I bet you think I came by to give you some sales pitch or bribe you with gumbo to make you work for us."

"I don't think that at all," I say.

"Good." She hands me a bowl and half of the baguette and uses a ladle to scoop a huge helping of gumbo from the Crock-Pot. "My family says my gumbo is better than any of those expensive white-washed restaurants around here."

I lift the bowl to my face and inhale deeply. It smells like fire and burns my nostrils.

"Honestly, I'm just glad I met someone I can talk to. I never get to talk to anyone around here but my family, and all they want to talk about is business." Olympia scoops out another helping into her own bowl and licks a bell pepper from her thumb. "I mean, I have my boyfriend here, but all he wants to talk about is the hotel."

"Your boyfriend . . . works here?" Dread settles in my gut. I already know her next words.

"Lamont," she says. "He works the front desk. You probably saw him when you checked in—tall guy with dreads?"

I take a big bite of bread and force myself to chew, even though it feels like paste in my mouth. Of course Lamont is Olympia's boyfriend. Zorie wouldn't be Zorie unless she set her eyes on a taken man.

"I see he hooked y'all up," Olympia says. "Lamont is good at recognizing good people. You must've made an impression on him."

I swallow my hunk of bread to stop me from blurting out that Zorie's boobs made the impression.

Olympia slides off her flip-flops and sits on the bed with her bowl of gumbo, tucking her legs under her. I don't know why I didn't notice it before, but one side of her neck is tattooed with Lamont's name. I need to warn Zorie as soon as she comes back.

If she comes back.

"So what do you ladies have planned while you're in our great state? Because I'm happy to be your personal tour guide," Olympia says.

I tear off another piece of bread but don't eat it. My stomach begs me not to. "Maybe."

She's quiet for a beat, watching me over her spoonful of fire. "You're right. You guys should get settled first." She shoves the spoon inside her mouth, and a trickle of gumbo juice slides down her chin. "By the way, I told my grandmother what you did to Uncle Delphin."

Panic grips my insides. Fucking great. It won't be Zorie that gets us kicked out of here. It'll be me.

"Please don't feel bad," Olympia says. "Mama fixed him right up. Gigi, my grandmother, was very impressed by you. She thinks you're a hero. Uncle D has been bringing hookers here for years—and with the hookers come the cops. Not the best look for a family business. But I think you finally scared him straight. You're tough. I like it."

The smell of gumbo makes me nauseated, and I'm one inhale away from vomiting all over Olympia's family's orange-and-gold carpet.

"Where'd you learn to defend yourself like that anyway?"

Zorie.

Prison.

I wipe my mouth with the back of my hand. She's fishing again. The woman is relentless. What part of none of your business doesn't she understand?

"Around," I choke out, followed by a loud belch. I clap both hands over my mouth, and Olympia giggles.

"I'm doing it again, aren't I?" she laughs. "I swear, it's like a disease."

Olympia reaches for the remote between us and aims it at the TV. It flickers to life after a few seconds, and a news anchor in an unflattering peach blazer appears onscreen.

"The search is still going strong for the duo known as the Wedding Crasher Killers," she says in her anchor voice. The same panic that gripped my insides moments earlier returns for an encore, this time squeezing them and making it harder to breathe.

"We should turn this off. The news is so depressing," I say.

"Wait, I want to hear this. It's all anyone around here has been talking about. These women are savages."

I reach for the remote next to her, but she grabs it and turns up the volume. Any second now, she'll realize one half of the savage duo is sitting next to her. If Zorie were here, she'd probably already have Olympia tied, gagged, and stuffed in the closet.

"The two women were last seen in Chickasaw, Alabama," the anchor continues. "Police warn the community that they are considered armed and dangerous and should be approached with caution. The women reportedly go by the aliases—"

"The pool!" I blurt out. "We should go to the pool!"

Olympia turns to look at me, her face contorted in confusion and curiosity. "It's kind of late, and I don't usually go swimming after gumbo, but if you like it, I love it." She turns off the TV with the remote, and I exhale a long sigh of relief. "You got a suit?"

"Left it back home," I say quickly.

She looks me up and down, her eyebrows knitted together. "You're, what? Size eight? Same as me. I'll hook you up."

I nod, even though I'm a size ten.

Olympia slides off the bed and slips on her flip-flops. I do the same and scribble a note on a piece of Queen's Inn stationery for Zorie: "At the pool. Be back soon." I place it on the bed so she'll notice right away when she comes back.

If she comes back.

———

Swimming while pukey is never a good idea. Every stroke inside the overly chlorinated pool brings on a new wave of nausea, but I force myself to power through. Stopping means talking, and I'm barely treading on dry land as it is.

"I forgot how much I love swimming," I say, trying not to submerge my head. Chlorine and my newly dyed wild-cherry hair are not a good mix. I swim away from her to the deep end, but she follows. "I was on the swim team at my high school," I tell her. "Almost won a scholarship."

That's a lie. I didn't *almost* win a scholarship. I *did* win a scholarship. That was when Zorie suggested we take a year off to see the country. "Your scholarship isn't going anywhere," she'd told me. "They'll hold it for you. Please, Kayla? I need you."

And like a dummy, I'd agreed, because I needed her, too. I'd never been apart from Zorie, and as much as starting a new life in a new state excited me, it also terrified me. Would our friendship survive the distance? Would living apart make us realize how different we were?

But Zorie was wrong about my scholarship sticking around. The university retracted it after my burglary arrest three weeks later. Maybe if I hadn't listened to Zorie and her ridiculous plans to crisscross the country, I'd be an actual college graduate right now, with my own lucrative job and my own fiancé to sit with across the table from Gloria and her goddamn fried fish. And maybe Zorie wouldn't be this looming shadow consuming every part of my life. That's the thing about life, though. There's no rewind button. Only a feeling of being in perpetual slow motion, like treading water before you drown.

"What school was the scholarship to?" Olympia asks.

I pretend not to hear her and push off the wall, propelling myself to the other side and climbing onto the edge. Swimming used to be my safe space. My oasis. It emptied my brain and helped me focus. But tonight, even my thoughts feel as if they're drowning and in need of resuscitation.

"I never got into swimming until Lamont and I moved into the hotel. I'm bored most days, so this gives me something to do," Olympia says. She glides to the edge of the pool and stares up at me. "Sometimes I worry about Lamont being bored. I caught him once with a guest in the laundry room. Almost pulled out that bitch's eyeballs with my bare hands. Mama and Gigi had to pry me off her." She dips her head back into the water and smooths her hair. "I black out when it comes to him. It's like I can't control myself, you know what I mean?"

You mean like almost plucking out another woman's eyes? Can't say that I do.

"Guess I've never had the opportunity," I say. I came close to losing my mind once with a guy I dated for almost a year. We even talked about moving in together, until I happened to see a text on his phone from his grandmother asking if she could ride his face. Turns out, all the so-called "family" contacts in his phone—his mother, sister, aunt, cousin—were covers for his side chicks. Looking back, it was actually pretty clever. Who's gonna be tempted to open a text from your man's grandma? I broke up with him and then bashed his car windows with a hammer and carved the word *asshole* into the hood with a screwdriver. That night, I became a living, breathing country song.

"You ladies wanna party?"

We both turn to see a woman and a man watching us from behind the fence. They look to be fresh out of high school, baby-faced, with bodies that have not yet been exposed to stress or cellulite.

"Depends on the party favors!" Olympia says.

The woman holds up a baggie filled with white powder and smiles.

"Set me up!" Olympia says. Then, turning to me, she asks, "You in?"

I shake my head. Drugs have never really been my thing. Sure, I've smoked the occasional joint with Zorie, but I always end up with a migraine after. Not worth the high.

"I don't think so," I tell her.

Olympia watches me for a moment, like she's taking inventory of my words. Then, smiling, she says, "You're right. We both need to be clearheaded for your interview with Gigi in the morning. See? This is why I need someone like you around. You can keep me from making bad decisions."

"That's a lot of responsibility," I say.

"Don't get me started on responsibility. Sometimes I think that's why Gigi won't let me work in the office. She doesn't think I'm responsible enough."

Her grandmother doesn't think her coke-snorting, eyeball-yanking granddaughter is responsible enough? Shocker.

"Grandmas can be a hard sell," I say. Not that I'd know. Both sets of my grandparents died before I was born. I wonder what it would've been like to have had someone else there when we lost Mom. Maybe then Dad and I wouldn't have drifted so far apart.

"You're right about grandmas," Olympia says. "Gigi is definitely a hard sell."

The coke couple have stripped down to their undies and are wading toward us, with the woman waving the baggie over her head and giggling wildly. Up close, they aren't as baby-faced as I thought. In fact, their faces are hardened and worn, with the telltale signs of premature aging around their eyes and lips. Nose candy does a body good.

"Who's ready for a bump?" the man asks.

I don't answer, too busy thinking about the fact that Zorie may have met her psychotic match in the form of a Haitian housekeeper with a talent for plucking out the eyeballs of her boyfriend's side chicks with her bare hands. I grab one of the towels from the stack in a chair and wrap it around my body. My borrowed swimsuit cuts into my flesh, and I can't wait to peel it off. "I'm going to head back now. Kind of tired."

Olympia nods and smooths back her wet hair with both hands. "I think I have a few more laps in me. Oh, and don't worry about the Crock-Pot. I'll pick it up in the morning."

She disappears beneath the water, and I watch her swim to the other side, her form strong and effortless. For a second, I'm envious of her. What's it feel like to be carefree? I doubt that feeling will ever return to me. Not with Zorie lurking around anyway. I pull my towel tighter to my body and cross to the gate. An older white man dressed in khaki shorts and a New Orleans Saints jersey watches me from his balcony.

"Lookin' good out there!" he calls down to me. "Bet you'd look real good up here, too!"

I pick up my pace, crossing to my room through the thicket of shrubs that divides the pool from the parking lot. I unlock the door quickly and slip inside, twisting the dead bolt behind me and sliding the chain lock into place. It's pitch-black inside our coffin of a room, and the air is thick with the smell of gumbo. When I flick the light switch, my note is exactly where I left it on the bed. Zorie is still MIA. Have I done this? Pushed her out of my life for good? Relief mixes with panic as I consider a life where Zorie no longer exists. Maybe she was right about me not surviving without her. I'd be forced to return to Redwood—to Dad and Gloria—with my tail tucked between my legs.

I sink down onto the bed in my wet suit and replay some of my last words to her. *"What I want is for you to have some goddamn remorse."* I'd be lying if I said I wasn't at least a little relieved that Zorie left me. *If* she left me. Sure, we've never been apart, but that was the old Zorie. The fun, easygoing Zorie, not this dark version who so easily wields a gun. No, this Zorie I won't miss. This Zorie I'll happily sever ties with.

I stand and start to peel off my bathing suit, when what sounds like laughter coming from the bathroom chills my insides and renders me temporarily paralyzed. I reach for the closest thing to a weapon I can find, which turns out to be the phone. Delphin's warning reverberates inside my head: *"Bat Chen an, tann mèt li."* If you hurt someone, you'll get what's coming to you. Is this my comeuppance waiting for me behind the bathroom door? Or maybe it's Delphin with his own bottle of whiskey to smash on my head. Not like I don't deserve it. *Bat Chen an, tann mèt li.*

I hold the phone out in front of me with both hands and tiptoe to the bathroom door. "Zorie, I swear to God, if you're in there and trying to scare me, I will kill you!"

Quiet answers me.

I stand very still, straining to hear what I'm convinced is the sound of splashing water.

"Hello?"

More quiet.

I take another step and pause. "I called the police, and they'll be here any second!" Then, feeling my threat isn't convincing enough, I add, "I have a gun!"

Light filters into the room from beneath the door, and I stagger backward. "Stop or I'll shoot!" I shout.

The bathroom door creaks open, and I brace myself for the big reveal on the other side.

"I knew you were lying about the gun," Zorie says. She leans against the doorframe, gawking at me as if I'm a stranger who somehow found myself inside the wrong room. Soap suds drip down her arms and legs, and she covers herself with a towel that barely wraps around her body.

"Why didn't you say anything? I know you heard me come in," I say and lower the phone to my side.

"I was busy." Zorie pushes open the door with her foot, and I see Lamont in the jacuzzi behind her. He doesn't look surprised or embarrassed when he sees me. More like smug.

"How are you liking your room?" he asks.

I stare at him, trying to make sense of what I'm seeing. Lit tea candles line the countertop, and a bottle of tequila sits on top of the toilet seat between two half-empty plastic cups.

"You can't help yourself, can you?" I say, shifting my gaze to Zorie. "It hasn't even been a day."

"Babe, do you mind if we finish this later?" she says to Lamont. Then to me, she adds, "Me and my bestie need a moment."

"Not a problem. Just hit me up whenever." Lamont stands, his body wet and shiny like it's dipped in oil, with his very large and very erect penis on full display. "You know where to find me."

I turn my back to him, and he laughs. So does Zorie. I stay like that, with my face practically touching the wall, until I hear the door open and close. When I turn around, Zorie is on the bed, smoking a joint and watching me.

"Way to be a cockblocker," she says.

I want to tell her that two of me couldn't block that cock, but I'm too furious to say anything other than "You're fucking this up!"

"You're such a child," Zorie says in disgust. "Sometimes I feel like your goddamn babysitter. You wouldn't know the first thing about survival without me."

"What exactly does survival mean to you, Zorie? Killing? Fucking? Or both?"

She rolls her eyes and flicks the joint's ashes into her hand. "That man you saw is so into me he's letting us keep this room for the next three nights—free of charge. That's survival."

"That's prostitution," I hiss through clenched teeth.

"Not that it's any of your business, but there was no sex. We went to dinner and came back to enjoy the jacuzzi."

"Naked?"

Zorie shrugs. "I didn't have a swimsuit."

She says this like I don't know her; like I haven't seen Zorie use her body to get what she wants since she first hit puberty.

"That man who's so into you has a girlfriend," I say. "A violent one, too. You better back off now."

"Or what? She's gonna put some voodoo curse on me?" Zorie laughs at the ceiling. "I think we both know I can handle myself."

I imagine Olympia pouncing on Zorie and shoving her thumbs inside her eyeballs so deep they pop out like a jack-in-the-box, with the bloody veins still attached. I shiver at the image. "Her family owns this hotel, and we need jobs. Be careful is all."

Zorie waves a dismissive hand. "You worry too much."

"And you don't worry enough," I snap. "I know about Aunt Ruby. You never told her we were coming here, did you?"

She gives a little laugh, followed by a half shrug. "Kind of hard to call a dead person, but then I guess you already know that, don't you?"

Zorie stares at me until I look away, my pulse throbbing beneath my skin. "All you do is lie! I thought the two of you were close. I believed you when you said this would be a good plan. A safe one."

"And it is!" Zorie jumps to her feet so fast the towel slips down her body and onto the floor. "Since you're so goddamn nosy, Aunt Ruby stopped talking to me when I was a kid because of something that went down with my granny. I thought maybe if I told you we were going to New Orleans to stay with her, you would feel better about leaving Redwood with me. But then, in Alabama, you seemed so unhappy, so I lied and said Aunt Ruby didn't want us there. I figured this gave you the out you needed to go back to Redwood and your dad." She pauses and inhales deeply. "Look, I'm trying to fix this. I found us this hotel, didn't I? And Lamont says he can get me a job as a go-go dancer at Club Bliss downtown."

"Of course he did," I mumble.

"Bet I make more money in a day than you do in a week scrubbing toilets." She stomps across the room to the bathroom and slams the door.

I don't follow her. When Zorie gets this worked up, there's no reasoning with her. It's best to keep quiet until she cools off, or strokes out.

Whichever comes first.

I'm patient.

CHAPTER TWENTY-FIVE

———

WEDNESDAY

Zorie is still asleep when I leave for the interview. This time I don't leave a note. She doesn't need a reminder that I'm moving on without her. I give myself one final look over in the mirror by the door before slipping outside. My outfit isn't exactly job-interview chic. Thanks to my lack of wardrobe, I'm forced to wear a pair of Zorie's leggings, still damp from my sad attempt at washing them in the tub, and a sequined blouse courtesy of Ruthann's closet. I did manage to do my makeup with what I could find in Zorie's bag. When I look at myself, I can actually see part of the old me again. Tired, but presentable.

Olympia looks less impressed when she sees me. She stops me in the office doorway, her face twisted in disgust.

"You can't meet my grandmother dressed like . . . that," she says.

I look down, suddenly self-conscious. "We were robbed at the last place we stayed. They took our clothes."

Olympia gives me a sympathetic nod. "Come with me." She grabs my hand, and I follow her to the laundry room behind the office. The suffocating smell of bleach inside the small space makes my eyes water and my throat burn. "There's always a good selection to choose from in here," she tells me, rifling through a basket.

"Are these guests' clothes?"

"Former guests." She hands me a brown skirt and a white sleeve-less blouse that looks two sizes too big. "Go ahead. Change."

I frown. "Here?"

"No time for shyness, girl. Gigi hates tardiness, remember?"

I slip off my sequined shirt and yank the white blouse down over my head. It swallows me whole. "I look like a marshmallow."

"You look employable. Now put on the skirt."

I do as I'm instructed and stand in front of her, looking like a sad cupcake. Olympia looks even less impressed by this outfit than my sequined number.

"You need shoes," she says, snapping her fingers. She takes off to the opposite end of the laundry room and grabs a pair of black bal-lerina flats from a box on the floor. "Here. Black goes with everything, right?"

I nod and slip off my flip-flops. The ballerina flats are tight and con-stricting on my feet, and I can barely wiggle my toes. I start toward the mirror by the dryer to check out the final look, but Olympia blocks me.

"No time." She grabs my hand and drags me behind her back to the office, where a black woman with fiery red locs is waiting behind the desk.

"You're late," she says, eyeing us both over the rims of her tur-quoise glasses.

"It's my fault, Gigi. Fashion emergency," Olympia explains. "Hope, this is my grandmother, Lenora Jean. And, Gigi, this is Hope. She's here for the housekeeping job."

Lenora looks me up and down. "Thought you said there were two of them."

"Just me," I say quickly. "My friend isn't feeling well this morning."

She sighs, looking agitated. "Very well. Follow me. We'll do the interview in the back."

I glance at Olympia, and she gives me two thumbs-up. "You've got this, Hope!"

Lenora is already halfway down the narrow hallway, and I hurry to catch up. The office is cramped with a twin mattress on the floor, two mismatched vinyl chairs, and a card table that I assume also functions as a desk.

"Please, have a seat," Lenora says, nodding at the chairs.

I sit down and fold my hands in my lap. There's no window, and the low ceiling makes the space feel confined and claustrophobic.

"I really appreciate this opportunity, Miss Lenora."

"It's Mrs. Jean." Lenora repositions one of the chairs on the other side of the table and sits. "You have no résumé?"

Shit. It's been years since I've been interviewed for a job and even longer since I've written a résumé. "I'm sorry. I can write one really fast," I offer.

She steeples her fingers under her chin and smiles. "That won't be necessary."

I follow her eyes to my left leg bouncing up and down. I cross my right leg over it and clasp my hands on my knee. "I can assure you I'm very experienced. I've worked at the same hotel for seven years."

Lenora takes out a notepad and a pen. "Same position?" she asks.

I wring my hands together, trying to decide whether her question is an insult. "I was actually up for a promotion but, um, had to leave unexpectedly."

Lenora is quiet for a moment as her pen moves quickly across her notepad. Probably writing "Liar" under my name in all caps. Then, pointing the pen at me, she asks, "And you're homeless?"

The question surprises me, even though it's true. I am homeless. And broke. I give a sheepish nod and mumble, "For now."

"I see." She nods slowly and rubs a finger under her chin as if considering my words. "Olympia likes you, so I'll make you a deal."

"I'm sorry . . . a deal?" I didn't come to this interview for a deal. I came for a job.

"I'll give you room and board at the hotel in exchange for work," she says.

I frown. "As in . . . I work for free?"

At this, Lenora laughs, and I see she's missing a front tooth like her granddaughter. Dental insurance is clearly not an employee benefit. "Baby, it ain't free if you have a roof over your head. I'll give you a weekly stipend for food." She leans forward on her elbows. "That's the deal. Take it or leave it. And for someone like yourself, I'd take it."

Something in her tone makes me think her words are a sort of threat. I rub my arms, suddenly very cold.

"Thank you," I say. "That's very generous."

Lenora smiles, looking pleased with herself. "We get a lot of strays around here, riffraff and such. This hotel used to be a classy place. Celebrities and politicians were always coming through. We were in all the tourist magazines." She pauses to gauge my reaction. I don't have one because it sounds like bullshit. "We were one of the first black-owned hotels in this county, but this new generation doesn't care about history or class. All you young people care about these days is Instagram. I told Olympia not to bring me any more strays, and she brought me you."

"I'm not a—"

She holds her hand up to stop me. "Everyone's a stray until they can confirm ownership."

I frown. "I don't understand."

"Identification, baby—Social Security card, license, you know, make sure you are who you say you are."

My stomach drops down to my borrowed ballerina flats. Identification. I might as well turn myself in now at the New Orleans Police Department.

"That won't be a problem, will it?" Lenora asks.

I shake my head. "Of course not."

"Good. Then you can start as soon as I receive your identification. Welcome to the team . . . Hope." She extends her hand to me, and I shake it. Her hold is tight and firm, but her touch leaves me feeling even colder than before.

═══

"I think I made a deal with the devil," I tell Zorie when I get back to our room.

She rolls over onto her back and rubs her eyes. "What are you even talking about?"

"I got the housekeeping job, but she's not paying me."

Zorie props herself up on her elbows and cocks her head at me. "Then how the hell is it a job? And what the hell are you wearing?"

I absently smooth the front of my oversize skirt. "I needed something presentable for my interview."

"And you chose that?"

I roll my eyes. "My clothes aren't the point, Zorie." I plop down on the bed and lean back against the pillow. The room is stifling despite the low whir of the air conditioner. I imagine coming home to this room for the next few months, the dank smell of it, matted carpet, and dismal gray color of the walls. "I was offered housing here at the hotel on the one condition that I work here. For free."

"That's some bullshit," Zorie scoffs. She kicks off the sheets and grabs her jeans from the growing pile at the foot of the bed. "Sounds like these people need to be reminded that slavery is over," she says, tugging on her jeans.

"What are you going to do? March into the office and tell them all to go fuck themselves? And then what? We're out on the streets again, trying to stretch what little money we have left after your little makeover?"

"Someone needs to tell them what's up," she says. Then, cutting her eyes at me, she adds, "You certainly didn't."

"Because none of it matters," I groan. "She asked for identification, and obviously that's not going to happen, so we're back to square one. Desperate." I close my eyes, feeling the familiar stabs of an enormous migraine on my skull. "The only job left that doesn't ask you to prove who you say you are is prostitution, and I'm not sure I have the stamina for that."

"You can work with me at Club Bliss. We'll do, like, a girl-on-girl routine. Men love that shit. We'll make so much money!" Zorie goes to high-five me, but I just sit there staring at her. "What? You don't like my idea? You worried about your body? Don't worry, you'll look hot with the right clothes."

"I want to do honest work, Zorie."

"Go-go dancing isn't honest work?" She uses her fingers to put air quotes around the word *honest*.

"You know what I mean," I say.

"No, I don't think I do, because what it sounds like is you think you're better than me."

I groan at the ceiling. Here we go again. It's the argument that never ends. "I just want to be a better person. No more lying or scheming. We've been given a second chance. This is our one shot to prove we can live an honest life from this moment on."

Zorie watches me, her face pinched. "You really want this bullshit housekeeping job?"

I shrug. "I think it'll be good for me. Like a penance or something, you know?"

She nods even though I know she doesn't have a clue what the word *penance* means.

"I think I might be able to help," Zorie says after a beat. She slips on a T-shirt that's several sizes too big, and I know immediately it belongs to Lamont. The cheater couldn't even be bothered to collect the evidence before leaving our room last night?

"Whatever you're about to say better not involve firearms," I say.

"Very funny." She rolls her eyes at me and sits on the edge of the bed. "I was talking to Lamont about our situation last night—"

"Zorie!" I squeal. "What part of 'wanted by the police' don't you get?"

"Will you please shut up and listen?" She sucks her teeth. "You get so worked up over the smallest things."

I check my mental list of the things I get *so worked up* over: murder, robbery, theft, the police—oh, and prison. Got it.

"Anyway, Lamont knows someone who can hook us up with new IDs, Social Security numbers, and even birth certificates," Zorie says, her eyes widening. "Girl! We can literally be reborn!"

She pauses and waits for my reaction to match hers. It doesn't, mostly because I'm pissed. "What reason did you give him for why we need new identities?"

"That's just it! He didn't ask." She says this with a kind of pride I don't understand. And then she has the nerve to smile.

"He didn't ask because he knows we're in deep shit. Innocent people don't need new identities. You have to start thinking, Zorie. You have to be smart."

She jumps up and points a finger at me, so close to my eye I think she might blind me. "I am smart. I'm a goddamn genius," she growls. "I've gotten us this far, haven't I? You should be thanking me, not insulting me."

I don't say anything, too busy avoiding having my eyes gouged out by the pointy acrylic nail aimed at my right pupil.

"Do you want the hookup or not? I told Lamont I'd let him know something by this afternoon."

My hand twitches. I'd do anything for a cigarette right about now. As much as I hate to accept help from a cheating asshole who's brazen enough to mess around with my roommate inside the same space as his girl's Crock-Pot, I need ID to work.

"How much is this going to cost?" I ask with a long sigh.

Zorie shrugs. "Nothing. Like I said, Lamont wants to help."

CHAPTER TWENTY-SIX

Apparently, Lamont's version of "nothing" means three thousand dollars.

"We don't have that kind of money," I tell him as he stretches out across our bed. In the past twenty-four hours, the guy has really made himself at home inside our room.

"What if I told you there was three thousand dollars at this hotel ready for the taking?" Lamont asks.

"I'd wonder why you didn't take it yourself." I push myself up on the desk next to the Crock-Pot, thinking he might recognize it, but he doesn't even glance in my direction. Lamont's bloodshot eyes remain on the ceiling, and Zorie's eyes remain on him.

"You think I could pull something off like that with my big black ass sneaking into guests' rooms?" He laughs, and so does Zorie.

"Well, you've certainly pulled it off sneaking into ours," I say.

Zorie shoots me a murderous look. "What Hope means is, how do we get our hands on this money?"

"This guest leaves his room every day from eleven to one. He keeps the cash inside a shoebox in the closet," Lamont says. "I'll give you a key, you go in, take the cash, and boom—new IDs by the end of the day."

I massage my temples, feeling the pressure between my brows increasing. "That easy, huh?"

"It can be."

Before I can tell him how ridiculous this all sounds, Zorie jumps to her feet and claps her hands. "We're in!"

"Hold on. You two are for real?" I slide off the desk and move in front of Lamont. "How do we know this isn't a setup? And how do you know this guest even has three thousand dollars?"

"Because I know." Lamont sits up on the bed and looks at me for the first time since he's been in our room. He looks older than I realized, at least in his forties, judging by that receding hairline. I wonder how old Olympia is. "Listen, I'm just trying to hook you ladies up. I got the hookup when I moved here, so now I'm paying it forward. Mrs. Jean is real careful about hiring people with shady pasts to work here. That's why most of us here are family. Last maintenance dude she hired was hiding cameras in guests' rooms and selling that shit online. She ain't trying to get shut down by the cops. They're already watching this place as it is because of that son of hers and his love of hookers. You want a new life? This is how it's done."

I look at Zorie again. She's practically foaming at the mouth to say yes. "If we do this, you can guarantee we'll have new identities—no questions asked?"

Lamont flashes a goofy grin that's not as convincing as I'm sure he thinks it is. "No doubt."

It all sounds so ridiculous: sneak into a mystery guest's room, rifle through their things, and find the mysterious shoebox full of cash. I press my lips together to stop the giggle forming in my throat.

"You in?" Lamont asks.

I hold his gaze and smile. "No."

He exchanges looks with Zorie as if waiting for her to interpret my denial. I say it again, louder, so there's no mistaking the single syllable.

"What do you mean no? This is easy cash," Zorie says.

"It's a setup," I say. "We go into that room, he calls the police."

Lamont leans forward on his elbows, cracking his ashy knuckles. "Now why would I do that?"

"Why *wouldn't* you do that?" I ask him.

"Guess that's what I get for trying to hook two sistas up." He stands and smooths the front of his wrinkled blue button-down shirt. "I'll be at the front desk if y'all need me."

"You're so sexy right now." Zorie leans in to kiss him, but he moves before her lips can land. I smile as she attempts to play off the moment by dabbing gloss on her pursed lips.

"You're a fool, you know," she says after Lamont leaves. "That money could've been an answer to our prayers."

"You honestly think if there was a shoebox with thousands of dollars in a guest's room that he wouldn't have taken it by now?"

"You heard him. It isn't safe for a black man to get caught around here." She slides the tube of lip gloss into her front pocket and folds her arms.

"Because he's so careful about keeping a low profile, right?" I laugh.

Seconds later, my smirk is replaced by shock as I'm shoved against the wall. Zorie stands within inches of me, her breath hot on my face.

"You can't stand not having control, even if it means saving your ass," she says through a smirk. "What's the matter? Still pissed I don't want to scrub toilets with you at this shitty place?"

I shove her away, and she staggers back against the bed. "Don't you ever put your hands on me like that again."

"Look who's finally growing some balls!" She laughs. "Proud of you!"

I grab the leftover crumpled dollar bills from Zorie's shopping spree off the nightstand and head for the door. If I don't get a cigarette soon, I might smother my best friend with her crop top.

"Where are you going, Kayla?"

I don't answer, and she doesn't follow me outside. There's a gas station on the other side of the hotel, and I pray they'll sell me a pack of Marlboros without ID. Lord knows the stress of the past few days has aged me at least a decade. I walk quickly through the maze of housekeeping carts parked outside room doors and am almost to the office when Olympia pops her head out of room 101.

"Someone's in a hurry this morning," she says.

I hold up the wad of cash in my hand. "Cigarette run."

"Don't waste your money. I got you." She reaches inside her housekeeping apron and removes a pack of Kools. "Here. Take it."

"I can't take your pack."

"I have plenty in my room." She takes my hand and places the pack in it. "My gift to you for impressing Gigi this morning. She really likes you, says you have good energy."

I give a nervous laugh. "Her detector must be broken."

"Not Gigi. She's good at reading people. Must be in our blood 'cause I knew right away you were good people." She smiles, and I'm once again greeted by her missing tooth. We stand there awkwardly, me with my charity cigarettes and Olympia with her methy grin, until the room door next to her opens. Two barefoot women stagger out, one holding what looks like a tangled hair extension and the other with an eyelash fringe stuck to her cheek. They stop briefly to look us up and down before laughing and stumbling away.

"Never a dull moment at the Queen's Inn," Olympia says with a shrug.

I watch the women make their way across the parking lot to an awaiting red Suburban and try to imagine a life here, surrounded by prostitution and adultery in a city known for debauchery. I'd never be free from the constant threat of the police sniffing around this place. Not to mention Zorie and her unpredictable ways. Once Olympia learns the truth about Zorie and Lamont, we'll be lucky if we're thrown out of here with at least one eye left between us. If I am ever truly going to be free and start over, I have to do it without Zorie.

"I should go," I say to Olympia. "Thanks for the cigarettes."

"No problem, and hey—don't forget to stop by the office with your ID. Gigi says you can start as soon as she clears you."

"On my way now," I say and turn in the direction of the office.

I don't realize I'm running until I reach the office doors and push my way inside. Lamont eyes me curiously from his clipboard as I struggle to catch my breath.

"Checking out?" he asks.

"I changed my mind," I say.

He lowers his clipboard. "About?"

"Don't play dumb." I lean across the desk as sweat drips down the sides of my face and pools in my cleavage. "I want in."

——

It takes Lamont at least fifteen minutes to walk me through the details of the plan and even longer for us to not get caught inside Lenora's office. He stands in the doorway, leaning out every few minutes to monitor the front desk.

"Room 227," he whispers, even though we're alone. "Get in and get out and then meet me in my room—239. I'll take you to meet the guy for your ID." He leans out the door again, then faces me. "You sure you don't want your girl to know? Y'all seem tight, like you don't keep secrets from each other."

"Positive. This stays between us."

He nods, and I force myself to believe it's genuine. Lamont slips me the key and points at the clock above the Coke machine. It's barely eleven thirty. "Better move your ass," he warns.

I stand and tuck the key inside my shirt for safekeeping before squeezing past him in the doorway. And then I spot her, watching us from the window.

Zorie.

"Go through the back. It's quicker," Lamont says, and nods at the door behind him.

I glance at the door and then back at Zorie, but she's gone. Or maybe it's my own paranoia creating images in my brain that look like Zorie. I push open the back door and sprint down the steps leading to a grassy area that separates two rows of rooms. A woman sunbathing on a yellow lawn chair eyes me curiously over her sunglasses, and I slow my pace to look less suspicious. Room 227 is the last room on the right, with a DO NOT DISTURB sign prominently displayed on the door handle. I'm thankful for the distance between me and the sunbather, but it doesn't stop her from watching me. She rolls onto her stomach with her face pointed in my direction.

"Housekeeping!" I yell loud enough for her to hear. She yawns, stretches, and rolls onto her back again, clearly no longer interested.

I knock three times, the way I always did at the Chamberlain, and then use my key card to open the door. The room is cluttered with old pizza boxes and overflowing garbage bags of clothes. The air smells stale. Mildewed. I pull my blouse up over my nose and feel along the wall for a light switch, knocking over a Crock-Pot in the process. Olympia is super generous with her family's gumbo. I return the Crock-Pot to its place next to the TV and try not to scream when a giant cockroach crawls out from inside. Surely three thousand dollars is enough to pay for better, roach-free accommodations.

Lamont said I'd find the cash inside a shoebox in the closet, but when I look in the closet, it's stacked with at least twenty shoeboxes. Even without a clock to keep track of the time, I feel it slipping away. I hurry to the closet, grab as many boxes as my arms will hold, and dump them onto the floor. Surprisingly, most of the boxes are full of shoes—men's shoes—but some are full of old receipts and napkins with names like Cheri and Britney, with little hearts dotting the i's. Who is this guy?

One by one, I open and close the boxes until I'm down to the last three. Two pairs of snakeskin Oxfords later, I reach the box I'm looking for. Carefully hidden beneath glossy Polaroids of half-naked women—seriously, who is this guy?—I find stacks of twenty-, fifty-, and hundred-dollar bills held together with thick rubber bands. There's a hell of a lot more than three thousand dollars stuffed inside this box. I may not need this shitty job or the fake ID after all. I dump them out and stuff as many of the bills as possible inside my bra and the waistband of my skirt. When I get down to the last four stacks, I search the room for a bag to stuff them in and find a brown paper bag with two half pints of gin inside. I remove one bottle, keep the other, and slip the cash inside. Walking out of this room with stacks of cash stuck to my sweat-drenched body is something I'm not entirely sure I can pull off. I stand and maneuver my legs in a way that feels more robotic than human. One of the cash stacks slips down into my underwear, and I struggle to move it away from the crotch vicinity.

After a ridiculous amount of wiggling and adjusting, I push the last of the boxes back inside the closet and make my way to the door, but it opens before I reach it. My bag of money and gin slips from my hand, and I jump back, startled, as Delphin stands in the doorway, squinting at me from underneath the Ace bandage that wraps around his forehead.

"This is your room?" I ask dumbly. The Crock-Pot, the Polaroids of half-naked women—of course it's Delphin's room, you stupid idiot. That cheating, receding-hairline asshole set me up.

"You lost?" Delphin asks.

I can smell the whiskey, like it's seeping out of his pores. "Olympia sent me in here to, uh, get something. I'm the new housekeeper."

"Is that right?" Delphin steps inside and closes the door behind him. "You find what you were looking for?"

"Yes, and now I'm leaving." I try to move past him, but he twists the dead bolt, and slides the chain lock into place.

"What were you looking for?" he asks.

"I . . . I can't remember."

Delphin smiles and staggers forward, steadying himself against the wall. "Can't remember," he repeats in a mocking, high-pitched voice. He leans in, and I see the two ugly pink scars stretched across his left cheek, like someone carved their initials into the side of his face. Olympia wasn't lying when she said he'd had a lot worse done to his face than a whiskey bottle to the temple.

"*Bat Chen an, tann mèt li!*" Delphin hisses at me.

The hairs on my neck and arms stand on end. "I'm sorry," I hear myself croak.

He smiles, smug and satisfied. I expect him to move away from the door after my weak apology, but he doesn't. I glance around the room for a potential weapon in case I'm forced to defend myself and settle on the Crock-Pot lid. Delphin looks down, following my gaze, and shoves the lid away from me, limiting my weapon options to the TV remote.

"You gonna hit me again?" he spits through clenched teeth. His expression changes, and he almost looks animalistic. He bares his teeth as if he's about to rip my flesh from the bone and then lunges at me, arms outstretched and fingers curled like hooks.

I stumble backward against the wall, and one of the cash stacks slips from my waistband and onto the floor. Delphin stops to stare at the cash between us, confusion and fury crashing into each other on his face.

"You stealing from me?"

All I can do is stare at him, which isn't a good enough answer. He reaches out and yanks me forward by the collar of my blouse, twisting the thin material around his fingers until it tightens around my throat. My breath hitches, but I try not to panic. No one knows I'm here except Lamont, who obviously planned this entire scenario. If Delphin kills me, he could easily dispose of my body, maybe even feed me to the swamp, and no one would be the wiser. I'd vanish. Disappear, like I never existed.

I think of Zorie and what she would do in this situation. Delphin's weakness is women, and Zorie can make even the most disgusting man feel like the most desired. I smile up at Delphin, then, licking my lips, say, "You're so sexy right now!"

My words surprise him almost more than they surprise me. Delphin loosens his grip around my collar but doesn't let go.

"What did you say to me?" he asks.

I clear my throat and channel my inner seductress. My inner Zorie. "I said you're sexy, baby. I've thought that since the moment I met you."

This time, he lets go. "Is that right?" He stares at me, his eyes wide and curious.

"You're so strong and powerful. I love that in a man. It's a total turn-on," I say, and glance behind him at the door. Even if I did my best Olympic sprint, I'll never make it past him.

"A turn-on, huh? Prove it," Delphin says. His hands move down my body and stop at my waist. Shit. Does he feel the money stuffed in my waistband? Is this the moment he takes his revenge? His *bat Chen an, tann mèt li!*

"Slow down, baby. We have time," I tell him. "Get on the bed. I want to give you a show."

Delphin narrows his eyes at me. He doesn't believe me, so I use the only thing I can think of to do the convincing for me: my mouth. I lean in and kiss him hard on the lips, trying desperately to keep his tongue from poking its way inside my mouth.

"Get on the bed," I whisper against his lips.

He smiles and kisses me again before backing away and positioning himself on the edge of the bed. I sway my hips to a silent Drake song, running my hands up and down my body while Delphin watches through half-open, glassy eyes. I turn my back to him, stick out my ass, and literally twerk for my life, then turn to face him with what I hope is a seductive and not a constipated smile.

"Lay back, baby, and close your eyes," I whisper.

Delphin flashes that familiar look of uncertainty, and I kiss him again. There's not enough mouthwash in the world to get rid of the sour taste of his mouth or the slobbery residue his lips leave behind. He leans back on the bed, grinning like a fool, and tucks his arms behind his head. I continue my awkward dance, backing up slowly and moving my hands up my thighs. Delphin licks his lips and reaches for something in the nightstand. A condom. Fuck. He really thinks this sad seduction of mine is leading somewhere.

"Slow down, boo. I'm not going anywhere," I tell him.

He ignores me and fumbles with his belt, tugging and pulling it into submission. If I don't get out of this room, Delphin is going to use that condom on me, and then a bath of boiling water will never make me clean again.

"Come here," he growls.

I turn to twerk again but hear the mattress springs creak and then Delphin's feet shuffling across the carpet. I immediately smell the sickening odor of him, like rotting meat.

"Enough! Take off your clothes, or I'll take them off for you," he says.

I look down, taking inventory of the dresser next to me: a comb, hair pomade, cocoa butter, a pair of tweezers, and a hand mirror.

I grab the mirror.

It happens lightning fast. The mirror strikes his left eye, and he staggers backward into a wall. But I'm not finished. I strike him again and again until the mirror cracks in my hand. One of the jagged pieces of glass lodges itself inside Delphin's cheek. His face will never recover from the scars I've created on it in the past twenty-four hours. He tilts back his head, allowing the blood to drip into his hair and down his neck. His face is as red and raw as hamburger meat. I rush past him to the door, struggling to unhook the chain lock, but even with his injuries, Delphin's reflexes are swift. He places a bloody hand on top of mine, squeezing until I whimper, and throws me back against the wall.

"The devil always collects!" he shouts.

The shattered mirror is at his feet, and I'm weaponless in this corner of the room. I start to scream, and he smashes my mouth with his hand. I inhale blood.

"You think you can steal from old Delphin?" he slurs.

If his bloody hand wasn't covering my mouth right now, I'd remind him that I *did* steal from old Delphin, and I almost got away with it. I bite down hard on his hand, and he slaps me, but his effort is clumsy, and he loses his balance and falls back on top of the bed and rolls to the floor.

"Asshole!" I shout, and kick him hard in the balls. At first, he doesn't move, and I start to second-guess my aim. But then Delphin hunches over, red-faced and crying. Bull's-eye!

"You bitch!" he shouts. He attempts to stand, but once again, his efforts are unsuccessful, and he collapses on top of the bed.

I'm at the door and miraculously manage to unchain the lock and run outside. The humidity stings my eyes, and I blink in the brightness of the afternoon. Sunbathing lady has left her perch on the lone patch of grass, and I feel a pang of disappointment. I'm alone. I run down the strip, terrified to look behind me and see Delphin and his crushed balls chasing me. In every horror movie in existence, the monster always manages to stay alive, even with a machete to the head. My legs move at full speed, pumping hard and fast, in the direction of the laundry room. I'm close enough to smell the bleach. And then an arm slides around my waist and yanks me into darkness.

CHAPTER TWENTY-SEVEN

———

Lights flicker on, and Lamont stands in front of me, serious and unsmiling.

"What the hell happened in there?" he asks. His tone is accusatory, and I find myself recoiling in the chair I've been forced to sit in, like a child being reprimanded by a disappointed parent.

"Like you don't know," I say, my voice cracking. "Delphin caught me inside his room, but I guess you meant for that to happen, didn't you? He could have seriously hurt me!"

Lamont lets out a frustrated groan and sinks down onto the bed, with his face in his hands. "Did you at least get the money?"

I frown. "What?"

He cuts his eyes at me and through clenched teeth asks, "Did you or did you not get the money?"

Clearly Lamont is incapable of a sympathetic response. I shift my weight in the chair, feeling the rough edges of the cash scratch my skin. "No," I say. "I couldn't get the money."

Lamont stands and paces in front of me. It's then that I notice the emptiness of the room. Everything is in its place, with no luggage or evidence that anyone has been inside the room until this moment. Even the vacuum lines on the carpet are perfect. I've cleaned enough rooms to know this one is unoccupied.

"I have to go," I say.

Lamont stops pacing and turns to look at me. "No."

It was such a simple and sure response that I almost laugh. I check his expression for any hint of a smile, but there isn't one. He stares back at me with a cold expression that makes every hair on my body stand at full attention. This is why he set me up. Not as some Haitian proverb about revenge, but so I could steal his girlfriend's uncle's money and bring it to him.

I start to stand, and he forces me back down into the chair.

"I knew you were the smart one," he says, smiling. "That friend of yours ain't got no head for business, but you know what's up."

"Rhonda will be looking for me."

Lamont laughs. "Rhonda . . . right. You don't have to worry about Rhonda. I took care of her."

I swallow hard. Is that an admission of something? Did Lamont just confess to hurting Zorie? "You . . . took care of her?"

He makes a gyrating motion with his hips. "Don't take much for her."

I wonder how he left Zorie. Probably fucked her into a stupor and now she's passed out in our room, tangled in their sex sheets. She won't come for me. No one will. For all I know, once Delphin's testicles recover, he'll be at the door ready to finish what he started.

"I changed my mind about the IDs, okay?" I tell Lamont.

"Changed your mind?" He strokes his goatee, watching me. An amused smile plays on his lips. "The thing is, I think you're lying."

"I'm not lying. I don't want the IDs."

Lamont slaps the heel of his hand to his forehead, laughing. "Not about the goddamn IDs! I think you're lying about the money! The question is, what are we going to do about it?"

I stare down at my hands, Delphin's blood staining my palms and caked beneath my fingernails. I'm tired of fighting. I've fought Zorie, Delphin, Frankie, hell, even Charles. At this point, surrendering feels like a relief.

"Fine," I say with a long sigh. "You want it. Take it."

Lamont nods, looking pleased. "Go on, then."

I stand and lift my blouse, exposing my waistband. Lamont waits, his unruly brows knitted in concentration. The bills stick to my skin, and I carefully peel them off.

"This what you want?" I ask. Then, yanking off the rubber band, I toss the bills at him. Lamont shouts every version of *bitch* at me, *cunt* being his favorite, and drops to his knees to collect the bills. I take this brief distraction as my last opportunity to get out of there and sprint to the door. It's time to leave the Queen's Inn and her royal family behind. Lamont is on me within seconds, grabbing at my clothes and pulling me back, but I don't let go of the doorknob. I unlock the dead bolt and yank it open only to see Olympia standing on the other side with her housekeeping cart.

"Hope? Lamont? What the hell is going on?" she shouts.

Lamont releases me, and I fall into Olympia's arms, hugging her neck so tightly I swear I hear her bones crack.

"One of the guests complained about loud voices coming from this room, but this room isn't registered to anyone," Olympia says. She pulls away from my hold, looking me over. "You hurt?"

"No," I say. "I just want to get out of here."

Olympia closes the door behind her and takes my hand. "Gigi is in the laundry room. If she sees the three of us coming out of this room, there will be hell to pay. We'll give it a few minutes and then leave, one at a time." Her gaze shifts to Lamont. "In the meantime, you want to tell me what the fuck you were doing in here with her?"

Lamont gives a sheepish grin and shoves his hands into the pockets of his jeans. "We were just having a conversation. Your girl needed help with a situation, and I was trying to hook her up. That's it."

If Olympia believes him, I can't tell. She turns to me and places her hands on my shoulders, her eyes serious. "From now on, Hope, if there's a situation you need help with, I want you to come to me, understand?"

I nod and let her guide me to the bed, where we both sit. She wraps both arms around me, cocooning me in warmth, and I let her. Lamont leans against the desk across from us, arms folded. He won't hurt me with Olympia here. I'm safe.

"I'm sorry about all this, Hope," Olympia says. She rubs my arms as if trying to make me warm. "Lamont is always doing the most. He knows how I feel about him being alone with female guests. I can't stand messiness, and he was so sloppy." She makes a tsk-tsk sound with her tongue. "Truth is, he should've tied you up first."

I jerk away from her, thinking I heard her wrong, and she shoves me back onto the bed, pressing down hard on my shoulders with the heels of her hands. For such a petite girl, she's freakishly strong.

"Where's the money, Hope?" she shouts, spit flying from her lips.

My heart stops. I'm dead. I must be. My God, she's in on it, too. The gumbo, the late-night swim, the job interview—all perfectly orchestrated to lure me into this fake friendship.

"Oh, come on, Hope, or whatever your name is," Olympia says, smiling. "Lamont told me you went through with it. Gotta say, though, I didn't think the rumors were true. Mama said Uncle D came into some money years ago because of some factory accident that messed up his face, said he kept it in a shoebox to pay his whores. And you actually found it. Well done, Hope."

I try to wiggle away from her, but her knee presses into my stomach. Lamont moves from his post on the desk and joins his psychotic girlfriend on the bed. With one swift motion, he rips the telephone cord from the wall and wraps it around my wrists, squeezing tighter and tighter until I beg him to stop.

"That's enough, Lamont," Olympia says. She reaches out to stroke my cheek, and I turn away from her touch. "I get it. You're mad at me. Right now, you're probably thinking, if I knew about my uncle's secret cash stash, why didn't I just take it myself? Remember what I said about beating the dog and waiting for its master? That's not just a Haitian proverb. We live by that mantra—it's our religion—and stealing from family is the worst karma you can get. But I can steal from you." Olympia climbs off the bed, and Lamont takes her place on top of me. He lifts my blouse and snatches the cash stuffed inside my waistband and bra.

"The thing is, Hope, you and your friend were already tainted," Olympia continues. "I felt your darkness as soon as we crossed paths in that parking lot. You're evil."

Lamont hands Olympia the cash, and she licks her fingers to count the bills.

"This all of it, Hope?" she asks.

"Yes," I say, my throat tightening.

They stand shoulder to shoulder, staring down at me as I do my best not to cry. I refuse to look weak, even if these are my last few moments alive.

"You're lying," Olympia says. "This is barely five hundred dollars. Where's the rest of it?"

"That's all there is!" I shout.

She grabs the waistband of my skirt and starts to yank it down, but I kick her hard in the groin, and she falls back against Lamont. Probably not the smartest move to make when my hands are tied together with a phone cord. Olympia regains her balance and limps toward me. I brace myself for whatever retribution she's about to deliver. I don't have to wait long. She slaps me hard across the face, and I immediately taste blood.

"Hold her feet," she says to Lamont.

I thrash my legs wildly, but he still manages to wrangle them together long enough to tie my ankles with his ripped T-shirt. Olympia hits me again, but this time she doesn't use her hand. Something hard strikes me across the forehead. A sharp pain runs down the sides of my face and neck. My vision blurs, and I'm dizzy.

"Take off her clothes. She must be hiding it on her body," Olympia says.

I try to roll over, but my body refuses to cooperate. As a final act of desperation, I blurt out, "My friend will call the police!"

I wait for them to untie me, to reconsider, but they laugh instead.

"Is that supposed to be a serious threat? Do you know how many times the police are here because of Uncle D? And yet here we are, still standing." Olympia drums her dirty fingernails against the wide gold buckle of a leather belt now sprayed with thick, wet, crimson streaks. "Look at you with your shitty hair and your fake-ass name. You really think we didn't know who you and your friend were the second you checked in? You have a car seat in your back seat with no kid, neither of you have IDs, and you get all nervous anytime I ask about your past. You know who acts like that? Criminals on the run. The way I see it, you've got a hell of a lot more to lose than me and Lamont."

Hot tears blur my vision, and I blink them away. "Fuck you!"

"Poor girl." Olympia crouches in front of me, her face contorted into an ugly snarl. "You beat the dog, and it turns out me and Lamont are the masters."

These are the last words I remember before darkness comes.

CHAPTER TWENTY-EIGHT

———

When I open my eyes, the room is dark except for the sliver of light from the window. A thick metallic smell hangs in the air. Like an old penny mixed with bleach. My forehead is wet, and there's a deep, pulsing pain around my wrists and ankles. It's quiet, but I'm not alone. I hear movement on the other side of the room. I roll onto my back, and a wet rag slides off my forehead.

"Please help me," I whisper.

"Who do you think untied you?" a voice answers me. I want to cry when I hear it. I'd recognize that mangled, rusty drawl anywhere.

"Zorie?"

"The one and only." I try to sit up but am immediately dizzy. "Careful now. You were knocked out for a long time," she says.

I search for her in the dark and find her arm, slick with sweat. "You're really here."

"Of course. Where else would I be?"

I can't see her face, but I know she's smiling. I smile, too. "How did you find me?"

"Every housekeeper knows you never leave your master key on your cart." She places a cold, wet cloth in my hand. "For your head."

"Thanks." I watch her shadow cross the room, squinting to make out her features, and though I can't be certain of it, I think she's naked.

"Want to hear something funny? When Lamont didn't come back to the room, I thought the two of you were getting it in. I looked all over this motel for the two of you, ready to call you out, and then I found you here . . . like this."

"I definitely was not getting it in with Lamont, but I was for sure getting my ass kicked," I say. "Speaking of my ass kickers, where are they?" A new rush of panic floods my body, and I look around quickly, thinking Olympia and Lamont are watching us from the shadows. My head still throbs from the crack of the belt buckle across my skull. I won't survive a second attack.

Zorie ignores the question, and I feel her hands tug at my arms, pulling me forward. "We should get out of here. We don't have much time."

A flash of light from outside illuminates Zorie's body, and I realize she *is* naked and that it wasn't sweat I felt on her arm. It's blood. She's covered in it.

"What did you do, Zorie?"

"We need to go. We've been in this room too long." Her hands tighten around my wrists, and she pulls harder, but I plant my feet on the carpet and hold my stance.

"What did you do?" I ask again through my teeth.

"Will you please move your ass and interrogate me later?" I jerk away from her and feel my way across the bed for the nightstand, finding the lamp and tugging hard on the string. It flickers on, and Zorie stands in front of me, trembling, her body glazed with blood as if she were painted with it. I scan her, head to toe, in search of a wound or some obvious injury, but find none. The blood doesn't belong to her.

"I didn't know what else to do, Kayla, so I tried to clean up." Zorie points to the housekeeping cart by the door, with Olympia's name written in slanted black letters across its side. Blood-soaked towels are piled on top of it, along with Ruthann's bloody *World's Best Grandma* T-shirt and Zorie's jeans. "But there was so much of it."

"We're gonna need more towels, Zorie," I say, but she isn't listening to me. Her eyes remained fixed on the cart.

"There was so much blood," she says again. "And you know what Leslie Grace says about bloodstains."

I nod slowly. "They're a bitch to get out."

It used to be a funny joke between us—Leslie Grace's never-ending pursuit of the perfect stain remover. But neither of us laugh this time. I force myself to stand on unsteady legs and take a tentative step forward. Zorie doesn't move or try to stop me. There's no point. We both know whose blood covers her, and whose DNA the police will scrape from the floor and walls when they discover the bodies.

"Zorie? Towels?"

She blinks at me. "I . . . think I used them all."

I follow the trail of blood to the bathroom door. Zorie's breath hitches. They are here.

"It wasn't my fault," she says quickly.

I touch the door handle, wait for her to stop me. She doesn't. The door doesn't open all the way. Something is jammed against it. I push harder with my shoulder and nudge the door open another inch. The metallic smell is stronger here. It swells in my nostrils and I choke back a gag. I spot a manicured foot with lavender-polished toes in a pool of blood. Beside it, a hand still clutching a fistful of bloody cash.

"Where is it?" I ask.

"Where's what?"

My throat feels tight and constricted. I might throw up. "The weapon, Zorie. Where is it?"

"I don't know."

"Zorie, if the police find it—"

"I didn't do anything!" she yells.

I stare at her. She's clearly in shock. "We need to get you cleaned up, and then we'll get out of here," I tell Zorie. I grab a sheet from the bed and drape it around her. "We're going to be okay. Don't worry." I take the corners of the sheet and swipe at her bloodstained cheeks, then her chest, where blood has pooled in her cleavage. "Did anyone see you come in here?"

Zorie shakes her head.

"Good. That buys us some time." I reach behind her to adjust the curtains, illuminating more of the room—more of us—in the late-afternoon sun. "I need to get you some clean clothes from our room. Turn off the lights and don't answer the door. Got it?"

"When I saw you on the bed, tied up and bleeding, I tried to wake you, but you wouldn't move. I thought you were . . ." Her voice breaks into sobs.

I guide her to the bed and crouch in front of her, placing both my hands on top of hers. "It's okay. I'm fine. You saved my life. I'll never forget that."

She sniffles and wipes her nose with the sheet. "You say that like you're not coming back."

"You know I am." I stand and start to walk away, but Zorie's hand grabs mine.

"You're coming back?" she asks.

"Of course." I squeeze her hand and smile. "You think you can get rid of me that easily?"

Zorie gives a weak smile in return and lets go of my hand. She doesn't believe me.

I don't believe me.

This is the way I will remember her, my best friend, trembling and naked with the blood of strangers drying on her skin.

"Hey," I say, studying her face. "Best friend's honor."

These three simple words are like magic. Zorie smiles, her eyes wide and hopeful. "You know you're my ride or die, right?"

I nod. "Forever."

I wipe more blood from her fingers, then her palm, where the rusty-orange color has embedded itself in the creases. I'd read some-where once that killing is a primal instinct. The urge is in all of us, some people are just better at suppressing it. Any of us could be a killer—the cashier at the grocery store, the nail tech, the barista at the coffee shop.

Your best friend.

These are my thoughts as I scrub Zorie's skin until it's raw—that my best friend gave in to her primal urge to kill, and that she could do it again.

"Are you mad, Kayla? Please don't be mad," Zorie says, watching me.

"I'm not mad." My voice is calm. Nurturing. It's my mother's voice, the one she used on me when I was terrified. "Clean yourself up, and I'll be right back, okay?"

"Okay," she says. "Be careful."

"Always."

I walk quickly to the door, thinking this is where our journey together ends. This is where I leave her—naked and blood-soaked in a rented room with two dead bodies bleeding out on the bathroom floor. It's the ending she deserves. Maybe even the ending I deserve. Maybe they'll think Zorie killed me, too, and fed my body to the swamp, my innards digesting in the belly of a gator.

"Kayla?"

I stop, but don't turn around.

"I love you," she says.

I nod, but keep my eyes on the door. If I look at her for even a second, I'll lose my nerve. I reach for the doorknob, hating how my bloody hand sticks to the metal. How much more blood will stain my hands if I continue this road trip to hell with Zorie? How many more bodies will we be forced to sacrifice in the name of survival? I take a deep breath and pull open the door.

This is where I leave my best friend, and where I find me.

CHAPTER TWENTY-NINE

—

The humidity is suffocating and makes running nearly impossible. But I don't stop. I can't. My blouse is soaked through and sticks to my skin. By the time I reach our room, I've already peeled it off, along with my bra. I wash off in the sink, clean my head wound, and dress in Zorie's crop top and jean shorts. If this were a movie, I'd scrub all evidence of us from the room, but there's no time for that. Miraculously I managed to hide a hundred bucks from Delphin's stash inside the bottom of each shoe. Between the room, Zorie's shopping trip, and what's left of our dwindling funds, that puts me at almost five hundred dollars. It's more than enough to get me out of here. I grab our bags and the car keys, give the room one last look, and slip the DO NOT DISTURB sign over the doorknob.

"Running from the police?" a voice says behind me, making me jump. It's the jersey-wearing, balcony-spying creep from last night at the pool. He grins at me from the bottom step of the stairs and takes a long drag from his cigar. "Didn't mean to scare you, darlin'. That's what my ex used to say if it looked like I was in a hurry, must be running from the police." He laughs as if it's even funnier the second time he says it.

"Have a good night," I say in my most polite voice.

He stands like he's about to follow me, but flicks the ashes of his cigar onto the breezeway between us.

"You're not traveling alone, are you?" he asks.

"I'll be fine." I take off toward the parking lot, struggling to keep both bags balanced in my arms. When Zorie's bag topples over, I'm surprised to see that the man from the breezeway is right there to help me collect the scattered items from the ground.

"You don't have to do that." The words come out more annoyed than appreciative, and I mean them to.

"I don't mind." He hands me Zorie's espadrilles, makeup bag, and hunting knife, which I slip into my waistband for safekeeping, then stands there as if he expects applause or maybe a curtsy.

"Guess I should hit the road." I step backward, and he steps forward, the toes of his New Balances inching closer.

"Care to join me for a nightcap before you do?" he asks.

"I don't think so."

"I knew you were a heartbreaker," he says with a smile. "The beautiful ones always are."

I ignore him and start across the parking lot, but he doesn't leave my side, matching my pace at an impressive speed. He lights a fresh cigar, tells me his name is Don and that he's separated from his wife. When he asks my name, I pretend I don't hear him. It's not a complete lie. I haven't heard much of what he's told me—I'm too busy watching the shadows for a tall, naked black woman covered in blood.

But I find Delphin instead.

He takes one disjointed step after another across the parking lot, stumbling into vehicles as guests evade him. One bikini-clad woman tries unsuccessfully to force her keys into the lock of a PT Cruiser, dropping them several times before finally opening the door and slipping inside. Delphin grabs at her, yanking the towel from her waist as the door slams closed in front of him. He leans against the car, pressing the towel against his wounded face, and lets out a loud, gurgled groan.

"What the hell is his deal?" Don asks, squinting.

Terror pulses through me as I imagine all the scenarios of a Delphin versus Kayla rematch. Not only will Delphin torture me if he manages to get his hands on me again—he will kill me. I don't want to go back to my room in case Delphin comes looking for me.

"On second thought, a nightcap sounds great," I say to Don.

"Well now, that's the spirit," he says with a wink.

He turns on the heels of his sneakers, and I walk the same path back to the hotel. We arrive at the bottom of the staircase at the same time, and I follow him up the steps as a prickly sensation runs down my arms and lifts the tiny hairs on the back of my neck. Something feels off. Strange. Like we aren't alone on the staircase. Like someone is watching me. I look behind me, glancing in every direction. I think of Zorie, safely tucked away inside the unregistered room of horrors. Delphin won't find her there, or the mutilated bodies of his niece and her boyfriend. Not yet.

"You coming, sweetheart?" Don asks.

I climb the stairs, taking two at a time, and pause at the top for Don to catch up. He's breathless when he reaches me and leans forward with his hands on his knees, hacking and spitting. I try not to stare.

"Damn cigars," he chokes out. "I really should quit."

I stare out at the parking lot again, anxious to get inside and away from the eyes I feel on me. Don unlocks his room and holds the door open. It smells like I imagine it would: cigars and sweat. A pair of flip-flops with black soles is next to his bed, along with something that makes my blood run cold—a shiny badge identifying him as Officer 8230 of the New Orleans Police Department.

"You're a police officer?" I ask, staring at the badge on his night-stand.

"Don't worry. I'm off duty, and I'm very discreet. I'll hide it if it makes you uncomfortable. I want you to feel as relaxed as possible." He reaches past me for the badge and tucks it inside the drawer.

"Now you see it, now you don't." Don lets out a low gurgling sound, like he's choking, but then I realize he's laughing and hacking up phlegm at the same time.

Fuck. Of all the perverts to meet tonight, I had to meet the one off-duty dirty cop.

"Oh wow. I didn't realize the time. I should probably get on the road before it gets too dark out," I say. I'd rather risk outside with Delphin than inside this room with Officer Don. At least Delphin might have lost too much blood by now to chase me. "Thanks for the invite."

Don slides between me and the door, smiling. "Shoot, I've done gone and made you all nervous, haven't I? One drink. It'll calm your nerves."

He places two plastic cups on the table by the window and gives each a generous pour of whiskey. "Here you are, my dear," he says, handing me a cup. "Cheers to new friends."

I down mine in one gulp and wince as it sets fire to my throat.

"Good, huh?" Don says.

He pours himself another cup and leans against the door, watching me over the rim. I'm not sure what to do with myself, so I sit on the edge of the bed and will myself to stay calm. It's clear he's not letting me leave. I am a stray he intends to keep.

"You know what we need? Music." Don opens his laptop on the table, and seconds later, the smooth sounds of Marvin Gaye float out from his speakers. Any other time, I'd find something like this hilarious, but watching Don and his big white belly sway back and forth off beat is just sad. "If you don't mind me saying so, making love to a beautiful black woman like yourself has always been a fantasy of mine."

A nervous laugh escapes me. "Is that right?"

"Listen, I want you to know I'm very clean, but if you want me to wear a rubber, I will."

I stop laughing. "Excuse me?"

"Oh, honey, this little innocent act you've got going on is real cute and all, but let's get this show on the road, shall we? Just popped one of my magic blue pills. I'm good for the next four hours."

"I'm not sure what you thought would happen here, but I'm not sleeping with you," I say, standing. My balance is off thanks to Don's whiskey, and I steady myself against the air-conditioning unit. The cool air feels good on my skin. Sobering, even. "Thank you for the drink, Don, but I have somewhere I need to be."

He frowns at me like he can't comprehend my words. "You're leaving? What's the matter, darlin'? I thought we were having a good time. Isn't that why you came up here?"

"I came up here for a drink."

"Looks to me like you came up here to be a dick tease." Don slams his laptop shut, and whatever version of him I'd met on the staircase immediately disappears. "I should arrest you."

"For being a dick tease?" I say and immediately regret it.

Don's face turns two shades of crimson, and he charges at me like an angry bull. I grab the hunting knife from my waistband and hold it out in front of me, stopping him in his tracks.

"Stay where you are," I shout. "I've had about enough of you men with your entitled cocks."

"I thought we were having fun here," Don says.

He takes a step forward, and I stab at the air between us. "I'm not kidding. I will cut off your dick and throw it over the balcony like it's Mardi Gras."

Don takes a step back, hands raised, palms forward. "Listen, it's late, we've been drinking, let's call it a night and go our separate ways."

"No," I say.

He lifts his eyebrows. "No?"

I think of the cash stuffed inside my shoes and the Buick out front. I need more resources if I'm going to put enough distance between myself and Zorie. "Give me your wallet, your phone, and your car keys."

"Don't you think that rate is a little steep? How 'bout I give you fifty like the others?" Don says.

"Something wrong with your hearing, Officer Don? I said give me your wallet, your phone, and your car keys. Now."

"Relax, baby. It's all yours. Whatever you want." He places his wallet, keys, and phone on the table and slides them to me. A thick gold band occupies the third finger of his left hand. I almost laugh at how predictable he is.

"Now take off your clothes."

Don looks confused, then smiles. "No offense, sweetheart, but my hard-on has left the building."

I take a step forward, feeling bold. "Do I look like I'm joking right now?"

His smile fades and is replaced by an annoyed expression. "Now wait just a minute here. I've played your little game, haven't I? You have my money, my keys, my phone—let's call it even."

"I can't do that."

"Can't or won't?"

"Both."

Don looks at the knife between us, then back at my face. I can almost see his brain calculating his next move. Should he reach for my knife? Call my bluff? His right hand twitches, and I tighten my grip on the knife's thick handle. Finally, after what feels like a minutes-long standoff, Don gives a defeated sigh and slides off his cargo shorts.

"You know, your generation of women has a lot to learn about life. You want to be strong and independent, but look at you—still got your hand out."

I roll my eyes. "Less talking, more stripping."

He pulls his jersey over his head and peels off his socks. "I raised two children, put them both through college, have a good job with a pension. I work hard, and sure, every now and then, I enjoy the company of a beautiful lady who knows how to keep her mouth shut and doesn't ask a bunch of questions. Guess this is my punishment for being a red-blooded man, is that it?"

Good God, I've had enough of Don's monologue. If I roll my eyes any harder, I'll taste them. "Get in the closet," I tell him.

He scratches at the white tuft of hair on his chest. "You really want to keep going with this?" Don asks, eyebrows raised. "I'd think long and hard right now, sweetheart. I have your DNA . . . your fingerprints. I'll find out who you are, hunt you down like a dog, and lock you up so fast you'll wish you'd just given me a goddamn blow job."

For a brief moment, I genuinely consider his words while my brain takes inventory of everything I've come in contact with since entering this room. Even if I wiped it down with a gallon of bleach, the room downstairs is saturated with evidence of our existence, and Don saw me leave it. I'm too far gone to have a change of heart now.

"In the closet. Now."

Don's smug expression twists into an angry scowl. Clearly Officer Don doesn't like taking orders, especially from a woman who doesn't know how to keep her mouth shut. He charges at me in his tighty-whities, arms outstretched, and I stab his hand. The knife pierces through his skin like a well-done steak. He stands there, eyes wide and uncertain, as blood fills his palm and drips down his forearm.

"You fucking bitch!" he growls.

"Next time, it'll be your heart. Now get in the closet."

This time, he doesn't hesitate. Don walks backward, cradling his wounded hand with his eyes still fixed on my knife.

"You're making a big mistake, sweetheart. If I were you, right now would be a good time to stop, turn around, and walk out that door, because unless you kill me, it's all over for you."

"I know," I say. "That's why I can't stop."

Don gives a defeated sigh and feels behind him for the closet door handle. "Last chance, sweetheart," he says.

For some reason, his words make me laugh. If Officer Don only knew how many "last chances" I've had, and yet, every single one brought me here, to this moment, with him. My last good place to stop. I think about Zorie's words to me the other night, how I love the chaos as much as she does. Maybe I do. Maybe I crave it. Need it. In a strange way, chaos is where I find control.

Like now.

"Get in," I say, smiling. And so there's no mistaking my command, I stab the air between us. The knife's tip grazes Don's swollen belly, and tiny crimson beads bubble to the surface. I try not to look apologetic as he staggers back inside the closet, with one hand pressed against his stomach and the other bleeding like a bad period.

"When I find you—" Don begins, but I slam the door before he can finish and slide the desk chair under the handle.

He wastes no time before jiggling the handle and thrusting his body against the door. The chair doesn't budge, but I add an extra precaution and move the desk in front of the closet. He'll kill me if he gets free, and he'll get away with it thanks to his shiny NOPD badge, which I slip into my bag along with some of his clothes. I leave his socks. Not touching those.

I cross the bags over each shoulder and step outside onto the balcony. The sun has disappeared behind thick gray clouds, making the once-vibrant colors of the Queen's Inn look dull and muted. I search the parking lot for any sign of Delphin or Zorie, but find only a black woman hurrying across the lot in her bare feet to a waiting red Mustang. If Delphin and Zorie are out there, they've blended into the shadows.

Something moves below me, reminding me that I'm not as alone as I think I am. I lean over the balcony and see our room door open. The same gurgled groan I heard earlier floats out from inside. Shit. Delphin.

I tiptoe to the other side of the balcony and consider my options. If I'm careful, I can climb down without being seen or busting open my head on the pavement below. Maybe. Hopefully. I adjust the bags and climb over the railing. It's rusted and wobbly, making me second-guess my decision, but I can't wait it out inside Don's room for Delphin to find me. No doubt he's found a master key and will search every single room until he finds me. He will have his *bat Chen an, tann mèt li,* and he will enjoy every second of it.

Trembling from head to toe, I try to find my footing on the splintered column and carefully make my way down, but slip and fall into the shrubs, banging my elbow on the edge of the concrete patio below. I lie there for a moment, wanting to scream. But I don't. I cover my mouth with my hands and swallow down the pain until I feel it burning deep inside my belly. This is where I leave it, where it boils and simmers. There's no time for pain.

I clamber to my feet, adjust my bags, and sprint toward the parking lot, ducking between cars and behind large shrubs until I reach the row in front of the office. I peer around the bumper of a minivan and see Lenora making her way to the laundry room with a clipboard. She stops mid-step, like she feels me watching her, and turns to peer out at the parking lot.

I start to hyperventilate and lean against the bumper to catch my breath. Get it together, Kayla. If I can just get out of this parking lot, I'll be okay. I have Don's money, his car, and no more Zorie messes to clean up or deranged uncles chasing me. I can start over, for real this time. I take a deep breath and pull myself to my feet. Then, aiming Don's key fob at the rows of cars in front of me, I press it. A metallic-blue Ford pickup lights up, and I run to it. The inside of the truck is littered with crumpled fast-food bags, Red Bull cans, and condom wrappers. The things Don must do inside this truck. I bristle and start the engine.

"You can do this, Kayla. You've got this," I say, and shift gears.

Lenora's attention has returned to her clipboard, and I wonder how long it will be before she discovers her granddaughter's butchered remains. Will she blame me and Zorie? Her strays? I press the accelerator and start to move forward.

CHAPTER THIRTY

I park inside an apartment complex on the outskirts of the city, thinking that if the bodies or Don have been discovered, the police will be headed for the interstate and back roads, not the River's Edge Housing Projects. My heart pounds painfully inside my chest. This must be what it feels like to have a heart attack. If I survive my heart exploding, starvation will surely finish me off. Maybe I should've called Officer Don's bluff and let him arrest me. At least I'd have a bed and three meals a day.

Beneath the mountain of McDonald's bags, I find half of a melted Snickers bar and shove it into my mouth, barely chewing. How am I going to do this? Live the rest of my life constantly looking over my shoulder and surviving on what little scraps I find? I lean forward and press my fingertips to my temples. Somewhere, Zorie is thinking the same thoughts. Have I done the right thing by abandoning her? She saved my life, and I left her behind with no money or means to escape. The least I could've done was leave the keys to the Buick in the room. Tears prick my eyes, and I blink them away.

I lean across the console, pop open the glove compartment, and feel around for any spare change Officer Don may be hiding, but find only a flashlight and a handful of receipts. I take out the flashlight and reach inside my bag for Don's wallet, aiming the light at the Velcro closure. Officer Donald Costello, Jr., is sixty-two years old, is married to a woman who wears pearls, and has two of the ugliest kids I've ever seen. He also carries only a Bass Pro Shops store credit card, a debit card, and thirty-two dollars in cash. Great. What am I supposed to do with thirty-two dollars? I open his phone, surprised to find it doesn't require a PIN, and scroll through his endless photos of black tits. At least he wasn't lying when he said he fantasizes about black women. The evidence is right there on his phone. I power it off and toss it out the window.

"I am so fucked," I groan.

As if in response, something rattles in the truck bed, making the blood freeze in my veins. I turn slowly and peer through the back window. Like the inside, the truck bed is full of fast-food bags and Red Bull cans, which explains the rattling. I twist back around, feeling stupid, and sink down into the leather seat. I need a plan. The police were obviously tipped off that Zorie and I are in the area, and by morning, New Orleans will be crawling with officers, the FBI, reporters—hell, TikTokers. I need to put some distance between me and the bayou. More rattling from the truck bed makes me jump. I look behind me, and the tailgate is down. Was it down before? I slide open the window to get a better view. The bed is covered with a blue tarp and streaked with something dark and wet.

Getting out to investigate would be stupid at this point, but common sense doesn't stop me from climbing out with my flashlight and walking to the back of the truck. I tug at the tarp, and it slides off the bed, revealing what looks like the remains of a dead animal. I let out a small scream and jump back inside the truck.

"We're going to need more than this to survive," Zorie says and holds up Don's wallet.

She's wearing a robe with the Queen's Inn emblem embroidered on the front. I aim the flashlight at her face, still caked with dried blood that settles into the deep grooves around her mouth when she smiles. She wants me to be shocked by her presence. I'm not. I expected her to be here, waiting for me. Waiting for us. KD+ZA.

"I told you not to leave the room," I say.

"You were taking so long . . . I got scared something happened to you," Zorie says. "And then I thought I saw a police car, so I jumped in the first truck I could find."

I make a face. "With that dead thing in the back?"

"Beggars can't be choosers," she says with a shrug. "I was planning to wait it out and come look for you, but then the truck started moving. Imagine my surprise when I saw it was you driving. We found each other again!" Zorie splays her arms and embraces me in a tight hold. She smells like decay. Death. "Hold up, I just thought of something." She pushes me away from her and studies my face. "I was coming to look for you, but you took off in this truck . . . without me."

It's pointless to lie. I did leave without her. But you can never leave Zorie. Pieces of her always manage to stay with you, no matter how hard you try to forget.

"Why would you do that, Kayla?" Her eyes fill with tears, and she sniffles. "You're my best friend. My sister."

"There was no time," I tell her. "I had to get out of there. I had no choice."

"Bullshit," she spat. "There's always a choice between what you do and what you don't do." She holds up the wallet again and flicks it with her thumb. "You clearly made a choice when it came to Donald Costello. What did you do, Kayla? Kill him? Or maybe you fucked him to get what you wanted?"

I stare straight ahead, clenching the steering wheel so tightly my fingers throb. "I got us both out of there, didn't I?"

Zorie grabs my arm, and I flinch. "You got *yourself* out of there." She leaves her hand there, and I imagine it around the hunting knife's handle, gripping it as she cut into Olympia's and Lamont's flesh.

"Fine. You want the truth? I did leave you because I can't do this anymore." I take a deep breath, then exhale hard. "I'm not like you. I'm not a killer."

"Neither am I," she says. "You know what your problem is, Kayla? You hide your darkness because you want people to accept you, but I know the real Kayla Davenport. The one who used to talk about poisoning her stepmom's coffee or pushing her stepsister down the basement stairs." She moves her hand down my forearm to mine and intertwines her fingers with mine. "That's the difference between you and me. I accept you for who you are, but you've never accepted me. Not fully."

"Those were the words of a dumb kid who was angry at the world for taking her mom. You know I'd never actually hurt Gloria or Candace."

"And yet you almost hurt Candace by rear-ending her with your car."

I lean back against the headrest and close my eyes. So much of my life has been about pretending: pretending to be happy while Mom was dying, pretending to be happy about Candace's engagement, and, even now, pretending to be happy to see my best friend next to me. What if hiding the dark, resentful part of me was easier than admitting I was more like Zorie than the Kayla I wanted people to see?

"Remember, you and me? We're the same."

Every decision I made as a kid, an adolescent, and an adult has been influenced by Zorie, or maybe I wanted it to feel like her influence because admitting they were my own decisions was too terrifying.

"I just want to feel safe again," I say.

"I know. Me, too. I'll always keep us safe." Zorie pulls out a wrinkled map. "I found it on that housekeeper's cart. It's our way to feel safe again."

I squint at the map. Mexico is circled in what I can only assume is dried blood.

"I figure we can stay overnight in Houston and drive to Mexico from there," she says, watching me.

"This is a joke, right?" I shift in my seat to look at her. Zorie holds the flashlight between us, and even though she's smiling, her eyes are sad. "Mexico? Really?"

She leans in close to me. The smell of her is nauseating. "Think about it, Kayla. If we stay in America, we'll always be looking over our shoulder for the police. But if we move to Mexico, we're free. We can do whatever we want."

I wait for her to laugh at the ridiculousness of her words, but she doesn't. Zorie holds my gaze, her expression sincere. "Do you know how far away Mexico is? How are we supposed to pay for gas? For food? Where would we even stay in Mexico? Oh, and let's not forget that neither of us speaks Spanish." I wave a dismissive hand. "Not happening."

"So what's your plan, then? Live in this truck? I'm sure it will make a lovely home." She picks up one of the condom wrappers from the floorboard and flicks it at my forehead. "Come on, Kayla. We can do this. We've already done it. Look at us, we're still here. Surviving."

"But I don't want to survive! I want to live!" I rub my eyes with the heels of my hands, feeling the weight of exhaustion roll over me. Last week, the only thing I had to worry about was making it through another one of Gloria's Thursday-night dinners, and now I'm being pursued by every police department across the deltas. I inhale deeply and consider my next words. "What if we turned ourselves in and . . . ended it all?"

Zorie shakes her head. "You must have a concussion from earlier, because you're talking out of your mind right now."

"I'm serious, Zo."

"So am I." Tears slide down her cheeks, but she doesn't bother to wipe them away. They drip down her chin and onto her robe in tiny pink droplets. "The only thing in my life I can remember that's never changed is you being there. Life doesn't make sense without you in it,

Kayla, and if we go to prison, it's over. All of it. I'll never see you again."

"You're really serious, aren't you?"

Zorie nods. "We're ghosts now. Back home, we don't exist—not like before. Look, I know you were scared when you left me earlier, but you don't have to be scared anymore. You and me, we're forever—and that's on God."

A black SUV drives past us slowly, its sound system making the truck's windows vibrate. Zorie and I duck down in our seats, and I reach for her hand. This is our life now, hiding in shadows, existing only inside the newest transformation of ourselves. I imagine our lives back in Redwood being picked apart and analyzed by people who claimed to know us and strangers who decided we were deranged and disturbed the moment our photos graced their screens. Dad will blame himself for the destruction of our family. Gloria will blame me. And they'll both be right.

"Aren't you tired of running?" I ask.

"What I'm tired of is the two of us constantly running toward the life we deserve and never reaching it," Zorie says. "I tried it your way. I stayed out of trouble . . . I held down a job—and for what? A paycheck that barely covered our rent? At least crashing weddings, we had a chance to have something, even if it didn't belong to us." She smooths out the map against her knee and runs a finger along the jagged line that divides Texas and Mexico. "Remember the other day when I said crossing into Louisiana would be like going into the future? Well, when we cross the border into Mexico, it will be like being reborn. Mexico is our chance to start over, Kayla. For real this time."

I lean against the door and try to imagine a reborn Kayla Davenport: a woman with her entire future in front of her and no criminal past or burden of guilt and shame holding her back. Hers is a life of opportunity, of new experiences and pure joy. This Kayla Davenport laughs more than she cries and smiles because her life demands it. I want that Kayla Davenport more than anything.

"How would we even do this?" I ask. "We barely have enough money to make it to the next city."

"Actually . . ." Zorie reaches into her robe pocket and takes out a handful of crumpled bills. "I found a few hundred in that housekeeper's laundry bag, and don't worry, we'll find a way to make more. We always do," she says, and places the bills on the console between us. "This will be the start of our brand-new lives—our rebirth. We're gonna be okay. I promise."

I nod, not because I believe her, but because I *want* to believe her.

"Okay," I say. "Let's go to Mexico."

Zorie's eyes widen, and she claps a hand over her mouth. Fat tears slide down her cheeks, and she sobs deeply. "This will be good for us. You'll see," she says between sobs.

Lightning flashes across the sky, followed by a clap of thunder that sets off a car alarm. I stick my head out the window and inhale. The air smells like rain. "If we're doing this, we should get on the road before it starts pouring," I say.

Zorie nods and fastens her seatbelt. "We're gonna be okay," she says again, but there's an uncertainty in her voice this time, even though she's smiling.

I start the truck as another flash of lightning illuminates the sky.

A storm is coming.

=

It takes us six hours, two driver changes, four Red Bulls, and three bathroom stops before we finally arrive at the Bull's-Eye Hotel and Casino in Houston. Zorie backs into a parking space between a Tesla and a minivan and cuts the engine. I search the dark parking lot for police cars. It's like a reflex now with every stop, trying to spot the cops before they spot us. We'd been careful on our journey, taking only the back roads and stopping at gas stations that were probably the scene of many crimes. And now we are here, in a nearly full parking lot, just asking to be discovered.

"We can't stay here, Zorie." I stare up at the hotel's marquee with the flashing neon bull's-eye next to a sign that reads NIGHTLY RATES STARTING AT $119. "It's too expensive."

"Didn't I tell you we'd find a way to make money? This is it." Zorie waves her arms out in front of her and waits for me to be impressed. I'm not.

"Let me get this straight. Not only do you want us to stay at a hotel we can't afford, but you also want us to gamble away our money?"

She shrugs. "You gotta spend money to make money." Then, with a wink, she adds, "Think of it as an investment."

I roll my eyes. So far, our trip has cost us almost two hundred bucks in gas and food, leaving us with just over six hundred dollars. At this rate, we'll be hitchhiking to Mexico. If we make it there at all.

"You know how good I am at blackjack," Zorie says. "Last time I played online, I doubled my money in, like, fifteen minutes. Let me do my thing, and I know I can do it again. I'll double—hell, triple— our money."

As much as I hate the idea of gambling what little funds we have left, I know we'll never make it to Mexico, or even survive once we get there, if we don't get more cash. Plus, I can't spend another second in the truck with Zorie smelling like she's rotting from the inside.

"Okay. Fine. But one hundred dollars is our limit in the casino. When our luck runs out, we leave. Deal?" I hold out my hand for Zorie to shake. This time, it's Zorie who rolls her eyes, but she shakes my hand anyway.

"Deal, bitch," she says with a smile.

I book a room with two double beds under Donald Costello's name and pay in cash. I tell the front-desk clerk I'm his wife, show her his ID, then slip her an extra fifty to let us check in early. She doesn't question it and hands me two keys for the sixth floor. I stop at the gift shop and buy some Bull's-Eye Hotel and Casino merch for us to change into and then slip Zorie in through the side doors. The total is almost one hundred fifty dollars for a few T-shirts, shorts, and two pairs of flip-flops with the silhouette of a bull on the soles. Isaiah should really consider a price markup on his supply. I briefly consider googling his name at the hotel's business center, wondering if he remained loyal to Zorie, but decide against it. Isaiah is the past, and Zorie and I are only looking forward from now on. I don't even know his last name.

We take the stairs to avoid drawing extra attention to the bloody woman in the dirty bathrobe and find our room at the end of a long mirrored hallway.

"Now *this* is a hotel room," Zorie says. She twirls around the room before diving onto the bed and spreading out. "I think I'll order chocolate chip pancakes with extra whipped cream, like your dad used to make whenever I slept over."

"Um, maybe you should take a shower first before you get your funk all over the covers," I say.

"Right." She gets back up and continues her twirls toward the bathroom, but stops mid-twirl at the doorway. "You'll still be here when I come out . . . right?"

I make a cross over my chest. "Best friend's honor."

"You said that last time."

I smile. "This time I mean it."

And I do.

CHAPTER THIRTY-ONE

THURSDAY

Zorie is gone when I wake up from last night's pancake coma. She left a note on the TV: "Casino downstairs." If anyone can stretch our meager funds from here all the way to Mexico, Zorie can. I stuff our belongings into a laundry bag, yank on my twenty-five-dollar shorts, twenty-dollar T-shirt, and fifteen-dollar baseball cap with the words I DON'T TAKE NO BULL, and head downstairs.

The casino is bigger than I expected, and it takes me an entire lap to find Zorie. She's parked in front of a slot machine, with giant leopard-print sunglasses and a sun hat that looks even more obnoxious than my cap. Together, we look like a couple of tourists, not criminals, which is the idea. But still.

"This one looks fun. Sit," she says and pats the stool next to her.

"How'd you do?" I ask.

Zorie shrugs. "Guess I'm a little rusty."

"Rusty as in you lost all our money?"

She rolls her eyes. "Rusty as in rusty. Now, will you relax and sit down? This will be fun, and we could use some fun, especially you."

I slide onto the stool between Zorie and an older woman with a buzz cut. She eyes me curiously when I sit down before moving her bucket of quarters to the opposite side of the machine.

"Okay. I'm sitting. How long are we doing this?" I ask.

"Until one of us wins."

I let out a long, exasperated sigh. "Let's just get this over with so we can get back on the road."

Zorie hands me her bucket of quarters, and I insert three into the slot. The machine lights up immediately, and I press the yellow button in the center. More lights, and finally two cherries line up next to a lemon.

"Guess I'm rusty, too," I mumble.

Zorie shakes the bucket of quarters at me. "Try again. I think your luck's about to change."

As if on cue, a woman in black fishnets and an unflattering dress that bunches at the waist sidles between us with a tray. "Can I get y'all a drink?" she asks.

I look at her, then at Zorie. "Kind of early for cocktails, isn't it?"

The woman grins. "Not if they're free."

"In that case, we'll take two whiskey sours."

The woman nods and smiles but doesn't move.

"She said two whiskey sours," Zorie repeats.

"Just need to see some ID," she says.

I make a show of searching all my pockets for my ID, then give the woman a mournful look. "Must've left it in the room. Can you let this one slide? We're on vacation. First time in Texas." I hold up a twenty, and the woman snatches it before I change my mind.

"One drink," she says.

"See?" Zorie says to me. "Told you your luck was about to change."

I go back to my game, this time with a slight smile on my lips.

Three whiskey sours and three hundred dollars in winnings later, I finally understand how folks can spend hours sitting on a painful stool and pulling a lever with more force than necessary. There's no thinking behind it, no distractions about Dad or what Zorie and I have done, just pull, wait, repeat.

"I'm gonna find a bathroom, and then you're taking me to lunch since you're clearly better at this than me," Zorie says.

I nod, but my eyes are fixed on the three flashing cherries in front of me. And just like that, I've won another fifty bucks.

"Looks like you're on a roll, honey," Buzz Cut Lady says next to me. She hasn't moved from her stool since I won my first fifty dollars almost an hour ago. I know she's waiting for me to leave so she can take over my machine. It's so obvious it's funny, and I bite back a smirk.

"So far so good," I say and reach for my bucket of quarters. The woman says something about me having a hot machine, but I've stopped listening. Something else has my full attention now. I wrap my arms around my bucket and focus on the TV behind the bar. A reporter with a heavily contoured face appears onscreen next to photos of me and Zorie with the chyron "Wedding Crasher Killers" beneath it.

"The Wedding Crasher Killers have reportedly been spotted in New Orleans and are the primary suspects in a double homicide at the Queen's Inn hotel located in the heart of the city," the reporter says in an ominous tone. "The murderous duo are Redwood Springs, Georgia, residents Kayla Davenport and Zorie Andrews. Residents in the surrounding cities and states should remain alert and contact their local police department if they encounter the women, as they are considered armed and dangerous."

A clip of Lenora appears, red-faced and tear-streaked and making a mournful sound I hope to never hear again. "They killed my grand-baby! *Dyabs!*" she shrieks before dropping to her knees with her hands lifted to the sky. A caption beneath the image translates *dyabs* to *devils*.

"*Dyabs,*" I repeat slowly.

"What'd you say, hon?" Buzz Cut Lady asks. She's moved her stool closer, our knees almost touching.

"I said I think I'm done for the day."

She looks almost giddy as I start to stand.

And then I hear Dad's voice, as clear as if he were right in front of me. "This isn't you, Kayla Renea," he says. I slump back down on the stool and look up to see my father seated in his favorite recliner and staring directly at the camera. At me. "Whatever has happened—whatever you've done—all can be forgiven. I'll help you. Anything you need. Just come home. Please, baby girl." A hand comes into frame and rests on his shoulder.

Gloria.

"Come home to your family," Dad says as the hand moves behind his head, stroking and scratching as if he's a Labrador. "I love you, baby girl."

The camera pans up, and Gloria is there, swiping at her eyes with one of Dad's handkerchiefs. She looks at the camera, all swollen-eyed and red-nosed, and says, "We both love you, Kayla. Come home."

There's something about the desperation in her face and voice that makes me believe her.

I take a deep breath and try to stay calm, but my bucket of quarters rattles inside my shaking arms. What if Zorie and I are making a mistake by going through with this Mexico plan? We've never even been anywhere outside Georgia—until now, that is. How would we even get into Mexico without IDs? And my $350 slot machine winnings won't sustain us. Maybe going home is the only way to untangle myself from this mess.

A hand touches my shoulder, and I jump, spilling some of the quarters.

"Relax, it's just me," Zorie says.

I slide off the stool to pick up the coins, but Zorie stops me.

"I got it," she says. She kneels in front of me and scoops up the small pile of quarters at my feet, then dumps them back into my bucket. "I think someone's had too many whiskey sours," she says, watching me.

"I'm fine. Just hungry." I glance back at the TV, and a man with a crooked smile is talking about the heat index reaching 110 degrees today.

"We better get you fed, then. I'm thinking Red Lobster. There's one close to here. We passed it last night."

I make a face. "You know I hate fish."

"Then order steak," Zorie says. She tilts her head and studies my face. "You sure you're okay?"

I nod and force a smile. "I'm great."

"Good, because today, we're celebrating." Zorie takes the bucket from me and leans in to kiss my cheek. "I'll go trade these quarters for cash and meet you at the side doors." She turns and walks away, and I stand frozen, watching her. A man in a cowboy hat follows too closely behind Zorie, and I have a sudden panicked thought that he might be an undercover police officer. My mouth opens to call her name, but he turns and embraces a woman wearing shorts that barely cover her ass. Zorie glances over her shoulder and blows me a kiss.

I let out a long breath and remind myself to breathe.

═══

My stomach is twisted in anxious knots by the time we reach Red Lobster. Zorie takes my hand as we wait in front of the hostess stand, looking more relaxed than ever, and hums along to the Taylor Swift song playing through the speakers. When she looks at me, I smile. Happiness looks good on her.

"You were right about today," I say to Zorie as we follow the hostess to our booth. The restaurant is empty and still smells clean and not yet fishy.

She slides in across from me and opens the menu. "What was I right about?"

"My luck changing."

"Damn right. Both of our luck is changing. I feel it."

The waitress places a basket of cheddar biscuits on our table, and we both nod our appreciation.

"I've done a lot of bad things, Kayla," Zorie continues. "But I think maybe there's still time to fix it."

I pull apart one of the biscuits and scoop out the insides with my fingers. For the first time in a very long time, I feel myself relax. It's really happening. Zorie is finally ready to end this road trip of horrors. We're going home.

"I'm proud of you, Zo," I say. "This is the right thing to do. Maybe the judge will show us some grace for turning ourselves in."

Zorie frowns. "Turning ourselves in?"

I stop chewing. "You said you want to fix things."

"Yeah, by moving to Mexico." She puts her elbows on the table and leans in. "Last night, I got to thinking about that field trip we took to the Railroad Museum in high school. The tour guide said most folks sneak in and out of the country by freight hopping."

"Would this be the same tour guide you made out with?" I ask.

Zorie rolls her eyes. "As I was saying before I was rudely interrupted, I did some research earlier at the hotel, and there are six train entrances into Mexico." She digs in her front pocket and takes out the map, then spreads it between us. "There's a city about five hours from here—Laredo. We can jump on the train there and jump off as soon as we cross the border."

I stuff more biscuit into my mouth. "Jump on and jump off, huh?"

Zorie gives me a weak nod.

"And what do we do when we jump off the train into the middle of nowhere? Do we call an Uber to pick us up?" I ask, spraying crumbs onto the table.

"God, Kayla. You're always so damn negative." Zorie sits back in the booth and folds her arms. "This is a good plan. It will work."

"It's not and it won't. First off, this isn't a movie, Zo. We can't jump off a moving train. We'll die. Second of all, we don't have enough money to survive. Between the hotel, the clothes, the gambling, and my winnings, we're right back where we started from, with only five hundred dollars."

"But we *do* have enough money," Zorie insists. She reaches inside her front pocket again, takes out a receipt, and slides it across the table. "See? We're good now."

I squint at it, confused. "This is a receipt for ten thousand dollars."

Zorie nods, grinning. "Turns out, if you win ten thousand or less, you don't have to show ID when you cash it in."

I almost choke on my biscuit. "You won ten grand? Why didn't you say anything?"

"Technically, they weren't my winnings," she says slowly. "Think of them as donations for our future."

She bites into a biscuit and waits for me to say something, but I'm in shock. We've spent the last few days looking over our shoulders for the police, and now Zorie has basically invited them to have lunch with us.

"You stole ten thousand dollars while we're wanted by the police for murder?" I hiss through my teeth. "Why are you always so god-damn reckless? Is this what our life in Mexico would be—you mak-ing dumbass decisions that put our lives in danger?" I squeeze the bridge of my nose and exhale slowly. "You never think about conse-quences, Zorie. What if someone saw you and turned you in or fol-lowed us here and they're waiting outside?"

"Jesus, you're so dramatic," she says, shaking her head. "No one saw me, okay? Most of them were too drunk to see straight."

"Oh my God." I clap both hands over my mouth and try to concen-trate on breathing and not screaming. "You did this to more than one person?"

Zorie smiles. "I did this to men." She picks up a menu as if we've finished our conversation, and I yank it from her. "Look, I told you I was rusty. My game was off, and I was running out of money. I saw an opportunity, and I took it." She folds the map and the receipt into two tiny squares and tucks them back inside her pocket. "How many times have I told you that men are simple creatures? You give them a little attention, look impressed, and suddenly they're in love. I played dumb and asked them to teach me the game, and when they weren't looking, I helped myself to a few of their chips. Why are you acting like this is a bad thing? This is the miracle we've been waiting for! Our prayers have been answered!"

I stare out the window at the parking lot, thinking how I never prayed for any of this, not getting fired, not Zorie giving away our emergency stash, and definitely not running over Amber Childress at her best friend's antebellum wedding. My prayers had been simple. I'd prayed for love, success, my dad's good health, and for Zorie and me to always be best friends. And somehow, my prayers have led me here, to a booth inside a Red Lobster in Houston, Texas, gorging myself on cheddar biscuits while Zorie and I contemplate freight hopping.

No, these were never my prayers.

"Remember when we were ten and I came to your house after my mom hit me and you said you'd always keep me safe?" Zorie asks.

"I do," I say, my eyes still on the parking lot.

"You did that for me, Kayla—all these years, you've kept me safe. And now it's my turn to do that for you."

I feel her hand reach for me, her fingers digging into my forearm until I look at her. See her.

"I know you're still pissed because I lied to you about Aunt Ruby, but I had to, Kayla, or else you never would've left Redwood with me. And then, when we were about to turn ourselves in at that gas station, you looked so . . . I don't know . . . relieved. All I've ever wanted was for you to be happy, and this wasn't making you happy. It was all over your face. So, I gave you an out and told you Aunt Ruby didn't want us in New Orleans."

"Your dead aunt didn't want us in New Orleans. Imagine that," I say.

Zorie's chin quivers, and she's quiet for a moment. "I fucked up, okay? A lot. But you know me, Kayla. I'm not a bad person. I know you think I hurt Lamont and that woman, but I didn't. I swear on my life. I was looking for you. I wanted to confront you about Lamont, but then I saw some old man going to town on him and that house-keeper with a knife. I don't even know how he could see what he was doing with all that blood covering his face." Zorie takes a long breath and shakes her head. "He just kept going at it, and I froze. All I could do was stand there while he stabbed them over and over again. And then he just . . . stopped. I swear he looked right at me, and I thought he was gonna do to me what he did to them, but he walked past me and out the door like I wasn't even there. And then I saw you on the bed, bleeding and not moving, and I thought I'd let you down. I didn't keep you safe."

My brain can't process the information she's feeding it. Nothing makes sense. Delphin killing his own niece after all that talk about the worst karma. And then I remember Olympia's words, so smug and self-righteous as she straddled me in the hotel room. *Stealing from family is the worst karma you can get.* Beat the dog, wait for its master.

"If we go to prison, who will keep you safe?" Zorie asks. Then, in a small voice, she adds, "Who will keep me safe?"

She leans forward on her elbows, head bowed, and sobs into her hands. For a brief moment, we are ten years old again and making a vow that's bigger than both of us. Every hope, fear, disappointment, and heartbreak I've ever experienced is tucked away inside my best friend. Safe.

"I will," I say.

Zorie looks up, confused. "You'll what?"

"I will keep you safe."

"You ladies ready to try our seafood sampler today?" the waitress asks, placing a second basket of biscuits in front of us.

"Could you give us a minute?" I ask.

"Of course. Take your time." Her eyes linger on me for a second, and a flash of something crosses her face. She offers a smile, but it doesn't match her eyes. They look almost frightened.

"I could use a sweet tea," Zorie says.

"Sure thing." The waitress backs away from our table slowly before turning on her heel and half walking, half running to the kitchen.

"That was weird," Zorie says.

I crane my neck to see the kitchen door and see the waitress's frightened face staring back at me through the window. "She knows who we are," I say.

Zorie waves a dismissive hand. "Bullshit."

"Didn't you see the way she looked at us just now? She knows." I slide out of the booth and dust biscuit crumbs from my shirt.

"What are you doing?" Zorie asks.

"Leaving. Unless you want the police to shoot first and ask questions later."

She rolls her eyes. "You're being overdramatic again. Sit down."

I look behind me and realize the hostess has disappeared and we're now completely alone inside the restaurant.

"We need to leave. Now," I say and grab Zorie's hand.

We run past a confused elderly man entering the restaurant and out into the parking lot. The Red Lobster is located inside a strip mall, squeezed between a Hobby Lobby and a flower shop, and several shoppers stop to stare at us as we zip across the lot to the truck. I don't want to die here in front of the Red Lobster and a bunch of wide-eyed tourists. They'll post pics of our bleeding bodies on Facebook and Twitter with #BLM. I don't want to be a hashtag. At this point, we're already destined to be Wikipedia entries.

And then I hear it, like a soft humming in the distance that slowly crescendos into a scream. Police sirens.

We reach the truck, and Zorie jumps into the driver's seat. She backs up before I can close the door, and one of my flip-flops slips off and onto the ground. We leave it and take off with our tires squealing on the asphalt. Shoppers jump out of the way, some stop to film us, and a few even give us a thumbs-up.

"Where to now?" I ask.

"I don't know. I need to think."

I glance behind us and see the flashing lights closing in on our truck. "If we stop now, they'll definitely shoot us." Zorie makes a sharp right into a mall parking lot, clipping the bumpers of an entire row of cars and knocking a woman carrying a small child to the ground. "Fucking awesome. They can add reckless endangerment to our growing list of charges."

We cross the parking lot to a construction site behind the mall. The truck jumps and shakes as we drive over deep grooves and uneven foundation. For a second, I think we've lost the police, but then I see the lights up ahead, and Zorie circles back toward the highway.

"What if we can't outrun them?" I ask, my hands tightening around my seatbelt.

"We will."

"But what if we can't?"

Zorie looks at me, her dark eyes blacker than I've ever seen them. "We. Will."

She veers off the highway and onto a back road with endless cotton fields lining each side. The truck jerks and sputters, and I'm beginning to lose faith in Officer Don's vehicle maintenance upkeep. Above us, a helicopter with the Channel 4 news logo stamped on the side hovers at a distance that seems way too close to be safe. My pulse pounds in my ears. No matter what happens, this will end badly.

"New plan," I say. "We need to get off this isolated road and back among people. They would never risk the lives of others if we're in a crowd and surrender."

"We're not surrendering!" Zorie shouts over the helicopter. "We're going to Mexico!" Even with the helicopter drowning out almost everything around me, I can still hear the desperation in her voice. "Do you trust me?" she asks.

I reach across the console for her hand and squeeze. "Always," I say.

"Then hang on." Zorie hooks a left through the cotton field and presses the accelerator all the way to the floor. With every bump, I say a silent prayer that there are no workers or animals hiding in the fields. Who knows how far this cotton field stretches or what's waiting for us on the other side. We keep going, leaving a trail of fluffy white clouds behind us.

"I want you to know that whatever happens, I love you," Zorie says.

"I love you, too."

The fleet of police cars closes in on our truck, and a voice over a loudspeaker demands we stop and exit the vehicle with our hands up. They're right behind us. It won't be long now.

"We have to stop the car, Zorie, or they will shoot us," I say.

"I can't." Her hands tremble on the steering wheel, and I lightly touch her forearm with my fingers.

"We're dead if we don't stop," I tell her.

Zorie stares straight ahead with a solemn expression. "We're dead if we do."

"This is your final warning! Stop the vehicle and exit with your hands up!" the voice says over the loudspeaker.

Panic seizes every inch of me. "We have to stop now," I say. "He won't ask us again, not with his words."

Zorie laughs, and a long string of saliva slides down her chin. "It was a good run, wasn't it?"

I smile at her. "So good."

"You think we'll be more famous than the Kardashians now?"

"Abso-fucking-lutely."

She slams on the brakes, and I lurch forward with my seatbelt cutting into my throat. Tufts of cotton land softly on the windshield, and we watch them fall, still and unmoving, as more sirens scream behind us.

"Guess this is it," I say.

Zorie nods. "Guess so."

I unfasten my seatbelt, watching her. She doesn't move. "You heard the man. Exit with your hands up," I say, and reach for the door handle.

"Kayla?"

I look back at Zorie staring at me, her eyes wide and intense. "You were the best part of my life," she says, her voice shaking. "I'm sorry for all this. I know this was never supposed to be your life."

I reach for her hand. "Hey, it was never supposed to be your life, either. We're gonna be okay, Zo. Whatever charges they have for us, we'll fight them. Together."

Zorie nods and takes a shaky breath. "Tell the police I did everything, okay? They'll go easy on you."

I shake my head. "I'm not lying on my best friend. Not again." I give her hand a small squeeze and push open the door.

"Tell them I did everything," she repeats, her voice smaller this time. Her hands press into my back, and I think she's reaching for a hug, but then she shoves me forward and out of the truck. My breath hitches in my throat, and I fall to the ground, landing on my knees. I push myself up on my hands, tears stinging my eyes.

"Zorie, no!" I shout, but she's too far gone to hear me. Three police cars take off behind her. Just like she wanted.

I hear the gunshots seconds later.

CHAPTER THIRTY-TWO

AFTER

Zorie is free now.

She was cremated on a Wednesday morning, the day of my arraignment. Dad brought her ashes home after her mother refused to allow any remains of her dead daughter inside her house. Miss Patrice told Dad that Zorie brought enough darkness to her life when she was alive, and she wouldn't be haunted anymore. Sad, but not surprising. Our home was the only place that ever felt like home to Zorie, so it only made sense for her to be there. Dad sent me a photo of the urn he bought for her. It's gold and engraved. Zorie Davenport, not Andrews. My sister.

Dad tries to visit at least once a week. I know the drive is hard on him, being three hours away. Gloria doesn't come with him, and part of me thinks he prefers it that way. He told me that after my call from the Cardinal Inn, the two of them argued for hours. Dad blamed Gloria for my decision to keep going with Zorie.

"If she hadn't mentioned that damn psych hospital, you would've come home, and those people wouldn't have been slaughtered in that hotel room," he'd said during our first visit. "That video we made for Channel 5 was supposed to be her way of making things right. A lot of good it did."

I'd watched him through the glass partition that separated us, thinking how wrong he was about Gloria's words changing my decision to leave the Cardinal Inn with Zorie. The truth is, I was always going with Zorie. We'd made a vow to keep each other safe—ride or die—even though, in the end, I failed.

I think about Zorie every day, how broken she was, how tortured. I'm thinking of her now as I wait for my attorney. Dad took out a second mortgage on the house to hire Jameson Flynn, Esq. One more thing to add to Gloria's growing "I hate Kayla" list. Should've known those tears were only for Dad. She was as cold as ever when she and Dad showed up for my arraignment. I'm sure she's found a comfortable place for Zorie's ashes, too. In the basement. At least Jameson is good-looking and not some old, crotchety man with hair coming out of his ears and coffee breath. I can hear Zorie now: *I object to my attorney being this fine.*

The door opens behind me, and Jameson walks in with his briefcase hanging from his wrist and an armful of files and papers. These days, I only recognize Jameson by his briefcase and files. They've become part of his wardrobe. He is a beautiful disaster. He pulls out the chair across from me and places his folders on the table between us, organizing them by color. The yellow folders are for updates about my case, green are for media coverage, and red are for Zorie.

"How are things, Kayla?" he asks in his thick New York accent. Dad purposely hired him because Jameson isn't from the South. He thinks New Yorkers are smarter. I'm not convinced yet.

"Things are . . . things," I say. "Not too bad for an inmate convicted of armed robbery, I guess."

Jameson doesn't laugh, or smile. I don't expect him to. He's always very serious. Maybe that's what makes a good attorney—a missing sense of humor.

"Dr. Jeffries tells me you're attending your sessions as scheduled," he says.

"Not like I have a choice, but yes."

Since being transferred back to Georgia from the only women's prison in the state of Alabama due to overcrowding, I've attended a total of nine sessions with Dr. Beverly Jeffries, psychiatrist extraordinaire. By the end of the first week, she'd diagnosed me with borderline personality disorder, PTSD, and depression and prescribed a colorful cocktail of happy pills. I've learned a lot in my sessions with Dr. Jeffries about accountability and accepting responsibility for the things I've done. She says healing can only happen when we look inward and accept the consequences of our actions. She likes to call decisions "pushes" because every decision moves the next, sometimes for better or worse, but it's always our choice to make. I know better than anyone how a single decision—or push—can move the next, and my decisions have always moved in sync with Zorie's. *"Remember, you and me? We're the same."* Dr. Jeffries brings up our friendship a lot. *Codependent,* she calls it, but I don't like talking about Zorie with her. Even with all the fancy degrees that decorate her office wall, she'd never understand Zorie like I do.

"I'll be honest with you, Kayla. A trial will be really tough to win without Zorie here to corroborate your story," Jameson says. "We have four dead bodies, and you were present at the scene of every crime."

"So that's it, then? I go to prison for the rest of my life for crimes I didn't commit?"

"Not necessarily." Jameson leans back in the chair and tugs his tie. It's purple today. Last time he was here, I told him my favorite color is purple. Jameson doesn't laugh, but he listens. "We can accept the plea deal the prosecution is offering, which would make you eligible for parole in . . ." He flips open the yellow folder and shuffles through the papers. "Twenty-five years."

"Twenty-five years? That's, like, a quarter of my life!" I shout. The correctional officer by the door takes a tentative step toward me, and Jameson raises a hand to stop him.

"You'll still be relatively young when you get out," he says, his voice low and calm. "It's a good deal, Kayla."

I lean forward on my elbows with my face in my hands. "I'll be middle-aged in twenty-five years. My dad will probably be dead."

"And you'll still have a life." Jameson drums his fingers on the table in an impatient kind of way, like he expects me to decide my future now.

"Can I at least think about it?"

He tugs his tie again. I'm starting to realize this is Jameson's tell when he's uncomfortable. I make him uncomfortable.

"You're in a lot of trouble here, Kayla. You violently assaulted a police officer with a deadly weapon. And then there's the matter with Paul, Ruthann, and their neighbor. As for the murders, the prosecution was pushing for a first-degree murder charge."

I stare down at my hands. The cuffs dig into my skin, and I wish they'd remove them for attorney visits. I'm considered a high-risk inmate because of the charges against me. The handcuffs keep me controlled. Safe.

"I told you what happened with Officer Costello," I say. "He would've killed me if I didn't get out of there."

"Is that why you robbed him?" Jameson sighs and massages the bridge of his nose. "Look, I'm obviously on your side here. I want to help you. I do. At the same time, these murders were incredibly violent. The couple at the Queen's Inn were stabbed over forty times combined. The female victim was almost decapitated."

My stomach turns. Until recently, I'd avoided the grisly details of the murders. I'd told the police about Delphin, how he'd assaulted me and then killed his family over some proverb about karma. They didn't even pretend to take me seriously or bring Delphin in for questioning. Of course, they'd have to actually look for him to do that since he's been missing since the night of the murders. Honestly, I doubt the police will ever look for him. Zorie as the beautiful crazed serial killer makes for sexier, more salacious headlines than an old perverted uncle who chopped up his niece and her boyfriend in a hotel room.

"How well did you know Zorie Andrews?" Jameson asks, watching me.

"I've known Zorie my whole life. She's my best friend." I shift in my seat. "She *was* my best friend."

Jameson reaches for the red folder. The Zorie one. "Did you know Zorie set her grandmother's bed on fire when she was ten years old? Her grandmother almost died. Seventy percent of her body was covered in third-degree burns. According to the child psychologist who interviewed Zorie after the incident, she did it because her grandmother wouldn't let her watch TV."

I hear Zorie's voice that night at the Queen's Inn: *"Aunt Ruby stopped talking to me when I was a kid because of something that went down with my granny."*

She set her great-aunt's sister on fire. Of course Aunt Ruby didn't want anything to do with her.

"I didn't know she did that," I say.

"The psychologist also submitted a report to the court stating Zorie exhibited traits of sociopathy."

"Sociopathy?" I repeat, the word thick and heavy on my tongue.

"In children, it's called conduct disorder, but can develop into antisocial personality disorder in adults," Jameson says. "It means people like Zorie act impulsively, break laws, and have no regard for their safety or the safety of others." He pushes a document across the table with the heading "American Psychological Association." "Does any of this sound like your friend?"

I stare at the document and the highlighted words: *manipulative, irresponsible, hostile, dangerous. Violent* is circled and underlined. Twice.

"What do you want me to say? That I should've known my best friend was a sociopath when we were kids?" I say, my voice trembling.

"Well, I didn't. Zorie was my best friend. I thought of her like a sister. For most of my life, she was my everything." I don't realize I'm crying until I see the wet spots on the table.

Jameson's face softens, and he slides the document toward him, returning it to its place inside the red folder. "Sometimes we think we know a person and then find out we didn't know them at all. It's even worse when that person is no longer around." He collects his folders, scribbles something on a notepad, and lifts half of his mouth into what I think is a smile. No wonder Jameson never smiles. It's unsettling. "Think about the plea deal, Kayla. It might be your only chance to get out of here someday."

=====

I think about Jameson's words as I'm escorted back to my cell. How well did I know Zorie? How well did she know me? Were we friends because we genuinely loved each other or because we needed each other? Maybe we were just used to each other. Dad would ask why I was friends with someone like Zorie, and I'd always say something generic like "Because I like her." The truth is, sometimes I hated Zorie, but I never stopped loving her. Ever. She was cruel and chaotic most days, and maybe I ignored it because she wasn't cruel to me. Maybe part of me knew even at an early age that being Zorie's BFF was a million times better than being her enemy. Maybe I'm the real sociopath.

My two cellmates, Jackie and Ana, are braiding their hair when the officer unlocks the cell and I step inside. It smells like shit, but it always smells like shit.

"Everything go okay with your lawyer?" Jackie asks. She's always very interested in my meetings with Jameson. Actually, she's interested in everything about my case. Like a weird, obsessed fan. When she first arrived to join me and Ana in our cell, she was quick to ask me about the murders. She wanted to know all the details—

the weapons, locations, last words. She practically foamed at the mouth if I mentioned Zorie. I've watched enough *Dateline* to know Jackie is probably a jailhouse snitch, so I keep my conversations with her censored.

"It was fine," I tell her and crawl onto the top bunk. Being an accused serial killer gets you first dibs on the top bunk. Still not sure what Jackie is in for. She won't talk about it. But Ana tried to kill her ex-girlfriend.

"I heard that Julianna chick might be transferring here because of overcrowding. Killing her best friend like that and then letting someone else take the fall? Man, that's fucked up," Jackie says.

"No, what's fucked up is the bride's husband messing with the best friend right up to the day of the wedding. I'd push that bitch in front of a car, too," Ana says.

I don't disagree. When the news first broke about Amber and Brett's affair, Zorie and I were suddenly exonerated by the court of public opinion. We were heroes for mowing down the homewrecking whore, until the real truth came out about Julianna framing us for murder. I wish Zorie were alive to talk about this. She loved twisted love stories. Dad asked me once if I think Zorie would still be alive if she'd waited for the truth, and I told him I wasn't sure. Maybe she was right about this eventually being her life, no matter what.

"If you need us to, you know, take care of anything with old girl, just say the word," Jackie says.

"I'll think about it." I push aside the mail on my mattress and stretch out. I get a lot of mail from men asking me to send them my panties. I always hand those off to Jackie. She loves stuff like that. Today's mail haul includes a letter from Dad, one from a New Orleans news station, and one from Candace. I open Dad's first, but it's not his handwriting inside. It's Zorie's. I sit upright on the bed and stare at my dead best friend's handwritten words in blue ink scribbled on a Dairy Queen napkin.

Dear Mr. Davenport,

I know I'm the last person you want to hear from right now, but since we both love Kayla, I wanted to reach out and let you know she's okay. She'd kill me if she knew I sent you this, but I know how much she's missing you right now. I promise, Mr. D, when all this blows over, you'll see her again. In the meantime, don't worry, I'll always look out for our girl!

Love,
Z

PS: Don't let your bitch wife see this.

I hold the napkin against my heart, pressing it into my chest as if to tattoo the words onto my skin. I want to scream at the unfairness of it all. Our ending wasn't supposed to be this. I was supposed to protect her. Keep her safe. She was my best friend—my person— flaws and all. Ours was meant to be a happy ending. After all the bullshit, we deserved a happy ending. I curl into a ball on my bed and tuck the napkin under my pillow. Candace's letter sticks to my elbow as I slide out my arm. She never writes to me. Her and Charles's Buckhead address is stamped on the front. He's using *doctor* in front of his name now. I roll my eyes and flip over the tiny blue envelope, which is already open. I'll never get used to having my mail opened and read by strangers before it comes to me.

Inside, I expect to find some long list of grievances about how much damage I've done to her reputation because of our stepsibling relationship, but there's no letter. Actually, it's worse. My dearest stepsister has sent me a wedding invitation. They've chosen a date in mid-August at the Ritz-Carlton for the nuptials. Fancy. Must've booked it before Dad took out the second mortgage. Not that it would've mattered. Gloria would sell her left kidney to give her daughter the wedding of her dreams.

I trace the invitation's gold calligraphy with my finger and smile. Funny how a single choice can determine your entire life. That day on the playground in first grade, I made the choice to be best friends with Zorie. She used to ask me how much I love her, and I'd tell her, "From here all the way to heaven." She'd laugh and say, "Then I hope heaven is a zillion miles from here!"

A zillion miles never felt so far away.

I check the box on the invitation next to "Declines with regret."

ACKNOWLEDGMENTS

—

Thank you to my parents, Thomas Dotson and Olivia Clay, for always being so encouraging and supportive. I will never be able to thank you enough for buying me my first typewriter instead of the Barbie Dreamhouse I desperately wanted. Thank you for being proud of me, even when I don't always think I deserve it. I love you both more than you know.

Thank you to my dream agent, Melissa Edwards, who truly made my childhood dream come true. I will be forever grateful for your email that summer and that first line. You get me, and most important, you get Kayla and Zorie. Your knowledge and experience in this industry is immeasurable.

Thank you to my brilliant and unbelievably creative editor, Sydney Collins. You understood the vibe of this book from the very beginning and have been its biggest champion since. I've said before that you have the best imagination ever, and it's so true. Kayla and Zorie's world would not be as bright, or as dark, without you. You are beyond talented, and I'm so lucky to have worked on this book with you. Thanks also to the team at Bantam Books and Penguin Random House, including, but not limited to, Abby Duval, Belina Huey, and Kim Walker. It still feels incredibly surreal to be a part of this imprint and publishing house. I am so thankful to each and every team member who gave this story life.

Thank you to my film and TV agents, Addison Duffy and Maialie Fitzpatrick, for your overwhelming enthusiasm for this wild story. I'm excited to work with you both.

To Kimberly Witz and Amy Tipton, thank you both for letting me vent as I clawed my way through the mountains of rejections and for your invaluable feedback. Kimberly, I have no doubt you'll have a book deal before you ever read this! To Pitch Wars (RIP) and Write-Mentor, thank you for connecting me with amazing mentors and an incredibly supportive writing community.

Thank you to my colleagues and fellow social workers, both past and present, many of whom I call my friends. I know I've been talking about my book dreams forever, and thank you for not rolling your eyes as I droned on and on. Your encouragement has kept me going, and I appreciate you so much for that.

To my sister, LaTonya, and my best friend, Kendra, thank you for always making me laugh and for being my biggest (and loudest) cheerleaders. You two have provided me with enough inspiration for a million characters. Seriously.

To my nieces and nephews, DaMichael, Cameron, Andrea, Olivia, Nehemiah, and Isaac, I hope you never stop dreaming big or trusting God. And to my four little squishies, I hope your parents let you read this when you're old enough and that your Cissy made you proud.

Finally, thank you to my friends, family, and church family who have prayed for me on this journey and who always reminded me to never give up. You have no idea how much this means to me. To my furry four-legged ride or die, Ivy, thank you for all the snuggles during my writer's block. I'll miss you forever and a day.

And to B.O., just because.

ABOUT THE AUTHOR

———

CHRISTINA DOTSON is a member of Crime Writers of Color and was a runner-up for the Eleanor Taylor Bland Crime Fiction Writers of Color Award. In addition to being a writer, she is a licensed clinical social worker and lives in Kentucky.

ABOUT THE TYPE

———

This book was set in Vendetta, a typeface designed by John Downer as an homage to the advertising signs painted on walls of old factories and warehouses of roadside America. Downer began his career as a journeyman sign painter, and Vendetta was inspired in part by the brushstrokes used in sign painting, which give this typeface its distinct angular character.